The First of the Attackers Arrived. . . .

They were small, swift birds with beaks and talons sharp as needles. They darted about the winged horse Bellimbusto, shrilling their wrath, plunging and diving at its eyes and neck and at the face and chest of Lodovico. They were worse than a cloud of enormous gnats and their attack was more determined, more deadly.

There were other sounds in the air now as the predators came upon them—hawks, falcons, eagles, powerful and restless as great cats, splitting the wind with faces like arrows. Their talons sank into flesh and their cries were screeches of loathing.

Lodovico began to lay about him with the flat of his blade, slapping the birds out of the air, sending them hurtling down. He could no longer aim to strike, but swung the sword wildly, praying that he did not touch his mount and end it for them both in one, long drop to the earth . . .

Chelsea Quinn Yarbro

Ariosto

*Ariosto Furioso,
a Romance for
an Alternate Renaissance*

PUBLISHED BY POCKET BOOKS NEW YORK

This is a fantasy. No one in it, by intention or implication, represents or is intended to represent any actual person living or dead. The author is aware of the anachronisms and inconsistencies functioning in this alternate Renaissance.

Another *Original* publication of POCKET BOOKS

POCKET BOOKS, a Simon & Schuster division of
GULF & WESTERN CORPORATION
1230 Avenue of the Americas, New York, N.Y. 10020

Copyright © 1980 by Chelsea Quinn Yarbro

ISBN: 0-671-83294-8

First Pocket Books printing April, 1980

10 9 8 7 6 5 4 3 2 1

POCKET and colophon are trademarks of Simon & Schuster.

Printed in the U.S.A.

for
C. D.
because it might have been
this way

PART I

La Fantasia

High, high overhead the horse circled slowly, majestically. He hovered on outstretched wings that glinted now black, now bronze, his beak flashing where the sun struck it in the splendor of the morning. Clouds fat and docile and pink as cherubs hung above him, and far below, the line of the coast was marked by a curling white mustache of breakers.

This was the land of the Cérocchi, a place of endless forests and broad rivers originating far inland, at fabled springs, guarded by immense and gorgeous citadels where lived sagacious wizards and golden emperors.

It was at the mouth of such a river that Nuova Genova had sprung up, a carnival gathering of piazzas and palazzos rising up like fingers at the end of a long, curving arm, a spit of land that reached into the sea from the marshy delta where the river bade a last, lingering farewell to the embrace of the land. In this location Nuova Genova beckoned the traveler in an eternal gesture of welcome.

The horse descended in lazy circles while his rider leaned back in the high jeweled saddle and plucked a few tunes on his chittarone and from time to time bent forward to admire the view as the city grew larger and more distinct. Now he could recognize the individual buildings by their distinctive features. There was the square façade of the Palazzo del Doge, as fitted this offshoot of Genova. Farther away but taller was the clock tower adorned with the five red balls of the Medici. Nearest of all was the palace of the Cérocchi prince, and as he passed over its timbered roof, women in fine garments of brocades, pearls and furs ran onto the gold-fronted balcony, shouting and pointing, their copper faces alight, their black hair framed by elaborate headdresses of feathers of every color, iridescent, now red and amber, now green and brass. Their voices drifted up to him, high and excited, in their unfamiliar tongue.

At last the horse landed, its gold-painted hooves and talons sinking into platinum-pale sand. Lodovico slung the chittarone over his shoulder by its long neck, then swung out of the saddle, one hand still firmly grasping the reins until Bellimbusto had furled his wings. He had seen many unwary riders taken by surprise when they had relinquished the reins too soon and had watched in helpless dismay as their mounts soared aloft, unfettered.

Already there were quite a number of people rushing out of the gates of the city to meet him, many of them handsome Italians, a few disdainful Frenchmen, and among the rest, bejeweled Cérocchi nobles. They were headed in this scramble by the members of the Signoria of Nuova Genova.

Lodovico stood waiting, his arms clasped over his chest, just below the gold-and-sapphire collar that commemorated his heroic command of the expedition to the great Oriental stronghold of the Thousand Golden Towers where he had defeated the Great Mandarin in single combat. He was dressed for flying, in a short velvet doublet over a shirt of pleated taffeta, slightly rumpled after long hours in his airborne saddle. His hose were stiffly padded and banded with gold-edged embroidery, and his leggings—what could be seen of them above high-topped cavalry boots—were of fine-knitted wool. His hair flowed in chestnut curls to his shoulders, and the velvet hat he now doffed was caught at the edge

of the brim by a jeweled brooch that held a long, lavish
ostrich plume.

"Look! Who they've sent!" cried the leader of the
Signoria to the others, his face filled with recognition
and pleasure. The secretary who trotted along beside
him turned to speak to the Cérocchi prince striding in
his wake. "It's Ariosto!" The others heard this and the
intelligence spread through the crowd as they hurried
forward even more eagerly.

When they were nearer, Lodovico spread out his
arms, a smile on his handsome face. "Good people of
Nuova Genova, I bring you greetings from il Primàrio,
the great Damiano de' Medici himself!"

The leader of the Signoria very nearly stumbled into
the magnificent winged horse as he came up to the
illustrious visitor. "Ariosto!"

Lodovico reached out to hold the old man up, laughing heartily as he did. The long-necked chittarone
thrummed against his back and his horse shied nervously. An easy pat from its master quieted the animal.

By now, many of the others had reached him, and
Ariosto had much to do to keep his spirited horse from
bolting while he grasped first one arm and then another
that was reached out to him. He heard his name in a
tumult of voices; his splendid eyes, the same chestnut
shade as his shining hair, shone with joy.

"Good citizens! Good friends!" the leader of the
Signoria called out at last as he turned to face the
gathering, motioning for silence with his upraised hands.
"You must step back. You must make room. Come,
make way for this great man." He motioned the people
away, but they were reluctant to leave. "We cannot ask
Ariosto to stand here on the beach like a vagabond."

"But I *am* a vagabond," Lodovico protested with his
most sincere smile. "Think how much of the world
I have seen, how few years I have been allowed to rest
with my beloved Alessandra, how I have gone first here,
then there, in the service of our great Italia Federata.
What am I, if not a vagabond, a rover?"

"A hero!" shouted several voices in the crowd, but

Lodovico shook his head, lowering his eyes. "No, no, good friends. I cannot aspire to so noble a name." He looked up keenly, feeling the renewed courage of those who faced him. "But I am here to serve you, and perhaps at the end of our struggles, we will all deserve that fine name. If there is glory, it must be earned, and I can see that none of you would turn from an honest battle."

This was greeted with such enthusiastic approval that Lodovico turned to the leader of the Signoria with an embarrassed chuckle. "What more can I tell them? My successes, such as they are, have been as much luck as any bravery on my part. Fortune is a fickle goddess, and may desert me at any time. For these good people, with so much of the right with them, they have no need of a champion. But if my presence means so much to them, then I will accept this great honor they give me."

The leader of the Signoria clucked his tongue. "You must not mind, Ariosto, if they express their faith in you. We have had little to encourage us since the prince here"—he nodded toward the tall Cérocchi who stood not far away, resplendent in feathers of many hues and beadwork of jade and chalcedony and ivory—"brought us word of the king of the Fortezza Serpente. When we sent our request for aid to il Primàrio, we had no idea that he would send you to help us."

Suddenly Lodovico's expression grew serious; even the winking light in his eyes was muted. "I have read the dispatch you sent. A terrible business, Podestà Benci." He looked down into the face of the leader of the Signoria. "I bring you the promise of Damiano himself that Nuova Genova will be protected with all the might of Italia Federata. As I left, orders were being sent to Venezia, commanding that nine troop ships set sail at once."

Andrea Benci's old eyes filled with tears of gratitude. "Nine troop ships!" he repeated, as if unable to believe the words. It was a litany of hope. "Oh, Ariosto, you cannot know what this news will mean to our city."

He beckoned to his secretary and repeated this information so that it could be issued as a public proclamation. He also motioned the Cérocchi Prince to come nearer, then gave his attention to Lodovico once more. "The Prince has sent word to the king of the Pau Attan north of here."

"And what was his response?" Lodovico demanded, a martial determination straightening his stance and lighting his features. He touched the chittarone slung across his back as if it were his great sword Falavedova now safely stowed in the wooden scabbard attached to his saddle.

"Alas, messages move slowly in this land. This is not Italia, where there are paved and guarded roads from Savoia to Sicilia. Here the men must make their way through the trackless forest. There are not only enemies of the Cérocchi to contend with, but there are dangerous animals and great marshes where seductive wraiths lure the unwary to terrible death." Andrea Benci sighed and crossed himself, then squared his shoulders. "No, we must not despair. Now that you are here, we will take heart again, I know it."

Lodovico gave him his wide, flashing smile, and wished that he could have more time to explore this gigantic, unknown land. If there were wraiths in the marshes and dangerous animals, he did not know how he would be able to resist them. If only he had not accepted the commission to lead the troops for il Primàrio! How he hated to turn away from such a challenge! He put his arm over Andrea Benci's shoulder and gestured toward the gates of Nuova Genova. "I've been in the saddle for two days," he said. "And damned uncomfortable it becomes after the first few hours. I would welcome a meal and a bath, and then, Podestà Benci, royal Cérocchi, we must talk strategy." He reached for the reins of his horse and led the celebrating populace toward the ornate gates standing open to receive him, armed captains saluting as he went through the gates, and calling his name.

La Realtà

"Ariosto!" the voice said more harshly, and an un-friendly hand was laid on his shoulder. "By San Giovanni!"

Lodovico opened his near-sighted eyes, blinking in the light. Beside him, the ink was dry on his quill. Somewhat belatedly he put his arms across the parchment pages in front of him. "I dozed off," he explained lamely.

Andrea Benci, personal secretary to il Primàrio, Damiano di Piero de' Medici, gave an irritated sigh as he looked down at the poet. "We are supposed to be in the loggia now. We're expected to help prepare the reception for the English ambassador and his mission. You, if it hasn't escaped your attention, are going to read the valedictory verses to them, welcoming them all to Italia Federata."

"I remember, naturally," Lodovico said with dignity, hating the superior air Benci gave himself, simply because he was closely associated with il Primàrio. "It's been difficult, writing the verses. Poliziano himself," he added in a mutter, "could not have found a word to rhyme with Wessex. Wessex!"

"Does that mean that the verses are not finished?" Benci, though an old man of sixty-two, stood very tall, with the hauteur of a born courtier.

"Oh, they're finished, such as they are," Lodovico growled. "I am only warning you that they are not as beautiful as I would wish. English is a terrible language for poetry. How can anyone write poetry in a language in which all the words end in *t* or *s* and half the vowels are left out altogether?" He made a show of gathering up the pages while he stuffed a few of the parchment sheets into the portfolio lying open on the table.

Benci gave him a look of polite condescension. "A great poet, laureate of la Federazione, stymied by a few unruly syllables?"

"Poetry isn't like yard goods: snip, snip and there is all you need for a sonetta. Poetry is the passion of the soul, a way for expressing things that cannot be said in the ordinary way. Daily life obscures so much. How can you cut lengths of cloth and think of the true nature of courage?" He saw that Benci's expression had not altered. "You are one of those cutting cloth, are you?" He heard Benci laugh indulgently, and realizing that there was quite a large ink smear on his sleeve, he gave a furtive twist to the material.

"You will have to change your garments, of course," Benci informed him sweetly and unnecessarily. Court receptions always required full formal wear, precisely the kind of clothes that looked most incongruous with Lodovico's rough-hewn features.

"Of course. I will not be long," Lodovico said in a firmer voice as he got to his feet. He hoped that Alessandra had remembered to restitch the knot of pearls to his sleeve. It was bad enough that the garment was over four years old and looked every hour of it; to have the jewels falling off it would cause the kind of snickering he loathed. There was also, he recalled with a rush of embarrassment, a wine stain on the hose where a clumsy servant had overset a tray at the last official reception. Perhaps he should rub wine on all of the stiff, slashed short pantaloons so that the mark would not be noticeable.

"We will begin in the loggia, so that the people will be able to watch il Primàrio receive the Englishmen."

Why, Lodovico asked himself, does Benci insist on calling Damiano il Primàrio, as if they had never exchanged more than bows? He nodded, to show he had been paying attention, though the pattern of sunlight on the inlaid floor was more interesting to him. The light was so narrow and intense that it seemed solid, like long, cloudy crystals thrust in at the window. There was little air in the room, so that the dust motes hung without motion in the stillness. He turned various similes over in his mind: Like topazes—trite. Like liquid butter—atrocious. Like the voice of bells and trumpets—perhaps. Like water from a golden spring—too precious. He sighed as the incomplete pictures jostled in his mind and the bar of light made a snail's haste across the floor.

Benci's voice reached him like the droning of a kitchen fly. "You will recite your verses there and then the entire train will move into the Grand Hall for the formal speeches. You will be called upon to read some of your own cantos after the meal. Perhaps the *Orlando,* though most of us have heard it before." His tone was snide. "You've been working on something new . . ."

"It isn't ready yet!" Lodovico said shortly. "I won't foist unfinished work on Damiano's guests."

Benci nodded condescendingly. "Il Primàrio expects you to sit beside the ambassador's secretary at the Great Table. That, of course, is the Chancellor, who is not here in his official capacity. We must be certain that we all remember this."

The bar of sunlight was thinner now, and reminded him of the light through yellow autumn leaves, or new-minted coins. On the whole, he liked the leaf image better, but thought that there had to be a phrase that had more translucence. Church windows were much too obvious and overused. Lodovico had stopped listening to the sound of Andrea Benci's voice. He had learned to endure this folly over the years, but he wondered what had become of those days when a distinguished poet like himself needed only a fine woolen lucco to wear for these occasions, for his genius was considered

more important than brocades, or whom he sat beside
at table. He rolled up the parchment sheets and turned
to regard Andrea Benci with what superiority he could.
"I will be ready shortly, you need not fear. You may tell
Damiano that I will not fail him, or that cursed English
ambassador with the impossible name. Wessex. Glennard. Sir Warford Pierpoint Edmund Glennard. What,
by God's Holy Wrath, am I do to with that?" Without
waiting for a response, he pushed passed Andrea Benci
and hurried from the study.

La Fantasia

They had feasted for the first part of the night, the
Italians, the few Frenchmen, and the Cérocchi vying
with one another in the sumptuousness of the foods
presented. All the dishes were displayed by gorgeously
liveried footmen. They carried each gigantic platter the
length of the hall, held aloft, to the accompaniment of
the musicians on the dais at the end of the huge room
who twanged and tooted and thumped for each new
temptation that was carried in for the diners' approval.
    Andrea Benci, in an outmoded and ill-fitting giornea,
sat to Lodovico's right and the Cérocchi Prince to his
left. Lodovico gave generous praise to the food and
its appearance, and he tasted every dish set before him,
but his mind was already engaged with strategy for the

defense of this city. The Fortezza Serpente was said to be dangerous and the men who owed fealty to its king were known for the fierceness of their wars and their scorn of pain.

"Honored Ariosto," said the Cérocchi Prince with great care in his pronunciation, "those of my nation are eager to aid you against these vile intruders. The king of my people, my father, has asked me to tell you that all of our warriors and wizards are at your disposal to command. Your fame has come before you, and your reputation. If Damiano de' Medici himself had come to us, we could not be more contented."

This expression of faith touched Lodovico deeply. It was a moment before he could answer. "Good Falcone," he began at last, using the Italian form of the Prince's name, "such a tribute coming from one so distinguished is a great treasure. You may be certain that I will do all in my power to be worthy of your trust, though it cost me my life, which is a paltry thing, when all is said." He took his cup and raised it to the Cérocchi Prince. "I pledge by this wine and by my honor that I will place you above my brother in my loyalty and affection so that together we may rid this splendid land of the odious forces of the Serpente." With a grand gesture, he tossed off all the wine in his cup.

Falcone reached to clasp him by the arm. His reserve, which was marked, had been set aside after Lodovico's great oath. His dark eyes glowed in his wide face and the jewel set in the fillet on his brow seemed to grow brighter. "Superb warrior!" he exclaimed. "My friend."

Their embrace was greeted by cheers from all those gathered at the feast. Even the servants raised their voices in approval, and two of the dogs scavaging under the long tables barked loudly enough to be heard over the commotion.

At last Lodovico turned to the assembly, his hands raised for silence. "Good friends! Citizens of Nuova Genova!" he shouted and waited for them to become quiet once again. "It is a fine thing to have such dedication, but it is better if we remember that it is God Who will give us the victory, if we are worthy. Let us all kneel and commend ourselves to His care for this great venture." Then, with profound humility, Lodovico rose from the table and went to the seat of the old bishop who served in the Cathedral of Santissimo Redentore. There he knelt with enviable grace, and lowered his head to be blessed.

The entire company followed his example, kneeling beside their chairs. Even the Cérocchi who attended listened in awe as the venerable Ambrosian priest pronounced his benediction in a surprisingly resonant voice. "You who will go among the servants of Satan," he thundered in Latin, "will take with you the shining sword of the Archangel Michael, for as Michael triumphed over the Devil and bound him forever in Hell with the Might of God, even so you, with the power of Virtue within you, will triumph over this vile spawn of Sin." He made the sign of the Cross over Lodovico, and then over the rest of the company.

The Cérocchi looked solemn, and the Italians were silent as they considered the dangers that waited for them. One of the Frenchmen was seen to turn pale.

Lodovico sensed this mood, and he looked at those gathered for this impressive feast. He was a fine sight—tall, magnificently attired, his collar with the Order of San Basilio hanging on a wide gold chain glinting in the torchlight, his face alight with zeal. His bright eyes rested a moment on the face of each of the men gathered in this hall. "Comrades! Do not let yourselves fall prey to fear now. It is certain that you know far better than I what we must face in the vast and unknown lands where the forces of the Serpente live. Yet, the falcon"—here he nodded toward the Cérocchi Prince—"has always been the enemy of serpents and he will strike valiantly at his enemy, with all the might of his blood and his honor. And are we not promised by God that those who fight in His name will have victory over their foes? Take heart then, my comrades, and be sure that our cause is just and our triumph assured."

Andrea Benci could not speak for the tears that rose in him. He took Lodovico's nearer hand and wrung it fervently.

"Oh, no, old friend, no weeping. This is a joyous time." He looked from the Podestà to the guests at the banquet. "For to how many of us is it given to face the enemies of God? Even those who will fall in battle, as must happen to some of us, surely, will have earned themselves a place at the Right Hand of God among the Saints and Martyrs. I tell you now, I would rather die transfixed by a Serpente lance than live to old age in decadent luxury and die forsaken by the world and the Glory of God. What true warrior could wish for any death but that gained in honorable combat? What true Christian could desire anything more than to give his life in a cause that is the same as the cause of God Himself?" He turned toward Falcone. "The Cérocchi follow their own gods, but we know them to be men of valor and worthy of this great task. Surely God will not despise them if they war on his behalf in this cause. Then let each of you Italians make a brother of every Cérocchi warrior, so that like the great fighters of old, like Achilles and Hector and that staunch Roman Horatius, like the great knights Roland and Oliver, like the Spanish Cid who drove the heathen from his land, we, too, may stand for all time as the measure of bravery and courage, of fidelity and devotion."

Falcone had come forward, the jewels of his clothes shimmering where the light caught them. Without a word, he took the dagger from his ornamented sheath and held it out to Lodovico.

"Ah!" Lodovico clapped him on the shoulder, took the dagger and kissed the blade before offering his poignard to the Cérocchi Prince. Falcone accepted the poignard and put it into his ornamented sheath, though it fit badly.

Now the hall was once again filled with cheers. The old bishop rose and pronounced the Benediction as

Lodovico heard his own battle cry *"Omaggio"* shouted back at him like the thunder of waves.

It was well into the night when the festivities ended and the men of Nuova Genova went to seek their beds. Lodovico stood in the empty hall, watching a few of the palazzo dogs fight over the remains of a haunch of venison. He had found he could not sleep, so full was his heart. His hand rested on the hilt of Falcone's dagger and he felt the same stirring of gratitude and humility that had nearly overcome him at the banquet.

"Troubled?" asked a voice behind him.

Lodovico turned quickly and saw Falcone standing in the doorway, a cape of tooled leather around his shoulders covering the finery he had worn earlier.

"No, not troubled," Lodovico answered after a moment. "I am often made to remember how fine a race men can be." He put his thumbs into the soft belt at his waist. "As I watched the men give their vows tonight, I was deeply moved . . . recalling it moves me now."

"Do you think it will go well?" Falcone asked, coming into the hall with silent tread.

"I hope it will." He stared down at the floor, doubts welling within him as he considered the magnitude of the venture. He had seen dedicated men cut down by the fearsome horsemen of the Great Mandarin as casually as a peasant scythed down grain. Though he would never say so aloud, he knew inwardly that the same fate could be waiting for all of them at the hands of the men of the Fortezza Serpente.

"Hope?" Falcone said gently.

"It's all I can do, my Prince. Flying here, I could see how enormous this land is. The wilderness is endless, and what might befall us there?" His handsome face was thoughtful now, and though there was no fear in him, he admitted to an inner caution. "You know this country far better than any of us, and certainly better than I, who have just arrived. I have heard tales of mountains and rivers so long and so formidable that

most will not dare to cross them. From the air such
things should be easier, but I would be a fool to say
that there is no challenge to us."

"Your mount . . ." the Cérocchi prince began, then
faltered. "We have only just seen horses in this land,
and your mount is more than that."

"He is part gryphon," Lodovico explained. "There
has long been a legend of this animal. It was said that
Roland himself rode such a horse, but there was no
proof. And then, when I was with the expedition in the
Orient, I learned more and eventually found the animals
in a remote valley high in the mountains. It took every
bit of gold I possessed to get two young ones, but I was
convinced it would be worth it."

Falcone's eyes glowed. "I have learned to ride a
horse," he said with a grin. "I am sure that I could ride
your animal as well."

The confidence of this statement made Lodovico
laugh. "I hope that you can. We will need men who
are capable of all military arts if we are to succeed in
our plan."

"The troop ships . . ." Falcone was serious once
again. "Are they coming, truly?"

"Yes. It takes time to cross the ocean, even when
the weather is favorable. Il Primàrio gave his word,
and that is the surest bond this side of the Word of
God." He saw the skeptical expression in the Cérocchi's
guarded face. "That's true, Falcone. Il Primàrio is a
good and just leader who does not treat his people
badly. He has said that the might of Italia Federata
will stand behind all those in Nuovo Genova and he
will not forsake us."

"But Italia Federata is far away, and we have heard
that there are other demands on il Primàrio. If other
matters intervene, we might be set aside . . ."

Precisely that possibility had worried Lodovico since
he had left Firenze, but he refused to voice it now. "He
is not the sort of man who abjures his promise."

Falcone's smile tightened and his lips grew thin. "I
don't know what to respond then. I do not wish to in-

sult you, Ariosto, but you must allow me my reserva-
tions."

Lodovico nodded. "I understand them, my friend,
far better than you might think. When I was far away
and fighting in the distant kingdoms of the East, I often
despaired. Yet dispatches reached us, and we were not
abandoned to our fates by our homeland. It's because
of that expedition that I can give you my word that the
troop ships will come, and if more aid is needed, we
will have it." As he spoke, he hoped inwardly that it
would be true. In the case of his Oriental expedition,
there had been the promise of treasure and the glory
of rediscovering the splendor of the East. But this unknown and uncharted land might prove to be another
matter if the campaign should prove to be long and un-
profitable. If that occurred, the Console of Italia Federata might move to withdraw the troops, leaving the
Cérocchi to face the men of the Fortezza Serpente
alone. No! He made a sudden gesture that startled
Falcone. He would not allow that to happen. If necessary, he himself would plead the case of the Cérocchi
and the men of Nuova Genova before the Console. He
realized that Falcone was staring at him, and he managed to smile.

"Your face . . ." the Cérocchi said tentatively.

"Not very pretty to look at, was it?" Lodovico asked
ruefully and stood straighter. "You must forgive me.
My thoughts are . . . scattered tonight. Tomorrow, when
my mind is clearer, we will talk again and you will
have the chance to look over Bellimbusto's points for
yourself." He put his hand on the shoulder of the
Cérocchi Prince. "It is an honor to be allowed to fight
with you, Falcone. Whatever the outcome of our battles,
I will always be proud to know that you were willing
to regard me as your comrade at arms."

Falcone nodded, saying nothing but touching the
poignard that hung in his dagger's sheath.

Andrea Benci was nodding in his chair before the fire
when Lodovico finally knocked at the door to his

chamber. "Oh, Ariosto. I had thought you might come earlier."

"I was with Falcone," Lodovico explained, an appreciative twinkle in his large, expressive eyes. "I must apologize for keeping you up so long, but I felt it was important to talk with the prince."

"Of course, of course," Andrea Benci agreed hastily. "You're quite right to do that. These Cérocchi are proud as Austrians. And I don't mind waiting."

Lodovico let that polite mendacity pass. "We must discuss what is to be done first. Certainly I must go and pay formal homage to Falcone's father. We must also think what is to be done with the troops when they arrive. They must be given quarters of their own and informed what rules obtain to them in the city."

Andrea Benci was wagging his head up and down, but it was clear that the old man had not considered the half of these problems. He gave a little cry of dismay and put his hands to his temples. "So much to do. So little time!"

The fire had burned low and the two lanterns were almost exhausted, so the room was very dim, but Lodovico thought he saw moisture gather in the old man's eyes. "There will be enough time," he said at his most reassuring.

"I do hope so," Andrea Benci muttered to the air. "I am afraid, Ariosto."

This simple confession filled Lodovico with pity for the old man. "We all know fear, Andrea," he said gently. "I have never been in battle when I was not afraid. You have a very real danger facing you and the outcome is unsure. In addition to that, there are many people here who depend on you for your wisdom and advice. Of course such responsibilities weigh heavily upon you—you are a good man and will not turn away from them." He sank into the chair opposite Andrea Benci, sighing as he did.

"But you," Benci protested, unbelieving. "You are a great hero. Surely you've mastered your fear?"

"I pray that I will, before every battle," he said softly,

looking at his clasped hands. "I know that I must not allow my fear to conquer me, for then I would be at the mercy of the enemy. Only they must be allowed to triumph over me, not my fear." His smile was sad. "I have too often seen what happens to men who surrender to their fears."

"If you are afraid, then how can the rest of us have courage?" the old man asked, bewildered.

"As I do—as any warrior does. You must learn not to be stopped by it, but to go on in spite of it." He studied the Podestà with compassion. "You've never had to face this before, have you?"

"Never," the old man said miserably. "I was not in Firenze when there was trouble with anyone. I've spent most of my life dealing with import and export matters, not wars." His arthritic fingers locked and unlocked as if performing a private ritual of their own.

"War is not really so different. Most of the time it is a dull thing. An army on the march is not much different from a group of merchants carrying wares, except that most soldiers are rougher men than merchants. We worry as much about food and bedding as you do, Andrea Benci. The rain wets us as much and is as annoying. The cold freezes us and the heat scorches us. You must not think of soldiers as men unlike yourself." He chuckled once.

Andrea Benci's brow furrowed. "As you say," he murmured. "I have little experience with soldiers. In Firenze, the Lanzi were not often involved with the merchants." It was almost an apology and the old man at last dared to meet Lodovico's eyes. "I will talk with the Signoria tomorrow."

It was good to see the Podestà put his mind to the task at last. Lodovico allowed himself the pleasure of being relieved. He felt now that Andrea Benci would be on the side of the fighters. To be sure of this, he added, "We cannot afford to lose this battle, not if Italia Federata is to have the lead in exploring this magnificent new land. The Spanish and the French

would like it if we failed. Therefore, we must succeed."

"Yes," Benci said, somewhat numbly. "There have
been Spanish vessels here from time to time. We have
not been anxious to let them land, but there was little
we could do without open conflict." He tried to shrug
this off, squaring his stooped shoulders for Lodovico's
benefit. "With you here, it will be different," he declared.

"I hope it may. That is why I was sent." Lodovico got
to his feet and favored Andrea Benci with a courteous
bow. "We must talk again, Podestà Benci, but tonight,
I am tired." His eyes sparkled as he looked at the old
man who was all but snoring. "A long flight like that
and I am exhausted."

"Um. Of course." The old man made a feeble gesture
of dismissal. "Don't stay on my account." His voice
had almost trailed away on the last words, and as
Lodovico reached the door, he could see Andrea Benci's
jaw drop onto his chest as he was at last unable to
resist the sleep that had been hovering around him.

Lodovico found his chamber. He could not bring
himself to wake the bodyservant who had been given
him, but tugged himself out of his clothes and stored
them in the trunk at the foot of the enormous bed he
had been provided. He could tell that the mattress was
filled with goose feathers and would be soft as merengue
to sleep upon, and that promise tempted him. When he
had donned his nightshift, he knelt and bowed his head
for his nightly devotions.

"In the Name of the Father, the Son and the Holy
Spirit, Amen," he said, as he had every night since he
was old enough to speak. "It has pleased You to send
me to aid these afflicted people in this strange and
distant land, away from my family and my country.
Whatever burden You give me, I will carry it with a
glad and humble heart and will, with Your help, so conduct myself as to be worthy of the honor. Should it be
Your intention to see me fall in battle, I ask that You
will forgive my sins, which must surely blacken my soul

and make it ugly to You, and will purge me of evil so that I will at last be sufficiently acceptable to You that I may stand in the splendor and radiance that endures forever. If my sins offend You too greatly, then I beg You will let my right arm falter so that I will die at my enemies' hands and be cast into the outer darkness." He stopped a moment, the terrible desolation of his petition weighing on him. The contemplation of that eternal isolation appalled him the way no armed enemy could. "Lord God, if You deem me worthy, spare me that." He had spoken more loudly than he knew, and it was startling to him. How must it feel, he thought, to be one of the warriors of the Fortezza Serpente and have nothing to meet at death but that awful, endless darkness? Hell, he knew, would be preferable. "I submit myself to Your Will," he whispered.

When he had finished his prayers, he rose and pulled back the coverings of the bed. The petals of sweet-scented flowers had been scattered on the silken sheets, and as Lodovico sank back into the lovely softness, he sensed he would have the same, wonderful dream again. There was a smile on his mouth as he let the perfume of the petals and the embracing luxury of the feather-bed lift and carry him into the delicious visions of his private paradise.

La Realtà

Alessandra had not repaired his sleeve, Lodovico noticed as he began to secure the fastening of his belted giornea. He saw that the brocaded panels of his bodice were more frayed than they had been a few months ago, and he sighed. There was a run in his silken calze-brache and the heels were sadly discolored. He consoled himself with the thought that his shoes, though scuffed, would cover the worst of that. He knew there was no way to repair the leggings in time for the reception, and the knowledge annoyed him. It was bad enough that he lacked inches and that his face was as rough-hewn as a bust by a novice sculptor; to have to dress shabbily was an affront to his dignity and position. He flipped the threads where the knot of pearls should have been and sighed more deeply this time.

He was attempting to arrange his unruly brown hair when his wife came into the room. "Good afternoon," he said, with a degree of affection as he tried to get the locks around his face to curl more tightly, as was the current fashion.

"Benci said that I can't come to the reception, or the banquet." She was a pretty, petulant woman with languorous eyes. Her body was opulent but lacked any quality of voluptuousness. She came up behind her husband and leaned her head against his shoulder. "I wanted so to see the English ambassador arrive. He's bringing an enormous number of men with him, they say. Some of them are very famous."

"That's true." He had given up on the curls and was running a comb through his short beard, painfully aware that he should have trimmed it that morning or the day before.

"What are the English like?" Her arms were still around his waist and she patted him before she stepped back.

"You've seen them before," Lodovico reminded her gently. "You said they all had red faces." It had been almost six years since there had been an official diplomatic visit from England, and this occasion, when King Henry was sending a full mission and his Chancellor to the Grand Duke of Muscovy with secondary visits at Firenze and Cracow, would be of much greater international importance, and therefore of greater ceremony than the previous visit had been. "Henry the Eighth likes these extravagant gestures," Lodovico added, as if he had been thinking aloud.

"They say he's a handsome man," Alessandra remarked, a teasing note in her voice. "It's a shame that he did not want to come as well."

"The King of England would not visit the Grand Duke of Muscovy, my love," Lodovico said as he threw down the comb. "That's the wrong precedent. Sending More is honor enough for a man who hasn't a real crown or kingdom to call his own." He bent down to try to adjust the sag in his silken calzebrache, and succeeded in making the run worse.

"Il Primàrio should see that you have finer clothes, since you're his official poet." She gave a significant look to her own camora, which was as out of fashion as the garments he wore.

"Alessandra . . ."

"It isn't right that we should be treated so," she insisted and folded her arms.

Lodovico agreed with her, but he said, "Il Primàrio has more on his mind than our wardrobes, wife. I may mention it to him. The trouble is, he's too much like his grandfather—oh, he loves the splendor, but most of the time he hardly notices what others are wearing. This is an important evening. He might be willing to listen to me if I point out the state of . . ." The words trailed off as he tried to fix a brooch over the broken threads where the pearls should have been.

Alessandra raised her head, not precisely defiantly, but not at all conciliating, either. "See that you remember. I am ashamed to be seen on the streets. We are not ragmongers. And as for Virginio . . . in case you had not noticed it, my husband, our son is growing and he needs larger clothes. I won't have him wearing those castoffs that we were given. You're a more important man than that, and deserve better."

It was true that Virginio was getting too big for all of his clothing again. A youth of fourteen now, he was getting more manly every day. It was time to send him to Roma or Paris or perhaps Milano or Pisa. He was ready to start his formal studies. Lodovico sighed, realizing that if his son was almost old enough for university studies, then he was older than he had felt himself to be.

"Have you decided where he's to be schooled?" Alessandra asked, with that uncanny perception of his thoughts she had often shown.

"Not yet," Lodovico answered, not wanting to discuss it when he had so many other things on his mind.

"I've heard that the schools in Germany are very good." She had taken the oblique approach, which was her favorite. Lodovico closed the clasp on the brooch and looked at her. "There is a civil war in Germany, Alessandra. You know that. It would be folly to send him there."

"But you'll have to decide soon. Arrangements have to be made if he's to be enrolled before he's sixteen." She was genuinely concerned. There was an anxious line between her brows and her voice had risen a few notes.

"I will speak to Damiano about it," he promised, knowing that until he did, she would give him no peace.

"I was hoping," she said in a different tone, "that you

would be allowed to spend part of the summer in the country. You keep saying that you are tired and want time to work on your new pieces. If we could have the use of one of the Medici villas, one of the small ones, nothing fancy, then you would have your rest and time enough to write without all these court functions taking away time." There was a tightness at her eyes. "I know that you do not sleep well, my husband, and that you are not as happy as you might be here."

"It's a busy year. Il Primàrio has need of me in these times." It was true—Firenze had seemed the hub of the world since 1530, and now, two and a half years later, there was no sign that the activity was diminishing.

"There are villas in the hills less than half a day's ride from the gates," Alessandra said with a touch of asperity. "If you must be near at hand, then let de' Medici put you in one of those."

"If there is an opportunity, I will ask about it. A summer in the country would be pleasant." He stood back and looked at himself in the small, expensive mirror of Venetian glass. He sighed his resignation and gave a last twitch to the brooch. The knot of pearls lay on the table where their luminous beauty derided him. As he put the mirror down, he accidentally scattered the pearls.

"Oh, no!" Alessandra cried as she saw the milky jewels rolling across the brightly painted floor planks. "Lodovico, how could you . . . your pearls!"

He shrugged and smiled. "It looks well enough with the brooch. I doubt anyone will notice." As he reached for the two scrolls he had tossed onto his writing table, he gave his wife a quick kiss, a kind of apology that she was not to be included in the gathering. He knew how much these occasions meant to her—far more than they meant to him. "I'll tell you all about the reception. Who was there, what they said, everything. I've promised to join il Primàrio and the English party after the banquet, but I won't stay too late." This, he knew, was a polite fiction. He had been looking forward to a long con-

versation with Sir Thomas More, whose writing he so
much admired.

"Remember what they're wearing," she reminded
him. "And tell me if that Wessex man is as handsome
as everyone has said. Some of those English are like
angels." She tweaked his beard. "But most of them are
pigs."

"Better for the angels." He laughed as pulled on his
soft velvet cap from which he had removed the bedraggled ostrich feather. "See what you can do with the
pearls while I'm gone. Perhaps you can put them on
the corsage of your blue brocade dress." It was her
newest, only three years old, and was quite flattering to
her, the blue making her rather pale eyes appear
brighter. "You can wear it tomorrow at the garden festival." He added then, more gently, "The banquet will
probably be terrible. You know what it can be like—
everything for show and nothing for taste and all of it
cold."

Alessandra gave a complicated little gesture and
waved him out of the door.

Cosimo, Cardinale Medici was waiting in the antechamber when Lodovico entered, and as soon as Lodovico knelt and kissed his ring, he said, "I don't know
what's got into Damiano, receiving the English when
the Pope is in dispute with the King of England." He
had piercing, somewhat protuberant eyes of a muddy
hazel color that always disturbed Lodovico. Those eyes
rested on him now, and the imperious voice rapped
out questions. "Has he said anything to you? Is it another one of his whims?"

"I don't know, Eminenza. I am only his poet, not his
adviser." As he stood he felt the run in his calzebrache
widen.

"Yet he discusses things with you," the Cardinale
insisted. "And this Sir Thomas More, certainly, is as
much a writer as a court official. It would be just like
Damiano to ask your opinion rather than mine. I tell
you, the Pope is distressed at this incident."

Pope Clemente VII had begun life as Giulio de' Medici, the illegitimate son of Damiano's great-uncle Giuliano, who had fallen under assassins' knives twenty years before Damiano was born. Both the Pope and il Primàrio were as fervently committed to their family as they were to their mutual dislike. Cosimo, being the most important member of the junior branch of the family, was often caught between the two powerful men.

"He hasn't discussed the matter with me, Eminenza," Lodovico said as evenly as he could, knowing Cosimo's capricious temper.

"He discussed banning slavery with you," Cosimo persisted, clearly expecting a response.

"He discussed that with everyone. It was a difficult question. Firenze had always permitted slaves. And it was his first major act after Magnifico's death." He wished he could escape from the scarlet-clad prince of the Church. "I know you felt he made the wrong decision, Eminenza."

"And you think he made the right one?" Cosimo demanded in his harsh voice that was more suited to a military leader than a churchman.

"I have said so. Because I would not like to be a slave." He tried to smile self-deprecatingly but could not quite manage it. "If you have argument with Damiano, why not speak to him?"

"I fully intend to, you may be sure of it. The boy has been avoiding me since I arrived from Roma. I won't tolerate many more insults. It is not only myself he affronts, but the Pope and Holy Church." It was typical of Cosimo to support his arrogance with all the political and spiritual weight he could muster. "He is walking a dangerous path, Ariosto. The Church has brought greater men than Damiano de' Medici to their knees."

Family quarrels always distressed Lodovico, and so he said nothing but, "An unfortunate situation," to Cosimo, Cardinale Medici before he went to the far corner of the room and pretended to study the new painting there. It was by Giovanni Rosso, and not entirely to Lodovico's liking. Forms seemed to be spilling out of the canvas, and the perspective was distorted to play tricks with the eye.

A moment later the door of the antechamber opened and Ippolito Davanzati came into the room. He was resplendent in a giornea ad alie of cut velvet embroidered with jewels, and was quite odiously handsome as well. At twenty-three, he was heir to the third largest fortune in Firenze. "Cardinale," he said as he genuflected perfunctorily and kissed the proffered ring. "Most of the others are gathering in the sculpture garden, though the artists aren't very happy to have it so. Would you let me have the honor of escorting you there?" His manner avoided insolence by the finest edge. At the last moment, he gave Lodovico his attention. "You're here too, are you, Ariosto? I was certain Benci had told you where you should be."

Lodovico despised these smooth-talking politicians. "I'm afraid he forgot to mention it," he responded with fierce civility.

"And perhaps your mind was on other matters," Ippolito suggested so kindly that Lodovico longed to slap his beautiful face.

"For God and the Devil!" Cosimo burst out. "Lead us to the others, Davanzati. The ceremony must be about to begin. We would be insulting"—he was clearly insulted himself—"if we were not there with the rest of the court to welcome the English, no matter how foolish and ill-considered their visit may be."

Reluctantly Lodovico followed Cosimo and Ippolito from the room, dreading the next few hours. He walked the familiar hallways of Palazzo de' Medici to the sculpture garden that opened on the Via de' Ginori.

It was a small courtyard, and much of it was given over to fine marble figures. Here Donatello had worked, and Ghirlandajo, and the young Michelangelo Buonarroti. A few of these masters' works were there, but more of the room was taken up by new, incomplete works of the latest Medici artists.

Today it was hard to study the sculpture, as the place was filled with the unacknowledged aristocracy of

Firenze. Lodovico knew most of them, loathed almost half of them, loved a few. He found himself a convenient corner and opened his scrolls as if studying his verses for the ceremony. In this way he kept himself occupied until the orders were given to proceed to the little piazza between Santa Maria del Fiore and the Battistero.

From the Porta Maggiore of the Fortezza da Basso, along the Via Faenza and the Via de' Cerretani to the steps of Santa Maria del Fiore and the doors that depicted the Gates of Paradise, the way was strewn with fragrant spring flowers. All of Firenze's sixty thousand citizens seemed to have come out for the day to view the procession of the ambassadors from England. Every window, every doorway, every balcony and available rooftop was crammed with people, and now, as the afternoon deepened and the rich golden shadows lay across the Arno valley, turning the houses the color of copper and their roofs the red of old wine, a hush fell at last.

Then la Vacca, the deep-throated bell in the tower of the Palazzo della Federazione, began its slow, mooing toll, and it was soon joined by the bells of Santa Maria Novella, Santa Trinità, Ognissanti, San Marco, San Lorenzo, Santo Spirito, Santa Maddalena de' Pazzi, San Jacopo Oltrarno, Santa Felicità, and the carillons of Santissima Annunziata and Santa Croce as well as the distant bells of San Miniato al Monte. It was a splendid, brazen cacophony, an ocean of sound merging and echoing down the streets as the first company of Firenzen' Lanzi entered the Porta Maggiore of the Fortezza da Basso. So great was the clamor of the bells that the trumpets and sackbuts of the soldiers' band were completely unheard, though they were loud enough to pierce the tumult of cannon in battle.

Between the Battistero and Santa Maria del Fiore, the welcoming committee stood. There were all the Console members who had been in the sculpture garden earlier, each in long and dignified robes with wide jeweled collars of office, a few wearing the various

colored ribbons of their particular Confraternitàs.
There were the senior representatives of the Artei, the
powerful guilds that were the commercial heart of
Firenze and Italia Federata. There were the Ducas of
Milano and Mantova, each with his own impressive ret-
inue. There were greater and lesser clergy—whole con-
stellations of bishops, priors, and priests, all in the
greatest finery the occasion allowed. With them, very
grand in red and tasseled hat, was Cosimo, Cardinale
Medici, his keen, measuring eyes flicking over the crowd
as he waited.

Andrea Benci moved among these diverse and occasionally hostile groups with astounding ease. He
chatted, arranged, informed, always unruffled, never
awkward. His giornea of wine-colored velvet was admired by everyone. He took this, and everything else,
in his stride, turning aside any and all compliments with
a graceful modesty that made Lodovico itch to strangle
him.

Somewhat apart from all this stood il Primàrio, Damiano di Piero de' Medici. At thirty-five, he was in the
prime of his life, a tall, saturnine man with dark hair
and straight brows. The mark of his Magnificent grandfather was on him, but it was less a matter of actual
facial resemblance—though he did have the wide Medici
jaw, long-lidded dark eyes and the firm, thin-lipped
mouth of that family—than manner. He carried a civic
staff in one hand and from time to time he tapped it
against his shoulder. Other than that one nervous gesture, he did little to show his impatience, but Lodovico
knew, after the close association of twelve years, that
il Primàrio was becoming very irritated. Damiano wore
his brocades with a nonchalance that Lodovico envied,
though he did fiddle with the stiff, gold-embroidered
tabard that was the only mark of office he would tolerate.

When at last the troop of Lanzi clattered and jingled
and trumpeted their way into the piazza, they were accompanied by cheers that almost overwhelmed the voices
of the bells. Damiano sighed and motioned to Lodovico

to join him as he moved to the front of the reception committee.

The Capitano of the Lanzi dipped his flag-tipped ceremonial weapon and climbed out of the saddle. "Primàrio!" he bellowed and was only just audible, though no more than ten steps away.

Damiano motioned for him to continue.

"The ambassadors from England!" He gave a sharp, unheard command to the mounted Lanzi, and they parted to allow a second party of horsemen to approach.

Compared to the lavish grandeur of the Italians, the English company was drab. At their head the Chancellor of England rode, and with ill-concealed relief, pulled his horse to a stop. He dismounted wearily, his dark brown, fur-collared cloak dragging on the ground as he came toward il Primàrio. His fine, sharp-nosed face set itself in a smile. "Primàrio de' Medici?" he said formally. "In the name of Henry Tudor, King of England, of that name, the Eighth, I greet you."

There was mischief in Damiano's dark eyes as he took the Chancellor by the hand. "You are welcome in Italia, Sir Thomas More."

More's somber features relaxed slightly and he reached up to straighten the square-cornered cap on his head. "I am mandated to present to you, Primàrio, Sir Warford Pierpoint Edmund Glennard, Earl of Wessex, Envoy to Italia Federata. Also"—he paused and indicated the oldest man in his party—"William Catesby, Esquire Royal to the former King, father of the Duke of Clarence and the Earl of Warwick."

"You are all welcome, were there ten times as many of you," Damiano assured him with half bows to the English party. "It is an honor to have such distinguished foreigners in our country. Lodovico Ariosto will express our sentiments for us."

Nudged forward, Lodovico ground his teeth as he reached for his scroll. His giornea seemed not to fit any longer. He was certain that it was a waste of time and no one would hear him. He paused while the trumpeters of the Lanzi played a fanfare and the bells were stilled, and then, hating the whole occasion, he began to read in a voice that was so strained and high that it was near cracking. What an ordeal it was, he thought, to read for these English with the impossible names.

La Fantasia

Falcone stood beside Lodovico's magnificent mount and stroked the glinting feathers of his folded wings. "He is amazing," the Cérocchi Prince whispered in awe for the third time.

"I've had him since he was a yearling. He was one of the two I brought down out of the mountains," Lodovico said, unable to keep his pride out of his voice. "You should have seen him then. He was all legs and feathers and every attempt he made at flying was simply pathetic." He gave the beaked and taloned horse another familiar pat on the neck. "He's fine now. On land or in the air, I've never seen his match. I can't imagine anything that could best him."

"We were shocked at the horses brought to Nuova Genova," Falcone said. "We'd never seen anything like them before, but this . . . He surpasses everything!"

"Yes, he is something special," Lodovico agreed. "I'd offer to let you ride him, but he doesn't take too well to strangers on his back. We might be able to ride him double. If we don't have to go very far, he should be able to carry two of us." While he was pleased that Bellimbusto was so much his own mount, he thought it would be a pleasure to see Falcone riding him in the sky. "Your name alone should give you the right to soar with him. A falcon like you . . ." He stopped in mid-sentence. "I'll send word to Italia. I'll tell them that you must have one of Bellimbusto's children."

"Are there more, then?" Falcone asked, his black eyes alive with wonder.

"Not very many, but they're breeding well. We've had good luck with the two I brought back. They produce about three offspring a year, and they grow fast enough. The real problem is taming them to ride. If you take a tumble when one of these animals is in the air, well, you might have time enough for a prayer." He chuckled, a full, rich sound that evoked an answering laughter in the Cérocchi Prince.

"Have you ever fallen?" Falcone asked, becoming serious once more.

"Only once," Lodovico confessed, his handsome features darkening with the memory. "Not very far, but far enough." That drop through the sky, when his heart seemed lodged in his jaw, the sickening impact in the field of ripening vegetables.

"You were very fortunate. I would not want to fall off such an animal." Falcone ruffled the feathers of Bellimbusto's neck. "I think such a fall would be formidable."

"It was that," Lodovico allowed with forced laughter.

"We will need much strength against the sorcerers of the Fortezza Serpente," he went on thoughtfully as he studied the folded wings and powerful hindquarters of the horse. "Their warriors . . ." He broke off quite suddenly.

Though the sun was warm on Nuova Genova and the distant waves were a soft, ecstatic sigh on the beach, Lodovico felt cold go through him. "What about their warriors?"

Falcone hated to show fear, and for that reason he

hesitated before he spoke. "They are giants, enormous, as strong as the bear and the panther together. They are armed with javelins and spears, and are all but impervious to us."

"Impervious?" Lodovico echoed. "I don't doubt you, but how can they be impervious? The Holy Roman Emperor in all his armor is not entirely impervious." He folded his strong arms on his chest and waited for the answer.

"They are coated with flint and frost," the Cérocchi Prince admitted unhappily. "When our arrows strike them, a bit of the flint breaks off, but the warrior is unharmed."

"There are cannon," Lodovico remarked. "It would be difficult taking them into the wilderness, but not impossible. If castle walls can be breached with cannon, then these flint warriors will be destroyed by a few well-placed balls, and your archers need not endanger themselves at all."

"I have seen your cannon," Falcone said slowly, little hope in his jet-dark eyes. "Against walls they are, as you say, most effective. But against tall, swift men, what can they do? I don't think your cannon can be maneuvered quickly enough to defeat them." He looked again at Bellimbusto. "These animals, well, that's another matter. With such mounts, we could defeat the flint giants, perhaps."

Lodovico's eyes widened at the thought of such a formidable foe. "Giants armed in flint and frost! Never have I faced such warriors. It may be as you say, and they will be the most difficult opponents I have ever encountered."

"They are that," the Cérocchi nodded mournfully. "Some of our most stalwart warriors have fallen to them. Then . . ."—his face was set with the horror of what he had to tell—"the sorcerer you call Anatrecacciatore takes the skins off our fallen men and with dreadful incantations and forbidden spells, inflates those same skins with the breath of his evil power and gives them

the ability to move again, but at his behest, so that they
enter the numbers of our enemies."

An Italian would have had tears on his face at such
a terrible revelation, Lodovico thought, but these
courageous, stoic Cérocchi would not so honor the evil
of Anatrecacciatore. "Have you the will to fight these
abominations, who wear the faces of your brothers?"

"Ah!" Falcone turned to Lodovico. "You understand.
Yes, that is the worst of it—that we must strike at those
who are most dear to us, and those who have had the
greatest respect of our people."

"Were you hoping, perhaps, that our men, being foreigners, would be able to battle the transformed warriors
without the hesitation that you, in your fidelity, must
feel?"

Falcone acknowledged this with a gesture. "It may
be foolish of us, but what can we do? I saw my own
cousin, whom I had watched die four days earlier, come
toward me with a maul raised to strike, and I did not
want to fight him. I felt my spear enter the flesh and
saw the thing collapse into a withered husk, and still
it seemed to me that it was my cousin who had died
afresh, though I knew it was his stolen skin only, and
the malefic will of Anatrecacciatore, not good, faithful
Boscoverdi who fell."

"You are a valorous people," Lodovico said, his voice
deep with sincerity. "It is a mark of your valor that you
do not willingly attack those known to you, though it
endangers you." He put his hand on Falcone's shoulder.
"We are together in this, good Prince. You and I will
find a way to defeat this evil, or no one will."

"I pray you're right," Falcone responded with a brave
squaring of his angular jaw. "You are new to this land;
you have nothing holding you here . . ."

"Except my vow," Lodovico put in, his fine eyes
blazing.

"Vows have been broken before. There was a promise
of peace between the Serpente and the Cérocchi. You
may still turn away from us and leave us to our fate.
But we Cérocchi—where can we go? This is the land

of our fathers and their fathers and their fathers before them. Our blood is mixed with the earth and we may not leave it."

"You have had my vow, Prince Falcone, that we will fight with you, and if God so wills it, die with you. The sorcerers of the Fortezza Serpente are spawn of the Devil and no Christian knight can call himself true and worthy if he turn from such combat. We will ride into battle side by side, and if we fall, it will also be with our faces toward the enemy and our banners high." He turned quickly back toward Bellimbusto so that Falcone could not see the moisture that shone in his eyes, for it would unman him to weep before this honest Prince.

Falcone put his hand on Lodovico's shoulder. "I will call you my brother, Ariosto, and will trust you with my life."

"And I you, Falcone," Lodovico said when he had mastered himself.

"But if you go, you endanger yourself," Andrea Benci said to Lodovico somewhat later as he sat in the audience hall of the Palazzo del Doge.

Lodovico shrugged. "Life is filled with danger, Podestà, and there is no avoiding it." He stroked his short, beautifully curled beard. "It is important that I meet with the King of the Cérocchi and, perhaps, his allies as well. The longer we avoid this discussion, the greater advantage to our enemies."

"You may be attacked. Wounded! Killed!" The old man's face was filled with terror at the possibility. "You're too valuable."

Lodovico let his eyes rest on Andrea Benci a moment. "I am here because il Primàrio was willing to risk me. How can you, or I, do less than honor his commitment?"

"He does not understand the situation here," Benci protested, his old hands tightening on the arms of his chair so that the blue veins and ridged tendons stood out in the skin like gold in quartz.

"That does not matter, Podestà," Lodovico said even more gently. "If I fail here, it will be my responsibility."

He looked beyond Andrea Benci, and there was a dreamy expression on his face. "In the end, it is a question of worth, of integrity. I could be named the greatest hero of Italia Federata, but if I turn from this war, then nothing would redeem my honor in my own eyes. In the end, it is myself who must answer to God for my actions: not you, not Damiano, not the Saints and Martyrs. You may order me to remain, and still I will go."

Podestà Benci sighed. "Very well, Ariosto. Go, if you must, but I pray, do not expose yourself to needless dangers."

Lodovico gave him an ironic bow. "I will keep what you say in mind, Podestà. It is certain that you wish me success." He stepped back from the frightened old man. "You have a garrison here," he reminded the leader of the Signoria. "You've relied on them in the past . . ."

"That was different," Andrea Benci interrupted, glowering. "They are good enough, of course. They've fended off occasional raiders and a few Turkish pirates, but that is not the same thing as protecting this city from the forces of a strong enemy."

"There is no indication that Anatrecacciatore is on the march," Lodovico said, trying to soothe the old man. "From what Falcone tells me, it will be many days before he can launch an attack against us."

"He's a *sorcerer*, Ariosto! Who knows what he can do! You've heard about the warriors of flint and frost? And the reanimated skins of fallen Cérocchi? You've learned of this and still say that we cannot be attacked?" Andrea's voice had risen to a shriek and he sank lower into his chair, as if hiding from the forces which he feared, even now, were gathering to strike at him.

"It is possible, I admit," Lodovico answered. "We must pray that he has not the power for such a move, or is still unaware of the resistance we're planning."

With a sudden burst of energy, Podestà Benci launched himself out of his chair, almost colliding with Lodovico. "We're desperate here. You know that!"

"Then the sooner I meet with the Cérocchi, the better," Lodovico said quietly as he led Benci back to the chair. "You must not let the people of Nuova Genova see you are afraid, for if they do, they will catch the fear from you, as if it were an infection, and you will be conquered by it rather than by Anatrecacciatore. If you cannot be brave for yourself, Benci, then be so for the people here."

Andrea Benci nodded, his head wobbling on his neck like the head of a poorly jointed doll. "Yes. For them. You're right."

"I'll make my journey as quickly as possible, you have my word, and will return as soon as I may without giving offense to the Cérocchi." He felt a great compassion for the Podestà. He had been an incisive and cold-minded diplomat in his day, but since age had taken hold of him, he had lost something of that cutting edge to his intellect. Before Lodovico had left, Damiano had confided in him that it would have been better, after all, if he had sent Andrea Benci to his family estates in Umbria, or appointed him Senior Envoy to the French court that was so much in the shadow of Italia Federata. "You have served our beloved country long and well, Andrea Benci," Lodovico told him, all the impatience gone from his tone. "Your love and your skill will guide you now, as they have so often in the past."

For a moment, Andrea Benci said nothing. "I've forgotten the way of it," he admitted in a small, timorous voice.

"No, you haven't," Lodovico said heartily. "You are merely out of practice. It will not take long for you to remember."

There was a pathetic gratitude in Andrea's smile. "Perhaps you're right," he said, and added in firmer tones, "if you're going to see the King of the Cérocchi, it would probably be best if you went now."

Lodovico could only admire the courage of that dismissal. He made a graceful bow and withdrew.

Bellimbusto attracted the attention of the entire Cérocchi city as he landed, both Lodovico and Falcone on his back. From everywhere the people came running, most of them shouting, all of them amazed.

"Dismount first," Lodovico said. "He's restless in crowds, sometimes, and may soar without warning."

The Cérocchi Prince nodded and scrambled hastily from the high-fronted saddle, turning to face his people as they gathered around the newcomers.

There were shouts of recognition, and after a moment a path was made for Falcone's father, the great Alberospetrale, King of the Cérocchi. Tall and straight, wearing his age in glory, the King passed through the throng with head high, the jewels of his leather giaquetta interspersed with porcupine ivory and the talons of eagles. As he drew near, Falcone dropped to his knee in homage to his father.

"Now let the gods be thanked: you have come again," Alberospetrale said in his deep, sonorous voice as he raised his son to his feet.

"With this splendid animal and this more-splendid hero, who is his master, to aid us," Falcone responded with pride. "We have been repaid in our good faith, for these valiant Italians have given their word that they will aid us in our struggles with the evil Anatrecacciatore and his terrible flint warriors. In token of their pledge, they have sent Lodovico Ariosto, who defeated the Great Mandarin himself in single combat."

The Cérocchi had quieted as Falcone spoke, and now there was a new energy in them as they stared at Lodovico, who had stayed in the saddle to control his restive mount.

"It is well," Alberospetrale intoned. "It is a great good and we are grateful to the Italians."

Lodovico murmured a few reassuring words to Bellimbusto, then came out of the saddle to kneel at the feet of the King of the Cérocchi. "Great Alberospetrale," he began, then looked up at the tall old man in his feathers and leather and ivory and jewels. "It is a humbling moment, to kneel before you."

Alberospetrale accepted this and indicated that Lodovico should rise. "You have brought two wonders with you—hope and that animal." He indicated Bellimbusto with a distinguished nod of his head. "I have never seen anything like him."

"There are only a few of them in the world," Lodovico informed the Cérocchi King with pride. "I was allowed to have this creature as my own in recognition of valor. Though it was too great an honor, I could not resist accepting him, so fine a mount is he." He reached out and patted the feathered neck.

"Ariosto tells me that it will be good to have his creature in battle," Falcone said, moving closer. "A few such animals as this one, and the flint warriors will not be able to stand against us."

"Excellent." Alberospetrale turned his hard, dark eyes on Lodovico. "I will not deceive you. The forces of the Fortezza Serpente are all armed and ready for war; since his army is made up of supernatural creatures, he need not worry about food and wounds and long marches, as we must."

"But he has to draw his power and contain the malefic forces he employs," Lodovico pointed out. "That in itself will make him vulnerable."

Alberospetrale agreed. "It is true, but without your help, we will surely be cut down so that our entire people are remembered only in legends." His kingly face was filled with a steady sorrow at the words. "We cannot prevail without you. Seeing you and this miraculous animal, I can almost dare to believe we have a chance against the Serpente."

Once again emotion threatened to overcome Lodovico. He could only bow in acceptance of this trust. "I will try to be worthy, great King. If God gives it to me, I will find death in your cause the finest triumph of my life."

Before Alberospetrale could speak again, the crowd parted and this time women approached. Falcone cried out as he saw them, and then went hastily to greet them, giving reverences to each of the women as they came up to him.

"This is my wife and daughter," Alberospetrale informed Lodovico, indicating the first two women. They were quite tall and handsome in that exotic way that reminded Lodovico of the women of the Great Mandarin. "Queen Giallopampino and Princess Ombrenuvola," he said as Lodovico bowed with consummate grace to each woman in turn.

The third woman hung back, and it was Falcone who brought her forward. "And this is my betrothed, of the Scenandoa people, the Princess Aureoraggio."

Lodovico was speechless. He had never before seen such a woman, one so lovely, whose every feature was in such perfect harmony with all the rest of her. Her dress was simple jeweled leather, and yet she outshone the Cérocchi women as a torch does a candle. At that moment, Lodovico wished for a quarrel to force upon his courageous ally Falcone only so that he could defeat him and claim this woman for himself. He bent to brush her hand with his lips. The fingers! Her touch! His pulse drummed in his temples like a call to arms. With an effort he relinquished the hand.

"I am a fortunate man," Falcone said simply, but to Lodovico he sounded intolerably smug and haughty.

"A very fortunate man," Lodovico agreed in a voice suddenly hoarse. "The Scenandoa, you say? I have not encountered them yet, I think."

Aureoraggio spoke then, and her voice was soft as the music of trees stroked by the springtime wind. The words, charmingly mispronounced, enchanted the great Italian hero. "We are the neighbors of the Cérocchi, and live three days' march from here. We are not a very large country, not nearly as vast as the land of the Cérocchi. We could not do you so much honor, but you would be the more welcome."

"If it came from anything that is yours," Lodovico managed to say with all the ardent gallantry that bloomed in his heart, "it would be a finer gift than any I have known, if it were only a drop of water."

Falcone applauded this. "They told me Lodovico is a great poet, but until now, I did not believe it." He said to his father, "These Italians have a reputation for their art, and I have seen their houses and know that it is true, but until I heard Ariosto speak, I did not know what orators they were."

Any tension that might have erupted between them dispersed as Lodovico remembered himself. He reached to slap an arm around Falcone's shoulder. "Come, I will need to find a suitable place for Bellimbusto and then, then there is the war, my friend."

"Bravely spoken!" Alberospetrale exclaimed, motioning to his selected knights to come forward. "These are the men who will go into battle with you. They will tell you what they have learned so that we may better prepare for the coming ordeal."

"I welcome their counsel with all my heart," Lodovico said loudly enough for all to hear. But as Lodovico followed the men into the Cérocchi fortress, he found new worry in his heart. What would he do, now that his strange passion was on him? Could he dare to look at Aureoraggio again, even hear the sound of her feet on the earth, the echo of her voice, and not succumb to her? Falcone was his sworn brother, a noble and valiant Prince, a respected leader of his people. Yet, oh, what was that when compared to the ravages of love and desire that Lodovico nurtured in his soul even as they consumed him?

La Realtà

The fish, predictably, was cold when it reached the High Table in the dining hall of il Palazzo Pitti. Lodovico could do little more than prong at it, letting the tepid sauce drop off the white, flaky perisco. Beside him, Sir Thomas More was attempting to make conversation with Cosimo, Cardinale Medici, but that wily prelate continued to avoid any mention of the English King's reprehensible and unforgivable marriage to the Boleyn woman.

"Talk to Damiano," Cosimo said at last with a quick, distrustful glance at his second cousin. "He is of the senior branch of the family and so is His Holiness. None of them pay much attention to the junior branch of the family."

Sir Thomas was shocked and for a moment could find no response that would not bring shame on the Cardinale, his host, or himself. He took a deep draught of wine and changed the subject.

Lodovico, bored and surly, plucked at the huge, gem-studded sleeve of the English Chancellor. "You've got to understand," he said loudly, to be certain that Cardinale Medici would hear him, "the junior branch is jealous. They've always been jealous. They've said that they could rule Italia Federata better than the senior branch. Not that they'll ever have the chance to do so,

God be praised. They mocked il Primàrio for not making himself a king when he had the opportunity. That gives you some idea of their feelings for the country."

Cosimo, Cardinale Medici, glared at Lodovico. "Poets are fools," he said sweetly.

"Anyone who speaks the truth is a fool," Lodovico shot back, and motioned for a servant to refill his wine cup. "Poets are cursed with clear vision, and a need to reveal what they see."

"Visions! As likely inspired by the Devil as . . ." Cosimo began, and farther down the table, Andrea Benci turned toward Lodovico, ire in his face. He was about to rise and remonstrate when Damiano said in his pleasant, easy tones, "My grandfather said much the same thing. And he was a poet himself."

At that moment, Lodovico could have kissed his patron. It was precisely this odd, generous quirk in the man that made Lodovico stay with him, though he hated civic functions, hated the silly formalities, hated the subtle cross-currents of rivalries and jealousies. When Damiano, with that casual, deft touch, turned defeat into victory, he felt his loyalty renew itself.

"He associated with poets, too," Damiano went on. "He was surrounded by them all of his life. They were his favorite society. And artists. Every variety of blessed madman. He used to tell me about the terrible argument that developed between Leonardo and Poliziano. Not that either of them was an easy man at the best of times, but in this instance they were very angry. My grandfather had come upon them in his library. They were shouting, apparently, and using words out of the lowest workman's tavern. The dispute concerned Buonarroti, who at that time had just returned from Roma. As you may know"—Damiano gestured expansively to his foreign guests—"my grandfather was his first patron. Michelangelo was every bit as unconciliating as a young man as he is now, and he and Leonardo disliked each other most"—he glanced at his Cardinale cousin out of the tail of his eye—"passionately. Poliziano championed young Buonarroti, which infuriated Leonardo. And apparently on this occasion, while exchanging epithets, they'd managed to disrupt the household. My grandfather told me that it was very nearly a week before the two men could speak to each other with anything approaching civility. Both Leonardo and Poliziano had his special genius, and both could be arrogant. Poliziano was not in good health at the time—indeed, he died the following year—and that made him more sharp-tongued than ever, which, in his case, is saying a good deal." He lifted his goblet. "To their genius, then, and we will do what we can to forget their faults."

The guests at the High Table obediently lifted their goblets and drank, and for an instant Lodovico was held by the gently reproving, sardonic look his patron gave him before he set down his goblet.

"Sir Thomas," he said to the Chancellor, taking Damiano's hint, "I have heard that there are men of great literary promise now at Oxford. Sadly, the only English poet I have read is the one called Chaucer, and only in translation."

Damiano nodded so slightly that it would not be noticed if it had not been looked for, then directed his attention to the Earl of Wessex.

In the expanded library of il Palazzo Pitti, two fires blazed in matching hearths at each end of the room. There were only ten people in the vast chamber, and all but three of them sat at the northern end of the room where Damiano was, in the best Firenzen' tradition, serving bowls of sugared nuts to his guests.

"I hope that you will remain here for a week at least," he said to the Earl of Wessex. "Il Doge of Genova will arrive here in four days, and you have so many maritime interests in common, it would be a pity for you not to have occasion to speak together." He waited while Sir Warford Pierpoint Edmund Glennard selected a candied walnut and ate it.

"Primàrio . . ." the Englishman began.

"No, no. I am Damiano to my friends. Il Primàrio, who is he but a puppet of the state? Damiano, however, is another matter. You will find Damiano much easier to deal with than il Primàrio, I give you my word." Behind the laughter there was steel and the English sensed it almost as quickly as the Firenzen', who had known it for years.

"Damian, then," Sir Warford said, dropping the final *o* as was the English habit. "I'm certain you understand that we are under orders from our King, and our time is not as much our own as we would like. We have been mandated to stay no longer in Federated Italy than three days, which will not enable us to be here when the Doge arrives."

"How unfortunate," Damiano said, intercepting a look that passed fleetingly between Sir Warford and Sir Thomas. "Il Doge will, I fear, feel slighted. Perhaps you may find it possible to remain here a little longer, in spite of your instructions. We had planned to offer you a full honor escort to the Austrian border, but it will not be possible to do that until our Lanzi return with il Doge." He leaned back against the side of the fireplace, his elbows propped on the ledge intended for lanterns.

Lodovico had to stifle a laugh, turning it into a cough, for which he apologized.

In that awkward silence, Cosimo, Cardinale Medici, came from the other end of the library where he had been deep in conversation with il Duca of Mantova and Ippolito Davanzati. His scarlet satin robes whispered on the floor as if he brought a nest of serpents with him. "Good cousin," he said to Damiano with a barely concealed sneer, "I fear I must leave this august gathering."

"How unfortunate," Damiano responded with no attempt to dissuade Cosimo.

"My Confraternità is holding a meeting, and since I am in Firenze, it is appropriate that I attend. Gentlemen . . ." He waited for the reverences of the other men in the library, locked eyes with Damiano once, then swept out of the room.

There was another long silence, then Sir Warford

cleared his throat. "Most commendable, attending such a meeting," he said.

"Do you think so?" Damiano made no effort to conceal his disgust.

"They're charitable organizations, aren't they?" Sir Warford asked, startled. "I understood that they were such."

"Ostensibly," Damiano answered with a sigh. "They do good work for the country, it's true enough. But that is not the purpose of the meeting tonight." He regarded his English guests a moment, then decided to speak. "Yes, the Confraternitàs perform many services for the state. They visit prisoners and the mad, provide clothing for the old and those in poverty. They house travelers and keep two hospitals for children. They also, some of them, have special meetings, such as the one my cousin is so anxious to attend tonight. I believe that this meeting will be for those who like to be whipped and sodomized, though I'm not certain. I do know that my cousin has a taste for whipping." He could not disguise his rancor, nor did he try to.

"But surely . . ." Sir Warford began, then broke off.

"There are other pastimes in the other Confraternitàs that are less distressing," Andrea Benci said hurriedly with a swift, reproving glance at Damiano.

"After all, a Cardinal . . ." Sir Warford made another attempt to assume a tolerance he was far from feeling.

"And a member of the junior branch of the family," Damiano agreed sardonically. "He has a great many reasons to wield that whip, or to lie under it himself." Suddenly, infectiously, he chuckled.

"Primàrio," Andrea Benci said in a tone that was dangerously like a reprimand.

"It is of no moment," Damiano said, his manner once again smooth as he turned the conversation into safer channels. "While you are here, you will doubtless want to inspect the various weavers' manufactures in the city. You will appreciate more fully why we continue to be interested in English wool."

* * *

The fires had burned down and the library was sunk into a ruddy gloom. Now only Sir Thomas More, Damiano de' Medici, Lodovico Ariosto, and Andrea Benci remained. Conversation had stopped some little time before, and the men sat in an unusually companionable silence. It was Andrea Benci who broke it.

"I fear age is catching up with me," he murmured. "The hour is long past when I should have sought my bed. With so much to do tomorrow, and the reception to plan for il Doge . . ." He got to his feet and nodded toward the other three. "Until morning then."

"God guard your sleep," Damiano answered quietly and watched as the old courtier crossed the library.

"Ariosto," Andrea said as he reached the door. "I would be glad of your company." He was issuing a command, but Lodovico chose to ignore it.

"I am satisfied where I am, Andrea. You must forgive me." He waited for Damiano's dismissal. If he left the library, it would be because il Primàrio himself had asked him to go, not because his too-autocratic secretary had ordered it.

Damiano said nothing. His eyes were fixed on the deeply carved door, and after a moment, Andrea Benci gave a hitch to his shoulders and left the three men alone. When the silence became oppressive, Damiano said, rather lazily, "And now, Sir Thomas, what is it you've wanted to say to me?"

Sir Thomas More was not startled by the question. "I was not aware that I was so obvious."

Damiano turned in his chair and gave the Chancellor of England a long, hard stare. "When you arrived this afternoon, I thought you were exhausted."

"I was," he admitted. "And my feet hurt."

"So." Damiano fingered the edge of his giornea's elaborate hem. It was a nervous, restless gesture. "I also noticed that you ate only half of what was set in front of you, and you've yawned away most of the evening. Whatever it is you wish to say in private must be very important to you." He had not altered his tone, but the words came faster. He waited while Sir Thomas gathered his thoughts.

"Primàrio," he said deferentially, "I must speak in confidence. It could be most unfortunate, should any of our conversation . . ." Though he did not look at Lodovico, it was clear that the poet's presence distressed him.

"Don't worry yourself about Ariosto," Damiano said rather brusquely. "He's overheard more state secrets than any of the spies at this court. I've never had cause to regret that."

Idly, Lodovico wondered if he should, for Sir Thomas' sake, find an excuse to leave, but he could not bring himself to do it. He admitted to himself that he was eager to know Sir Thomas' secret. He settled back in his chair and studied the embers of the dying fire.

"Very well." Sir Thomas rubbed at his stubbled cheeks. "You know, of course, of my King's dispute with His Holiness." This was a statement of fact. All Europe knew of it. "I am supposed to press Henry's interests with you, as you know. But I'm afraid that I am prey to grave doubts about His Majesty's conduct. I have not been able to accept the new conditions of worship we've been given. I cannot accept his divorce. I cannot tolerate his break with Rome."

"Are you saying that there is rebellion brewing in England?" Damiano asked with a deceptive lightness.

"No, not precisely. That is, there may be, but I know nothing of it, if there is. No. That was not my purpose in speaking. You see, Primàrio, I find that I cannot remain in England. If I do, I must surely defy the King, and he will destroy me. I could reconcile myself to that fate, I think, if I didn't have a wife and family. In conscience, I could not ask them to live in the shadow of my ruin." He spoke quite calmly, as though he had long since made up his mind.

"I myself am not on the best of terms with His Holiness," Damiano said coolly. "I doubt if I could convince him of anything at the moment."

"I would not ask that," Sir Thomas responded quickly. "I was not aware that there were such difficulties,

and I confess I had hoped that there might be a way . . .
But no matter. What I am asking you, Primàrio, Damian, is the right to remain here in Italy. Catastrophe
awaits me at home. Here, I may live and continue to
work. Perhaps I can help Henry to be reconciled with
Rome."

Damiano made a noncommittal sound, then asked,
"And your family?"

"They are at the moment in the Netherlands, visiting
friends."

"How providential," Damiano said, laughing softly.
"You are a very subtle man, Sir Thomas."

"My wife agreed that it was a fortuitous time, since I
was going to be gone so many months in any case. It
would not take them long to come to me here, if I were
to send them word they were wanted." He smoothed the
fur edging on his long gown and at last looked toward
Damiano.

"I see." Damiano fingered his neat, short beard. "You
realize that, given my difficulties with the Pope, your
presence could be something of an embarrassment to
me?"

Sir Thomas stared at his hands in his lap. "Until this
evening, I was not aware that your relations were so
strained. I felt, since you're blood relatives, there would
be a closeness . . ." He could not go on.

"You say this, coming from England where Plantagenet cousins killed each other for more than eighty
years?" Damiano clearly did not expect Sir Thomas to
have an answer to this challenge. "It was clever of
Richard to make Henry Tudor his heir. It prevented
more bloodshed."

Sir Thomas started to rise. "I see. I am sorry that I
importuned you in this way, Primàrio. I beg you will
forget . . ."

"Sit down, Sir Thomas," Damiano interrupted him
sharply. "I haven't refused your request." He waited
while the older man sank back into his chair. "You
are certain you stand in danger from your King?"

"As certain as I may be outside of a cell." There was

a fatalistic expression in Sir Thomas' face, and his words were flat and toneless.

"You are a valuable man to Henry. Do you think he would overlook your worth for nothing more than pique?"

"I am positive he would."

Lodovico longed to ask Sir Thomas what it was about Henry VIII that made him so sure of the King's enmity, but knew that he could not speak without angering his patron. He set his mouth in a tight, closed line, and listened.

"Positive?" Damiano repeated skeptically. "A man who has been of service as long as you have? He must be very serious about his break with the Church."

"He is very serious about the child that Mistress Boleyn carries," Sir Thomas said grimly. "One of the unofficial reasons for this mission to the Grand Duke of Muscovy is that Henry hopes for an alliance there. If the child is a male, then Henry wishes to betroth him to the oldest of the Grand Duke's daughters. If the child is female, she will eventually be the Grand Duchess to the Grand Duke's heir."

"From what we know of the Grand Duke, none of his children have survived infancy," Damiano remarked, but there was a keenness to his face that revealed his newly-kindled interest.

"Yet one of them will probably survive, and Henry dreams of a bond there." Sir Thomas sighed heavily. "What I have told you is treason."

"Then why have you spoken?" Damiano asked, his large brown eyes darkening.

"How else am I to convince you of my sincerity?" This time Sir Thomas actually rose from the chair. "You will want to think over what I have told you, Primàrio. I am, I need hardly remind you, at your mercy. Should you decide to reveal to Henry all that I have told you, my fate is sealed, and it is a dire one."

"For the sake of the Virgin, sit down!" Damiano burst out. "You have no idea what I am thinking. I am not your capricious Henry Tudor. Sit down!" He waited until Sir Thomas obeyed him. "The peace we have negotiated with the Turks is a perilous one," Damiano told him when he was confident that Sir Thomas was listening. "It could be easily overset. If Muscovy and England were to form an alliance, and if Poland could be convinced to join with them . . ."—he shrugged extravagantly—"then our little treaty would be at an end in less time than it would take the parchment to burn. And if we have to take up a sea battle against the Turks again, we will have to cut back our exploration in the New World, and leave it open to the predatory Spaniards."

Sir Thomas listened in dismay. "But the betrothal of children, that could not . . ." He stopped. "Yes, of course it could."

"Indeed," Damiano agreed. "I do wish my twin had survived. There is more than enough work here for both of us." He tapped his long fingers together in an attitude of prayer. "You are to journey through Poland, are you not, on your way to Muscovy?"

It was a moment before Sir Thomas answered. "Yes."

"I see. I assume that your purpose is more than mere formality."

"I can't tell you . . . I've compromised my mission enough already. But what you surmise is not unreasonable." There was a leather wallet attached to Sir Thomas' belt and he opened it to draw out two small scrolls impressively sealed with ribbons and wax stamped with the Great Seal of England. "One is for Poland, the other for the Grand Duke."

"I see." Damiano brushed a straggling lock of dark hair from his brow. "I feared that this might happen, but I didn't think that Henry was prepared to go so far."

Lodovico had known Damiano long enough to recognize the worry in his voice, though there had been almost no alteration of tone. His brow furrowed in sympathy.

"Well." Damiano stood at last, and walked to the fireplace. "I am very much in your debt, Sir Thomas.

Without the intelligence you've given me . . ." He turned abruptly. "You may remain here in Firenze for the moment, though I would prefer you continued on with your mission to learn what you can of Poland's and Muscovy's reaction to Henry's proposals."

"You are asking me to spy for you," Sir Thomas said very calmly, his face a polite mask.

"That's true," Damiano said tersely.

"Spying is ugly work," Sir Thomas muttered.

"War is uglier," Damiano snapped. "You've thrown yourself on my mercy, Sir Thomas. All right, I will take you in, though the Saints alone know how I will deal with my Papal cousin over it. But you've revealed a nest of demons where I thought there were only discontented children. And by God, Sir Thomas, you will aid me now." His soft voice was urgent as he spoke. "If you need a sop to your conscience, consider what might happen if you remain here. Henry will realize that you have thrown in your lot with me, and he will have to press for more forceful arguments. If you continue on with the mission, and return by way of Italia Federata, what can he suspect? Particularly since I will send him my official request that you do so, and tell him that I look forward to your return."

Sir Thomas regarded Damiano, respect in his angular face. "You make it difficult for me to refuse," he said grudgingly.

"I should hope I make it impossible," Damiano answered at once. "I meant what I said, Sir Thomas: I am in your debt. I trust you will forgive me what what I ask of you." Suddenly his grand manner was gone, and Damiano faced the Chancellor of England without any artifice at all. "Do you know what Italia was like before the federation? It could be like that again—a collection of petty kingdoms and dukedoms and counties and republics, all yapping at one another's heels like curs in the street. The civil war in Germany is a good reminder of what could occur here. I love this country to the point of idolatry, and I would sacrifice myself, or you, or Lodovico or any other one I love before I would allow her to be torn asunder by war. If that means that I must make you a spy and myself a hypocrite, I will. If it's any consolation to you, my wife and two of my daughters have been my spies before now, and Pia is a nun, Sir Thomas." He spoke of his younger daughter, who had taken the veil some three years before. "If she could risk eternal damnation for the unity of Italia, why should you balk at a sensible mission like this one? You are known to be an intelligent man, Sir Thomas."

"You possess a strange humility, Primàrio," Sir Thomas said with a sour smile. "You give me no choice, which is doubtless what you intended."

"Until you spoke, I had no reason to ask anything of you," Damiano protested with perfect civility.

"I wonder." Sir Thomas stood slowly and gave Damiano one long, measuring look. "I will go to Muscovy for you, and I will be your tool, Primàrio. When I return I will tell you what I have learned. In exchange, I expect you to send for my family at once, so that I will find them here when I return. I'm certain you can find a plausible excuse to offer my King for your invitation. If they are not here when I return . . ."—he put one hand to his head, as if to touch his thoughts and give them shape. "I would think that the Pope would find my story enlightening."

"I see," Damiano murmured. "Then we understand each other, Sir Thomas."

"And may God have mercy on us both," Sir Thomas answered heavily, and crossed himself.

Damiano kicked at the embers with the toe of his soft leather boot. He had said nothing in the half hour since Sir Thomas More had left the library of the Palazzo Pitti. Lodovico had sat watching him, compassion and distress struggling within him. He could find no words to express his emotions adequately, and kept his uneasy silence as the room grew cold.

Finally Damiano looked up. "He's right. I had intended to ask him to gather information for me." He struck the mantel with the flat of his hand, disgust marking his strong features. "He has contempt for me, but that's deserved."

"He doesn't understand, Damiano," Lodovico said, feeling the terrible superficiality of his words.

"And you do?" Damiano very nearly laughed. "Don't protest, my friend. It's useless to protest." He came away from the fireplace and stood staring down at Lodovico. "My grandfather's best friend was a poet. I hope I am not being a fool to emulate him."

"Am I your best friend, Damiano?" Lodovico asked, his pleasure dulled by the suspicion that Damiano was mocking him.

"After what you've heard tonight, I pray that you are." He smiled unpleasantly. "I meant what I said to Sir Thomas—I will sacrifice anyone I must in order to keep this country united. You will do well to remember that."

Lodovico felt an instant of intense fear. He knew beyond doubt that Damiano was perfectly sincere, and he tried to bury the fear under self-deprecating laughter. "If the death of a poet will change anything, then my life is yours to use as you will." As he said it, he remembered that Damiano was a powerful man, larger and heavier than he himself. All he would have to do would be to lock those long fingers around his throat and that would be the end of him. He got quickly to his feet. "I haven't betrayed you before, Damiano, and I will not do it now." His voice shook, but it was from terror, not fervor.

"If you are not in earnest, you will regret it, my friend." Damiano scrutinized Lodovico's face, then, apparently satisfied with what he had read there, he put an arm around Lodovico's shoulder. It was an effort for Lodovico not to cry out at this sudden, threatening familiarity. "It's late, and you will want to seek your bed. Doubtless Alessandra is impatient to have you with her. If she is anything like Graziella, she will be pestering you until dawn about the kinds of shoes the English wear."

Somehow Lodovico was able to snicker at this, and said with the assumption of sophistication he did not feel, "Wives are often so, Damiano. You know how curious women are."

"None better." Damiano gave a sage nod, then changed again with that mercurial temper that often baffled his associates. "That's unfair. If my wife were not the woman she is, and had been willing to go to France for me to listen to the gossip at court, we might have had soldiers in Torino ten years ago." His arm fell from Lodovico's shoulder. "I am grateful to Graziella and Pia and my lovely Carità. They've been more loyal than my sons ever were." As always when Damiano mentioned his sons there was a fleeting anguish in his face. He turned away from Lodovico, gesturing toward the door. "It's nearly morning and if either you or I intend to be civil to our visitors, it's time we were asleep. I don't like to ask this of you, Lodovico, since I know you'd rather spend the time on that new work of yours, but do you think you might find a way to turn out some simple ballade lyrics? The musicians have been protesting at doing the same songs over and over. Maffeo says that he can set the words to tunes quickly."

Though Lodovico did indeed resent the intrusion on his time, he said, "I'll do what I can, Damiano. Maffeo might have asked me himself."

"But you could have refused him," Damiano said mischievously. "You would not refuse me, however. Or so I hope."

Lodovico gestured fatalistically, thinking as he did that this strange request, coming from Damiano in this way, flattered him, and though he could not admit it, he said, "It will be my pleasure."

"I doubt it, but I thank you for doing it." They were at the library door now and Damiano stopped, giving Lodovico one long, searching look. "I wish I could send you with the English to Muscovy, my friend."

"Send me with the English?" Lodovico asked, dumbfounded. "But why?"

Damiano's face darkened. "A reluctant spy is dangerous. If there were someone else to keep watch . . ." He shrugged. "I'll have to find someone. Perhaps young Ippolito Davanzati."

"That fop!" Lodovico burst out, injured that Damiano would place more confidence in that beautiful shallow young man than in himself.

"Precisely," Damiano agreed. "He's rich, self-indulgent, vain, and venal. Hardly a man Sir Thomas would confide in, or trust. Ippolito hates me. If he were convinced that the journey to Muscovy would in some way harm me, he would be eager to go. My Cardinale cousin would insist upon it." He put his hand on Lodovico's shoulder. "You're too much my friend, and that would make you an object of suspicion, which would endanger you, Sir Thomas, and the mission."

"I am willing to face danger," Lodovico said quietly, but with a certain frightened pride.

"You may have to yet," Damiano said, and under his jocularity there was a steely grimness. "It isn't necessary now, but it may come to that."

"Damiano?" He could sense a retreat in the other man, and wondered if, inadvertently, he had annoyed il Primàrio. He fixed his thumbs in his narrow, rosetted belt. "Tell me how I am to assist you and you may be sure I am your man." He winced as he heard the fabric at his waist tear, then looked down, chagrined, at the dangling brocade belt.

"San Pietro del Pescatori!" Damiano stared and laughed, brown eyes sparkling. "What are you wearing such old clothes for? I know that poets are said to be unworldly, but Lodovico, this . . . ?"

"It's the best I have," Lodovico said stiffly as he gathered up the ruined belt.

"Then order something new. I can't have you looking threadbare. It makes me appear mean. Tell Rodrigo to make you something appropriate. Two giorneas and one of these French-style doublets." He shook his head. "Those doublets. If they get any shorter, we'll have to pad our bums as well as our thighs and calves. You've seen what the English are wearing now—codpieces like

Turkish cushions! That monstrosity that Sir Warford had on . . ."

"Outrageous," Lodovico nodded, though he had been more amused than shocked by the English fashions. He realized, irrelevantly, that Alessandra would be delighted to hear of Damiano's instructions. "My wife and son could use new garments," he ventured.

"Of course. You needn't wait for me to give you permission. Let Rodrigo know when you've decided you want something more. You're not unreasonable in your demands. Two new suits of clothing in a year is quite acceptable; three, if there are state reasons for the third."

Lodovico inclined his head. "As you wish."

"Lodovico," Damiano said kindly, "you're not here on sufferance, and I won't deny you any sensible request. But I can't watch over you either. If there is something you require, give the order for it. If you have doubts, ask me, but don't wait for me to authorize it before you act. I have too much on my mind for that."

"Thank you," Lodovico said, not certain why.

Damiano's long hand dropped. "Watch More while he's here, Lodovico. I want to know what he does."

"As you wish." Even as he accepted this assignment, he felt some of the pleasure of his meeting the Chancellor of England go out of him.

"It's not what I wish, but what I must do." Abruptly he turned and pulled the door open, and without another word strode away down the hall.

La Fantasia

Somehow Lodovico survived the evening celebration with the Cérocchi, but much of it seemed a dream. He could not look at Aureoraggio without feeling his love go through him like a lance. When she moved, the earth trembled. When she spoke, the wind was hushed and the water in the nearby river was silent. Like the sunbeam for which she was named, she shone among the others. Nothing was more graceful than the motion of her hands. The very air was perfumed by her breath.

There were endless speeches, or so it seemed to Lodovico as he sat in the great hall of the castle of the Cérocchi King. Ballads were sung of the exploits of the heroes and the perfidy of their enemies. Great scholars told of the history of this gallant people and the priests commended them to the care of the Cérocchi gods. Through it all, Lodovico struggled with himself, forcing his eyes not to look at Falcone's betrothed, stilling his voice so that he would not declare his love, or betray himself to his valiant comrade.

Toward the end of the gathering, the great wizard-priest Cifraaculeo rose and came to the hearthside. He was ancient, gnarled as a Grecian olive tree and of the same silvery darkness. Unlike the others who were garbed extravagantly, he wore only a long, simple robe of supple, white deerskin. A cap of long pheasant feathers covered his steel-white hair. As he approached the hearth, the Cérocchi grew silent.

"I have listened tonight," Cifraaculeo began in a voice high and quivering with emotion, "to the reminders of our glory and the bravery of our people. This good Italian"—he acknowledged Lodovico with a grave gesture—"has brought us pledges that inspire us all. The water is wide, Cérocchi, and the wiles of the enemy are endless. Though we wish for the promised allies who will be our brothers, still it is not wise to place faith in them until we see them gathered before us. No!" This last was to Lodovico, who had risen to protest. "I do not dispute your honor. I wish only to remind you all of the treachery of Anatrecacciatore. Think of his power, his malice and his goals. Even now, speaking here, we are in danger. Who among us is invulnerable to his great magic? Think! Who can be sure that an evil ghost sent to watch and listen has not entered his body and is at this moment letting Anatrecacciatore overhear every word we speak? Who? I have my spirits to protect me, but so subtle is our oppressor, so versed in loathsome spells, that no one can be inviolate. Take my warning to heart, for I give it with the last of my hope. If we fail here, then we are doomed forever." He had raised his hands in a gesture not unlike a Papal benediction.

"Cifraaculeo!" Lodovico cried out in answer to this. "I am a foreigner here. And though it may be as you tell us, yet I think that a sorcerer would not know how to possess me or any of my countrymen. We do not know your ways, and that in itself may protect us."

"Bravely spoken!" Falcone said.

"Bravely and foolishly spoken," Cifraaculeo corrected him. "Ignorance is no protection. How can you resist an enemy you do not know, cannot see, have not identified?" His questions brought a rustle of uncertainty to the gathering. "Yes, you think of this, do you not? You see now that your promised aid might be worse than no aid at all." He turned toward Falcone and his father Alberospetrale. "You are to lead us, you stalwart men, and our warriors will follow you loyally. But still we must be warned that they are placing themselves in danger, for it may be that the Prince and the King have been possessed by the hideous imps of Anatrecacciatore, for the purpose of destroying you all."

"Wait!" Lodovico commanded, and got to his feet. "It is not fitting that I speak so to you, venerable Cifraaculeo, and did not my honor move me, I would refrain now. But though you give good counsel, and warn us of the hazards around us, still you give us a greater disservice, for if we cannot trust one another, we cannot go into battle. Those who fight side by side are brothers, and as brothers they must trust each other." He turned, regarding each Cérocchi warrior in turn. "Who among you is willing to stand at my side in battle?"

Half of the men responded loudly and Falcone leaped to his feet with a great shout.

Lodovico seized Falcone by the arm. "Yes! And I have called you brother," he declared, trying fruitlessly to turn the image of Aureoraggio from his mind as he met Falcone's eyes.

"And will the rest of you feel so when the man beside you plunges his lance into your vitals?" Cifraaculeo asked, his demeanor changing as rage filled him. "I do not wish to be the last wizard-priest of the Cérocchi, but I tremble. You wish to war against a terrible evil, and for that each of us is grateful. You will not triumph, however, if you deceive yourselves. You have seen the warriors of flint and frost, and know their relentless force. You have had to battle the inflated skins of your dead comrades, and known only sinking horror at such combat. And that is only a part of Anatrecacciatore's strength. He will send you dreams of slimy, gobbling horror that will drive you to madness. He will visit you with fires and rains that will turn your line of march into endless desolation. Every creature in the forest will be at his command, and there will be ravening wolves, monstrous bears, enraged panthers—even the squirrels will be your tormentors."

"Then why do you wish to fight at all?" Lodovico demanded of the Cérocchi, turning his back on Cifraaculeo. "If there can only be death and defeat at the hands of Anatrecacciatore, why do you not flee now? It may be that your wizard-priest is right. Yet I would rather die opposing those who would destroy me than perish from my own cowardice."

This last word stung the Cérocchi. An angry mutter rushed through the warriors and one or two put their hands to their daggers.

"Yes, draw your weapons, Cérocchi," Lodovico said. "Better to draw them and die honorably than listen to despair. I tell you this: it may be that the forces of Anatrecacciatore will overwhelm us all and we will fall to the last man on the field of battle. It *may* be. But if you do not fight, then that death is utterly assured." He folded his arms on his chest and the Order of San Basilio glowed in the firelight. "If it were my choice, I would go to battle alone and unarmed rather than turn from such a fight. In our holy writing, we are told that a shepherd boy with a rock and a sling brought down an armed and fearsome giant. If that can happen to a youth of Israel, it can happen to the warriors of the Cérocchi." He felt Falcone's arm on his shoulder as he returned to his seat, but all that mattered to him was the smile that Aureoraggio bestowed upon him.

Alberospetrale was on his feet, motioning the suddenly noisy gathering to silence. "What this foreigner has told us is right. We deserve nothing more than dust if we will not protect ourselves and our land. Yet, Cifraaculeo is also correct, for there is more danger here than comes from spears and arrows. We must be on guard at all times. For that reason alone, let our wizards, with Cifraaculeo to supervise them, employ all their arts for every protection known to them. Let them petition the gods of the earth and the air to aid us."

Cifraaculeo heard this and bowed his submission, but as Lodovico watched him, he thought he had never seen a more cynical expression in a human face.

"What is it you fear?" Falcone asked Lodovico two days later as they strolled down the street of the armorers. Here men sweated over their forges, tempering metal with the blood of goats and hardening wooden staves in beds of hot ashes.

Lodovico did not answer at once. "I fear, I think, the doubts that Cifraaculeo has sown. I have listened to your warriors at night, and though I am inexpert in your tongue, still I know the sounds of anxiety, and I have heard them too often." He pulled at the short curls of his neat beard. "If I had not been assured to the contrary, I would think that your wizard-priest was with Anatrecacciatore rather than you Cérocchi."

Falcone was shocked and did not respond for a moment. "It's unthinkable. He's been the servant of our King and our gods for all of his life. Oh, I agree that he has not been useful of late." His laughter was brief and strained. "He's an old man and his visions trouble him. His warnings are well taken, for there is always danger from the magic of Anatrecacciatore."

"Perhaps," Lodovico said slowly. "The ways of our peoples are often dissimilar, and it may be that I am refining too much upon what I have heard." Again he pulled thoughtfully at his beard. "I will have to warn my men of these things. I'm afraid that my Italians . . ." —he made a gesture of dismissal—"they might not understand why you allow your wizard-priest to say such things to you on the eve of war."

"And do not your priests speak with you?" Falcone gave him a startled look. "I thought, after the banquet . . ."

"Our priests shrive and bless us, they do not predict disaster. Every soldier will confess and his sins will be forgiven so that he may battle with a clean heart and the praise of God on his lips." Lodovico recalled his guilty love that so thoroughly possessed him, and he was not certain he dared confess it, for he could not, in honesty, say that he repented it. He mastered the sudden tremor within him. He had never before fought with sin on his soul.

"We do not do these things," Falcone said thoughtfully. "I have seen a mass. Andrea Benci tried to explain it to me. I see why it is desirable to drink the blood of your Great King, because that is the way to strength, but why was there no other sacrifice? A god who is to help you in war should not be offered mere bread. He needs something better to bring his help— a horse or enemy prisoners."

Lodovico threw back his head and laughed. "No, no, you don't understand, my friend. God has already had His blood sacrifice in His Own Son. He asks no more of us than that we live as His Son taught us, in harmony with one another."

Falcone's brow furrowed. "In harmony? Yet you pray to him when you go to war?" He sighed in exasperation. "No, Ariosto, do not try to explain it to me. From what I know of your achievements on the field of honor, I cannot doubt but what your god assists you, and that you are a credit to his power, but if he desires that you live harmoniously, I don't understand it." He had been staring straight ahead, preoccupied. Then his expression lightened. "Beloved!" he called out as he saw Aureoraggio approach them.

The sight of her almost stopped the breath in Lodovico's throat. He burned and froze at once as she glanced his way. "Falcone," she answered in her voice that no music could equal. "And the good Ariosto. I have been thinking of your words the other night, and they have given me heart."

Speaking with an ease he did not feel, Lodovico said, "If you would be more inspired at such a gift, I would lend you mine as well, to keep your heart company."

"Again the poet!" Falcone grinned. "It is a great kindness of you to treat my Aureoraggio with such courtesy. Sometimes, being away from her own people and not yet at home among mine, she feels a great loneliness and sadness, and there is little I can say to comfort her. You, however, being another stranger, and with charming ways, have lightened her sorrows." He took Aureoraggio's hand in his. "For both of us, I thank you for your generosity."

While Falcone spoke, Lodovico had been able to

smother the fury that had surged up within him, and
he mumbled a few, graceless words of disclaimer.

"I was so afraid," Aureoraggio said to the both of
them. "While Cifraaculeo was describing the wiles of
Anatrecacciatore, I was terrified to think that he would
point to me, and declare that I was part of his minions.
I am a stranger here. None of the men spoke of it, but
it struck me almost to the heart."

"He could have easily singled me out," Lodovico told
her hastily, wishing he could enfold her in his arms
and kiss away her fears. Had he known at the time that
Cifraaculeo's rantings had caused her one moment of
distress, he would have flung the old fool into the fire
for her.

"I thought that he would," she confessed, lowering
her eyes. "And Falcone has said so many things in
praise of you, it made me think that we were all in
great danger."

"My betrothed and my friend!" Falcone exclaimed
earnestly. "I would not have tolerated the loss of either
of you. My father would stand by me in this, I know."
He touched the jewel-spangled belt he wore where
Lodovico's poignard hung in its ill-fitting sheath. "Cifraaculeo is wise, but often knowledge creates a new
foolishness."

Lodovico nodded, then turned away suddenly. By
way of excuse for this departure, he said, "I must see
how your armorers are doing with the designs I gave
them." In reality, he knew he had to get away from
Aureoraggio, for his passion was dangerously near over-
whelming him. When she had given him that tender
look, standing so near, he had wanted to fall at her
feet. He knew that to do so would be disastrous, yet
disaster had never seemed sweeter.

The next day a runner arrived from the city of the Pau
Attans with dreadful news. He had stumbled into the
Cérocchi fortress in the hour before sunset, and by the
time dusk had come he was dead.

"Did you see the wounds?" Falcone asked in a hushed voice as the priests chanted for the runner.

Lodovico nodded soberly. "I saw them."

"Those are the marks of the warriors of flint and frost. That sharp cut, like a rodent's teeth, with the blackening of frost." Falcone had removed a jewel from his cape, and this he went to place in the dead runner's hand.

Softly, so as not to interrupt the Cérocchi rites, Lodovico began the Requiem, his head bowed.

As the wailing of women rose in the night, Cifraaculeo addressed the assembled Cérocchi. He was magnificent in his long white robe and pheasant feathers, and his voice rang.

"There is to be no peace here!" The words cut through the cries and lamentations. "The gods have declared it!"

This awful announcement was met with renewed keening.

"We have brought the evil to us. It will not depart." He stood back and sprinkled sweet herbs on the body, then knelt to kiss the ground beside it.

"If the flint warriors have already reached the Pau Attan," Falcone murmured, "there is less time than . . ."

"I know," Lodovico responded softly. "We cannot wait for the troop ships to arrive from Venezia, but must prepare with what we have here."

Falcone made a despairing sound in his throat. "If they come upon us now, we will be more helpless than a child abandoned in the forest."

"How long do you think they will take to get here? Two days?"

"I don't know," Falcone admitted. "I would have thought it would be more than ten days, but if they are already upon the Pau Attan, who can say?"

Lodovico nodded toward Cifraaculeo. "Could he tell you, through his spells? If he insists on meeting ruin with such determination then let him use his skills to our benefit." Already his fertile mind was working again. "If you think they won't be here for at least two davs, I can take Bellimbusto back to Nuova Genova and bring their Lanzi here on a forced march. We could not return in one day, but in three we can cover the distance. I'll send the horsemen ahead, and you will have them, at least."

"Is it possible?" Falcone asked. "It would mean that Nuova Genova would be left unprotected, and la Signoria might refuse to do that. I could not blame them for that, when such horror is loose in the world."

"They will send the Lanzi," Lodovico vowed grimly, determination and purpose uniting in his heart. "If I have to force them with my sword, they will come."

"That would not be a promising beginning," Falcone said with a miserable attempt at a smile. "This was not what we agreed upon."

"That doesn't matter," Lodovico responded, his face set in decisive lines. "I was sent here to lead troops. Those were my specific orders from il Primàrio himself. It may not be what la Signoria had intended, but that's not important. We have a pact to honor, and I will see that it is done."

The chanting had become louder and now a procession of priests was coming along the wide road that wound through the Cérocchi city from the temples in the east to the fortress in the west. These men were a magnificent sight, walking in single file at a dignified pace, each holding a staff with the representation of a god upon it. Their robes were of soft leather the color of new-minted coins. They each wore a headdress of porcupine ivory which clattered softly as they walked. Their voices blended in the steady beat of their chant and their steps. Many of the Cérocchi lining the road lifted their arms as the priests went by, and cried out to them.

"My father will have to hear of this," Falcone said, when the priests were past. "I cannot act without speaking to him, and I would wish that you would give him the benefit of your counsel."

"I'm anxious to speak to him," Lodovico said quickly. His fine brown eyes were alight now with the promise of battle, and as he walked beside Falcone, there was a power in his stride that promised well for the fight to come.

"What if these warriors are truly indestructible?" Falcone asked, grimacing at his own apprehension.

"The Fortress of the Thousand Golden Towers was impregnable, I was told," Lodovico responded. "There were those who were willing to believe it and did not put the matter to the test. I was not so complacent." He still felt the thrill he had known as the huge doors of hammered gold had burst asunder and he had been the first over the dazzling wreckage. How good it had been to fight them! He had known a joyous pride then and the blood sang in his veins now at the memory. The Great Mandarin in garments that put his ruined gates to shame had mocked him from the farthest tower, but that derision had stopped when Lodovico's ensanguined blade had claimed his life as the price of his mockery.

Behind them, the priests began a slow, solemn dance for the benefit of the gallant soul of the Pau Attan runner.

La Realtà

All the guards and the English visitors had been sent away from the loggia of the Palazzo Pitti, and the public doors were circumspectly closed for the arrival of the outraged Doge of Genova.

He walked like a pouter pigeon and was much the same shape. His face was that of a demonic baby. He toddled wrathfully up the length of the loggia and confronted Damiano, pudgy hands on his hips. "A fine reception, Primàrio!"

Andrea Benci had been attempting to placate il Doge of Genova most of the morning, without success. Now Damiano smiled with deliberate charm and opened his hands helplessly. "What can I do? They are promised to Poland, and cannot remain more than another six days. You must understand that part of the demands are those of the weather, as they want to reach Muscovy before the cold comes, and with the civil war in Germany, how can they be certain of a rapid journey into Poland?" His voice was easy, his smile indulgent, but Lodovico could see that Damiano's hands were clenched on the arms of his chair.

"It's an insult to the Pope!" il Doge insisted.

"Ercole, their King, has turned away from the Pope. What do you expect the English to do? If they wait for a Papal visit, they are defying their King—if they keep their visit brief, they have a reasonable excuse to avoid seeing the Pope. These are good men, Ercole. They are in a difficult position." Damiano was running out of patience and his words came more quickly though the tone was even.

"And what of the rest of us, pray?" Ercole Barbabianca demanded, his small, brilliant eyes glittering.

"We share that awkwardness, of course. And such outbursts as yours do not make the situation any easier," Damiano added with a touch of asperity.

Doge Barbabianca rounded on Damiano. "I came here on very short notice, Primàrio. Most of my court cannot join me. For that reason, Genova is forced to make a poor showing, and with our shipping contracts in such disorder . . ."

Lodovico raised his untidy brows. So that was the problem. No wonder the choleric Doge was so distraught. He moved forward in his chair to listen.

"If it's any consolation to you, Ercole, Venezia has not had time to send anyone, and Doge Foscari is away in Cyprus. You're in a far less awkward position than they are."

"Venezia!" Ercole scoffed, but with an element of satisfaction. Before the federation of Italia, only eighteen years ago, Genova and Venezia, the great seagoing republics, had maintained a bitter rivalry for half a millennium. Il Doge of Genova licked his lips. "I did not realize that Foscari was still in Cyprus. A pity."

Neither Damiano nor Ercole was deceived. "Of course," Damiano said with a slight, sarcastic smile.

"And the English will be here for another what— five days?" Ercole tapped his dimpled chin with a stubby finger. "Something might be accomplished."

"Sir Thomas More should be willing to discuss shipping contracts with you," Damiano said, and there was the hint of a sigh in his voice.

But Ercole was not mollified. "And what good will that do? He's to go to Poland and then to Muscovy to meet with the Grand Duke. He will be gone for most of a year. Anything can happen in that time."

"He is capable of sending messages and dispatches," Damiano reminded him with spurious patience. "Ercole, think! If you insist on making an issue of this visit, there will be a great deal more than embarrassment to deal with. If you insist on bringing your supposed slight to the Pope's attention, how can Clemente react, but with the full weight of his authority? He will have no choice." He paused, and said in a colder tone, "How little it would take to end our federation. And Italia once again would be at the mercy of every external enemy because we would all be occupied in destroying each other. Or have you forgotten what it was like?"

Ercole was somewhat taken aback. "Don't be silly, Damiano," he blustered. "You're magnifying this out of proportion."

"*I'm* magnifying it?" Damiano was incredulous.

"And you haven't considered my position," Ercole insisted. "I'm here with an insignificant escort, with only my nephew for companion, my court has been left behind, and my Console, and they are *not* pleased, I am asked to deal with a Chancellor of England who will be out of the country for a year, and with a King who is in open defiance of the Pope." Il Doge recited his grievances with perverse delight. "If I did not know you better, I would think this was purposefully done. I suppose I should be grateful that we're not at war with France, as well."

"By the Body of God, man!" Damiano erupted, coming to his feet and approaching il Doge. "What would I have to gain by that? I'd be demented to slight anyone in Italia Federata. It's petty and mean-spirited of you to think this of me." He paced away down the loggia, then came back, and it was clear that he had once again mastered his temper. He ran his hand through his jaw-length dark hair. "Ercole, hear me out, and then if you want to go sulk with your current . . . nephew, that will be all right with me."

The pugnacious attitude of il Doge was not promising, but he said, "Very well, Primàrio. I will listen."

It was a few moments before Damiano began. "Suppose, my friend, that we decide to make an issue of the English visit, with full civic and federal ceremony and all formal visitations. Suppose, again, that we prolong the visit, so that it is acknowledged as a full and official mission to la Federazione. Clemente will know of this, and will not have the luxury of ignoring it, as he can now, and will have respond in some way because of the action King Henry has taken. The most obvious form of action would be the withdrawal of Papal support of la Federazione. Because la Federazione would be compromising the Pope. And soon we would all be at each other's throats, as we were before. Ercole, I beg you, swallow your pride for a few days, as I have swallowed mine."

Ercole shrugged. "It's difficult . . . " he began.

"Of course it is difficult. We're simply a brief stop on a journey. We can't be anything else." Damiano grinned. "I haven't been asked to assist in the negotiating for English wool. We're leaving that to the Artei, so that the contracts are wholly commercial, without any taint of diplomacy."

"Does the Chancellor of England deal with merchants?" Ercole sniffed.

"No. Sir Thomas is a scholar. He's been reading and talking with Ariosto there." For the first time Damiano acknowledged Lodovico's presence. "He's with the masters at l'Academia today, talking philosophy."

Ercole was taken aback. "What will the Pope say to that effrontery."

"The Pope will keep his peace, if he's wise," Damiano said through tightened teeth. "So far Sir Thomas has defended Roma, at great risk to himself. Clemente knows this." At the thought of his cousin, he felt a touch of spite. "Clemente may prefer Cosimo to me, but he keeps to the senior branch, being of the senior branch himself."

Il Doge removed his square, flat-topped hat, as a gesture of capitulation. "I will watch for a day, and then we will speak again. You have my word that I will not exacerbate the problems here." He glanced at Lodovico and gave a significant, questioning wag of his head.

"Lodovico is a poet, not a politician," Damiano said quietly. "Quite refreshing, believe me."

"You Medicis and your poets," Ercole said, and for the first time he laughed. "Your grandfather was worse, I understand. It must be something in the blood."

"So it must," Damiano concurred. "I am grateful to you, Ercole."

"See that you remember it," il Doge said with a wide, malicious smile. Then he went toward the door, for all the world like a ship under sail. "If I find you're deceiving me," he called as a parting shot, "it will be the worse for you."

"No doubt," Damiano murmured wearily as he gave il Doge a half bow. "You see?" he said to Lodovico when the door was closed. "They're all like that. I had Gianpiero at my side before Mass this morning. He feels that Padova was insulted because their delegation did not arrive until after the English got here, whereas Sforza and Gonzaga were here in advance." He crossed the marble floor slowly, his face expressionless with worry. "Milano. Mantova. Padova. Modena. Rimini. The d'Estes are unhappy. What do they want me to do?" He lifted his hands and let them drop down against his thighs. "My good cousin Cosimo is entertaining a French Archbishop this evening, which is intended to be a slap in the face to me and the English. There's nothing France would like better than to see an end to the federation, and if they can also embarrass the English, it's an added pleasure."

"Why don't you speak to him—to Cosimo?" Lodovico had fallen into step beside Damiano as he sought the small door at the far end of the loggia that led to his study.

"My grandfather taught me never to acknowledge a wound. If I mentioned Cosimo's latest treachery, he would know that his dart had hurt me. Like Clemente, I will pretend that I don't know there's a gauntlet at my feet, and perhaps we can scrape through again." He opened the little door and motioned Lodovico to precede him. When he pulled the door to, he locked it carefully.

Lodovico took one of the two chairs on the far side of the writing table. He could not forget the contempt in Ercole Barbabianca's face when Damiano had introduced him. It stung him as deeply as laughter could. He tried to smooth his straggly beard and thought again that it ought to be trimmed.

Damiano had taken his single, high-backed chair and was reading the various letters and petitions stacked neatly on the writing table. The third letter made him snort disgustedly. "My wife's brother," he explained curtly. "He's in Pamplona now. He wants me to endow a monastery there. That would truly put the seal on disaster." He sailed the letter to the far side of the table for Lodovico to examine. "Padre Humilidad indeed! Lazaro Frescobaldi is a sham, and always has been.

How Graziella can be so true-hearted and he such a rogue, I will never understand."

"In Spain?" Lodovico said, disbelieving even as he read the letter. "But the Pope has put all Spain under interdict," he protested. "What can Lazaro be thinking of?"

"His own advantage. When has he ever thought of anything else? First it was that monk Luther in Germany, and now Hieronomites in Spain. It's a good thing his father's dead and cannot be shamed by him." Damiano's face had flushed with anger. "Don't mention this to Graziella, will you, Lodovico?"

"Why should I?" Lodovico asked, genuinely confused. He had little contact with Damiano's wife and on the rare occasions when he did, his wits had a tendency to fail him. Beautiful women often flustered him, and Graziella Frescobaldi was reputed to be the loveliest woman in all of Italia Federata.

The harsh lines left Damiano's face. "A courtier would have the answer to that question, but I am pleased that you don't. My wife is an intelligent woman, and devoted to this country, but there are those who would use her scapegrace brother to coerce her . . ." He did not finish, but turned and stared out the window. "It happened once. In France. Never let her know that I told you." Suddenly he cleared his throat and picked up the next sheet of folded and sealed vellum.

At sunset the Venezian envoy arrived with a party of ten men-at-arms and a dozen courtiers. He presented himself at once to Damiano in the loggia of il Palazzo Pitti where il Primàrio's guests had hastily assembled. Damiano had hurriedly changed into a giornea ala scala and taken his seat in the loggia a scant ten minutes before the Venezian company came in through the street doors.

"Primàrio, on behalf of Doge Foscari, greetings from Venezia." The envoy, Sergio Vanazza, was a tall man, fair-skinned and light blond, as were many of the Venezians. He wore the badge of the Leone di San Marco on a heavy gold chain around his neck and carried the staff of his office.

"Our greetings to him," Damiano said, with a side-glance at the irate face of Ercole Barbabianca. The Genovese Doge had turned an unhealthily mottled shade of plum as he watched the Venezians introduce themselves.

"The occasion of an unofficial visit from representatives of the King of England must be a pleasure to us all," Sergio Vanazza enthused.

"You will allow me the pleasure of making you known to Sir Thomas More, Chancellor of England; Sir Warford Glennard, Earl of Wessex; and William Catesby, Esquire Royal," Damiano said, in a tone that suggested he would rather have surrendered to the Turks.

"A great honor!" Sergio exclaimed, bending his knee to Sir Thomas. It was a courtesy far beyond that required by custom, and it set the hall rustling. Ercole Barbabianca could be heard to swear comprehensively.

Lodovico, standing near il Primàrio, saw the annoyed frown that flickered across his face and was gone. He took the scroll from the sleeve of his lucco and asked in an undervoice, "Do you want the verses now?"

"No, I want to be at table. Still it might be as well if you read them. Anything to stop this debacle." He put one hand to his eyes as Lodovico drew back, aghast. "Pardon me for that, my friend," Damiano said very softly. "By all means, read the verses. Perhaps then Vanazza will cease this display."

Lodovico accepted the instructions and stepped forward, holding up the scroll as much as a gesture to get attention as to prepare himself. He saw that the Venezian Envoy had got to his feet and was looking thunderous. " 'On How Venus, Goddess of Love, Was Born of the Sea at Venice,' " he announced in a loud, harsh tone, and waited while the gathering fell silent.

When the messenger arrived from Napoli, Damiano flung the book he had been reading across the room and almost overturned his chair as he rose. "Now Napoli! Damn every one of them to perdition!" He walked the length of his library and glowered at Andrea Benci. "I suppose I'll have to receive him," he said darkly.

Benci's expression was wonderfully smooth. "He has come a long way. It is not his fault that his King sent him." The old courtier folded his hands at his waist and waited with maddening politeness.

"All right!" Damiano muttered, adding to himself, "Who is doing this? Why?"

Though Andrea Benci, who was across the room, did not hear this, Lodovico, who had risen at Damiano's outburst and stood little more than an arm's length away, did. He wished he could question il Primàrio, but concern stopped him. Andrea Benci was in the room and the messenger from Napoli was eager to be presented.

"Bring him in here. I won't snap his head off. Apologize that I am not more formal. Tell him that we don't have official court functions on Wednesdays, or something similar. Heaven forfend that he should think he has been insulted." As soon as Andrea had closed the door, Damiano put his hands to his head. "I am going distracted!"

At that, Lodovico decided to speak. "You think that someone is doing this? How can you discover who it is?" He decided not to offer comfort, since he did not know how it would be taken.

"No. No, I don't." He breathed deeply, and then straightened himself. "Someone must be doing it, though, and doing it to embarrass la Federazione. First Genova, then Venezia, then Rimini, and now Napoli. We'll have the Pope on the doorstep next and all the demons in Hell will be on us." Damiano began to pace. As he walked his simple, short, woolen guarnacca swung above his knees making a gentle, rushing sound. "This was supposed to be an unofficial visit. That way we did not need to risk challenging the Pope. Now everyone in Italia seems to know of it, and unless the English leave quickly, Clemente must notify us of his displeasure."

"But who would want to do this?" Lodovico asked. "War is one thing, but why bother with . . ."

"Why waste the money and lives in a war when there are other ways of fighting? Why do you think I want Sir Thomas to bring me news of Russia and Poland? I had hoped that Poland, being Catholic still, might refuse to be allied with the Russian and English churches, but for that I'd need Clemente's cooperation, and now . . ." He stopped at Lodovico's steeply-canted desk and leaned against it. "I think that the Pope would say prayers of thanksgiving if that alliance is made only to repay the injury he thinks he has received from me."

"You can explain that to Clemente, surely," Lodovico said, putting his book aside.

"Can I?" Damiano asked sadly. "Should I even make the attempt?" He grimaced and was about to say more when the door opened again and Andrea Benci escorted the messenger from Napoli into the room.

"Oh, God," Damiano said in an undervoice to Lodovico as he recognized the man. "He's a cousin of the della Roveres." That family had been the sworn enemies of the Medicis for five generations.

"Primàrio de' Medici?" the messenger said with the slightest of bows as he came into the library.

"Good day to you, Adriano Montini," Damiano greeted the arrival with courteous reserve. "Your King has somewhat surprised me." As he spoke, he strolled toward the visitor, his hand out for the scroll Adriano carried.

"It is my King who is the more surprised, Medici," was the sharp return as Adriano Montini slapped the scroll into Damiano's outstretched hand. "A visit from the Chancellor of England, and the King of Napoli was not informed?"

"A very brief, very unofficial stay on a journey to the Grand Duke of Muscovy," Damiano answered, sounding fatigued. He opened the scroll and read it. "Your King is a master of the invective," he observed when he had finished. "Pray, what does he want of me, other than my abject apology?"

Lodovico wanted to protest the idea. He locked his hands on the tall desk and kept silent. If Damiano had wanted his defense, he would have indicated it.

"I recall that when Henry broke with Roma, it was your King's opinion that none of us have any dealing with the English whatever. In not informing His Majesty of Sir Thomas' visit, I had hoped to spare his feelings." This was said so very smoothly that it was more condemnatory than wrath would have been.

"This is another matter," Adriano snapped, but there was trouble in his faded brown eyes. "Manrico has been King less than two years, and with the new laws of the federation, his position is ill-defined. This is just another example of the ambiguity of his position."

"You have that wonderfully well rehearsed," Damiano approved. "My congratulations."

"If you intend to scorn my King . . ." Adriano's round face darkened and his voice took on a strident edge.

"Nothing of the sort," Damiano assured him. "I have been trying to honor each member of la Federazione as he indicated he wished to be honored, though in this instance, I seem to have failed most reprehensibly." He held out the scroll to Lodovico.

"Damiano?" Lodovico asked. He had never been given an official document by il Primàrio, and he was not certain if that was Damiano's intention now.

"Take it; take it." When it was out of his hands, he gave his attention to Adriano Montini again. "Since you have come, you must meet the English, and give them whatever tidings Manrico has seen fit to send, providing they're civil."

Adriano looked about to strangle, but managed to say, "It is not for you to question what my King says to the English."

"Oh, yes it is, as long as the English are my personal guests." Damiano managed to laugh in his familiar, easy way, though Lodovico could see how much it cost him. "Remember that: the English are guests of this city, not Italia Federata. Firenze and England have done business for centuries, and it is good that the Artei leaders have the chance to deal with them personally from time to time."

"If they are bargaining, why are you not with them?" Adriano demanded.

"I should think that's obvious. They're doing commercial contracts, not diplomatic ones. How many times will I have to explain that? I don't know how so many of the regional rulers of la Federazione got the impression that there was more to the visit than that." He gave Adriano a sharp look, then addressed his secretary. "Andrea, take this man to the dining hall and see that he has a decent meal. If the inns on the road are as bad this year as they were last, he must be faint from hunger."

It was a dismissal, but one that Adriano Montini was not apt to dispute. He bowed, a little more deeply this time. "I am grateful, Primàrio. I trust that you will reserve some time for me while I am here so that this misunderstanding, if there is a misunderstanding, may be ended."

"I would welcome it," Damiano said earnestly, and watched until the messenger and his secretary had withdrawn. "A misunderstanding. That is one word for it."

Lodovico heard the implacable note in Damiano's voice, and did not speak. In his hand the scroll from Manrico II, King of Napoli, dangled unread. He saw the lines deepen in Damiano's brow and felt his own forehead contract in sympathy. "Is there anything . . ."

Damiano looked up swiftly, as if he had forgotten Lodovico was with him. His frown grew thunderous, and then faded as he said ruefully, "You know, I never intended to drag you into this. I was only doing as my grandfather suggested. He used to tell me that the love of learning and intellect banishes the love of politics—according to il Magnifico, those who love politics are the ruin of nations and those who hate them are the salvation, for only they seek true and workable solutions." He walked down the library to where a tall portrait hung over the smaller fireplace and stared up at the face there. "He was sixty-seven when that was painted. You cannot imagine how thin he had become in those last years. Enrico fleshed him out some, but I remember how gaunt he was. He talked a great deal about Poliziano that last year. He missed him, and loved him. He told me to marry a Firenzena, that the family was getting its blood too much diluted by Roman Orsini. He insisted that my father's second wife be Firenzen'. My mother was a Rucellai. My wife is a Frescobaldi. My daughter Carità is the wife of a Strozzi. What could be more Firenzen'?" His gaze lingered on the exhausted, regal face of Lorenzo, whose large, dark eyes seemed intensified by his pale skin and fringe of pewter hair. "He hated going bald, but he refused to wear a wig." He stepped back a few paces, still watching the portrait. He shook his head once, twice. "I wish he could advise me now. These last few days, I've been going over in my mind all he told me. If only I could get to the bottom of this!" Abruptly he turned away from the portrait and came back to Lodovico. "He can't answer me, and I've worn myself out trying to find someone who can—and will."

"The English will be gone in three days," Lodovico said with what he hoped was encouragement.

"That's something," Damiano nodded slowly. "But whatever it is, it won't stop because they're gone. It's like a river in winter, Lodovico. This is simply one of the places it has broken through the ice. Whether you see the river or not, it is still there and it still flows, no matter how deep the snows are." He looked down, then inhaled sharply. "I should not have given you that," he said as he held out his hand for the scroll.

"I didn't read it," Lodovico hastened to reassure him.

Damiano laughed bitterly. "That's not my concern. It is only that now everyone will think you read my scrolls and dispatches."

"But I don't," Lodovico protested, thinking for the first time that perhaps Damiano did not trust him. A swift stab of disappointment went through him, but he banished it resolutely.

"That's not what will be believed," Damiano said thoughtfully.

"I'll tell them the truth, then. And if you deny that I'm given any of the documents . . ." He was cut off by Damiano's laughter.

"Then it would *certainly* be believed. If you deny it and I deny it, why, there'll be no way to convince them that you aren't wholly in my confidence." He stopped and looked at Lodovico. "That wasn't meant as it sounded. You are, in fact, in my confidence, but not in the way most of the world interprets the word. Lodovico, I wish I could protect you from the malice that you haven't earned but will receive nonetheless. I can't do that. It's the price of my friendship, I'm afraid." He offered the scroll. "Would you like to read it?"

Lodovico gave his shoulders an awkward hitch. "I suppose not, if it only insults you."

Damiano tossed the scroll onto the writing table across the room. The scroll skidded on the polished wood, rolled, and fell to the floor. "Damnation! It shouldn't have done that." He lifted his eyes to the elaborately carved ceiling, an expression of abstraction on his face. "I think," he said after a pause, "I think that you and Alessandra and that boy of yours—Viriginio?—Virginio, will go into the country for a month or so. You could use the writing time, could you not?"

"Yes, of course, but . . ." Lodovico knew that Alessandra would be delighted with this news, and realized that though it was something he had thought he desired himself, now that the opportunity was presented to him, he did not wish to have it. "Wouldn't you rather have me here?"

"For myself, yes, but for you, no. I'll lend you the old villa at Fiesole. That way, if I need you, you will be only an hour away. You can work there, and for a time you need not be bothered with the suspicions of the men of the court." He looked over the racks of books and said, "That early book of Nicolo's, you've read it?"

"Yes." The word came out more sharply than he had intended, but his passionate dislike of Machiavelli had not died with the man.

"Yes. It's a pity he's not around. Oh, the book is infuriating, but it is good counsel in an emergency, and that is what this is, my friend. I may send for Guicciardini, though I'd rather keep him with Charles while the German war continues." He caught the distress in Lodovico's eyes. "Don't fret: I'm not casting you aside. I am only trying to gather what protection I can."

It was an effort for Lodovico to accept this gracefully. "If there is to be a battle, I would rather be allowed to fight," he said, getting to his feet and straightening his shoulders. He wished that he made a better showing, that he was taller and stronger and keener of eye, but there was no way to change himself. He was about to put his thumbs through his belt, but remembered at the last moment what had happened before, and let his hands hang at his side.

"It's not that sort of fight, I fear." Damiano bent to pick up the fallen scroll. "This time, it is more subtle, like a plague spreading through us. It is as deadly as war, and is conducted by similar rules, but like a disease, it contaminates everything it touches. For my own sake, I would like to think I've spared you that, and I will, for as long as it is possible to do so." He had put the scroll on the table and now he opened it idly and glanced over the message. "When it is no longer possible, you would do well to fear me."

Lodovico held himself rigid, but inwardly, his spirit sagged. He had no words to offer Damiano that would ease him, and now it seemed that his presence was not required. His jaw tightened against an absurd impulse to protest.

"When the English have left us, I will make arrangements for you to go to the villa." Damiano rolled the scroll once more.

"I . . . thank you." Lodovico could not bring himself to say more.

"Do you indeed?" Damiano laughed shortly. "Not now, perhaps, but you might, one day."

Before Lodovico could think of a proper response, the door opened and Andrea Benci announced the arrival of Ippolito Davanzati.

La Fantasia

Podestà Benci's wizened face was pasty white as he listened to Lodovico's report. At the end of it he tottered to his feet and came across his council chamber, his expression anguished. "We must leave. That's the only thing to be done. How else will we be safe? We must leave quickly."

"Leave?" Lodovico burst out, horrified at what he heard. "It is precisely now that we must stand and fight! How can you think of leaving when we would be abandoning these noble Cérocchi to ruin and destruction?" He went on his knee to the leader of la Signoria. "You are a man of honor, Podestà Benci. You are revered for your wisdom. How, then, can you think of leaving the Cérocchi, even for a moment?"

"But Anatrecacciatore," Andrea protested. "You've told me what the runner from the Pau Attan said before he died. Ten of their villages have been decimated and their capital city is under siege—if it hasn't fallen already," he added darkly. "For the love of the Virgin, get off your knee, Ariosto."

Lodovico rose gracefully. "I must make you understand, Podestà," he said urgently, his words vibrant with purpose. "I have given the Cérocchi my word that we will stand by our agreements with them . . ."

"You have what?" Andrea Benci exclaimed, stepping back in horror at what he heard. "What possessed you?"

"Nothing possessed me," Lodovico said, his chestnut-colored eyes graying with suppressed rage and disgust. That this old man should be so powerful, and so afraid! His shapely musician's hands knotted themselves into soldier's fists at his side. "There are cities in the world where Italians are regarded with contempt as a race of spineless merchants. Always in the past I have defended my own, but seeing you, Podestà, I realize that their accusations and disparagement were correct."

This cold condemnation brought Andrea Benci up short. He regarded Lodovico with loathing, his features changing swiftly from abject fear to haughty anger. "Spineless merchants, when we have half the world in our hands?"

"But it wasn't the merchants who took that world," Lodovico reminded him. "There were no merchants with me at the Fortress of the Thousand Golden Towers, only my warriors, who were not afraid to fight, though they knew many of them would not live through the encounter." He had to blink back tears at the memory of those fine, courageous men who had fallen to the soldiers of the Great Mandarin. If only he could have half, a third of their number with him now, in this new and unexplored land!

Andrea Benci sneered, but his voice cracked. "It is not your decision to make, Ariosto. You are not mandated with the safety of Nuova Genova. When you have lived as long as I have, you will learn that what men like you call cowardice the rest of the world calls prudence."

"That may be," Lodovico said as he followed the old man across the room. "But I do not anticipate an old age. Old age is the reward of a safe life, and it has never been my goal to live safely." He folded his arms across his chest. For a moment he sincerely pitied the old Podestà, who had so little steel in him, but it was an emotion he could not indulge, else the Cérocchi, Nuova Genova, and all of this wondrous land would be lost.

Once seated, Andrea seemed more confident, as if the chair were imbued with the power of the state and could bolster him up. "You have only that messenger's word that the warriors of flint and frost have wrought so much destruction among the Pau Attan. In the confusion of battle, it may have appeared worse than it was. I have heard from the captain of my Lanzi that it is easy to be mistaken in battle." He offered this argument in an unsteady voice. He could not bring himself to meet Lodovico's eyes.

"You did not hear the messenger, Podestà Benci, and I did. A soldier knows when a report is genuine, and I have never before heard such conviction on a man's lips as I heard then. He died to tell us of the fighting." His words were low with feeling and he wished fervently that he could have brought the dying Pau Attan runner to this old man to tell his story again.

"What do you want me to do, then? I must call the Signoria to meeting, of course, to hear how we may best evacuate the city . . ." His suddenly rapid babble was interrupted by Lodovico.

"*No!* I tell you that you will not leave! If I must destroy every ship in the harbor to keep you here, I will. Pray don't think that I exaggerate. I have sworn fealty to Falcone"—he blotted out the image of Aureoraggio that rose in his mind—"and I will not be forsworn for you or anyone. When Damiano sent me here, it was because he knew that we could no longer haggle like merchants." He put one foot on the first step of the dais. "I am empowered to assume command of your troops, and if you make it necessary, I will do that."

"God have mercy on us," Andrea muttered as he

crossed himself. "You're a madman. Il Primàrio cannot have intended you to do this."

"Mad? If to love honor more than life is madness, then I most certainly am mad." He threw back his magnificent head and laughed heartily.

"Raving, too," Andrea said under his breath as he regarded Lodovico with something between abhorrence and awe.

"No, no, old man, not raving." He managed to stop laughing to speak again. "You cannot know how I feel now, because you have never known the joy of hazarding your life for glory."

"Joy?" Podestà Benci demanded.

"Yes, joy. There is nothing more intoxicating, except the fulfillment of love. If I could trade every moment of danger for a year of peace, I would not do it, not if it meant losing that superb elation that one knows only with a sword or his beloved in his hands." He stepped down off the dais. "Call la Signoria to meeting, and quickly, for we have little time to prepare. And tell them that we will not turn away from this land, for it is not only the land of the Cérocchi, it is the land of Italia as well that we defend." He walked swiftly across the hall and did not pause to listen to Andrea Benci's sputtering objections. He was determined to speak to the captain of the Lanzi before la Signoria gathered.

Massamo Fabroni was a soldier of the old school—rough of face and speech, touchy in matters of honor, inwardly and outwardly scarred by his profession, and thoroughly pragmatic. He stood, hands clasping his belt, head erect, facing Lodovico at the entrance to the barracks of the Lanzi.

"We must talk, you and I," Lodovico said with an appreciative grin to the captain.

"If you would have it," Massamo said, standing aside to let Lodovico enter the common room of the barracks.

It was a low-ceilinged, large place, with three hearths and a number of low tables and benches where most of the Lanzi spent their idle days. It smelled strongly of wine and leather and sweat, all the odors mixing into a rich, earthy pungency that to Lodovico was the essence of bravery as incense is holiness to a priest, and just as sacred. There were perhaps fifty men taking their leisure after their midday meal. Some of the soldiers were engaged in polishing their arms and armor; a few were dicing; in the far corner two men sat at a small table, grimly arm wrestling; nearer the door, half a dozen soldiers shared the last of a small barrel of wine, singing boisterously over their cups. They had given little heed to their captain until he rapped out to them: "Rise!"

There was a moment of hesitation, then a startled scramble as the soldiers got to their feet, abandoning their activities as they looked toward the door.

Today Lodovico was not so grand to see as he had been upon his arrival, but he was still impressive.

"Ariosto has returned to us and has news!" Massamo Fabroni moved in Lodovico's wake, and his announcement captured the attention of all the Lanzi.

"Yes," Lodovico said pleasantly. "I have just come from the capital city of the Cérocchi where they have had news from the Pau Attan. The forces of Anatrecacciatore are on the march. They have already sacked many of the cities of the Pau Attan and they will turn next to the cities of the Cérocchi and the Scenandoa. We have sworn to aid the Cérocchi in their struggle with these hideous foemen, and if you are with me, we shall." He could see their eyes filling with that steely light that would carry them to triumph in battle.

"What about the troop ships?" a well-weathered sergeant asked from the bench where he had been repairing the grip of his sword hilt.

"We have been promised more troops, but even if they depart in all haste, they will not arrive here for many days. We must act now, and though there are few of us, we will have to stand with the Cérocchi. Each of us must hold his life precious and sell it dearly to those who oppose us." Lodovico began to walk around this common room, his tread firm and his motions decisive and brisk. "I have heard that when this city was founded there were those who opposed you— not the Cérocchi, but others. Some of you will remember those days. So must you fight now: Anatrecacciatore is a wizard of enormous power and immense evil. His warriors are creatures that are as terrifying as they are dangerous. We cannot win if you lull yourself into the belief that since these people do not have cannon and other firearms they are therefore easy to defeat." He paused and watched as the various soldiers reacted to his words. One man with a vicious scar across his nose and cheek let out a terse laugh, another patted the mace that hung from his belt.

"Those of you who have fought in this wilderness will have a better understanding than the rest of the particular difficulties that will confront us in our campaign. It would be well for you who have fought in the forests to tell those who have not what you experienced." He recalled, as he spoke, how valuable his guides had been in the Orient, for they knew the trackless deserts and cloud-shrouded mountains and had been able to make the way easier.

"What has la Signoria to say to this?" Massamo demanded abruptly.

"La Signoria has not met and I have yet to discuss this with them," Lodovico answered, his face revealing how little he thought of la Signoria.

"They may refuse to let us follow you," Massamo warned and was supported by the murmur of many of the Lanzi gathered there.

"It matters little what they decide. I am a Commendatore Generale of the armies of Italia Federata, and as such, am empowered to declare martial law. So far I have refused to do so because I did not want to alarm the people here any more than necessary, but if la Signoria attempts to thwart me, they will find that their powers have been suspended. I will admit," he said, more mildly, "that I would not like to take such drastic action. It would be better if la Signoria sees wisdom and votes to honor the pledges they have made to the Cérocchi. But we must not let our oaths be abjured by those old men. Remember that you are paid by la Federazione, not by la Signoria, and that you are sworn to uphold the word of il Primàrio as well as the word of the Doge of Genova."

"The powers of the Doge are strong here," Massamo said, simply stating a fact. "If we act in a manner contrary to their orders, we could be considered mutinous, and they would be justified in leaving us here or having us killed."

This time there was louder confirmation from the soldiers, and one of them lifted his arm in a rude gesture.

Lodovico heard him out, and made no attempt to deny this. "Yes, they could declare you mutinous, but my word before il Primàrio will be final. You are protected, so far as Italia Federata is concerned. What we must do now is make certain that la Signoria does not give us any more interference than is absolutely necessary."

His listeners gave grumbling consent to this, but there was a new excitement among them that was as charged as the air of a thunderstorm. Laughter, eager and ferocious, was mixed with their breath and one or two gave it voice in soft, potent bursts.

"It must be war," Lodovico declared, his rich voice ringing in the low-ceilinged room. "Any other course is despicable. When I was with the Cérocchi, one of their number cast doubts on us, saying that we might change our minds and withdraw from this land. There are those of la Signoria who would wish to prove that calumny true and brand us with traitorous treachery before our good allies." He felt the color mount in his face at the mere thought of this shame. He raised his head proudly. "I refuse to be branded a coward by doddering old men who have never swung a sword in their lives!"

A roar of approval met this and Massamo Fabroni put one enormous hand on Lodovico's shoulder.

"Those of you who have seen the Cérocchi know what superb warriors they are and will be proud to fight beside them. The forces of Anatrecacciatore are subtle and vile beyond anything I have known before. For that reason, I have little blame for Podestà Benci and la Signoria for their timorousness. They see the power and the evil of the sorcerer and their bones turn to milk within them."

"Or to cheese," said a wit among the soldiers. Laughter boomed through the common room.

"They are doing as they think they must," Lodovico said when there was quiet again. He had been laughing with the rest and his voice was not entirely steady. "Do not treat them with scorn or contempt because they are not brave. It is not the merchant's part to be brave; it is the soldier's virtue." He heard a muttered objection and he added with utmost sincerity, "No, no, my friend. Don't let yourself be seduced by your own stalwart heart. You must be willing to understand why they fear, for that understanding will give you wisdom and strength, both of which we will need in abundance if we are to come through this campaign with victory." He spread out his arms, as if waiting to embrace the room; dedicated himself to uphold their honor.

Massamo said quietly, "How dangerous is it, truly?" There was no fear in that gravelly voice, but there was circumspection and Lodovico was grateful for it.

"The danger is great," Lodovico conceded. "We won't tell la Signoria that," he added with wicked delight, punctuated with a deep chuckle that was echoed by many of the others. "Even if you, each of you, decided not to fight"—his tone revealed how unlikely he knew this was—"still, I would have to return to the Cérocchi and join with them in battle, so grave is the threat and so worthy is the cause." He gave a reminiscing smile. "I did that once, when I was younger. I had only Falavedova," he said, patting his sword, "and two horses. The opponents were the gigantic Turks who spin like the dust storms in the desert. Being young and inexperienced, I climbed to the crest of a ridge . . .

Yes, I know," he said ruefully as he heard the shocked reaction of the soldiers. "I have said I was inexperienced. I gathered up rocks to throw and knelt to commend my soul to God, for I was certain as a man may be that I would die that day. The gigantic Turks came at me as endless and relentless as the sea, and I fought until it seemed there was nothing in the world but what my sword could strike at. I had been wounded, and that dreadful weakness began to possess me, so that I sensed that it would have to end soon."

"Did your soldiers return?" Massamo asked. He, like all the others, was caught up in this story.

"No. They did not. But I was aided." He nodded slowly, thinking back to that bloody hillside and terrible foe. "There was a sudden disturbance and then a troop of soldiers came over the crest, and at the sight of them, the Turks stopped spinning and gazed at the newcomers with mind-chilling terror. Then they fled in disorder as the troops, all on fine white horses, swept up the hill, passed me and pursued them down the far side, killing every hapless Turk they came upon with the greatest skill I have ever seen."

"Who were these soldiers?" the old sergeant demanded to know.

"I wondered that myself. At the time I was faint and I collapsed before I could see more. But later I awoke in their camp, and I was taken to the captain who had led the attack. And it was then I realized that these were the famous Amazons."

"Amazons!" Massamo cried out. "I don't believe it!"

"Nor did I, at first. But as I recovered from my wounds, they gave me more than ample proof that it was so. I could wish them with us now. I had the pledge of the captain, who is named Zaidorah, that if I should ever need a fighter to stand beside me, she would be honored to have it be her." When indulgent mirth greeted this, Lodovico responded testily, "We have battled together since then. I have seen her face a line of Mandarin cavalry without flinching, and I cannot make the same statement for myself. I know that I

faltered when the battle was most fierce and the sun
was scorching the sky, when my troops were beaten almost to their knees and my head was filled with thirst-
born visions. Then Zaidorah proved her worth beyond
any price, for she castigated me and showed me by her
example what it was to fight bravely. Her sword never
stopped until she had cleaved a path of bodies that
led from our lines to the very tents of the enemy."

The few ribald comments that had been made at the
beginning of his reminiscence had stopped and now
the men stood in awed silence.

"A woman like that . . . " Massamo began, as if to
make up for his earlier derision. "A rare thing. It would
do my heart good to see her in battle."

Lodovico grinned at that, his handsome features
becoming more attractive, his fine white teeth neatly
framed by his dark beard and curling mustache. "No
man ever had a better comrade at arms, I will tell you
that. It does my heart good to think of her."

One of the older soldiers was not convinced. "I had
heard that the Amazons gelded any male they caught.
You haven't the look of it."

"They do occasionally castrate their enemies, but I
was not that. Their Queen, in fact, said that I was almost brave enough to be a woman."

The laughter this time was rollicking and the men
thumped each other on the back and stamped on the
floor at the thought.

"If you had seen those women fight," Lodovico said
rather sadly, "you would not laugh."

The old sergeant was the first to speak. "Women on
a battlefield, any part of a battlefield, are bad luck."
He was supported by murmured agreement and a few
of the Lanzi crossed themselves for protection. "I've
seen many a fight ruined because there were women
about," the sergeant declared.

"Have you?" Lodovico made an unpleasant gesture.
"You may wish before this war is over to have the
advantage of just one Amazon. The only ones who

suffered when I fought with the Amazons were the Turks."

This brought a flood of other questions, and Lodovico looked about for a bench where he could sit to converse with the soldiers. He set his mind to the task of recounting tales of adventure and battle, of exploration and glory, and found himself well-rewarded by the bright faces of the soldiers who listened to him. It was a pity he had left his chittarone, since he thought, with sardonic self-mockery, that all that was needed was a little music to make his stories complete entertainments.

The bishop's secretary was a gray-eyed Frenchman in a cassock which he wore as if it were sewn with pearls and diamonds. He gave Lodovico a haughty stare and addressed him in Latin. "The bishop is at prayers. You haven't an appointment."

"The bishop knows I must speak to him." Lodovico maintained an attitude of respect in this vast Cathedral of Santissimo Redentore. While it was true that the man wearing the cloth was an arrogant fool, Lodovico knew that the cloth itself was worthy of homage.

"Perhaps tomorrow, after mass," the secretary suggested with a slight curl to his lip.

"Perhaps as soon as you announce me," Lodovico responded with forced good manners. "Devoted as you are to your faith, you have probably not heard that we are all in mortal danger. And though the promise of heaven is sweet and those of us who trust in the mercy of God will go gladly down to death, still, there is a powerful and malignant enemy who stalks us even now. It would be wise, I think, to inform the bishop of this."

The Frenchman had turned a pasty color as Lodovico spoke, and stammered a few words. "This way, Ariosto. Yes. The bishop. This way." The long nave of the cathedral echoed with the sound of his voice, making the stammer come back in eerie whispers.

As the door to the bishop's private quarters was

opened, that upright old man could be seen on his
knees before a crucifix in a small chapel that adjoined
his study. When the Frenchman called him in a discreet
undervoice, the bishop crossed himself and got to his
feet. "Ariosto," he said in those vibrant accents that
Lodovico remembered from his first evening in Nuova
Genova.

"Eccelenza," he said, kneeling to kiss the episcopal
ring that was extended to him. "I fear I have grave intelligence for you."

"As I thought." The bishop motioned Lodovico to a
chair before removing the stola from his shoulders,
gave this into the Frenchman's keeping. "You've been
with the Cérocchi."

"Yes, I have," Lodovico said, and once again
launched into the tale of his stay in their city. He strove
to bring the bishop a sense of the terror that the Cérocchi lived with daily, and their courage in facing it. He
told the Ambrosian prelate of the despair preached by
Cifraaculeo and the stern bravery of Alberospetrale.
He touched only once on the women, and the color of
his face darkened as he spoke the name of Falcone's
betrothed of the Scenandoa. He told of the preparations for war and described the arrival of the runner
from the Pau Attan, and the obsequies that were given
him.

Through it all, the bishop listened in silence, his old
eyes revealing little, as if he were hearing confession.
He was of a noble house in Brindisi and allied by marriage with the Ducas of Ferrara, and there was as much
warrior as priest in him. Once, when Lodovico described the marshaling of the Cérocchi troops he had
watched, the icy eyes had flared with reminiscent
warmth.

"There you have it," Lodovico declared at the end
of his narrative. "I have tried to make Podestà Benci
understand, but his fear is in him like a rot that devours
his vitals. Without your help and your alliance, I fear
that the Cérocchi must suffer. I have with me a mandate
from il Primàrio empowering me to take command of

all troops, but I know that if la Signoria were to oppose me"—he shrugged and averted his eyes—"what can we do alone?"

"You are not alone," the bishop said resonantly. "You have the might of God with you, and nothing will prevail against His strength." The old face was set in militant lines. "Those who war for the Right will be upheld and those who are in the ranks of Satan will be cast down into the Pit forever." He paused for a moment, and when he spoke again there was an impishness in his demeanor that Lodovico had not seen before. "I think Andrea Benci will be convinced: he will not have you alone to contend with, but me."

La Realtà

Alessandra was delighted at the news. "The villa at Fiesole? It's wonderful. I was there with Graziella once, and it is quite charming. It sits on the brow of the hill, you know, and has a beautiful garden with two fountains." She beamed at her husband. "Think of the work you can do. No more need to find something to rhyme with Wessex."

Lodovico was not listening to her. He sat on the edge of their bed and stared toward the window which faced the back of the Palazzo Pitti where gardeners were working on pruning the formal shrubbery. He put up his hand to shade his eyes, hating to admit that it was shortsightedness and not the sun that made the distant figures blur. "Yes," he said remotely when he realized she had spoken. "I'll be close enough for him to reach me on short notice, of course." This last was said slowly, uncertainly, as if to reassure himself.

"But he won't have to, will he?" Alessandra asked, becoming anxious. "Lodovico, you need time to do your work, and you won't get it here. Il Primàrio demands so much of you."

"I don't mind," he said, looking at her at last. "Your new dress is very becoming. I like that color green."

She smiled at this, then looked away. "La Duchessa wore this shade, I remember. It went so well with her yellow hair."

Lodovico recalled Lucretia Borgia, Duchessa of Ferrara vividly and with as much real affection as Alessandra did. "Yes. There was that one silk gonella, with the Venezian sleeves edged in sapphires and emeralds. She always wore it when she presided at the great festival at Easter." She had been his first real patron, and though he privately had thought her somewhat stupid and weak-willed, he had felt that her enthusiasm for his work was genuine and it had meant a great deal to him when he was younger. Even then he had admitted to himself that the beauty that had been so famous was fading, that her bleached hair was an ugly color and that her reputedly seductive voice was merely a little hoarse. He forgave her all these shortcomings because she had been kind to him. Fleetingly he wondered if that was the same reason he liked Damiano.

"Your new clothes will be ready in another two days," Alessandra was telling him, interrupting his thoughts. "It's a pity that you won't have the new giornea for the last banquet for the English. Well, there will be other times, and the English have no taste in clothing anyway." She rose and went across to the window, taking an obvious delight in the new camora she wore. "You're deep in thought, my husband. Will you tell me?"

Lodovico looked up. "What?" He smiled as if to

pass this off. "I'll have to do another few ballades for the consort and I have my verses in my mind." He got to his feet slowly. "I hope you don't mind my pre-occupation." Making a vague gesture with one hand, he added, "As you say, the English will leave soon and Damiano has many things he requires of me before we leave for the country."

Alessandra's expression changed to one of indulgent tolerance, such as mothers show to clever children. "Surely poets are not given the same tasks as courtiers."

The image of Andrea Benci, tall, smooth-spoken, capable, wholly contained, filled his mind. "No," he said in a strange tone. "There are other tasks given to courtiers." He went to the door, attempting to whistle the new tune Maffeo had written, and cudgeled his brain for words to set to it, but found none.

"I'll give orders that our belongings are to be packed," Alessandra called after him, as if expecting to be contradicted.

"Certainly," he replied. "I won't be able to give it my attention for a few days yet. You might ask Virginio to help you."

"Boys are useless at packing. Give them a flower and a shield, and they'll put the flower on the bottom every time." She gave an exasperated shake to her head but there was an undertone of pride in her voice.

"And poets, I assume, are worse?" His chuckle was gentle and she took no offense at this challenge, but waved to him as he left the room.

Twilight had fallen by the time Lodovico had prepared the new verses for the musicians, and though he was not satisfied with them, he knew they were sufficiently polished to be acceptable to Maffeo. He drew a deep breath and let it out slowly. At least in the country he would have time to rework his poetry again, which he longed to do. It had long become something of a joke with the writers and scholars in Firenze that Ariosto was revising his great *Orlando* again. He smiled a little sadly, and turned his thoughts to his new *Fan-*

tasia. Would it ever be ready, good enough, recognized? He was not certain that it mattered.

There was a sound at the door, and then it was opened a little and Lodovico could see the back of Andrea Benci as he stood there, one hand on the latch, his back to the library, his voice lowered in curiously furtive conversation.

". . . if there's a reconciliation, it will come too late if you act now."

The other speaker said something, but Lodovico was unable to hear it. Fascinated, he rose from his chair and approached the door, taking the precaution of removing a book from one of the slanted racks and opening it at random.

". . . it need not be dangerous for . . . and the end of summer might be better . . . if there is suspicion later . . ." Benci's tone had grown quieter still and Lodovico wondered if he dared to press his ear to the door to listen.

Again the unknown and garbled second voice spoke, this time more vehemently.

Benci gave an irritating laugh. "You're fleeing from shadows," he said nastily and pushed the door open a little more.

Lodovico barely had time to jump back and spread the book he carried in his arms before Andrea Benci saw him. Il Primàrio's secretary stopped a moment and regarded Lodovico with a strange, angry expression. "Ariosto," he said after a moment.

"Benci," he responded, affecting surprise.

"I did not know you were here," Andrea remarked and Lodovico felt his face grow cold, though the room was pleasantly warm on this spring day.

"I was reading," he said unnecessarily, holding out the book as proof. For the first time he noticed that it was on the breeding of farm animals.

"For your next epic?" Benci inquired gently.

"Oh, no," Lodovico said with a laugh that sounded like a death rattle in his own ears. "Damiano is lending me his villa at Fiesole, and I thought perhaps I'd better

learn something of the livestock there before I have to
live among them." It was a rather neat lie, he congratulated himself as he thought it over.

"A practical poet. Amazing." Benci had come a
little farther into the library. "Il Primàrio is not here?"

"As you see." Lodovico indicated the room with a
nod of his head. "I think he's closeted with the Venezians and Genovese at the moment. He mentioned that
he had to postpone his meeting with the d'Este boy who
arrived yesterday night." He thought it odd that Damiano's secretary was unaware of il Primàrio's activities for the day, but did not want to mention it.

"Of course. He should also be spending time with
Cardinale Medici. We must get through this ill-advised
English visit with as little offense to the Pope as possible, but now, with all these delegations . . ." Andrea's
hauteur became more marked. "I can't think what il
Primàrio can be doing, extending his courtesy at a time
like this." His mouth closed sharply, as if he wanted to
trap all the words behind his teeth. "I'll leave you to
the breeding of . . . swine." He pulled the door open
again and left the room abruptly.

Lodovico stood for some little time, watching that
door. He was certain that his presence had made Andrea
Benci leave. He knew that the elegant courtier was
angry with him, but no matter how he thought, he
could think of no good reason for it. True, the night
before Lodovico had made a number of jokes at
Andrea's expense, but none of them were disastrous,
and all of them, he had to admit, he had made before
and Andrea had endured them with a patient, contemptuous indulgence. Why had Andrea left the room?
What had he interrupted or prevented? Was it only the
secretary's arrogance that made him leave, or was there
some more sinister reason? He put the book on farm
animals back on the rack and sank into a chair near
the longest writing table. It was foolish to think that
there was any malice in what he had overheard. Courtiers were always involved in various petty intrigues,
and that had been the case for as long as he could

remember. To whom had Andrea been speaking? He
had said that there might be a reconciliation, but it
would be too late? Was some hanger-on anxious to gain
the attention of one of the women? Had one of the
Ducas asked about a feud with another, or between two
different noblemen? Was it a husband concerned for
his wife? A father for a child? Was Andrea part of
another attempt to bring Damiano and his son Leone
together again? The young man was living in Austria,
and it might be that with the English going to Poland
there were those who would wish to convince the father
and son to speak again.

The day was advanced into the late afternoon by the
time Lodovico left the library, discontented and more
perplexed than when he began to puzzle out what he
had overheard. He had thought he might mention it to
Damiano, but at last had rejected the idea. What would
he tell il Primàrio? he asked himself sardonically—that
he had overheard a courtier saying something about
danger? He could hear Damiano's kind, condemning
laughter in his mind and he flinched at it. No, he could
not endure that.

He resolved to put the matter out of his mind and
went in search of Sir Thomas More.

Lodovico found the Chancellor of England near the
Mercato Nuovo watching a troupe of acrobatic dwarfs
performing. He laughed heartily at their antics and when
they had finished, threw them a handful of coins before
turning to speak. "I have a dwarf of my own in England," he confided. "A good enough jester, but nothing
like these splendid little men."

"Indeed," Lodovico said, because a response was
clearly indicated. He locked his hands behind his back
and fell into step with Sir Thomas.

"We English do love our grotesques, but not in the
morbid way that the Spaniards do." He turned toward
the Ponte Vecchio. "It's nearly sunset, and yet the hills
are full of light. In England, you know, the sky is not
this vital blue and our days fade gradually. In summer,

our twilight continues for hours, but in winter, in winter there is little more than a few hours of light in the day, and most of that filters through rain and snow." He smiled. "When I first thought of leaving my home, it filled me with sorrow. Now, though I know I will miss the gardens and our pale sunlight, I can see that there will be real pleasure here, and that this beautiful land is not the prison I feared it might be." He looked toward the hills on the south side of the Arno. "I have been assured that my family may live quietly here, though it hardly seems possible. Considering what Damiano has done these last few days, I cannot imagine this place being the place for retired living."

"Then you are set on returning here." Lodovico was somewhat startled to realize that he took so little satisfaction in learning this.

"Yes. I have spoken with Damiano again, and I am willing to do what he wishes. He has also said that he will address the Pope on behalf of my King, which was more than I expected."

It was so like Damiano, Lodovico reflected, to offer a man an unpleasant choice, and then, when it had been made, to sweeten that choice with an unexpected reward. They stepped onto the Ponte Vecchio with its houses and shops.

"London Bridge is like this, but longer," Sir Thomas said as he glanced at one of the tiny storefronts. "I have heard that there are men and women who are born, live and die on London Bridge without ever setting foot on either bank."

Lodovico was longing to find out more about Sir Thomas' second interview with Damiano, but decided he could not press the matter. "I have heard the same of the people here, but I confess I do not believe it. There are no priests on the bridge and they must attend mass at some time."

"True," Sir Thomas agreed, walking a little faster as they passed a tavern. "It will be dark soon, and we should not be abroad."

"We have nothing to fear," Lodovico promised him.

"You are known to everyone in Firenze, and none of them would dare to touch you. It would be too dangerous for them. Now, if it were one of the lesser courtiers, or myself alone, perhaps there would be some danger, but not until night has fallen."

"Damian is fortunate to have such law-abiding subjects." The doubt in his tone was not disguised.

"Oh, they are not particularly law-abiding, and they are not his subjects. It is simply that they know that il Primàrio does not want his guests abused, and if they are, some of the entertainments will be gone from Firenze. Damiano heads the Console of la Federazione, but that does not make these people his subjects. Firenze is a republic."

"And that humble man lives more lavishly than the King of France," Sir Thomas said with no condemnation.

"He has a large fortune," Lodovico agreed. They were almost off the Ponte Vecchio now, and it was apparent that the dusk was fading rapidly into night. "I should call for a torch bearer, if you like," Lodovico said. "It's not far to the Palazzo Pitti, but if you would like the way lighted . . ."

"As long as you know the way, I can see no reason . . ." Sir Thomas never finished his sentence. There was the sound of running feet behind them, and a warning shout from a fisherman near the bank of the river, and then two men in long masks and carrying cudgels raced up to them, their weapons up.

"That's the one," the larger of the two men growled, and to Lodovico's horror, pointed not at Sir Thomas, but himself.

"Catch the other!" the other muttered, and with startling, terrifying swiftness, rushed at Lodovico.

There was a brightness before his eyes, and a sound of ships colliding, and Lodovico fell into a heap on the street flagging. The last thing he noticed was the distress in Sir Thomas' eyes.

*   *   *

His head was bandaged and his face ached in a way he had not thought possible, worse than when he had had a diseased tooth rot in his head. He had a book open before him, but his eyes ached too much for him to read in comfort.

"Well, Master Ariosto," the physician announced after he had looked into Lodovico's eyes and had a look at his chamber pot, "I will not bleed you today, since the last cupping appears to have done the trick. You must have a very thick skull, or your brain is so strengthened with study that you resist anything that can be given with a club."

Lodovico tried to smile at this ponderous humor, but abandoned the effort. "I thank you for your care," he muttered, recalling how much he hated physicians.

"Il Primàrio has been asking after you, and I know that he will be pleased with my report." The physician was preening, taking a personal pride in Lodovico's improvement. Lodovico wished he felt strong enough to pull his long nose off his face.

"When will I be allowed to get up?" he asked the physician through a tight jaw.

"I think that we will consider tomorrow possible. You will be allowed to sit in a chair for a few hours, and then you must return to your bed. If that is successful and there is neither fever nor flux, in a few days after that, we will allow you an hour in the garden, and if that is not detrimental, then in a week you should be able to resume your work for il Primàrio." He folded his hands on his paunch.

"And Sir Thomas?" He could not recall hearing what had become of the Chancellor of England. If there had been murder done, he knew it would be his fault. He should never have exposed them both to attack in that stupid way. He had been warned that there were enemies in Firenze and had chosen to forget it. If Sir Thomas were dead, Lodovico thought that Damiano might well, and justifiably, hold him responsible.

"He and the rest of the English mission leave today. He sent his regrets to you, of course, and said that he was sorry that you would not be able to speak with him again until he returns from Muscovy."

"But he's all right?" Lodovico could not keep the relief from his voice as he sat up in bed. "He wasn't hurt?"

The physician wagged his head ponderously, as if his skull were filled with jewels or, Lodovico added inwardly, lead. "No, by the Grace of God he was spared. There were those on the Ponte Vecchio who saw the attack and came at once to aid you. There was a great cry set up and the Lanzi were sent for at once. A fortunate thing for you," he went on sternly, "as the blow you suffered was severe."

"But Sir Thomas was not harmed." He felt foolish asking the same questions, but the physician seemed reluctant to answer.

"Not harmed, no. Had his dirk out in a moment, I understand. That was lamentable, because he should not have been carrying it at all. He claimed he'd put it in the sheath without thinking, and everyone's willing to believe it, but il Primàrio knows that it was not quite that way." Again there was the slow, portentous nod. "Just as well, really, but very awkward."

Lodovico touched the bandage that wrapped around his head like a dubious wreath. "How long did . . . You haven't said how deep my swoon was." If the English were leaving this very day, he must have been unconscious longer than he thought. He was certain he could recall being bled the day before, but that would not be time enough for the mission to plan its departure.

"Yesterday you wakened. I bled you for the first time the day before that. I wanted to do it sooner, but there was so much suffusion of the countenance that it could not be done safely. You had a deal of fever then, but it passed quickly enough, and delirium is not unusual at such times." The physician sighed and put one large hand on Lodovico's shoulder.

"I was delirious?" Lodovico demanded, ignoring the hand. "For how long?" What had he said? He felt a chill spread through him, for there was so much he might have revealed.

Apparently some of this concern was on his face because the physician gave him a kindly smile. "I know how you men close to il Primàrio are, always chary of your secrets. Well, and that's probably a good thing. Il Primàrio himself was aware of the danger. Andrea Benci sat with you while your thoughts and tongue wandered."

Lodovico tried to picture that tall, old courtier sitting beside him while he tossed and mumbled, but could not. Surely such a task was beneath him. "Benci."

"The rest of the time your wife sat with you. She, I may tell you, is a sensible woman, not like those who flutter and whine when they see a little blood. She claimed she was distraught, but I could wish more of those I visit to have such distraught wives." His rumble of laughter was like everything else about him, weighty and large.

Lodovico felt himself flush. He had not asked about Alessandra.

"You are fortunate in your wife, sir. Most fortunate." The physician's eyebrows rose significantly, then beetled down for emphasis.

"Yes," Lodovico agreed, but could not bring himself to say more. Alessandra was a blessing, he insisted in his mind, and even as he admitted it was so, he was touched with irritation. Competent, affectionate, intelligent Alessandra, who had lived with him, married him, given him Virginio—she should have married a politician or a merchant or a professor, not a poet.

"There, you're tiring already," the physician said with gloomy satisfaction. "I knew how it would be. You're to rest, Ariosto, and tomorrow we'll see how you go on. I will tell the cooks that you're to have barley broth and an infusion which I will provide them. Your wife can look after you. I know you'll have the best of care from her."

"Yes," Lodovico said again, feeling foolish.

"That was a nasty blow," the physician added as he

went toward the door with stately steps. "Men have died from less. Be aware of that, while you recover. This was no little thing. I've closed the gash with silk, and in a few days I will remove the threads."

Lodovico felt a dizzy, sinking sensation churn in him. "How long was the . . . gash?"

"Nearly as wide as my hand," he said, presenting a palm for his inspection. He was at the door and made no attempt to come back toward the bed. "I say this to you so that you will not treat my instructions lightly. I tell you for your own good that it could have gone badly for you."

"I see." Lodovico leaned back against his pillows and let his book slide to the floor. He told himself that the giddiness he felt came from his hurts, but he knew that it was from fear.

An orchard surrounded the formal gardens of Palazzo Pitti so that the morning was filled with the scent of apple blossoms as well as that of roses. The morning was warm and promised a hot, lazy afternoon.

Lodovico sat by the high, clipped hedge, a writing case open on his lap, a half-filled vellum page before him, his quill clogged with dried ink. His eyes were dreamily fixed on the Fortezza di Belvedere higher up the slope, and beyond it, crowning the knoll, the Romanesque splendor of San Miniato al Monte. He hummed occasionally, though he was not aware of it.

A shadow fell across him and Lodovico looked up, thinking that he had been forgiven at last and that Damiano had sought him out. But the face was framed by silver hair, and that lean, elegant figure was not il Primàrio, but his secretary, Andrea Benci. Lodovico swallowed the disappointment that flooded him and regarded the old courtier.

"I understand that you sat with me while I had fever. I thank you for that." He closed his writing case and attempted to smile.

"It was necessary. Since il Primàrio has seen fit to take you into his confidence, someone has to be certain that nothing he has told you reaches the wrong ears, even by accident." The asperity of these words startled Lodovico.

"It was not my intention to be attacked or be cudgeled, believe me." He did his best to keep his tone even, but his breath came a little faster and he could feel color mount in his face.

Andrea Benci sighed. "Of course not. But you behaved very stupidly, exposing yourself and Sir Thomas to great danger."

"I realize that," Lodovico responded sharply. "I was terrified for Sir Thomas when I came to myself. I didn't want to . . ." He stopped abruptly and looked away once more.

"Well," Andrea said in a more conciliating tone, "Sir Thomas was not hurt and there was no serious trouble after all."

Lodovico wanted to object to that, but held his tongue. He put one hand to his newly-trimmed beard and gave Andrea a measuring look. He knew that would draw attention to his face, which was what he wanted to do. A few hours earlier his mirror had shown him eyes surrounded by purple that was fading now to a yellow-green as well as three abrasions, on his cheek, his temple and brow where his face had struck the paving stones as he fell. "No," he said after a moment, when he was sure that Andrea had looked at his face. "There was, as you say, no serious trouble."

Andrea Benci had the grace to cough, but there was no other indication that Lodovico had embarrassed him. "Sir Thomas asked that he be remembered to you. He said that he enjoyed your company."

"I enjoyed his," Lodovico said at once. "It was an honor to meet him. I look forward to his return."

"For San Stefano's Stones!" Andrea burst out. "Be a little thoughtful in what you say."

Lodovico frowned. "The mission is coming back through Italia Federata after the visit to Muscovy, is it not? That was what I was led to believe." His expression was ingenuous but under his assumed innocence,

Lodovico was angry. He may have babbled while in the grip of fever, and he had never before cared much for the political maneuvering that was meat and bread to Andrea Benci, but he knew enough to keep his silence on Damiano's behalf. He gave himself the pleasure of adding, "You were the one who made the plans for that visit, weren't you? I seem to recall Damiano saying he had given that task to you."

There was a moment of silence between them, then Andrea sighed. "Yes. But, Ariosto, guard your words. There is too much at stake here for you to speak unwisely."

"Because I am a poet does not necessarily mean that I am also a fool!" Lodovico remonstrated, getting to his feet as he spoke. "I would also suggest to you that the garden is not a place for this discussion. If you wish to carry this talk further, we should retire to a more private place." There was a high, clear sound in his skull, but he did his best to ignore it. "I am at your disposal, Benci."

The courtier looked about uneasily. "You're right. I will talk with you later. It will not do for us to be seen together for too long. The wrong assumptions might be made."

"Oh, come," Lodovico said, beginning to think the whole thing had gone too far. "With Sir Thomas gone, where is the danger?"

Andrea Benci crossed his velvet-clad arms and gave Lodovico a hard stare. "We're assuming, naturally, that the men who attacked you were after Sir Thomas. But what if they weren't? What if you were their target, Ariosto? What then?"

The sun dazzled behind Andrea Benci's silver head, and Lodovico could not see his face to discover whether he was being mocked or not.

PART II

La Fantasia

For three days the warriors had been gathering. There were many of the Cérocchi from their various, far-flung cities in the forests; Pau Attans in their thick leather armor, greedy for revenge; Scenandoa spearmen in breastplates of porcupine ivory and collars of cat claws to indicate merit and rank; Cesapichi with their long lances and stiff shields of boars' hide; the Cica Omini cousins of the Pau Attan with their great maces and mauls: Cicora in high, jewel-studded boots and armed with javelins and bows; pikemen from Annouaigho far to the south; Onaumanient, more of the Pau Attans' cousins, these men carrying tall bows and wicked knives in their wide belts; and a small band of fighters with short curved daggers from the city of Giagaia in the north. They were a stirring sight, these proud and dedicated men, coming together, old feuds forgotten, so that they could meet the real enemy, Anatrecacciatore and his terrible, unhuman army.

Lodovico and Falcone stood together on the steps of Santissimo Redentore and watched while the warriors filled the piazza. Two rows of Lanzi flanked the great companies of these forests. Alberospetrale waited somewhat apart from his son and the great Italian hero. His old face was thoughtful as he stared out at the armed men. To Lodovico's chagrin, Andrea Benci had refused to attend the ceremony and was in the Palazzo del Doge, sulking.

"Is there word from Italia Federata yet?" Falcone asked in an undervoice. "I have heard that a ship put into port today."

"A French ship, unfortunately," Lodovico sighed, one hand resting on the hilt of Falavedova. "I spoke to the captain earlier, but he has been trading for furs much farther up the coast, and has seen few other ships these last three months, so my news is more current than his. I have sent a dispatch with him, telling him that it is urgent that it be delivered, and pledging my word that he will be rewarded for delivering it promptly. But how soon can that be?" He tried to keep his own apprehension from his tone, but knew that it was reflected in his fine, bright chestnut eyes. "I have not wanted to tell our fighters this. At such moments . . ." He shrugged.

"Yes, that is wisest," Falcone said heavily. "I will admit that when I saw the ship, though I knew it was impossible, I hoped that it brought us men and weapons."

"Well, we will have to do with what is here," Lodovico said, putting one hand on Falcone's shoulder. "Surely it is possible for men such as these to defeat Anatrecacciatore."

"Defeat him or die," Falcone muttered, then looked into Lodovico's face. "Don't chide me for my fears, Ariosto. I've had less time to learn to accept them than you have."

Lodovico's face filled with compassion. "And you have a great deal more to lose. That's very true. I have asked myself whether, if this were Italia Federata, I would be doing more." He paused and looked over the troops with narrowed eyes. "I have not been able to answer that question, but I give you my word that I want this land to be as sacred to me as my own."

"But why?" It was the only time Lodovico had heard real doubt in Falcone's voice.

"Because, my friend, if I cannot uphold my honor

here, then I can uphold it nowhere. The coward who
says that he can fight only on his native soil gets no
respect from me. How could I feel otherwise?"

"There is Podestà Benci to give you an example,"
Falcone said with a nod toward the Palazzo del Doge.

"He's an old man," Lodovico said, but the words
did not sit well with him. "He is like those who have
been in battle too long and find it difficult to move, let
alone think. I saw a battle-toughened captain in such a
state once. He sat on the ground and let the dust run
through his fingers, like an infant at play. Something
very like that has happened to Benci, I fear. Everywhere he turns he sees defeat." He had shut the memory of David Campolargo's collapse out of his thoughts
until now, but the image returned as sharply as if he
had just looked away from the scarred veteran as he sat
in the dirt, a vacant smile on his weathered features.

"If he cannot or will not fight, then he should make
way for those who can and will," Falcone burst out.
"The first officer of the Cesapichi was insulted by
Benci's attitude, and he will not be the only one to
feel so." Falcone's jewel-studded leather armor flashed
as he moved in the morning sun. His handsome countenance was brooding and his eyes seemed to darken to
black. Deliberately he turned his back on the Palazzo
del Doge.

"Contain your anger, Falcone," Lodovico said softly.
"I agree that it would be best if we could post Benci
back to Italia Federata, and the dispatch I sent with
the Frenchmen requested just that, but until he goes,
there is nothing to be gained from this show of hostility.
It can only make matters more difficult for all of us.
The Lanzi are bound by their oath and their contracts
to obey the Podestà and la Signoria. We must have
those Lanzi in battle. If, in order to have them, we must
show a servile face to a frightened old man, where is
the harm, so long as the Lanzi are with us?"

"If the frightened old man were my father, would
you still say that?" Falcone shot back, and then ground
his teeth, as if to mangle the words he had just spoken.

"I doubt if your father would be so paralyzed with fear that he would behave so. I did challenge Cifraaculeo, when he could find no worth in our struggle. It must be the same for all of us, my comrade, or there is no point in taking to the field for death, as death will have already touched us." He motioned toward the piazza again, seeing the Onaumanient company talking easily with their cousins, the Cica Omini. The Onaumanient had unstrung their huge bows and were engaging in friendly arguments with the Cica Omini about the relative merits of the bow and the maul. It was the sort of quarrel Lodovico had heard many times before, in many lands, and as always, he took heart at this gallantry.

Alberospetrale interrupted Lodovico's reflections. "I have not seen Coltellomelma," he said as he approached Lodovico and Falcone. "Have you spoken to him, my son?"

Falcone's brow tightened. "Coltellomelma, no." He cast a quick, anxious glance over the piazza as if he might not have seen all the men there. "He is the great captain of the Cicora, and a famous hero. I assumed that he . . ." Falcone stopped, then looked toward the ranks of the Cicora. "Nembosanguinoso is there, but not Coltellomelma."

"I have spoken with Nembosanguinoso, but he said nothing about Coltellomelma not being with them." The King of the Cérocchi made a sudden, imperious gesture at a Cicora officer and stood, straight and commanding, while the man he had singled out stepped onto the cathedral steps. He addressed the Cicora in his language, and Falcone moved a little closer to Lodovico in order to tell him what passed between his father and Nembosanguinoso.

"He is saying," Falcone murmured, "that we were expecting to have Coltellomelma to command the flanking forces, which he has done before with great success. Nembosanguinoso answers that he has not seen their great captain for more than ten days. He is telling my father that Coltellomelma set out then to meet with representatives from the Cioctau and Iustaga in the city of Naniaba. 'We have had no message from him since he left us.' My father is asking if there has been any attempt to reach him. Nembosanguinoso says that there has not been time, because the call to muster came before they could send runners after him. He also says that there were three men from Eiche-Ah who offered to carry a message to Naniaba, since they had planned to go that way."

"And of course, there has been no word from the men from Eiche-Ah," Lodovico added fatalistically. "How near to the forces of Anatrecacciatore are these cities?"

"It is hard to tell," Falcone said softly, sounding angry in spite of this. "If the warriors of flint and frost have come far, then none of the cities are safe, and that includes this Nuova Genova. Naniaba is well fortified, but we know what these warriors can do." He made a gesture of helplessness, then forced himself to be less despairing. He met Lodovico's eyes. "It is a worthy battle, is it not? To face a foe of this strength, surely our stand against him is necessary?"

Lodovico's smile was valiant and sad. "I know why you ask, and I suppose it is good to do so." He paused a moment as he looked at Alberospetrale and Nembosanguinoso. "I believe that if I shirked my duty to you and this battle I could never deem myself worthy to hold a sword again. Surely there is no fight more honorable than this one."

Alberospetrale had overheard this, and now he turned to Lodovico with an expression that was almost a smile on his noble face. "Yes, what you say is good, Ariosto. If you will bring this fire to the battle, then the warriors of frost and flint cannot stand against you, or against any who also hold that fire within them."

Beside the King of the Cérocchi, Nembosanguinoso lifted his head, and though he obviously could not understand the words, yet something of their sense was communicated to him, and he raised his head with pride.

"I can only pray that God will give me the strength

and courage to be worthy of your praise, good King."
He bowed his head and saw the jewels in his collar of
the Order of San Basilio glisten in the sunlight.

Then the doors of Santissimo Redentore were flung
open and the great procession emerged to the accompaniment of trumpets, organ, and the singing of sweet-
voiced boys.

To the east of Nuova Genova the campfires of the warriors glared in the night like the eyes of wild animals.
Lodovico paced the ramparts of the city with Falcone,
his eyes looking beyond the ragged patches of light to
the vast blackness of the great forest. "How close do
you think they've come, my friend?"

"Close enough," Falcone said. He was wrapped in
a long cloak of white deerskin that was embroidered
with his falcon insignia. He looked older in this uncertain light, as if the coming of battle had tempered and
aged him between dawn and sunset.

"Do you think there will be more companies arriv-
ing? You have said that messengers went out to more
than a dozen cities." He remembered the way the runners had set off and once again he admired their bound-
less courage.

"We don't know how many of them reached their
destinations," Falcone reminded him in somber tones.
"And what they found when they arrived. We will not
know for some time yet, I think. Until you are willing
to get your mount and fly over the forests."

The night wind smelled of the ocean, of distance and
salt. It came fresh from the breakers that pawed at the
beach, rushed through Nuova Genova, then ruffled
the campfires of the warrior companies before hurrying
into the trees, spreading excitement as it went. Lodovico
drew his soldier's cloak·more tightly around his shoulders. "I must do that at first light," he said, as much to
himself as Falcone. "Bellimbusto has been fed and is
ready to fly. I wish that there were time to get you
another such mount. Two of us in the air would be
better than one."

"And I long to ride him," Falcone confessed with a half-smile.

"I know. Well, we must hope that there will be time to get you your own horse." He turned away from the fires and the dark toward the city. There were bits of carnival sounds in the night, and pockets of torchlight showed that the revels had not yet ceased. "It is good that the men have this chance for pleasure, but I hope that they will not drink too much," Lodovico said a few moments later as he and Falcone passed over the roof of a busy tavern.

Falcone's thoughts were similar to Lodovico's. "I was just thinking that I wish it had been possible to marry Aureoraggio before we left to fight."

At the mention of that name, Lodovico's hands tightened and a tremor compounded of desire and rage shook him. "Yes," he said when he was certain he could speak without betraying himself to his friend, "I know what it is to long for the embrace of love. When death is so near, then love is with it. I struck down a man in battle once," he went on in a different tone in order to put out of his mind the shining vision of Aureoraggio, "who begged me to carry a message to a woman he had known many years. He said that he had always loved her, but had never found the chance to tell her, and now that he was dying, he wished that he had spoken. When I found this woman and gave her the message, she wept and asked me why he had remained silent, for she had loved him with her life and had been afraid to let him know." He shook his head slowly. The thought of Aureoraggio had not left him. He saw her face in his mind even as he recalled the tears in that haughty Austrian woman's eyes as he brought her the dying wish of her friend. Would he, he wondered, send such a message to Aureoraggio? Should he speak to her now, and beg her to say nothing to Falcone? No, no. He knew he must not. It would be too great a burden to place on those fragile shoulders. His love was not welcome, was not lawful, and for that, he knew he must keep his silence though it gnaw like a rat in his vitals.

"Ariosto," Falcone said sharply, and frowned as Lodovico turned his burning eyes on him.

"My mind . . . was elsewhere," he said thickly, and forced himself to grin. "My wife, Alessandra, has often complained that in my worst moments, I am no better than those men below us."

"Ah. You miss her comfort. She is a long way from here." The sympathy in Falcone's eyes was so genuine that for an instant Lodovico thought himself a traitor to this honorable Cérocchi.

"Yes, she is a long way from here." Lodovico turned away to hide the expression he knew was on his face. His next words were muffled. "The comfort of love—how I long for it."

"That is the poet in you," Falcone said in an attempt to lighten Lodovico's mood.

"That is the man in me, Falcone. As it is in you." He choked back the confession that threatened to spill out of him. He would not share that burden, he reminded himself with inner fury. His passion was secret and must remain secret until his life was gone. Quite suddenly he turned on his heel and strode away down the ramparts, calling back to Falcone, "I must see to my men. I fear they will be too far gone in drink unless I stop them now, and they must not begin a march with aching, dull heads. I will speak to you again at first light."

Falcone did not answer, but stared after him, marveling at how well Ariosto carried his responsibilities, and wishing that he, too, possessed that calm, self-sufficient bravery that made Ariosto the hero he was.

La Realtà

Below and to the south Firenze lay like a child's toy. Lodovico leaned on the wall that surrounded the villa's garden and stared down at the red-tile roofs. The afternoon was hot so that the air sang with it, and even the breeze was still. Only the lazy splash of the fountain broke the high, singing silence.

Stripped to his stiff-padded hose and shirt, Virginio drowsed under an ancient laurel. A book lay open on his chest, the Latin title stamped on the spine declaring that the forces in nature cannot be denied. Lodovico read these words, studied his son's sleeping face, noticing the first darkening shadow on his upper lip. Very softly, so as not to wake Virginio, Lodovico laughed.

A crunch of footsteps on the gravel path claimed his attention and he moved quickly to find out who had come to see him.

"Lodovico," Damiano called, frowning as he was motioned to be silent. "There is someone here?"

"Only Virginio. He's asleep." Lodovico pointed to a bench some distance along the wall. He could feel the smile that stretched over his face, and tried not to be too delighted that his patron had come to talk to him. Over the last month he had seen Damiano but once before. That had been a hurried meeting in Firenze before he had left for the villa and at that time il Primàrio seemed distracted and brusque. Now there was a welcoming embrace and a Medici grin as well as a stifled laugh at the sleeping youth.

"I hope that isn't how he plans to study," Damiano said softly as he allowed Lodovico to lead him to the bench. "I know he wants to absorb learning, but I doubt that's the best way."

Lodovico sank onto the bench, suddenly aware that his old guarnacca was not really suitable for entertaining il Primàrio, and he began to apologize.

"Sweet Virgin, don't speak so. I'm dressed for hunting, myself," he said, pointing out his drab giaquetta and straight-collared shirt. "I must say, I like this French fashion in high boots." His were of soft doeskin and were held up by straps that tied to his belt. "We went through brush this morning, and I've learned the worth of these for my shins. Not a scratch on me." He leaned back, propping his elbows against the top of the wall behind him. "A pleasant place, Lodovico. How do you like it now?"

Puzzled, Lodovico looked away over the little garden toward the fountain. "As you say, it is pleasant."

"You are getting work done?" Damiano's eyes were squinted against the sun, revealing nothing of his thoughts.

"A fair amount. Not as much as I had hoped, but . . ." He gestured inconclusively. "Alessandra is overjoyed. She likes raising poultry and growing herbs."

"And Virginio, I see, is given over to study." Again he gave his wide, thin-lipped grin.

"As you see." Lodovico smiled because it was expected of him, but his eyes were vague.

"Have you decided which school he is to attend?" Damiano asked after a moment.

"Paris. I think it might be well for him to see another country, and Germany is out of the question. They're almost as bad as Spain." What was it that Damiano wanted of him? Lodovico wondered.

"I had a report from Guicciardini last week. He says that the followers of that heretic Luther burned another

one of Savonarola's monks' schools. I must say," he
went on with a hint of a sigh, "I am glad that grandfather had Savonarola thrown out of Firenze when he
did. He was quite mad. The Germans are welcome to
him."

"He's very old," Lodovico pointed out. "When he
dies, his followers will lose heart or go over to Luther."
It was a popular belief, one espoused by Cosimo, Cardinale Medici.

"Where is the improvement? Instead of fighting
among each other, they will be fighting everyone else."
Damiano's voice had grown sharp and Lodovico saw
the long-fingered hands tighten on his belt.

"Is that what Guicciardini thinks?" He did not know
what Damiano wanted of him, so he echoed what he
heard, wishing he dared to ask il Primàrio what was
disturbing him.

"He is not pleased. Those damned German princes
are up to something again, and this time they're talking
to Spain about it, whatever it is. There've been meetings
at some schloss in Saxony. Ever since the Habsburgs
settled the Bohemian question, they've been pushing for
an alliance with Spain. With themselves to head it, of
course." He added this last with unaccustomed bitterness.

"But Spain is under interdict. Surely Clemente would
promulgate a Bull . . ."

Damiano drew a long, weary breath. "If Luther's
followers have their way, Germany will be under interdict as well. I don't think we can hope that Luther's
followers will take on the entire might of the Spanish
Dominicans." He turned his eyes toward the fountain,
his face blank. "Nails of Christ, what am I to do?"

That softly voiced question disturbed Lodovico more
than any outburst would have. He tried to find a comforting phrase or two, but they eluded him.

"France has already sent envoys to the Sforzas in
Milano. There is the gentle suggestion that Milano withdraw from la Federazione and ally with France. Il Duca
hasn't answered yet, but he may accept. He's angry

enough to do it. Venezia has refused to quarter Milanese troops. Foscari has said that he would as soon
have the horse if he must have the Trojans." He reached
over absentmindedly and pulled a branch from the
shrub by the wall and began to tear the leaves from it.
"Genova has also been approached and il Doge is still
fuming about what he thinks was a slight when the
English were here. He was honorable enough to send
me a note about the French. Ercole Barbabianca may
be a pompous ass, but he is an honest one." One of the
twigs was bare now and Damiano began on another. "I
wish I knew who informed Foscari and Barbabianca
about the English visit. Someone is working against
me." He flung the little branch away quite suddenly.

Though the afternoon was hot and still, Lodovico
felt a chill go through him as he looked at il Primàrio.
"Surely there was no secret. You stated that it was an
unofficial . . ."

Damiano cut him short. "Yes. I explained my reasons,
and I thought that the matter was obvious enough. But
somehow my Ducas and Doges and Princes don't believe me. And at least one of these men has hinted that
he has his information on excellent authority."

"The Pope?" His Holiness was the only authority in
Italia Federata who wielded more power than his cousin.

"I don't think so. My various cousins in the Church
don't think so, unless they mention Cosimo, who is certainly feeding the flames. He makes no secret of that."
Damiano got abruptly to his feet. "There must be
someone . . . German? French? Spanish? If la Federazione were ended, they could pick the bones of Italia
together." He began to pace, his feet grinding on the
loose pebbles of the walkway. "This morning, Paolo
brought me word that he caught the understeward passing notes to one of the d'Este's grooms. D'Este! I can't
go to Ferrara and demand an explanation. D'Este's my
friend." His voice caught and he stood still a moment.
"Or he professes to be my friend. So does Barbabianca.
Perhaps Foscari is the more truthful, because he offers
no false coin."

Lodovico stared at Damiano, thinking that he ought to do something or say something that would solace the man. He stammered a few words, then closed his mouth as Damiano began to speak again.

"All the time we were hunting, I was trying to make sense of this. I very nearly took a bad fall on a jump a novice could handle. That's when I decided to come here. You won't carry tales. Thank San Dismo you're not a politician." His hands slapped his sides. "I am to a point where I guard what I say in confession for fear it will work against la Federazione."

"Damiano," Lodovico said, unable to hide his shock. "You cannot do . . ."

"Graziella says that I do not talk in my sleep, and for that I am grateful, but Minetta told me once that I did. I have given her a house in Ravenna and enough money for her to be comfortable the rest of her life. What else could I do?" He ran one hand through his hair. "There are times I fear that I am going distracted. What sort of trust is it that cannot survive a visit from the English?" His laughter was a little wild and Lodovico felt a new sting of alarm within him. "Lodovico, I pray you, with all my heart"—there was no mistaking the sincerity in his voice—"do not doubt me. Don't stare at me that way. And for the Passion, don't pity me."

"I don't pity you, Damiano. But I am concerned. You come here unexpectedly, and tell me such things . . ."

Again Damiano interrupted. "You haven't been in Firenze for more than a month. There are times I wish I hadn't sent you here. I've wanted to talk with you. But so far . . . All this I've been telling you has been building like the power in one of Leonardo's old toys. You know the Confraternità that goes in for those masked orgies? I almost went to their last one. Imagine being covered by a black silken sheet with only one, crucial hole, and the attention that is so extensively lavished on what is revealed there. I haven't allowed myself more than three cups of wine in a day so that my tongue will never be unguarded. An orgy, though, where there are no faces—a whole world of nothing but genitals." He went and sat on the wall, his back to the valley and Firenze. "I used not to understand why so many of my . . . associates chose to attend these evenings, but I do now. Giordano told me once that he was addicted to the gentle whips of his Confraternità and I was horrified. Giordano is a powerful man, handling enormous amounts of money and endless responsibility. Yet, like my Cardinale cousin, he seeks the lash. I have scourges enough in my life, but I know now that it would be easy to succumb to that other."

Lodovico had sat very still as Damiano spoke. When he was certain that il Primàrio had finished for a while, he said, "Where is the harm if you do that? You say yourself that it attracts you. Where is the difference between that and Minetta, except in numbers?" He was surprised to hear how calm his voice was and how reasonable he sounded.

"The illusion of anonymity," Damiano mused. "It would be only an illusion, and I would be a great fool to make myself so vulnerable. A careless word, or a ruthless man with a knife . . ." He shook his head. "There must be a place in Italia where there is escape from all this. A monk's cell, perhaps." He laughed at himself. "It's a lie, my friend. I don't truly desire escape, only a little time to set the burdens aside, not discard them altogether. That, in part, is why I came here, why I sent you away from Firenze."

Over the valley two larks were ascending, singing. Lodovico heard them and turned to watch their flight.

"I have a new mistress," Damiano said after a moment, an edge of scorn in his voice. "A pretty puss she is, too, rapacious as they come but randy as a hare. She cares only that I bring her presents and keep atop her for an hour. In my way, I am grateful to her." His heels clacked against the wall.

Twice in his life Lodovico had taken a mistress, and one of them was Alessandra. There had been other women, of course, their pleasure purchased in taverns or demanded of servants. Yet he had never heard Damiano speak cynically of the women he had kept until now. There were other men who were both callous and cruel and Damiano had always looked on them with subtle contempt. Now he was speaking in the same tone. Lodovico scowled at the empty spot of air where the larks had been. "Why do you keep her?"

"She's stupid and she's safe," Damiano snapped. His heels thumped on the wall in a slow and regular rhythm. "I needn't think around her. Do you know what luxury it is not to have to think?"

"Thinking is a joy," Lodovico said to the air, bewildered.

"If your thoughts are full of the things that give you the rewards of wisdom or the delight of entertainment, it probably is. I've forgotten such pleasures. My mind is filled with reports and rumors and plans and worry. Thought is a trial for me. When I came here, I was hoping that I could put it all aside and discuss, oh, the classics or what that new Polish essayist has said about the work of Dante." He pushed himself off the wall. "And I have only myself to blame that we haven't talked of such things. I have been speaking almost since the moment I arrived. I can't say you distracted me, surely." He touched his hands to his wide, prominent brow.

At last Lodovico felt he could address Damiano. "Come. A little time, Damiano: we'll tell Alessandra that you will take comestio with us. There's plenty of chicken and bread was baked yesterday. And," he went on more lightly, "this *is* your villa. Eat with us. I won't ask you about anything but Plato, if you like." Inwardly, he was astounded at his own ease. He put his arm through Damiano's as if he had been doing this every day of his life.

Damiano made no protest. "My grandfather loved the country. He used to threaten to stay at Ambra forever. It was impossible, but he longed for it as long as I knew him." With his free hand he made a sweeping gesture that took in all of the little garden. "What more native land does a man need than this?" The question was obviously rhetorical.

"I suppose it depends on the man," Lodovico said as he turned at the fountain and guided Damiano toward the side door of the villa.

All that was left on the table was a platter of melon slices soaked in wine. The courtyard was fallen into welcome shadow and the worst of the day's heat was over. This being an informal meal, Alessandra sat at the table with the men. The sleeves of her camora were pushed up to her elbows and she was as much at ease as her husband, her son and their guest.

Damiano had spent the meal regaling them with stories that even had the two servants laughing. Now he sat with a cup of wine before him, one foot propped on the chair Virginio had vacated. "Lodovico, you've proved your worth again."

"I?" Lodovico blinked. He had been basking in il Primàrio's attention, which he admitted he had sorely missed. "By telling the cook to grill some more sausage?"

"That, and other things." He emptied the cup and reached for the jug to fill it again. "I'm half-drunk, full, and content, and I haven't been that for longer than I care to think of. You've listened to my tales without asking me once about any other business. You're literate and articulate and . . ." He broke off, staring across the courtyard. "I'm a fool."

This last puzzled Lodovico. "What?"

Damiano waved his hand. "Nothing. Nothing. Jumping at shadows." He drank again. "Would you be willing to send your groom to Firenze tonight, just to let Benci know where I am? I left word that I would be back for the evening meal, but tonight, I think, I will sleep here, in that little room overlooking the orchard."

Though he had appropriated that room for his study, Lodovico turned to his steward, saying, "You know the room. Prepare it for il Primàrio."

"And the material that is there?" the steward asked with a wholly expressionless tone.

"Surely it can be put on the shelves there." Lodovico glanced at Alessandra. "Unless you have another suggestion?"

"There are shelves enough, I think." She was enjoying herself tonight, sitting with the men, her elbows propped on the table as she drank her wine.

"Of course there are," Lodovico said quickly. "Bruno knows where he should put things." He felt then that he had to excuse his outburst and turned to Damiano. "I'm afraid that there may be some clutter in the room, but if that will not displease you?"

"Clutter?" Damiano chuckled. "Books, papers, poetry, how nice to have them around me."

Virginio rolled his eyes skyward with the eternal dissatisfaction of the young with their elders. "My father is very messy. He says it helps him think."

"What do you know of it, lad?" Lodovico asked, not very sharply. "You have yet to acquire the habits of scholarship. When you do, then I will listen to your strictures." He smiled to soften this rebuke, remembering how his father had terrorized him, and how he had promised himself that he would not do that to his own son.

Damiano cut this short with a reminiscent twinkle and a light word. "My grandfather used to insist he was a neat man, but I can remember how the papers piled up like snow on his writing table. He knew exactly where everything was, however, and so, no matter how chaotic it seemed to the rest of his family, and I include myself, for him, it was neat. He hated not being able to put his hands on things at once." He drank again, sighing happily as the wine spread its magic through him.

"Let me fill your cup once more," Alessandra said, and reached for the jug before Damiano could help himself. As she poured, she said to her husband, "There is a Spanish wine in the pantry, sweet and white. Why don't you open it now so that we may pour it shortly?"

Even as he felt indignation within him, Lodovico

recalled that it had been the custom of the high-ranking of Firenzen' society to serve their guests at meals. He rose without a murmur of objection and went into the villa, to the kitchen.

His cook looked up, startled, from where she was sitting with two men who were unknown to Lodovico. Her face turned an astounding shade of mulberry and she stammered, "These are my . . . cousins, who came to see me. I didn't think . . . it was wrong to feed them." She gave a miserable smile and crossed herself.

Lodovico looked at the two men, noting that one of them wore the somber rough homespuns that were the uniform of a traveling priest. The other man had on a leather apron and might have been a smith, judging from his massive shoulders and thick-muscled arms. He motioned to his cook and when she came nearer, said, "I won't mention it to my wife, but if I find that the best of our food is gone, you will hear about it."

The cook's blush was fading to a cheesy pallor, but she managed to say a few words of thanks.

The priest had got to his feet and had begun to explain his exact degree of relationship to Lodovico's cook, but stopped when Lodovico said, "All the world has cousins. Neither of you is a young man, and since you seem more hungry than amorous, I will make allowances for this visit. But in future, you must send a request before you visit your cousin. While this is usually a peaceful household, there are times we would rather not have unexpected guests, even in the kitchen." His mind went back to the courtyard where Damiano sat at his ease.

"Of course, master," the cook muttered, turning to bustle back to the table and her cousins. The priest took his seat and remarked in a fairly loud voice that Maria had been safely delivered of a boy the week before, and the smith added that his mother had feared for Maria's life, but she had avoided childbed fever this time.

Lodovico was not listening to their conversation,

since family gossip usually bored him. He opened the door into the pantry and looked for the jar of wine Alessandra had mentioned. At first he did not see it, and then he thought to look in the shelves behind the locked spice chest. Sure enough, there were eight large jars of Spanish wine and four more of Umbrian red. He reached for one of the jars, changed his mind, and took two.

The conversation had become more quiet and desultory in the kitchen, and Lodovico was pleased to nod and hurry on. He did not like to intrude on his servants' lives, and his cook, he knew, was a gifted and oddly temperamental woman.

"You took your time," Alessandra said as Lodovico came back into the courtyard.

"I had trouble finding the wine. The steward hides it well." He put the jars on the table and began to peel the hard wax from the mouth of one. "It will be ready to drink in a moment," he assured Damiano.

"Fine," was the response, and il Primàrio held out his cup to Alessandra. "I am going to regret this in the morning, but for the moment, this is heaven."

Alessandra's laughter was a trifle too loud, Lodovico thought as he pried the cap off the wine jar. He sniffed at the contents and was relieved that the scent was good. There had been a bad jar in the last lot; he would have been shamed to have another for Damiano.

"I've always liked to sing," Damiano said meditatively as he stared up toward the darkening sky. "I haven't much of a talent for it, but it's been an enjoyment to me. I haven't sung in weeks."

"Sing now," Alessandra urged, and Lodovico knew she would boast of it for days.

He sat still, shaking his head. "No, no, I think not. I suppose my courage is lacking. I'm certain I would squawk like a duck, being so out of practice."

"I doubt it," Lodovico reassured him as he sat down once more. Not waiting for Damiano to make up his mind, he began in his own, rather thin baritone, " 'Non so che altro paradiso sia,/quando amor fussi sanza gelosia./Quando amor fussi sanza alcun sospetto,/lieta sario la vita degli amanti,/e'l cor pien di dolcezza e di diletto/da non aver invidia in cielo a' santi./Ma, lasso a me, cagion di quanti pianti/e questa maladetta gelosia!' "

Damiano had joined in the last few lines with uncertain harmony. At the end of it he reached for the newly opened jar and refilled his cup. "It does me good to hear that old song. 'Quando amor fussi sanza alcun sospetto,/lieta sario la vita degli amanti,' . . ." He sighed, and did not finish the stanza.

"That's beautiful," Alessandra murmured, looking across the table at her husband. "Don't you think so?"

Whatever Lodovico might have answered—and he had no idea what to say to her—was interrupted by the young Virginio.

"It's *stupid!*" he burst out. "Who can love without jealousy? Who would want to? It sounds silly, to be unsuspicious."

"How do you know, puppy?" Damiano demanded, the mischievous light in his eyes once more.

Virginio set his jaw as his face went rosy as a bake-stove. "I know something about it, rest assured," he announced with what he had intended to be hauteur but sounded much more like petulance.

"I thought so, too, at your age," Damiano said kindly, but still amused. "I don't know how my grandfather bore with me." His voice changed and he laughed easily. "Yes, I do. He remembered his own youth, as I do. Those lyrics of his were written when he was older and had learned better." He drank his wine slowly and deeply. "It's going to be a beautiful night, I think."

Lodovico watched as Damiano rose and went toward the edge of the courtyard where the end of the garden offered a sliver of a view of Firenze, lying below them. He had often stood there himself, seeing the city darken at evening, watching the distant, pale glare of windows and entrance torches that marked the streets, listening to the tolling of the bells in sudden, solemn conversation.

"Damiano," Alessandra called after him, but Lodovico put his hand on her arm and motioned her to silence. She gave her husband an abrupt, troubled look, then shrugged.

"I'm going in," Virginio declared, and almost overset the bench he had been sitting on in his haste to leave the courtyard.

"A difficult boy, these days," Alessandra sighed as she looked after her son. There was no anger in her. She started to speak again, then lapsed into silence as she heard a door slam.

"He will be off to his studies soon, and that will end these displays of his," Lodovico assured her as he got to his feet. "He thinks he is bored here, and so he tries to liven his days." He took up the cup Damiano had left behind, refilled it and his own. "He will treasure this summer later, but now it only distresses him because he is certain that life is passing him by."

"That's ridiculous. He's hardly old enough to shave." There was an unbelieving sharpness in Alessandra's tone, and she at last looked into Lodovico's eyes. "It *is* ridiculous, isn't it?"

"Of course it is," Lodovico said sadly, "but at that age, there is such urgency. It is later that we learn to savor our days." He turned away from her and walked across to where Damiano stood, silently looking down on the soft, distant lights of his city, lights that warmed the spring darkness the way the little candles before their shrines relieved the darkness of San Lorenzo, Santa Maria Novella, Santa Croce, San Marco, Ognissant, Santa Trinità, and all the other churches of Firenze.

Damiano's face was sullen as he stared upward at Andrea Benci. The old courtier had not yet dismounted, though he had arrived some little time before.

"We have need of you, Primàrio," he repeated in a manner that was at once demanding and subservient.

"I appreciate that," Damiano snapped back, putting one hand to his aching head. "I only wish that you had not been quite so prompt in the exercise of your duties. And you need not remind me that my Cardinale cousin would be insulted if he is kept waiting—he is insulted by my existence; he's made that very plain." He looked back toward the passage to the courtyard. "We are having soft cheese this morning. Come eat with us."

"I broke my fast two hours ago, Primàrio." There was a tone in his voice that implied that Damiano was being lax because he had not done the same.

From his place by the door, Lodovico called out, "We would be pleased if you would join us. The cook can press some fruits for you, Benci."

There was a swift look of approval from Damiano that delighted Lodovico even as Andrea Benci said, "I haven't the time. Perhaps another day."

"Don't be churlish," Damiano admonished him. "Lodovico does well to ask you, and it is not kind of you to respond in such a manner."

Andrea Benci blinked, unaccustomed to being addressed in that way, and straightened himself in the saddle. "I must refuse this kind offer," he said stiffly. "Someone must make the proper preparations for il Cardinale. I fear I cannot stay if His Eminence is to be greeted as he deserves."

"Do as you think best," Damiano said, resigned. "I will be along when I am done. And I remind you that we're not to see Cosimo until prandium, which gives me ample time to finish my meal here, ride back to Firenze, change my clothes, and spend a little time in my study before my cousin requires me." He made a gesture that dismissed Benci, and came down the path toward Lodovico. "What you told Benci about the pressed fruit—will you have her press some for me? My head is filled with devils this morning."

"Certainly," Lodovico said, feeling lamentably pleased with himself for being able to continue his private conversations with Damiano despite the demands of il Primàrio's high office. He nodded toward Benci as he stood aside for Damiano to pass through to the courtyard and was amazed to see fury on the secretary's face, and a naked jealousy that was subtly twisted with gloating.

La Fantasia

Bellimbusto rose eagerly into the air, curvetting playfully after his lazy days in the Nuova Genova stables. His enormous wings thundered like well-filled sails, and they smoldered black and bronze as the sun struck him.

Lodovico felt the same elation as his splendid mount. To be airborne again! To set forth at last toward the enemy! His laughter was deep and full. He hated the waiting, the endless delays and preparations while the enemy made undiscovered progress. He was in his element, and laughed once more as he looked around at the thinning morning mist and the receding ground.

Now he could see the first rise of mountains in the distance, looking a furry blue. Here and there bands of green showed meadows and fields among the trees, and the glint of silver, like carelessly flung coins, marked the course of the river that curved its way from the mountains to the ocean.

Below and behind him were the lines of his troops.

Falcone rode with Massamo Fabroni at the head of the soldiers. The Cérocchi prince was mounted on a huge red stallion that Lodovico had admitted he would have chosen for his own had he not been riding Bellimbusto. The old Lanzi captain was mounted on a rawboned liver-chestnut known for his unflagging energy and uniformly bad temper. They were a strange pair, to be sure, but the men behind them were certainly as ill-assorted as their leaders. Yet, thought Lodovico as he brought Bellimbusto wheeling in an enormous circle over this unusual army, with the help of God, they might yet emerge the victors. The implacable enemy could be overcome.

As the shadow of Bellimbusto's wings passed over Falcone, he looked up and lifted his bow in solemn greeting. Lodovico returned the salute and added one for Massamo Fabroni, then set his mount's head toward the west.

Up here the winds were singing high, taunting songs that Lodovico knew well presaged a storm. To the south he could see an ominous dark line in the under-bellies of towering, pink-shot clouds. The air itself crackled its anticipation. There would be time enough to make a good advance, he hoped, but this night they would have to stop early and make a secure camp. Fleetingly he wondered if Anatrecacciatore had called up the storm to harass the men who rode against him. It was possible, he knew. He had seen just such sorcery in the land of the Great Mandarin, though there the storms had come snaking in out of the desert, hot and treacherous as Turkish bandits. Here, the land was vaster and more verdant, yet Lodovico sensed that Anatrecacciatore would turn this to his advantage if he could.

As Bellimbusto's wings strummed the air, Lodovico found himself remembering the leave-taking of that morning. He had no one to embrace him with the tenderness and fervor that so many of the men inspired. He had stood a little apart, desiring no pity for his isolation. But Falcone had found him, and had brought

Aureoraggio to him. What torment he had known in that instant! He had been near to forgetting himself, but instead had murmured a few courteous remarks to the Scenandoa princess before thanking the Cérocchi prince for his consideration. Now he could see Aureoraggio's face in the clouds, could hear her soft accents in the crooning wind. He told himself sternly that he should be watching the ground beneath him, not dreaming of that unattainable maiden. He sat straighter in his saddle and was glad that he had not brought his chittarone with him, for this way he had no excuse to lose himself in music.

Some little time later, he was far ahead of his troops on the ground. The forest rolled out below him, endless, with fewer and fewer clearings and cities to be seen. Lodovico marveled at the immensity of it. What would the lone traveler be faced with in that forest below? It was a sobering reflection. These forested mountains, resting in their blue-green haze, how often had they swallowed up men with the same casual ease that the sea devoured sailors? He looked toward the west where the mountains were higher, more formidable, and tried to remember what he had been told of the rivers that lay beyond.

He was distracted by the sound of birds, a joyous, shrill sound that seemed to well out of the trees below him. Lodovico leaned back in his saddle, delighted to hear the twittering chorus. He was astounded when, in the next instant, Bellimbusto let out a distressed cry and dipped suddenly before striving desperately for greater altitude.

Lodovico gripped his saddle with both hands, staring around in bewilderment. He tried to speak reassuring words to his mount, but in a moment his tongue cleaved to the roof of his mouth as he saw thousands, tens of thousands, hundreds of thousands of birds erupt from the forest beneath them and begin a frenzied upward assault. The sound that up until that time had charmed Lodovico now took on the sinister characteristic of a war cry.

Valiantly Bellimbusto drove upward, his wings thundering his fear. Lodovico gave him his head and moved high in the saddle to give him more upward balance. The sound of the birds grew louder and louder, a terrible shriek like the mightiest storm wind.

The first of the attackers arrived, the small, swift birds with beaks and talons sharp as needles. They darted about the hippogryph, shrilling their wrath, plunging and diving at the eyes and neck of Bellimbusto and at the face and chest of Lodovico. They were worse than a cloud of enormous gnats, and their attack was more determined, more deadly.

Fumbling for his great sword Falavedova in the ornate saddle scabbard, Lodovico was struck for a moment at how absurd it was, being high in the air battling sparrows, larks and linnets. These were creatures of beauty, of delight, not of this savage assault. He could feel blood on his face where the birds had struck and gashed him. Even as he dragged the sword from its case, Lodovico wondered how he could use it against such little, rapid foes. The long blade was designed to shear through armor, not feathers, to strike down soldiers, not songbirds. He felt helplessness as he saw the steel flash in the sunlight.

There were other sounds in the air now as the predators came upon them—hawks, falcons, eagles, powerful and restless as great cats, splitting the wind with faces like arrows. Their hooked beaks and keen eyes were quick to use the smallest weakness, quick to rip and tear. Their talons sank into flesh and their cries were screeches of loathing. Lodovico felt Bellimbusto lurch and scream as two white-headed eagles gouged for his eyes. The fabulous mount slid sideways on the wind as if seeking to escape from the tormentors that filled the air so densely that it was impossible to see what lay more than an arm's length ahead. Infuriated now, Bellimbusto flailed out with his taloned front quarters and flung one of the fulvous-feathered eagles spiraling toward the forest that they could not see beneath them.

Though it offended his soldier's pride, Lodovico began to lay about him with the flat of his blade, slapping the birds out of the air, sending them hurtling down. He could no longer aim to strike, but swung the sword wildly, praying that he did not touch his mount and end it for them both in one, long drop to the earth. Was this what the minions of Hell had endured at the hands of the angels? he wondered for an insane instant. With each swipe of his sword, he could feel the press of feathered bodies, hear the chorus of the wounded, but he saw little, and he felt as a blind man must when set upon by marauders. He yelled encouragement to Bellimbusto and sensed the answering strength.

Yet it was not enough. The larger, heavier birds were on them now, the geese, ducks, plovers, and turkeys. They were more dangerous than the hawks and the eagles not only for their greater size but for their ferocity. Three enormous golden swans began to worry at Bellimbusto's hindquarters even as the geese plucked at the black-and-bronze wings. Bellimbusto howled in protest, his gilded rear hooves striking out uselessly, sending him and his rider lurching through the sky.

In panic Lodovico almost dropped Falavedova as he clung to the high front of his saddle. His vision was blurred and his arms were so sore that he could not bear to lift them. With more determination than he had known he possessed, he forced himself to hold the sword and to stay in the saddle as Bellimbusto rose sharply and dropped with sickening quickness, seeking to rid himself of the birds. There was still force in these movements, but Lodovico knew that it could not last much longer.

"Down! Down!" Lodovico shouted hoarsely to the hippogryph, and fought both dizziness and swifts as his mount descended. He tried to clear his eyes and his thoughts. A little more time and the ground would rush upon them and they would be in the murderous branches. He set his knees against the heaving flanks and steadied the animal even as he guided him toward the forest below. There was a chance, he realized, one chance. He had seen a river sliding under the trees, and knew that there might well be beaches or grassy stretches near it.

The claws of a hawk raked his forehead and blood poured over his face, clouding his eyes. Impatiently he wiped it away with his sleeve and at the same time brought Falavedova around to hack at the bird. He knew a moment of gratification as the hawk faltered and fell, and then he felt the battering of goose-bills on his legs.

Below the forest waited, the trees offering the spurious comfort of their leafy crowns that surely concealed deadly limbs capable of breaking him and Bellimbusto if they could be lured onto them. A woodpecker landed on his arm and began methodically to peck at his flesh. That beak, used to drill holes in trees, was hideously efficient on his shoulder. With a sense of revulsion that horrified him, Lodovico pounded the bird with the hilt of his sword and tore it away from him.

Still the trees covered the river, and still Bellimbusto, exhausted and harried now nearly to the limits of his legendary strength, flew lower and lower. The birds circled around them, their wings and their cries louder than any tempest Lodovico had ever known.

He reeled in the saddle as a wild turkey blundered against him, thrashing wings at his head. Lodovico took Falcone's dagger and stabbed blindly at the enormous bird and was rewarded by feeling it go limp in his grasp. He was about to thrust it away when he knew that he would have to sleep in the open that night, and determined that these birds would feed him and Bellimbusto. He shoved the turkey against the knot of blankets at the back of his saddle, and began to slice at the myriad attackers. He fared little better with the dagger than he did with his sword, but he found that working the two blades together gave him a measure of protection he had not had before. With an effort he shouted heartening words to Bellimbusto and sensed his mount's understanding in the renewed surge of power from the huge wings.

At last he saw a narrow stretch of sand, and he gave the signal to the hippogryph to descend. In dismay he saw that there were ducks on the riverbank and as they neared them, the ducks rose up in a body. It was more than he could endure, he feared, and he felt his heart grow cold in his breast. He brought his bloody hand, with Falavedova still clutched tightly in his wounded fingers, up to cross himself. He had failed his men and his God. He wondered if he should drop his weapons and give himself up to the fury of the birds.

Then he saw that the ducks had flown in terror, away from him and the faltering Bellimbusto in their fearsome cloud of screeching, chattering, infuriated birds. The ducks had fled! His face set itself in a hideous smile and he began once again to hack at the feathered adversaries around him.

Even as Bellimbusto's gold-painted talons touched the sand there was a shudder of thunder in the air. Lodovico was out of the saddle at once, crouched low to fend off the continued attack.

It never came. The birds stopped, hovered in confusion, and then with strange cries, flew away from the spot and each other in terror, as if suddenly brought to their senses of the enormity of their unnatural transgressions. Lodovico stood still, one hand on Bellimbusto's reins, and stared at the sky, empty now of everything but the thunder.

He landed the next morning in torrential rain near the camp his troops had set up. There was a great bustle to meet him, and shouted questions that were stilled when the men were close enough to see the tatters of his clothes and the bruised lacerations of his face and body.

"I must see Prince Falcone," he said in a voice that was cracked with exhaustion. "Where is he?"

A number of the men pointed the way to the Cérocchi's tent, and just as Lodovico stumbled forward, the men parted as Falcone himself approached. "What happened? Why didn't you return . . ." His demands ceased as he caught sight of Lodovico.

Lodovico lifted one blood-caked, shaking hand to his forehead. "I met with opposition," he said, hoping to make light of it. He felt fear sink cold fingers into the vitals of the men around him, and he knew that he had to dispel it at once. "It seems Anatrecacciatore has a certain humor about him."

"The soldiers of flint and frost?" Falcone asked, the very name making his words soft.

"Oh, nothing so grand as that. A flock of birds." He knew he could not venture laughter, so he contented himself with a shaking of his head.

"Birds?" Falcone echoed with a swift glance at the men. "Birds did that to you?"

"Well, there were a great many of them," Lodovico allowed. "You know, targets that small are damned hard to hit." He was relieved to see the men lose some of the rigidity his arrival had occasioned. If only his voice did not sound as if it belonged to an enormous frog. He had not been able to do more than make the most cursory examination of his injuries, but he had a fair idea that he was not a pretty sight.

"Birds." Falcone came forward now, and clapped his arm around Lodovico's shoulder, more gently than it appeared, and still Lodovico could not entirely disguise his wince when Falcone's arm touched him. "You must tell me more of this." He looked toward Bellimbusto, standing in the rain, bedraggled feathers and matted hair making that glorious animal seem a discarded toy for a god. "Your mount . . ."

"I must see to him," Lodovico allowed wearily. "He must be dried and stabled and fed. When I have done that, I will be with you in your tent. If you will tell Fabroni and your father that we must speak, I will be with you directly." His every joint ached, but he refused to limp. He waved to those warriors he knew and called a few greetings as he turned to lead Bellimbusto

to the northern edge of the camp where the Lanzi
horses were sheltered.

"But you are certain that the ducks did not attack you?"
Cifraaculeo demanded for the third time.

"They flew off," Lodovico answered patiently, though
his body hurt and he was almost too tired to speak.
He had been in Falcone's tent for several hours and
had yet to be given food or the opportunity to bathe
and change his clothes. He reminded himself that his
report was more important than his comfort, but his
weary sinews protested inwardly.

"But the other birds came at you in a body."

"I have said so," Lodovico responded more sharply.
"I did not have time to determine how many of what
bird attacked me, and I confess that I have not yet
learned all the varieties of fowl that live in this land,
but I assure you that there were a great many. Geese,
swans and other water birds among them, but not
ducks." He had asked once why that should be important, and had been given no answer. Now he repeated
his inquiry. "You have laid a great deal of importance
on these ducks. Why is that?"

"Anatrecacciatore is the Duck-Catcher," Falcone explained in spite of the fulminating glance cast on him
by Cifraaculeo. "There has long been speculation about
his name, but no answers. From what you have told us,
it would seem that he has control over the birds of the
air, all but the ducks. It may be of use."

It seemed to Lodovico that much of his fatigue had
evaporated as he heard this. "He has no power over
ducks? Do they inevitably flee him, do you know?"

Cifraaculeo glared down at the Italian hero. "We
believe this is so."

Lodovico got to his feet, uncaring of the protestations of his muscles and joints. "Why was I not told
this earlier?" he wanted to know, looking from the
Cérocchi Prince to the high priest. "If the ducks are not
under his influence and always flee him, then they will

be our advance scouts. We need only see where they
are . . ."

"They flee from us, too," Falcone reminded him,
though there was a guarded expression of hope in his
black eyes.

"But, listen—they will fear Anatrecacciatore more
than us, will they not?" He saw the tentative nods of
agreement and hurried on. "We must set out flanking
scouts, so that nothing will be missed. If the ducks flee
toward us, then we know that the sorcerer's forces are
on the march. We'll need a system of signals that will
not alert the enemy to our tactics, and that way we will
gain still more time. Unless Anatrecacciatore can command every other creature in the forest, we will have
gained an advantage. With so malefic and subtle an op-
ponent, we must have more intelligence if we are to
defeat him.".

Falcone's face grew sharper as Lodovico spoke. "It
is well," he said after a moment. "There are men of
the Scenandoa who are noted for their skill in scouting.
They will be glad to do this, for they have suffered
much at the hands of Anatrecacciatore."

"Yet these forests are vast," Lodovico said, feeling
he had to interject a word of caution. "It would be an
easy thing for all of us to blunder through them and
never engage the other side in battle, so that in the end
all each had to show was fatigue and field losses."

"Do not underestimate Anatrecacciatore," Cifraaculeo said gloomily. "He will know where we are and
what we do, no matter what precautions we take. He
will strike when it suits him, after we have gone far,
when the spirits of our men have become disheartened,
when each band of warriors is full of rivalry with all the
others, so that they will not fight together, then, then
Anatrecacciatore will send his invincible armies against
us . . ."

Lodovico interrupted this catalogue of woes. "If his
warriors are invincible, as you say, there is no reason
for him to wait until we are lost in the forest and without provisions, weapons or morale. All he need do is

send them crashing down upon us now, conquering your men near their cities so that plunder as well as victory is close at hand. If he must lead us far into the wilderness, it is only that his strength is not so vast as we have been led to believe and either he must fight on his own accursed ground, as the wizards of Russia did, or his troops are not invincible and he must stay near the source if they are to triumph in battle." As he spoke, he could feel more hope surge through him. Yes, he saw that their cause was not entirely lost. While the birds had attacked him and Bellimbusto dropped through the air, he had feared that there would be no way to conquer such a powerful sorcerer, but now, hearing the words of the high priest and listening to the warnings, he realized that they had some small chance for success. His great heart was lightened and in his soul he thanked the mercy of God for this information, and begged forgiveness for his doubts, and the great sin of despair.

"Then it is folly to proceed!" Cifraaculeo cried out. "Each step takes us closer to his power, giving him more of an advantage!"

"Perhaps." Lodovico took a turn about the tent, his mind too preoccupied for him to admire the appointments of tooled leather and embroidered cloth. "Still, we dare not expose your homes to the full attack of his forces. There must be a way . . ." He glanced down and saw a mouse hidden in the fold of the tent cloth. The animal did not move as Lodovico approached it, but stared upward with eyes shiny as black glass. "Strange," Lodovico mused as he paused near the little animal. "Strange."

"What? . . ." Falcone started forward but Lodovico waved him back.

"In a moment, my friend." Quite suddenly he moved, scooping the little rodent from the fold in the cloth. The mouse made tiny shrieks of rage and tried to eat through glove-leather into Lodovico's palm with its teeth. Lodovico swore but refused to drop the animal.

"I have found a spy, I think," he said, feeling something between terror and amusement.

"A spy?" Falcone asked, bewildered, as Lodovico approached him. "What spy?"

"I have a mouse in my hand. It did not run when I came near it and now it is biting me with the will of a tiger." He felt the blood run out between his gloved fingers and had to resist the impulse to crush the creature in his hands. But that, he knew, would be foolish, for if it were truly under the control of Anatrecacciatore, such an act would free the sorcerer from the little body and give it the chance to inhabit another. Such as Falcone. Such as Cifraaculeo. Such as himself. He ground his teeth and looked at the high priest. "Who among you knows the rituals to make such animals speak?" At his words, the mouse was still.

"I do. And there is one more powerful still with the Cesapichi who is known everywhere for his gifts." This last was told reluctantly, though it was certain that Cifraaculeo did not relish the talent himself.

"Bring him. This mouse, absurd thing that he is, may yet be more important to us than all our warriors, horses, and weapons combined." He did not look to see which of the two Cérocchi obeyed his instructions, but set himself the task of holding the suddenly active mouse while it scrabbled on his bleeding leather-covered palm, biting, scratching, for all the world like a marauding wolf seeking escape from a trap.

La Realtà

It was one of those lachrymose summer storms that
flailed in out of the west, wrung its gray fingers over
the Arno valley, and spent itself in hysterical flutterings
against the hills. Lodovico sat at his desk and listened
to the last of the rain as it spattered on the shutters. A
book lay open before him, but he had not been reading
it for some time.

"Husband?" Alessandra called from somewhere beyond this little haven. "Lodovico?"

He roused himself from his thoughts and answered,
"In my study, my dear." He heard her as she trudged
up the narrow stairs and the rap of her knuckles on the
door. "Come in." The small courtesy both pleased and
annoyed him. He knew she was coming to him, had
heard her approach the door. What would have been
the point in refusing her entrance?

Alessandra came into the study, an expression of
ill-use on her face giving her somewhat bland appearance a character that it rarely achieved otherwise.
"There is a messenger below. He says he must speak
with you."

"A messenger? In this weather?" He was at once
startled and wary.

"You weren't reading?" Alessandra asked, indicating
the darkened room and the unlit lantern.

"Reading? No. I was . . . thinking." Lodovico smiled apologetically. He always found it difficult to recall himself when his thoughts had been broken into so abruptly.

"Well, then." Alessandra stood aside in the doorway, doing her best to conceal her impatience. "The man told me it is urgent. You should hurry, I think."

"Of course," Lodovico murmured, setting aside the vellum pages he had stacked by his elbow. "Yes. Tell him I will be there in a moment. I've had a great deal on my mind . . ."

Alessandra's gesture was exasperated and resigned. "Don't be too long, husband," she admonished him affectionately as she closed the door behind her. Lodovico could hear her steps retreat down the hall to the stairs.

Lodovico stood alone for a moment, one hand on the frayed standing collar of his guarnacca. He gave the garment a peremptory tug and pulled at the sleeves of his shirt so that they puffed out at the simple slashing. His stiff-padded knee-length hose were rumpled and he supposed his calzebrache were sagging. He had often wondered how men like Andrea Benci always contrived to look so neat. There was never an unwanted crease in Benci's clothes, his leggings never twisted or sagged or ran, his shirts never had spots and the complicated slashings on his guarnaccas and giorneas were always stylish. His barber never hacked his hair to uneven lengths and his little beard was always perfectly groomed. Lodovico tugged at his beard; the stiff hair refused to lie down. He decided to leave his cap where it was and reluctantly left his study for the receiving room below.

As he came into the entryway, he saw the messenger waiting. He was a tall man wearing a long cloak that was dripping steadily onto the stone floor. There was a harassed look to him, as if this were not the only unpleasant errand he had run that day. "Messer' Ariosto?"

"I am he." Lodovico performed the most minuscule of acknowledgments.

"I am Renaldo Tommassini," said the other, as if the name should mean something to Lodovico.

"I don't believe we have ever met," Lodovico said after giving the man's face a quick scrutiny.

"We have not," Renaldo answered shortly. "I am sent by my uncle. I thought you would have heard of me."

"Your uncle? I'm afraid I . . ." He knew he ought to offer the man the warmth of the fireplace in the receiving room, and belatedly he gestured toward that chamber. "Perhaps . . . you might sit down. I could send for hot wine?"

"Thank you, I would like that." There was a thawing in the imposing young man. "It was a hectic ride here."

"These summer storms. Very unpredictable." Lodovico called to Alessandra, "Have Nerissa heat and spice some wine for this poor man."

"I have already spoken to our cook," Alessandra responded primly, adding in a slightly injured tone, "I will leave you to your discussions." She turned away toward the back of the house before Lodovico could think of anything to say.

"Good," Renaldo sighed as he began to pull off his sodden garments. "We must speak in private, Messer' Ariosto. It is important that we are not disturbed."

Lodovico was genuinely puzzled. He had received a few messengers from Firenze since Damiano had visited him three weeks ago, but none had come in such weather and had insisted on so much secrecy. "If it is that private, we may retire to my study. It isn't very warm, but I know that . . ."

"No, no," Renaldo Tommassini protested, raising his gloved hand. "Here will be well." He cast his cloak onto a table near the fireplace and spread it out to dry. As he tugged the gloves from his hands, he remarked, "The approach to the villa is wet as a creekbed."

"So it is." Lodovico took the chair farthest away from the fire and sat, waiting. "Have you letters for me?"

"Letters?" Renaldo was startled. "There are things one does not put in letters, at least not when there are messengers who are discreet." His smile was condescending and there was disdain in his tone. "You must allow that there are men whom it is not wise to trust, even with letters."

"Certainly," Lodovico answered automatically, and could not understand why Damiano had employed this self-important young man on such a mission. He had his answer at once.

"I am employed by Andrea Benci, the personal secretary to il Primàrio . . ."

"I know Benci," Lodovico said mildly, satisfied that Damiano had not intended this Renaldo as an insult. "I am surprised that he would send you, or anyone, to me."

For the first time Renaldo Tommassini seemed distressed. He sank into the chair by the fire, clasped his hands, then rose again. "It is a most delicate matter. I'm sure you can appreciate that."

"I hope so," Lodovico assured him, feeling baffled by the man's refusal to get to the point.

"It is not what Andrea Benci wishes to do, but he has orders, you understand." Renaldo took his seat again and stared at the fire. "I am told that you are somewhat in il Primàrio's confidence, so I will speak freely."

If this was an example of his free-speaking, Lodovico thought, he would be astounded at what Tommassini considered obtuse. "I would appreciate that."

"It is Sir Thomas More," Renaldo exclaimed, and clasped his hands together in an attempt to restore his formidable manner.

"What of Sir Thomas? I beg you not to speak in riddles. If there is trouble, tell me at once." His voice had gotten louder and he made a stern effort to control it. Had anything befallen the Chancellor of England?

"Have you had any communication with him since he left Firenze?" Renaldo demanded, sitting forward, his chin thrust out. Lodovico stared at him, thinking that the young man had a very Medici jaw, and tried to determine to his own satisfaction which Medici had seduced his way into Tommassini's family. Lorenzo or his brother Giuliano, perhaps, or Damiano's father, Piero. They were all possibilities. . . .

"What?" he asked rather suddenly, realizing that he had been staring and had not properly heard the question.

"I said, have you had any communication with Sir Thomas More since he left Italia Federata?" This was said with exaggerated care, as if Renaldo had decided that Lodovico was deaf or foolish.

"Why do you ask?" He had not meant this as a challenge, but from the way Renaldo's expression hardened, it was clearly interpreted as such.

"Andrea Benci knows that you were visited by someone carrying a letter. When he was not notified of it, he grew concerned."

Lodovico wanted to know by what right Andrea Benci could demand this or anything of him. It was Damiano who trusted him, Damiano who was his patron, his friend. He considered the letter that had been given to him a few days before, brought by a monk traveling from Poland to Roma. He was startled to hear himself say, "I have heard nothing from Sir Thomas recently. Damiano was given the last letter I received."

Renaldo was taken aback, but was able to disguise it quickly. "We had heard you were sent a letter."

This stung Lodovico, and instead of apologizing and telling the brash young man the truth, he found himself infuriated that his privacy had been violated. He sat straighter, making up his mind to complain to Damiano at the first opportunity. "I did have a letter from Poland, it's true. It came from a scholar there who wishes to translate some of my poems, but has no complete editions. He wants me to send him one." He reminded himself that he would have to send Jerzy a copy of one of his volumes. His longtime correspondent would not mind receiving it.

"A Polish scholar," Renaldo repeated softly.

"I will be happy to supply his name, if it is required." Lodovico's tone was icily polite, more out of anxiety than anything else. If Renaldo insisted on seeing the letter, he would surely be revealed as a liar, and he knew that once Damiano heard of this, he would lose all trust in his poet-friend.

Apparently Renaldo read other import into his words. He, too, sat straighter. "I was not suggesting that there was any dissemblance. A man of your literary reputation must often receive such requests." He spoke more surely now, as if he had convinced himself of Lodovico's honesty. An expression between anger and disgust hovered on his face, and then, with a great effort, he schooled his features to a pleasant smile. "What a day to come on a fool's errand."

"It is unfortunate," Lodovico agreed promptly, vastly relieved that this Renaldo Tommassini would not insist on pursuing the matter. He was gratified to hear Alessandra's firm steps in the hall.

"Hot wine," she announced as she came into the chamber without knocking. "Nerissa has also insisted on serving little cakes with fruit to go with the wine." She held the well-laden tray in both hands and glanced at the table in some aggravation. "Certainly the cloak must remain spread to dry. Where shall I put this tray?"

Lodovico indicated the seat of another chair. "It will do. This is not comestio or prandium, and Tommassini's is not a formal visit." He tugged at his badly-trimmed beard. "Do you disapprove, Signor' Tommassini?"

"No, not at all." Renaldo looked up at Alessandra, a curious expression in his narrow eyes. "A pleasant villa, Donna."

Alessandra gave him her most complacent smile. "Truly. We are fortunate, my husband and I, that il Primàrio knows his worth."

A warm, private pride filled Lodovico as he heard Alessandra speak. It was remarks of that sort that reminded him why he loved her. He looked squarely at Renaldo Tommassini. "You will have to tell Andrea

Benci that his zeal has been misplaced. A pity." Lodovico folded his arms.

"He was most anxious for word from Sir Thomas More," the young man said, beginning to appear less formidable.

"As am I." Lodovico wished now he had taken the time to change into his lucco, the one with the embroidery down the front panel. The garment was warmer than his guarnacca, more prosperous-looking and of a cut and style that would make this young upstart tender him more respect.

"Certainly you must be. I will tell Signor' Benci that you have heard from a Polish friend." He accepted the cup that Alessandra held out to him but his face had darkened, and it was plain that he felt much put upon. "In such instances, however, zeal cannot be displaced." The tantalizing fragrance of the spiced wine took his attention and he drank deeply, gratefully.

"If you were willing to ride out here in the rain, you must certainly believe that." He held his cup for a little time, not wanting to appear too eager in the presence of Renaldo Tommassini. He was still confused by his own mendacity and for that reason, if no other, hoped to put a stop to any more questions.

"There is much unrest in Italia Federata," Renaldo announced, as if he expected Lodovico to contradict him.

"I have heard that, and seen it." He touched the place on his head where the cudgel had struck. "When you consider how much is at stake in this country, it is not surprising." The wine was hotter than he had anticipated but he drank it with an unreal ease. It would not do to appear at a disadvantage now. He set the cup aside and said in a crisper tone, "Well, if that is all you came for, I am sorry to be such a disappointment. However, I have my work to attend to and if you will be good enough to forgive me . . ." He had risen before Renaldo had time to respond.

"But the cakes, my husband,"Alessandra protested, shocked at this churlish behavior.

"When my mind is active, food does not attract me," he informed her and their guest. "Perhaps later." He was almost to the door.

"Messer' Ariosto . . ." Renaldo Tommassini began, torn between his sense of duty and the lure of the hot wine and cakes.

"If I had anything to tell you, believe me, I would be willing to discuss the matter with you at whatever length il Primàrio required. But since I do not, really, I must . . ." He was out the door and moving quickly toward the stairs. He had not thought to escape so easily, but he could feel his resolution beginning to wane, and feared that with wine and cakes in him, he would blurt out the truth. Yet the greatest puzzle remained within him—why had he lied at all?

Sir Thomas had written in Latin, since he had little Italian and Lodovico no English. The letter had been scribbled in haste and sealed five times. The English Chancellor was deeply troubled, and confessed this to Lodovico in terse phrases.

"I am torn with doubts," Sir Thomas confided. *"My heart is not my own. I fully understand the danger in which D. dM. stands, and I most truly feel sympathy for him, and wish to aid him. Yet how can I, when to support D. dM. is to defy the Pope, and I have already defied my King for my faith? Respected Ariosto, I will tell you that I believe that young Davanzati who accompanies this mission is spying for Cosimo, Cardinal Medici. Whether or not you choose to reveal this to D. dM. will be up to you. I cannot have such an act against the Church upon my conscience. I pray daily for wisdom but God has not granted my prayer. My daughter has written from Amsterdam to say that she and my wife and family will shortly leave for Firenze, and by the time this arrives, they may have already reached Italy. For their protection, I must continue to work on D. dM.'s behalf, but for the sake of my soul and the tranquillity of my mind, I should offer this*

breach of faith up to His Holiness and beg his forgiveness for my treason."

Should he, Lodovico wondered, inform Sir Thomas that Damiano was aware of Ippolito Davanzati's work? Would Sir Thomas feel relieved or the more betrayed? He tapped the parchment and stared with supreme abstraction at the half-closed shutters. Where did his own obligations lie? Foremost he would serve Damiano, but in these circumstances he had no idea which way was best. He was still smarting from the shoddy treatment he had been given—sending one of Benci's lackey-courtiers, indeed! He had drafted two letters of complaint to Damiano and in the end had destroyed them both. Undoubtedly il Primàrio had his reasons for using that officious young man, or had not thought the matter important enough for a more impressive messenger. With an effort Lodovico swallowed his pride and resolved not to mention the matter to Damiano. To make much over such a little thing! Men of the world did not allow such matters to distract them.

He was still sitting, alone, in the dark, when Virginio scratched at the door and entered the room without waiting to be bidden.

Lodovico looked up sharply, as if he had been startled out of sleep. "What?" he asked, passing a hand over his face.

"I had to talk to you," Virginio said as he pulled one of the chairs nearer his father's worktable. "Why haven't you lit a lantern? This place is as dark as a tomb."

"Um." Lodovico reached automatically for the flint to strike a spark, but as he did, he said, "You want something of me, then."

"Yes, I do," Virginio began confidently, then stopped and stared down at his hands. "Father, look." Again he faltered. "When I'm in Firenze, everyone says . . . They all laugh . . . I'm treated like a bumpkin because I live in the country!" he burst out.

"In a Medici villa only an hour from the Porta San Gallo," Lodovico reminded him.

"That doesn't matter." There was the beginning of sulkiness in his words now. "You don't understand what it's like."

At that Lodovico could not stop himself laughing. "But I do," he said gently when the mirth had cooled. Now that the lantern was burning he could see that his son was truly distressed. "I said much the same thing to my father and he undoubtedly said the same to his, and one day your son will tell you that you don't understand. I am not laughing at you, my boy, I am . . ." He was what? he asked himself, staring at the flame in the lantern. "Amused? Heartened? Pleased?" He tried each of the words out and then gave up. "Don't mind me, Virginio. My thoughts have been far away and are slow coming back."

His son sighed with impatience. "I was in Firenze yesterday and it was terrible. Now that Adriano Montini is setting the pace for everyone . . ."

"Adriano Montini?" Lodovico cut him off. What was the Neapolitan courtier doing in Firenze now? Damiano had told him that Montini was part of the della Rovere family. Why would Montini live in the city of his rivals?

"He's a fine man," Virginio insisted, staunchy defensive. "He has suppers and entertainments. And there are scholars there," he added as if to bolster his argument. "I talked to one fellow from France the other night. He told me a lot about the Université in Paris. They've had an influx of Spaniards recently, because of the interdict."

"Have they?" Lodovico was not truly listening. His mind was occupied with the matter of Adriano Montini.

"There's a Moor there who lectures on history, and René said that everyone goes to his talks, though the man's Latin is unbearable." There was excitement in his face now, and some of his guarded attitude faded. "René knows one of il Primàrio's sons . . ."

"Did he have the gall to say so?" Lodovico asked, aghast. "In Firenze? It will get back to Damiano. What can Montini be doing?"

"He's visiting Firenze to see how matters are going for la Federazione," Virginio said patiently, as if reciting by rote. "He was sent here by the King of Napoli, who can't attend meetings himself."

"He sends a della Rovere to a Medici city. He has more than mere observation in mind." Lodovico got up suddenly. "I must go to Firenze. I'll have to see Damiano."

Virginio's face fell at once. "But I have to talk to you!" he declared. "There are things I need to . . ."

"This is more important," Lodovico said curtly.

"But it's night," his son persisted. "Open the window. The sun's been down almost an hour. You can't ride to Firenze in the dark, even if it is a short distance. You always tell me how dangerous it is." He had got to his feet and stood near the door, as if to block the way. He was not certain himself whether or not he would actually oppose his father physically, but his need was strong. "You have to listen to me."

Lodovico looked toward the shutters and at the lantern and told himself that he was too lost in his thoughts. The boy was right—it would be folly to ride in the dark, and by the time he reached the city walls, the gates would be shut for the night. "Very well." He returned to his chair. "What is it, Virginio? Is it about Adriano Montini?"

"Yes, in part," Virginio said at once, pleased that his father seemed to grasp his interests.

"In part. What else?" He had to concentrate on what the boy was saying because his worry very nearly distracted him.

"I've had an offer from . . . well, it doesn't matter who, but a friend in Firenze . . ." The enthusiastic light was back in Virginio's eyes and he leaned forward, elbows on knees, his hair curling over his forehead.

"It does matter who, but we will get to that in a moment," Lodovico interjected.

Virginio started to protest, then thought better of it. "Well, this friend has said that I may stay with him until it is time for me to leave for Paris. I'll have a chance to talk more to René, so I won't be a total novice when I get to the Université, and I won't miss three days out of four in Firenze." His jaw tightened at this last.

Lodovico felt Sir Thomas' letter under his hand. "Who is this generous person, and is it your friend who offers, or a family?" He took care to be certain there was no severity in his voice.

"Well, it is my friend's offer, but his sister assured me that their mother would be delighted to have me." Now the words came out in a rush and there was a slight reddening of his face that was not entirely the work of the lantern light.

"A sister and a mother as well," Lodovico observed, not quite concealing a smile. "Who are these good people? Unless Adriano Montini has brought most of his family, I doubt he's the one . . ."

"No, no, not Montini." Virginio could not quite meet his father's eyes. "He would not have me, anyway. He's older and . . . richer."

"And higher ranking, yes." How sensitive the boy's honor was, Lodovico thought as he looked at him. Though he was not a boy anymore. Already the man in him was honing his face and drawing his limbs out. When he returned from the Université he would be like a stranger, or like someone known long ago.

Virginio cleared his throat. "The mother is Ottora Piaggia."

"Benci's cousin!" Lodovico exclaimed. He felt himself touched with anger, though he did not know why. He told himself it was his distress at the afternoon's visit, but the anger was not cooled.

"Lietiza," Virginio went on, "she's the daughter . . ."

"I thought she might be," Lodovico answered with gravity, trying to believe that it was only natural that his son would be drawn to young women, and that it was better he pass his time with a well-bred girl than tupping the expensive whores of Firenze.

"She's spoken to her mother, and she told me this

afternoon that I would be welcome." He hesitated. "Tancredi gambles. I thought you'd better know."

"I see." Lodovico had heard about Tancredi Scoglio, and knew that he was his widowed mother's greatest worry. "And you, Virginio?"

"Well, I've tried it," he admitted fearfully. "I won quite a bit at dice once, but I lost it. It made me feel light-headed, seeing that money in stacks and watching it change hands as if it were pebbles. I didn't believe it was happening. And then, when I had the money in my hands, it was as if it were on fire, or enchanted. None of it was real. I drank half the night—I know I never told you about that—and the next day I tried again, and it all went, fast as water. I wanted to go on playing," he said in a low, shamed voice, "but Tancredi told them I was your son, and they wouldn't let me because they said you hadn't enough money to pay for my losses."

Lodovico sighed. "It's true enough. Men with patrons may live well enough, if they are circumspect. Whatever riches I have are between the covers of books, my son, not in gold." He regarded the averted face and felt himself ache for his wounded boy. To have his pride so harshly used—he had known a similar blow himself, when he was slightly younger than Virginio. At the time he thought he would never recover from the disgrace, and later, when he learned that no one had paid the least attention to his terrible humiliation, he had been poisonously furious.

"So you don't need to worry," Virginio went on, as if he had not been listening to Lodovico. "I won't embarrass you by running into debts at dice. Tancredi has money from his father. Bernardo Scoglio," he added haughtily, as if to rebuke his own father, "was a very wealthy man. Tancredi has a sizable fortune."

"He does now. But the dice will rob him of it." He felt fatigued. "What you want, then, is my permission to go to Firenze until it is time to leave for Paris, because you are certain that you have earned the contempt of your fellows for living here in the country, and because you are terrified that you might miss something if you are not inside the city walls."

"Tancredi's mother has invited me," Virginio reminded him forcefully.

"So she has. Ottora Piaggia. The Piaggias did very well when they married her off to Scoglio. Don't put too much hope in Lietiza, Virginio. She will do for a flirtation, but her mother has her eye on others to be her husband. The way matters stand, the girl will not be allowed to marry anyone but a rich man." He also hoped that his son was not yet thinking of marriage, not with the years of studying that lay ahead of him. A scholar without a patron had little to offer a wife except his books and poverty.

"I don't want to marry, not yet," Virginio said, shocked at his father's suggestion. "Lietiza is a very lovely girl, and enchanting"—he had assumed a worldly manner that was almost ludicrous in its seriousness—"but she is not for me. We trifle with each other, nothing more."

"Don't let her mother hear you say that," Lodovico warned. "You will find that your invitation has been cut short if you say such things where Ottora can hear you. Perhaps you shouldn't say it to Lietiza, either. No matter what she tells you, she may nurture hopes."

Suddenly Virginio laughed, not with his newly-learned sophistication, but with genuine mirth. "She does nurture hopes, but not of me. She is infatuated with Ippolito Davanzati, and with him gone to Muscovy, she wants diversion. She likes me because I am smarter than her brother, and so is she, and she enjoys playing jokes on him."

"She yearns for Davanzati and teases her brother for poor wit?" He was amazed. "Ippolito Davanzati is crafty, but I have never heard anyone foolish enough to praise his learning or his intellect." He remembered the last time he had seen the beautiful young courtier. At that time Davanzati was dressed for riding, but even then his mantle was of sculptured velvet and the wool of his thick calzebrache was embroidered where it showed above his tooled leather boots. He had sat his horse with arrogant ease and only the most censorious would have been cruel enough to point out that the gelding was more suited to a palsied old woman than this magnificent youth.

"Women are fools: you know that." Virginio became suddenly austere. He sat straighter. "Will you let me go, father?"

"To a house of Andrea Benci's cousin?" He knew that it was not wise to impose his own struggles and conflicts on his boy. "If you understand that you are to accept nothing but their hospitality, I will consider it. I want to hear what your mother has to say before I make up my mind. A mother, you know, has a special vision."

"She'll want me to stay here because I'm going away," Virginio muttered, looking toward the lantern again. "She keeps talking about it as if I'm never coming back."

You're not, Lodovico thought. You will not come back as this lad on the brink of manhood. When you return, you will be someone else, and we will not know you. "Don't blame her for that. All mothers share her fear when they love their children."

Virginio's expression showed that he thought this was a frightful burden for any child to carry. "You'll talk to her, though?"

"Of course. I have told you I would." He got to his feet, indicating that their discussion was at an end.

"I'm going into the city tomorrow," Virginio added, some of the defiance back in his eyes.

"Very well. Unless there is more rain, there should be no difficulty." He put his hand on the doorlatch.

"You'll explain to her." He could not entirely conceal his anxiety, and Lodovico felt his heart go out to the boy.

"I will do my best. And I will tell her that since you will not see Firenze again for two years at the least, it might be wise to let you have more time there." It might also, he added to himself, ease the pain of parting. And perhaps, his thoughts continued, and he hated himself for them, having Virginio in Firenze, he would know more of the intrigues he had been so eager to escape.

La Fantasia

Lincepino, the great wizard of the Cesapichi, placed the mouse in a cage of woven bark, and surrounded it with a circle of water and a number of torches. He tossed strange-smelling herbs onto the fire and he chanted, conjuring the soul in the mouse to come forth.

The little animal sat in silence, unmoving but unafraid, its eyes fixed on the wizard with searing hatred. Once it bared its teeth and made a sound not unlike a cat hissing, but the rest of the time, it was ominously, threateningly still.

Lodovico waited in the shadows, apart from the Cérocchi and the Cesapichi, studying all they did and thinking of the many strange ceremonies he had witnessed in his travels. What he saw now fascinated and revolted him. The mouse, he knew, was unlike any mouse he had ever seen. More than that, it distressed him greatly to watch the animal sit in the cage, responding with such ferocity while Lincepino stood over him chanting in guttural accents. The herbs gave off an acrid, bitter smell as they burned and the other men waited with ill-concealed avidity in their eyes. What were they waiting for? Lodovico asked himself, and had no answer.

Lincepino threw other more noxious substances onto the torches and his peculiar songs grew higher, more frantic. Near him, Cifraaculeo watched, a worried frown deepening in his face. He turned for a moment to Falcone and gave a hopeless, minute shake of his head.

Then the mouse screeched with terror and turned away in the cage, whimpering and biting at itself with its sharp teeth while over the cage a mist was gathering.

Slowly, horribly, the mist grew denser, coalescing. It elongated, and as the torches flickered low, it began to assume a shape. First there were the long, fearfully thin arms that reached out of the mist, with fingers that seemed to extend endlessly, clutching, rending. Then the shoulders, wider than Lodovico had ever seen, ridged with muscle that made the gauntness of the body more impressive and more horrible. The chest was ridged by the ribs, long and lean to the point of emaciation. Narrow hips appeared with the bones thrusting at the flesh like inner blades. There could be no doubt of the apparition's manhood, for he was lavishly endowed, the organ long and flaccid, the testicles hanging behind massive as goose eggs. At last the head and face formed in the mist. There was a high, noble brow in a narrow head, the hair raising like a crest or old halo. The nose was long, prominent, the cheeks high with the skin pulled tight beneath them. The mouth was firm and compressed with an expression of the utmost malice. Finally the eyes shone in the mists—deep-set, dark, and vile.

Lincepino moaned and his chanting ceased altogether. Cifraaculeo stared at the thing that had come forth from the mouse and he closed his eyes at the enormity of it. Falcone inadvertently stepped back and cried aloud when his foot touched the base of one of the torches.

"Anatrecacciatore?" Lodovico whispered, unable to speak any louder.

Cifraacuelo, aghast, nodded.

The mists were growing denser, becoming palpable. In the tent the torches nearly guttered and the stench that filled the place had little to do with the herbs that Lincepino had burned. The presence was miasmic, seeping out to touch each of them in turn.

"No!" Lincepino shouted, and at the sound of the shout, the others were released from their thralldom. The wizard of the Cesapichi grabbed for certain objects he had set before the torches and these he held aloft while barking out terse phrases that Lodovico could not understand.

Something of the loathsome manifestation responded, for the light returned a bit, and the form in the air trembled as if disturbed by a wind.

"What is he doing?" Lodovico murmured to Falcone.

"He is binding it so that it cannot harm us. If it had reached us . . ." He broke off, nearly retching at the thought.

"How does he control it, if Anatrecacciatore is such a great power?"

"Every wizard has his weakness, surely you know that," Falcone said in spite of the utter condemnation in Cifraaculeo's expression. "No matter how great his power, in some way Anatrecacciatore is vulnerable. You yourself know that his power does not extend to ducks. It may be that because of his name, the ducks are sacred to him and cannot be bound by his power, since it is from them that it was drawn."

The figure now was more defined, almost solid, its baleful eyes hot with rage. It struggled against the invisible bonds that held its tenuous shape and though silent, it seemed to roar with frustration. Lodovico was apprehensive, for he sensed that this formidable sorcerer might have more power than even Cifraaculeo credited to him. He watched the arms raise up as if to strike, and encounter a barrier. The spirit turned as if seeking to find its tormentors, and there was no pleading or supplication in its manner: here there was imperious and virulent enmity.

Lincepino positioned himself out of the light, and there was sweat on his body now that had the scent of fear in it. The wizard of the Cesapichi trembled as he chanted, his voice on a higher, less certain pitch.

"You idiot!" Cifraaculeo spat at Lincepino. "He will find your terror and the binding will fail!" The high priest of the Cérocchi took up a set of wooden clappers and began to circle the ring of torches, adding his own words to the spell that bound the sorcerer. He went quickly and with a sharp, angry step, but Lodovico could see the shaking of his hands that went beyond the rattling of the wooden clappers.

"Merciful and Omnipotent God," he said softly as he crossed himself. "You Who see our plight, send us Your strength or surely our souls are lost forever to the forces of Hell. If it is Your wish that I and these good men suffer the pangs of damnation, then I submit humbly to Your wish. Yet I pray that we are not beyond Your thought and out of mind in darkness, and that You will send Your angels so that the Sword of San Michele will strike again for us against this devil's spawn as it struck down this sorcerer's parent. In the Name of Your Son, Who came to save us, I ask this. Amen." Again he crossed himself, resigned now to accept whatever heaven decreed. His heart was not calm, but he felt a greater certainty, knowing that he had survived with miraculous aid in the past. He took the dagger Falcone had given him and began to draw a line around the torches so that now the sorcerer was bound by steel as well as fire and water.

Cifraaculeo stopped his singing a moment to stare at the Italian. Then, as if sensing some worth in this action, he continued his mystical offices, this time with more determination. His hands no longer shook.

The apparition could not move quickly, being made of mist, but it drifted slowly to find the source of this new irritation. When it faced Lodovico, it stopped and there was in that lean face an expression of such wrath, such inexorable venom, that Lodovico nearly dropped the dagger he held as he was caught in the light of that malevolent gaze. It took the whole force of his will for him to look away and to resume his task, though he felt the excoriating hatred in those phantom eyes follow him, implacable in their villainy.

His face was ashen when he at last stood erect, the circle completed. Lincepino nodded toward him once, a new respect in his noble face. Even Cifraaculeo gave him a grudging nod of approval.

"What did you do?" Falcone demanded softly, who was not as reticent as the other men to acknowledge Lodovico's service.

"It is a protection known in my country. I should have thought of it sooner. It has saved me before." The first time, in the trackless desert, when the ancestral spirits of the Great Mandarin had been sent against him, he had contained them with this trick. He put his hand on Falcone's arm. "But I tell you, I have never known such potent evil before in all my travels."

"You do well to acknowledge that, pale one," said the phantom, though the lips did not move. The voice spoke out of the air, out of the very fabric of the night. It was deep and strong as a bell, and as sweet. It was a voice for a Prince, for a Pope, for a seducer. It went on, "You have evaded me before, but I warn you that I will not let you escape me again. And you, Cérocchi, Cesapichi, you puny men of little talent, hear me. For the moment you have restrained me, but it will not happen again. You think you are safe, that my power cannot touch you." The laughter that followed this caused Lodovico's very bones to turn cold.

There was a cracking sound and a sudden, violent wind that rocked the tent and extinguished the torches and that was gone as quickly as it had arisen. In the next instant the three beams that supported the tent broke and toppled, falling as if to strike down the men who stood, stupefied, within it.

*   *   *

They examined the husk of the mouse, for it seemed to be no more than skin and crumbing bones. Cifraaculeo looked grave and for the first time held his pessimistic tongue.

"Do you think he will be back?" Falcone asked the question that filled the others' thoughts but which they would not voice.

"He can," Cifraaculeo said grimly and glared once again at Lodovico as if the Italian had in some way put them all at a disadvantage.

"What will we do, if we can't contain him?" The Cérocchi prince grasped the dagger Lodovico had given him in a futile defiance. "If there are no weapons that will defeat him and he has power more than he has already shown . . ."

"Good friends," Lodovico said as he put his hand to the jeweled collar that held the Order of San Basilio, "what choice have we? Either we go forward and meet the forces of this tremendous evil or we lie here craven, worse than that mouse cowering in a burrow, and we leave ourselves open to any attack that he may send against us. What will he decide upon next? His is the Fortezza Serpente, so it might be the snakes he uses. Or what of bees? Imagine the sky covered with bees in swarms darker than storm clouds and more painful and deadly than the lightning. I have already learned what he can do with birds, and that was against only one man. What he could muster to stop this army, I dare not consider. We must advance or we might as well begin our epitaphs at this moment, and name ourselves cowards." He had not meant to speak so sternly, but now his blood was up again. He held the mouse in his hand and felt the little creature which seemed much like a rotten, furry grape. What monstrous horror would so abuse those little animals? "We are simply more mice to him, in his arrogance. I, for one, will not wait for that malefic presence to poison my soul. If I must give it up to God, so be it, but let it be as it was given to me, untainted by any sin but those I have committed, not that execrable sorcerer."

"You humble me," Falcone said quietly. "You are right. No," he added to the other two men, "do not dissuade me. It is time that I remembered what I am. Let you, wizard, and you, high priest, do all that you can to counteract the strength of Anatrecacciatore, with prayers and invocations and spells. I will go into the field, as a Cérocchi Prince must, and I will take my soldiers with me, and fight beside this Italian hero who has done so much for us." He had crossed his arms over his muscular chest and stood, legs apart, head proudly high.

Cifraaculeo lifted his arm as if to strike the son of his King, then dropped his hand. "If there are gods and powers and spirits enough left in this land to aid you, then you have my word that I will do all that I can to invoke them on your behalf. But you go to your death, Falcone, and I am not the only one who will mourn for you."

At those resigned words, Falcone nodded somberly, and whispered "Aureoraggio."

That name filled Lodovico's being with a warmth like the sunlight she was called. He knew that his face reflected this sense and it was with misgiving that he faced his friend Falcone. That beautiful woman flooded his senses and the world was made of her. How could he continue to prevaricate? When would Falcone see the truth, and what would he do then?

"Our friend is already fired with zeal," Falcone said, misreading the light in Lodovico's eyes and the brightening of his face. "He is willing to take up this fight in a land that is unknown to him. What else can we do, but emulate his example?"

Now Lincepino attempted to recover his confidence. He squared his shoulders. "Surely it will be difficult for us to battle such a formidable sorcerer, but it is as the pale man says, the alternative is to live as the mole does, in the darkness of the earth, to be blind and debased. I have gone in my magic with the moles, and the rats and the vermin of the earth, and it is not the life for a man." He picked up two wide bracelets made from the hollowed bones of deer and boar, strung with jewels and mystically painted wooden beads. These he tied to his arms and gave a single nod.

"The life of a man is better than the life of a mole," Cifraaculeo agreed as he shook the wooden clapper he still held. "It will be difficult in the days to come to remember that, when the dead outnumber the living and we see the skins of our brothers filled with sorcerer's breath and sent against us, but I will not retreat."

Falcone smiled as he took Lodovico's hand. "It is settled, then. We march at dawn."

Lodovico woke in terror, then realized that it was only the chirping of birds before dawn that he had heard, and not the clarion of another attack. He sat up slowly, drawing the three sewn wolf pelts around him against the chill. His face was still sensitive from the beaks and talons that had raked it, but he knew that he must shave and trim his beard if he was to make a creditable appearance. He shook off the last of his sleep and got to his feet, yawning as he stared out the tent flap into the camp.

There was a slaty light in the clearing, and the many campfires were dead or dying, sending up blue ribbons of smoke into the dew-laden air. The woods around them rustled with wind and far off the brook was scolding its way between the banks. There was a moist smell in the early morning, as if the mists above the trees had caught the scent of earth as if it were a gigantic tent. Across the camp, beyond the tents and the little hillocks of sleeping soldiers, there was the looming mass of the forest. Here and there a branch reached into the clearing as if to tempt the men there into the green depth. But on this morning, with white wraiths of vapor winding in flocculent streamers among the trees, the wood offered more than the velvet stillness of a day verging on dawn. Now there was a subtle danger, as if those insubstantial fogs would trap and bind anyone sufficiently foolish to venture near them. Lodovico drew the wolf pelts more tightly about him and walked back into his tent and began to look for his razor.

By the time he had shaved and trimmed his beard, the camp was already awake. The few men who had stood guard were grumbling loudly in complaint from the hours they had passed in the clammy fog, and berated the fortunate ones who had slept.

Fires had been rekindled and the first odors of cooking mixed with the mists, imbuing the brightening morning with trout and wild pork.

"There you are," Falcone said at the door as he came into Lodovico's tent. "After last night, I felt you must surely have spent the night in the tent of your priests."

"I did go to confess," Lodovico said as he pulled his mantled guarnacca of tooled leather over his silken shirt, "so that if I fall in battle, I will be as free of sin as a decent man may be. After that, I knew it would be wisest to sleep. We will have a long day, I think."

Falcone nodded. "How were your dreams?"

He had dreamed of Aureoraggio, of her radiant face suffused with adoration and love, of her eyes gazing into his with that candor, that limpid purity that had captivated his heart. "I have forgotten them."

"I wish I could forget mine," Falcone sighed. "All night I was tormented with visions of Aureoraggio so that I thought my heart or my loins would burst." He did not see the distress in his friend's eyes, and he went on, "There are many things I would sacrifice to conquer this foe of ours, but after last night, I know that my manhood is not one of those things."

"Truly," was Lodovico's curt answer. He took his time fixing his belt and the scabbard that lay across his back to hold Falavedova so that he would be entirely composed when he faced Falcone.

"Do you ride Bellimbusto today?" Falcone asked, a little wistfully, when Lodovico indicated he was ready to leave.

"On the ground. After the beating he took in the air, he will need some little time to recover." As he passed out of the tent, he clapped his hands and pointed to the Lanzi corporale who had been appointed to wait on him. "You may dismantle my tent and pack my belongings. We march in two hours. Be certain that all are ready."

The corporale, who was called Antonio and came originally from Torino, saluted smartly, as if to show the Cérocchi Prince how a real soldier behaved.

"Your men are strangely trained," Falcone observed, though it was hardly the reaction that Antonio had hoped for.

Some of the oppressiveness of the morning fell away from Lodovico. He saw the first coloring of the dawn spreading across the eastern sky like blood from an opening wound, and he thought it was a good omen, for the night had been passed in safety, and surely the portent favored this army and was against the forces of Anatrecacciatore. He put his arm around Falcone's shoulder and began to explain how the salute had come about and added fanciful tales of the confusion that had been rampant before the custom of raising visors had begun. He had the satisfaction of hearing Falcone laugh aloud as they made their way through the camp to the tent of the leader of the Pau Attan.

La Realtà

Margaret Roper had much the look of her father. She was not particularly tall, her hair was brown and her eyes the same clear, direct blue-gray of Sir Thomas'. Her dark clothing was distressingly English and her stiff skirts made the crinkling sound of bending chain as she curtsied to Lodovico.

"San Jacopo!" Lodovico said quietly, blushing at this remarkable show of respect. "No, no, dear lady, you must not." He hurried across the reception room and extended his hand to her. "Believe me, it is not deserved. For Damiano, perhaps, or the Ducas and Contes and Doges and Princes, yes, certainly, but for a poet . . ." He tried to laugh and very nearly coughed.

"My father has praised you highly, Messer Ariosto. He has said that you are the greatest Italian thinker since John Picus." She would clearly brook no opposition in this matter. Whatever her father told her she was willing to accept as true.

"John Picus?" Lodovico repeated blankly. "John Picus?" Then he sorted out the name. "Ah! You mean il Conte Giovanni Pico della Mirandola e Concordia. Yes, indeed, a most gifted, wonderful mind. It is a pity that he died so young. I wish I had had the chance to know him. He had the look of an angel, that one." He had seen many of the portraits of the fair-haired,

fresh-faced young man. It hardly seemed possible that
so formidable a wit and so erudite an intellect lay behind that mild and beautiful exterior.

"My father is his greatest exponent in England,"
Margaret Roper informed Lodovico, standing with her
hands folded across the front of her ugly dress, her stiff
kettle headdress covering all but a few wisps of her
hair. There was a severity about her that went beyond
the brown stuff garments and the austerity of her expression. Lodovico thought that such a woman might
have better been born male, for few women had the
opportunities for learning that this woman so truly
craved.

"Do take a chair, Donna," Lodovico offered suddenly, remembering his role as host. "I am indebted to
il Primàrio for sending you to me for this day, though
I am not entirely sure why he did."

Margaret selected one of the high-backed chairs
and settled primly on it. "I understand that Damian
Medici has struck a . . . bargain with my father." From
her tone, Lodovico was certain that Sir Thomas' daughter was apprehensive about the matter. "He said that
you have been in communication with him and would
give me news of him . . ." Her voice became very small
and she blinked back tears. "The King, you know, is
not pleased with my father. When he married that
terrible Boleyn woman, they had a . . . disagreement."

"So Sir Thomas has said," Lodovico said gently,
knowing what fear those few words concealed. "He informed Damiano that it might be dangerous for him to
return to England. That, I understand, is why you and
your mother, indeed, all your family, have come to la
Federazione."

"Yes." She nodded as if her head were a fragile cup
balanced on a little tray. "He does not want us to suffer
on his account." The clear eyes were suddenly fiery.
"But I would, Messer Ariosto! If my father was in
danger, I would suffer any—*anything* to save him!"

Lodovico could well believe it. "Be calm, Donna.
You are here so that it will not be necessary for you

to make such a sacrifice." He did not know how to deal with this woman, he thought. She reminded him of what he had read of the early saints, who sought out tribulations so that their faith would be all the stronger for testing. "Dear lady, what can I tell you that will ease your heart? Would you like to see the few letters your father has sent to me? I have one here . . ." He rummaged around on the littered tabletop, and at last found the folded parchment sheet under three discarded pages of abortive poetry. "Here. You will want to see what he has to say." He offered the letter to her.

"Thank you." She took the letter and opened it eagerly, reverently. "He hasn't written to us, you know, since he sent us to the Low Countries. He thought it was wisest." She stifled a sound that was very likely a sob. "I beg your pardon, Messer Ariosto. I am not behaving well for you."

"Nonsense," Lodovico protested weakly. "What shall I do for you, if not share your father's letters?" He smiled at her, and wished that he had a way to contact Sir Thomas. He had questions about Margaret Roper, and though Sir Thomas had spoken of her with affection, Lodovico had no feeling for the woman. The English were very different from Italians, he knew, and for that reason, he could not trust his complicated reaction to Margaret. "You'll see that there isn't much in the letter, really. The German States are still battling, but that is a continuous process. He mentions that Sir William Catesby is ailing, but a man his age is going to have difficulty on such a journey. It is a wonder that your King Henry allowed him to go."

Margaret looked up from the page. "Sir William Catesby was the Esquire Royal to Richard Plantagenet when he made Henry of Richmond his heir. One of his conditions was that Sir William was to maintain that post for as long as he lived, and that his sons were to be ennobled. When Richard died, Henry of Richmond kept Catesby on, though there was little affection between the men, and Henry the Eighth loathes the man. He has been looking for years for an excuse to be rid of Catesby. It's a pity," she added after a moment "Sir William is one of the last of them, and a kinder, more loyal man does not breathe on the earth. When it seemed that war between the Tudors and Plantagenets was inevitable, Sir William stayed by Richard."

"Did you know Richard?" Lodovico asked, recalling that the last Plantagenet king had been in correspondence with several of the members of Lorenzo's court.

"No, he died before I was born. Catesby said that after Richard's wife and son died, he was a changed man. It's strange for a King to love his wife, but Richard did love his Anne and it was his greatest pain to lose her, and then their son. His nephews had been poisoned, and he felt that in order to avert more suffering, it would be wise to arrange for a peaceful transition from Plantagenet to Tudor." She pursed her lips. "Is that how it seemed to others? Or did it smack of surrender?"

Lodovico had seen a few of the letters Richard Plantagenet had written in the last two years of his life, and had found them inexpressibly sad. "Was he a good King, this Richard the Third?"

"Yes," Margaret said quickly. "And a courageous one. My father met him when he was young and said that few men had seen so far beyond the limits of their reign. Richard had a census taken, you know, and reorganized the treasury on more realistic lines. He also began the new processes of Parliament. It's unfortunate he died so young, but he had long been afflicted with a wasting disease . . ." She stopped, her keen eyes meeting Lodovico's. "I have heard that Lorenzo sent him three of the best Italian physicians."

"I have heard that, too," Lodovico said, as if this tenuous bond made them closer. He was struck suddenly by the vulnerability of this woman, and realizing how cast adrift she must feel, he was determined to give her his full sympathy.

"But Henry is not pleased with Sir William because he was part of all that, and so, he sends him with my father into Russia." She spread the letter again, reading it with close attention. "I am surprised," she said when she was halfway through, "that the Polish escort should have come as far as Udine to meet them." She read a little further and smiled. "Ah. I see here that my father feels that it was more than an escort. *'For if Russia and England do form an alliance, Russia may well press westward into Poland, and with war in the German States, it will fall to Poland and Austria and Hungary to stave off that giant country. It is the dream of the Grand Duke of Muscovy, so they say, to unite all the Russias under his banner—a foolhardy plan on the face of it, but perhaps not impossible. The Great Khan accomplished far more with much less. If it comes to that, Poland, Austria and Hungary will have to stand not only against Russia, but, I fear, against the Turks as well, for I doubt the truce would be honored at such a time.'* He is most probably right. Or does it seem otherwise to you, Messer Ariosto?"

Lodovico gave her a self-deprecating smile. "I am a poet, Donna Margharita. I have no feel for politics. I can see that there is danger, of course, as any sensible man must, but whether Poland and Hungary will become allies against Russia . . . How can I tell?"

"Well, it would appear that the Poles had business in Austria already and came into Italy as an excuse." She finished the letter and folded it carefully before handing it back to Lodovico. "I thank you, Messer Ariosto. It does my heart good to read my father's letter. I feel less lost because of it."

This admission of hers touched him. "For the daughter of my friend, it is a small thing to do. If you require more of me, you have only to ask." Yet he said this in a perfunctory way, knowing that it was expected of him, and being confident that there was little he could do.

"I know you are busy with your poetry now, and I would not interfere with that, but . . ." she said in a rush, her face suddenly rose-hued.

Lodovico looked at her askance. "My work is going well," he said, "but there is much to be done on it." He wished he had some finished pages to show her, but most of them were in his study on the floor above.

Margaret arranged herself on the chair so that she looked almost childlike. "Messer Ariosto, I would like to learn to read Italian."

"What?" Lodovico stared at her, not certain she was serious, and very much afraid he would laugh. It would be a great cruelty, he said to himself, to laugh at this earnest young woman, and it would be a disservice to Sir Thomas. "There are better teachers than I am, Donna," he said, his caution making his voice breathy.

"I know there are those who can teach me the words. I have read much of their works in the past months. I realize that, given a year or more, I would learn a great deal on my own. But I would still not be able to express myself with elegance, with learning, in a way that my father would wish. It is true that there are others who know more of teaching, but no one knows more of the language than you do." Her head had come up again, and her steady gaze burned into Lodovico's weary, tan eyes.

"I see." He came back into the room and drew up a chair for himself. "Did Damiano suggest this?"

"The Premier approved my request." She was quite autocratic now, and her voice had become hard. Lodovico recalled the deep, orator's tone of Sir Thomas' voice and thought it a pity that his daughter was not like him in that way. "I am determined to learn, Messer Ariosto. If you will not teach me, then I must find another, for I am determined to be proficient by the time my father returns."

Lodovico gave a gesture of helplessness. "You see where I live, Donna. I am fully an hour away from Firenze. If you wish to come here, then, of course, I will be happy to teach you, though you may find that I am not as adept as many others are. However, let me recommend to you that you find someone in Firenze, an educated man, a priest, perhaps, who can school you in the ordinary forms of the language. Then, when you come to me, we will not have to waste time on simple things." He smiled in what he hoped was a cordial manner. He felt his hands go cold as he waited for her answer.

"You don't wish me as a student?" She made the question a challenge. "I will bring a maid as I did today. There is no way my visits can be considered improper. You may command your wife to sit with us while I have your instruction."

"No, no," Lodovico protested, and this time he did laugh. "You misunderstand me entirely." He tried to picture in his mind Alessandra sitting through long afternoons devoted to verbs and poetic structure, and the amusement made him lighthearted for the the first time since he had set eyes on this unnerving woman. "Donna Margharita, I have said I will teach you. But you will not want to come here every day."

She caught her lower lip between her teeth. "No," she admitted when she had considered the matter.

"Therefore, choose a day. That day will be yours, every week you desire my tuition. That is more possible, is it not? And while you are in Firenze, you will find another master for those days you are not coming to me." He leaned forward, realizing that it would be stimulating to teach this daughter of Sir Thomas More.

She gestured an acceptance. "I am at a loss here," she said after a moment of silence. "I have not been separated from my father before."

"But there is your mother, your sisters, your brother, your husband."

"She's not my mother," Margaret said firmly. "I love Alice Middleton dearly, but she is my father's second wife. Though she has been generous with us, as many another woman might not have been. She is much devoted to my father."

"A second wife," Lodovico mused, somewhat surprised. "Still, Donna, you are not alone." He was pleased that he had been able to admonish Margaret so gently. It was wrong to upset Sir Thomas' daughter.

"But I am!" she burst out and, to Lodovico's dismay, began to weep. "I've always been with him. I have cared for him, read with him. I washed his hair-shirt, fasted when he did . . ." She put her hand to her mouth as her sobs grew louder.

Lodovico felt clumsy. Had an Italian woman burst into tears he would have known what to do, but with this self-possessed Englishwoman, he had no idea what to say, what to do, how to act. Tentatively he put one hand on her shoulder, and was rewarded by a moan. "Donna . . ."

"I'm so distressed," Margaret wailed, and gasped in an attempt to control her tears.

"Naturally," Lodovico said vaguely, wishing that Alessandra would come and help him in this difficult situation.

"Messer Ariosto . . ." she said, catching her breath in high, anhelous whimpers. "I never . . . I didn't . . . *Forgive me!*"

Lodovico patted her shoulder and murmured some inanity. How much he wanted to leave the room! "Dear lady, you shouldn't worry." It sounded woefully inadequate to him, but apparently it was sufficient comfort for the daughter of Sir Thomas More.

"I will be myself in a moment," she promised as she sat upright again. "I rarely . . ." She made a motion with her hand. "We English are a sentimental people, and . . . and I have often seen others weep, but I hate to do it myself. It is so lacking!" She had taken a folded cloth from the wallet at her belt and she stabbed it at her eyes as if to frighten the tears away.

"We Italians also weep, Donna," he said with a self-deprecating smile. "For joy, for sorrow, for beauty, for pleasure, for anger, for pain . . . there is no occasion that an Italian cannot weep for it."

An unsteady smile wavered on Margaret's lips. "You're a very generous man, Messer Ariosto." The worst of her crying was past now, and though her breath came shakily, there was no renewal of her sobs. "This is not the way I had hoped to conduct myself before my teacher," she went on a moment later, with more confidence.

"You reassure me," Lodovico said fervently and sincerely, and was astounded when Margaret laughed.

"Oh, how good of you to make a joke of it. My father told me you are kindness itself, and I know now it is true." She made a wad of the cloth and returned it to her wallet. Her smile was still not entirely successful, but it was undoubtedly genuine.

Relieved, Lodovico got to his feet. "If you are ready, Donna, I would be honored to present you to my wife." He felt, he thought, as if he were entertaining a noblewoman, easily overset and inwardly distraught. Margaret Roper was young, but her manner was that of a matron. "And while we walk, perhaps you will select the day you wish me to instruct you?"

Margaret nodded. "I will. After this display, I am flattered that you will have me."

Lodovico wanted to put that episode behind them as quickly as possible, and so rather than comment on her words, he said, "And after you have had some refreshment, then I will bring the rest of your father's letters to read. It will please him, I know, that you have seen them."

Tancredi Scoglio leaned precariously out of the saddle and wagged a finger at Lodovico. "That son of yours . . ." he said, slurring the words.

"What about Virginio?" Lodovico had hurried into the courtyard as soon as he had heard the wild hoofbeats. It was late and a single torch blazed in the entrance to the villa. "What has happened to my son?" It was difficult to speak, and his mind was filled with memories of Virginio toddling through the little house in Ferrara; Virginio in a meadow; Virginio playing impromptu calcio with other boys in the innyard near Bologna; Virginio at his studies, his tongue sticking out with concentration; Virginio playing the lute badly but with determination; Virginio lying under the laurel tree, an open book on his chest . . .

The laughter that greeted this question was immoderate. "Sly, very sly, that Virginio."

"San Giorgio, if there is anything . . ." Lodovico made a fruitless attempt to catch the reins of Tancredi's high-bred bay, but the horse, already overwrought from the furious night ride, reared and scampered away from him.

"Capezzoli della Virgine!" Tancredi swore as he tugged at the reins to bring his horse under control again.

"What has happened to my son!" Lodovico shouted, and then was silent, realizing that he did not want Alessandra to overhear if the news were terrible.

"Joined a Confraternità, the lucky bastard!" was the answer at last, and Lodovico was filled with an inner sickness as he recalled in his mind the various activities of the Confraternitàs that had little to do with charity.

"Which one?" he asked softly.

"Worried, poet?" There was derision in the voice now, and a kind of triumph. "There are more than thirty to choose from, and each has its own . . . rituals." He hooted loudly and his horse bucked.

"Which one?" Lodovico demanded, coming up to the horse, heedless of the danger from the steel-shod hooves.

"The best, the best, only the best. He can whip a Prince of the Church if he chooses!" Tancredi was clearly enjoying himself. "He couldn't get into the one that uses the black cloth—even our Cardinale can't aspire to that."

"Per Dio, keep your voice down!" Lodovico said sharply. "Half the countryside will be awake if you keep on."

"Don't you want them to know?" Tancredi yelled, bringing his horse up close to Lodovico. "Don't you want the world to know that your boy lies down for such high-ranking men? Let a Cardinale bugger you and no one will burn you for sodomy." He wheeled his horse again and brought it within an arm's length of Lodovico. "He's either a damned catamite or he's very, very clever." He reached for a wineskin that dangled from his saddle and pulled the stopper from it. "He can advance himself a long way on his stomach!" It took two attempts to get the spout of the wineskin to his mouth, but when he had it there, he drank deeply, noisily, then flung the empty thing away.

"You are mistaken." Lodovico spoke coolly. He had had a moment to master himself, to calm his fears and his anger. "If my son has joined a Confraternità, as you say, it is not for the purposes you imply."

"Why else join?" Tancredi asked, and at last lowered his voice. "I tell you, poet, that your son is at this very moment closeted with his Confraternità . . ."

"It is not possible," Lodovico cut him off. He was contemptuous of this drunken young man now. "It is very expensive to join such organizations, and I know well that he cannot afford it."

"There are ways to get the money," Tancredi said nastily. "He has a great deal to offer that those men would like—youth, a handsome face. One of them might be persuaded to pay his fees for certain private considerations." He tugged his horse around again. "Ask him yourself." He pulled his horse up tightly. "Ask him yourself!" he shouted and set his spurs to the horse's flanks, sending the terrified, exhausted animal springing forward out of the courtyard and down the hill toward the road to Firenze.

Lodovico stood in the courtyard, one hand clutching the front of his houserobe. He told himself that everything Tancredi had said was the result of the wine. The youth was jealous, or merely playing a malicious prank. He reminded himself that he knew his son, and it was impossible that he would ever allow himself to be so used, so seduced, so debauched. Yet, he knew that Virginio wanted wealth and was easily swayed by admiration and flattery. Faults of youth, he told himself, but it would be a simple matter for an older, more ruthless, cynical man to manipulate such a boy as his son . . .

It was cold in the courtyard, he realized. A wind had come up and had banished the heat of the day. He turned as if on ice rather than the courtyard flagging, and made his way back to the entrance of the villa. His mind was restless, febrile. He had forgotten to bring down the books for Margaret, and she would come in the morning. No, it was two more days until she arrived. There was need to order more parchment, since his supply was low. He could send a note to Virginio . . . He wanted another edition of Greek poetry. No, not Greek. It was the French, yes, the French who interested him.

He was halfway up the stairs when he came to himself again. Then he stood still, his hands on the railing, his face wet though he did not realize he was weeping. He knew he had left the door open and unbarred, and he forced himself to walk down the stairs once more, close the door and set the heavy bar in place.

As he got into bed, Alessandra asked him sleepily, "Who was that?"

"No one. Just a mistake."

"Was it a messenger?" She had turned toward him and even in the faint light he could see she was watching him closely.

"Not exactly." He wanted to sleep. He had never been so weary.

"Was the news bad?"

Lodovico gestured futilely to the darkness. "He was drunk. Very drunk. He made no sense." He let himself be comforted with that thought. Tancredi had been drunk, there was no doubt, and what he had said had happened might well be nothing more than wine fumes. Still some doubt remained. "I may go to Firenze tomorrow. Or the next day."

There was no answer from Alessandra, who was already asleep again.

Two days later Virginio appeared at the villa. There were dark smudges under his eyes and an unhealthy pallor to his skin, and when he spoke, it was in short, ironic bursts that were oddly frightening coming from so young a man.

"You've got to speak to him," Alessandra insisted on the third day. "He must talk with you. You're his father." She was dressed in a countrywoman's smock of undyed linen that gave mute testimony to her work in the farmyard. "He's hardly eaten since he came back. You saw his face. What if he's ill?" Her hands moved erratically, as if eager to escape her body.

"I don't think he's ill," Lodovico said quietly, but wondered if it might be so. He welcomed the idea. "I'll do what I can to find out," he said with more firmness than he felt.

"Today, husband. This afternoon." Though she said it kindly, Lodovico knew it was an ultimatum, and that if he did not speak to Virginio, Alessandra would. He dreaded what she would do if it turned out that Tancredi had spoken the truth.

"Yes. This afternoon." He kissed her affectionately. "I'll go up now, if you like." He had seen Virginio slip away to his bedchamber some little time earlier. It would have to be done eventually, he said to himself, and so it might as well be done now. Reluctantly, he turned away from Alessandra and sought out his son.

Virginio was lying on his bed, face pressed against the pillow, his leggings unfastened and his boots on the floor. The petulant expression he had worn earlier had darkened to the curious cynicism of youth. "Archangeli," he groaned at the sight of his father.

Lodovico paused with one hand on the doorlatch. "You're awake."

"Of course I'm awake. What does it look like?" He turned onto his back and stared up at the patterns on the ceiling.

"Your manners are atrocious, Virginio," he remarked, knowing that his, in their own way, were as bad. "If this is the way you plan to behave in Paris . . ."

"Paris!" Virginio scoffed, as if he were speaking of China.

"You will leave in less than a month." He came across the small chamber and looked down at his son. "Tancredi Scoglio rode out here a few nights ago. He had

had a great deal of wine. He told me a few things that . . . distressed me. If you know what matters he . . . mentioned, I want you to deny them if you can."

"Tancredi. That sot!" Virginio lifted his arms and let them pound back into the bed.

Lodovico hardened his heart. "I forbade your teachers to thrash you when you were young, because I had hated being beaten when I was a student, but if you persist in this way, I will take a rod to you, my boy." It was the right of fathers to do so, though Lodovico had rarely exercised that right.

Virginio laughed unpleasantly. "I'm nearly as tall as you are, and I'm not soft with study."

This defiance stung Lodovico to the depth of his soul. He was not aware he had lifted his arm, he did not feel the movement until his open hand struck his son's face with desperate force.

Father and son stared at each other, each amazed, each filled with a sense of loss. It had been many years since Lodovico had struck Virginio, and then it had been part of his task as a father. Now it was something else entirely. Neither had expected this, neither had wanted it, and yet it happened.

"Iddio." Virginio at last put his fingers to his jaw and turned away from his father.

Lodovico stepped back aghast. He was breathing quickly, a dizziness jumbling his thoughts and making it impossible for him to frame a response. "Now then," he said unsteadily. "You'll answer me, Virginio. Or you will . . ." Or he will what? He did not know.

"Or what? You'll disown me?" His young face was set now, closed against his father.

How could he disown Virginio? "I want answers."

Virginio attempted a sarcastic laugh and failed. "You don't know what that could mean. You don't know what I'd say."

"I've already heard what Tancredi reported. I will suspend my judgment until you've spoken. If you aren't willing to tell me, what must I believe?" He wanted to beg his son to forgive him, to open his heart to him, but it was like shouting across an abyss where the words were lost and only the echoes, broken shards of what was said, could reach Virginio on the far side.

"Believe what you want." He reached for another pillow and began to hammer it with his fists. "You believed Tancredi, didn't you?"

This is not what Lodovico had intended at all. How had he let it come to this, in so little time? Virginio's mouth was sulky, but there was something of the boy he had been not so long ago behind his slightly averted eyes, some of the look he had had when he had been shamed. Seeing this and recognizing it, Lodovico's resolve crumbled. "No, Virginio, I did not believe him. But what made him say it?" There were tears welling in his eyes and he pinched the bridge of his nose to stop them.

"Say what?" He went on pummeling savagely at the pillows.

Lodovico forced himself to an outward calmness. "He came the other night, very late. He said that you . . . that you had been taken into a Confraternità. He mentioned a Cardinale. I inferred it was Cosimo de' Medici. You know what they do? Not the public charity, not the banquets, but the other side of it. You're old enough."

"I've heard rumors," he answered testily. "That's all there is in Firenze. Just rumors."

"What happened, Virginio? Tell me." He took a step nearer.

"Nothing happened!" The words were soft but had the impact of a shout.

Lodovico waited in silence, wishing he could find the right phrase to break down the resistance Virginio had built up.

Where argument had not succeeded, silence did. Virginio turned to the mound of pillows he had battered into a lumpy wall behind him, and after a while, he began to speak. "I thought they liked me. I really thought they did. Tancredi was pleasant and his sister made me laugh and let me open her bodice when she'd had a few cups of wine. Their mother was good and smiling. I thought they liked me."

Lodovico knew what it was to be stung by hypocritical friendship, and remembered the terrible sensitivity of his youth. He said nothing.

"That uncle of theirs," Virginio went on after a bit. "He's always so attentive."

"Andrea Benci?" Lodovico asked, trying to discount his own—jealous?—dislike of the man.

"The one who's il Primàrio's secretary, yes. He came to the house very often, and paid a lot of attention to Tancredi. Sometimes he'd lecture him on the way he lived. He kept saying that if he didn't do something about his gambling and drinking and whoring he wouldn't be able to advance himself later in life. He held me up as an example once and Tancredi didn't like that."

So far Lodovico was able to sort out all the *he*s and *him*s, and resisted the urge to correct his son's form. Now that his anger was over, Lodovico let himself sit on the foot of the bed. "What more?"

"After he told Tancredi that he should be more like me," Virginio said, a thoughtfulness replacing the wounded tone he had been using, "Benci took more of an interest in me. You know, he talked to me. I thought it was wonderful that someone as important as he was should talk to me." He snorted out a bitter laugh. "What a fool! He invited me to the Palazzo Pitti, and I was sure that it was because he'd decided I was brilliant. Insead, he introduced me to Cardinale Medici. We had melons out in the gardens and the Cardinale was even nicer than Benci had been. And I was taken in by it! I could see myself advancing right up through the civic government into the Signoria. I imagined that I would be their protégé. I thought that because Benci was disappointed in Tancredi, he'd decided that I would be a worthy successor." There was as much embarrassment as self-condemnation in his words, and he dared not meet his father's understanding eyes.

"And what then?" Lodovico's heart was sad but

serene. What he had been told was wrong, and his son had not been debauched and corrupted. Whatever else Benci and Cosimo de' Medici might have done, they had, between them, made certain that Virginio would keep away from their influence.

"There were little favors. I kept telling myself that it was because I *deserved* them, and that the recognition I wanted was coming to me." He turned onto his back and stared blankly upward. "And then Tancredi got nasty. I reckoned he was jealous, and thought nothing about it. That was before the Cardinale invited me to a banquet of his Confraternità. Tancredi told me what took place afterward, and I said that had nothing to do with it." He sniffed like a child and his voice, which had for the most part steadied downward into manhood, cracked. "I was wrong."

Lodovico nodded gently. "Your vanity is more hurt than your virtue, Virginio." He stood and looked down at his son. "It is a lesson that we all learn, who live in the shadow of the great ones. You must decide for yourself how much of yourself you will trade for advancement and favor. There are many young men who would have accepted the Cardinale's offers."

"I know," he admitted, torn between disgust and compassion. "I saw a number of them. What worried me the most is that most of them are intelligent and competent. They have real ability, and yet this is the way they seek to advance. I'd heard about that. Everyone hears about it. This minister or that representative or such-and-such a bishop bought his greatness with his body. It's whispered about at school and in church, but that's not the same thing as *seeing* it happen."

Which of his son's companions had made that decision? Lodovico wondered. He had observed such arrangements many times in the past, and could recall at least three successful protégés who had turned on the men who had advanced them once they had reached sufficient power to be able to afford revenge.

Virginio ran his hands over his hair. "I want to be in Firenze. It's boring here. But I don't want to be around Benci or the Cardinale. I don't think I want to be around Tancredi, either, not if he thinks I lay down for Cosimo."

"What do you want, then?" Lodovico asked, and without waiting for an answer, made the suggestion that had been forming in his mind. "Would you prefer to leave for Paris? I could spare a few more fiorini d'or so that you could travel a bit in France. I will ask Damiano for a man to accompany you. He'll agree to that." If it were necessary, Lodovico would tell il Primàrio what his second cousin had attempted to force upon Virginio. As long as the boy was reluctant, Damiano would help him to get out of range of the wily prelate.

Though it was difficult, Virginio managed to smile. "I've been sitting up here since I came back waiting for you to throw me out. I know about what Tancredi told you. I thought after that you wouldn't listen to me."

Lodovico bent to embrace his son, thinking as he did how tall he had grown. "I've known you longer than Tancredi," he reminded Virginio, and stood back. "Nerissa has made a berlingozzo. Will you come and eat some of it for her? You know how cooks are about food—you refuse a meal and it is worse than demeaning a gift."

"I'll be down shortly." He sat on the edge of the bed. "I can't present myself looking like this. I must have a clean shirt somewhere." This was said with a naïve vanity that pleased Lodovico very much. It was reassuring to know that Virginio cared about his shirts.

"I'll take your message to her," Lodovico said from the door, and gave himself the pleasure of smiling as he pulled it closed.

A new and enjoyable atmosphere of camaraderie and trust grew between Lodovico and his son for the next five days, and each reveled in it. Then Margaret Roper rode out from Firenze for her lesson in English and the good fellowship ended abruptly.

"I've met you, I believe," Margaret said to Virginio

in frosty accents. There was less than a decade of difference in their ages, but Margaret spoke with the confidence her father had taught her, and Virginio, still longing to strike out on his own, begrudged every hour of study and experience Margaret possessed.

"Yes, I was there with friends." They stood in the antechamber where Lodovico gave the young woman her lessons. Neither wanted to be the first to sit.

"You occasionally visited Cardinal Cosmo, I understand," she said and only the lifting of her brows revealed her disapproval.

"Sometimes," Virginio admitted.

Lodovico watched them from the door, dismayed. He had been looking forward to this day, envisioning it as a greater opportunity for sharing his new intimacy with his son. He tucked the volumes he carried under his arm and came farther into the room. "You know each other?" he asked, as if he had not heard the uncordial exchange.

"Yes," Virginio said. "I'm going riding this afternoon, father," he went on in a different, uncaring tone. He had said earlier that he would enjoy learning a little English from the daughter of the Chancellor himself.

"If that is what you want, Virginio," Lodovico said, hoping that his disappointment was not too obvious.

"It's fine weather. I've been poring over books for days. I need to get out." He gave Margaret the shortest of bows, refused to kiss his father's hand, and left the room with unbecoming abruptness.

"I upset him," Margaret said after a moment as she sank onto a chair. "I hadn't realized he was your son. I would not have spoken to him as I did . . ."

"I heard nothing that would . . ." Lodovico hastened to assure her, but she cut him off.

"No, not now, earlier. The secretary of the Premier— Andrew, his name is, I believe. He presented your son, and apparently thought I knew who he was. I didn't. I had heard a rumor . . ." Again she stopped and stared down at her hands in her lap. Today she was dressed more in the Italian style, in a rust-colored gown with a stiff lace collar. Her hair was still covered, as was the custom with many married women, but instead of the stiff kettle headdress, she had a simple chaplet of gold net. Lodovico realized that she was really quite pretty in a solemn sort of way.

"I know something of those rumors. But you know rumors," he said lightly, quoting his son without being aware of it. "Firenze is full of rumors. Nothing but rumors."

"I . . . I didn't mean . . . It is none of my affair, Messer Ariosto." She could not bring herself to look at him.

Lodovico took the chair across the table from her. "My dear Margharita, don't trouble yourself. You have my word that my son is not what you were led to believe. You have lived in a royal court, and this is not so different. You must not be surprised to hear everyone's reputation shredded and carded like wool." He chuckled gently at his own witticism.

"I must beg your pardon," she said in very good Italian. "I have forgotten charity and the nature of courtiers. Andrew said that it was not as it seemed, but I felt it was good manners only."

"Andrea Benci?" Lodovico asked, startled. He did not want Benci defending Virginio after he had treated the boy so shabbily. He refused to think that it might have been an apology. Benci was a political creature and apologized for nothing unless it could be used to later advantage.

"Yes." She looked up, trying to put herself at ease. "Italia Federata is still strange to me, and so I don't always see how very like England it can be."

Lodovico smiled at this, then set the leather-bound volumes he had been carrying on the table. But even as he began to point out examples of phrasing and erudition in the work of Poliziano and Ficino, he could not still a question that nagged him—if Andrea Benci was the political creature Lodovico believed him to be, what could he gain by maligning Virginio?

La Fantasia

By nightfall the odd army had reached low hills, and it was at the crest of the highest of these that Falcone and Lodovico ordered that camp be made. The night was clear and perfumed with flowers and other rare fragrances that were new to Lodovico. The ferns and mosses glistened with evening dew as if they had been sewn with diamonds, and the trees nodded in the low wind. There were blossoms everywhere, but hidden, as if unwilling to show themselves to ordinary mortals. It would have been idyllic but for an ominous tinge of green in the sky.

There was an evening meal of venison and grouse and pork and white fish, and afterward the soldiers gathered in coteries to brag and sing and gamble through the evening hours. Lodovico and Falcone strolled around the camp, and later, they went to be blessed by the officers of their religions.

"But I don't like that sky," Falcone said later. It was dark and yet the distant clouds were shot with light. This was no approaching storm, but something more.

Lodovico fingered his beard. "I've been watching it," he said evenly. "If we were at sea, I'd take in most of the canvas, but here, I don't know what to think."

"There are no night birds," Falcone went on. "I've been listening for them."

"They don't want to come near the camp," Lodovico suggested, though he did not believe it himself.

"We heard them last night." The Cérocchi Prince stood still, his head cocked to the side, for all the world like the bird for which he was named. "There's nothing. It's quiet. Hardly a rustle anywhere. What forest at night is so quiet?"

Lodovico shared his concern. "Have you spoken to Cifraaculeo? Has Lincepino said anything?" Though he did not like either the Cérocchi high priest or the Cesapichi wizard, he respected their integrity and trusted them to be truthful in these matters.

"No. I couldn't find Lincepino. When I went to Cifraaculeo, he did nothing more than invoke the gods for me, and then returned to studying the stones he carries." This concerned Falcone a great deal, for his eyes narrowed to slits and his brow drew inward, puckering the skin above his nose. "I wish that my father had come with us. He is wiser than I. Yet one of us . . ."

"One of you had to stay behind to govern your people, and it is better that you, strong and young, should be in the field, and that Alberospetrale, touched with age, should remain where his experience and understanding will be the most needed." Lodovico gave Falcone's shoulder a compassionate pat. "I know what it is to leave those you love behind." He dared not think of that too long, for as he spoke the words, the face of Aureoraggio shone before him and he longed for her as intensely as he longed for the benediction of heaven.

"Ah. To you, I must appear contemptible. This is my own land, not the home of a stranger, and yet I hesitate in the face of the danger that threatens it." Falcone looked across the camp toward a place where Pau Attans watched Italian Lanzi play at dice. One of the French soldiers had lost a pair of silver spurs and the betting was growing heated as other fighters wagered various weapons in place of coins.

"I think that had better be stopped," Lodovico said

quietly, a somber note in his words. He had often seen
that gambling could be more divisive than the most
subtle strategy of the enemy. With a sign to Falcone, he
made his way through the men to the place where the
soldiers gathered, shouting.

"And I'll bet my steel helmet," a burly Lombard was
declaring as he approached.

"Done. This gauntlet . . ." What the gauntlet was
forfeit for or against was never revealed, for at that
moment, Lodovico broke through the press of men,
bent down and seized the leather cup that held the dice.

"What has possessed you?" he inquired gently of his
soldiers, his voice in contrast to his brilliant eyes that
raked over them. "We are hunting a most deadly foe,
and all you can do is cast bits of bone to see how quickly
you can throw down your arms. I am ashamed of you,
my Lanzi. See how the warriors of this country conduct
themselves, with dignity and circumspection. They stand
and watch you, but they take no risks. Have you forgotten that at any time we may be set upon by gigantic
opponents of flint and frost who are so ferocious that
legend has claimed they are invincible? Have you forgotten that?" He looked from one man to another, and
not one was able to meet his challenging eyes. He took
the cup and flung it far away, so that only a slap of
leafed branches revealed its passage.

"Capitano . . ." one of the Lanzi objected, getting to
his feet and folding brawny arms.

"Do you question me?" Lodovico asked this soldier,
a wide, martial smile on his mouth. "Or would you
prefer to save your strength to battle the deadly forces
that even now move against us? If you are so foolish
as to desire to fight me, don't hesitate, I pray you. Let
this be settled now."

The Lanzi grumbled an incoherent protest, but his
hands did not move toward his weapons, nor did he
take the belligerent stance of a brawler.

Then one of the French mercenaries got to his feet.
There was a pile of winnings beside him—coins, a saddle, a short sword, and a boar spear. He hooked his

thumbs in his belt and regarded Lodovico with a sneer. "There is more to be won, Ariosto."

"I say that there is not," Lodovico responded at once. He could sense violence in the Frenchman and felt his body tighten in anticipation. It would take more than words to persuade the man.

The Frenchman swaggered forward a few steps, a rictus smile on his swarthy face. When he was slightly more than an arm's length away, he took a stance, legs apart, and rocked on his heels. "Who are you to give us orders? We hear a great deal about your supposed bravery, but where are the deeds to prove it?"

Cries of protest and approval came from the Lanzi, and a few of them withdrew judiciously, recognizing the danger. Massamo Fabroni put up his hand as if to bring a halt to the impending battle.

"No," Lodovico said, stopping Massamo. "I will not have my courage doubted. If this man insists that we put the matter to the test, so be it." He was already tugging off his guarnacca, which he flung to one of the Lanzi corporales near at hand. "Hold this for me," he said, and gave his full attention to the Frenchman, who was untying the lacing of his farsetto.

"Well enough, Messer' High-and-Mighty Hero," the Frenchman mocked as he began to turn up the sleeves of his old-fashioned shirt. That garment was none too clean and the number of stains and patches it had made a melancholy pattern that was too easy to read.

Lodovico secured his rolled cuffs at the elbow with silken ribbons. The medals on the fine gold chain shone and winked in the luxurious mat of hair on his chest. He saw with consternation that there were Cérocchi and Cicora in the crowd gathering around them. It would be a difficult matter to keep the fight private.

"Fear defeat, do you, Ariosto?" the Frenchman taunted him as he took up his fighting posture; slightly crouched, his arms held out and curved forward, ready to seize and crush. He moved lightly for a man his size, and the firelight lent a statuelike bronze color to the thick muscles of his neck and chest and arms.

"Every man fears defeat," Lodovico answered coolly, "when it faces him." He, too, fell into the attitude that the Frenchman had adopted. He was aware that the Frenchman was bigger and heavier than he, but was probably slower as well, depending too much on bulk and brawn and not at all on wit to win.

The opponents circled each other warily, and the men watching sized up the fighters. One or two called out bets, but Massamo Fabroni quickly stopped this. "Honor is at stake here—nothing else."

It was the Frenchman who made the first move. He lunged forward suddenly, his arms swinging and grasping. It was an overconfident maneuver, the careless tactic of a man who was not used to skillful fighting. Lodovico sidestepped him easily and twisted the Frenchman's nearer arm to pull him back in position. The Frenchman howled and swore, his free arm windmilling in an attempt to land a blow on his tormentor's body. It was an easy thing for Lodovico to evade these reckless flailings, and he grinned as he stepped back from the Frenchman.

There were Cesapichi soldiers in the crowd now, and talk spread through the encampment that there was a battle among the foreigners. More of Falcone's army hastened to watch.

Lodovico and the Frenchman had resumed their careful circling, and again it was the Frenchman who attacked first. This time, he kicked out forcefully, trying for a shin or a knee or the groin. Lodovico skipped lightly away and the Frenchman, carried by the force of his motion, came near to falling. This brought a scattering of appreciative laughter from the men watching. Lodovico frowned as he heard this, for he sensed it would enrage the Frenchman.

He was correct. This time the Frenchman did not wait for a favorable moment. He charged Lodovico, head down, more like an angry ram than a soldier. His large arms reached out, and this time he caught Lodovico around the waist and bore him backward toward the cooking fire.

Now the place was alive with shouts, and Massamo Fabroni strode forward to break up the fight.

"*No!*" Lodovico ordered. "This must be finished!" Even as he cried out, he swung his legs off the ground so that the Frenchman, already bent nearly in half and running, had to take all of Lodovico's weight onto his shoulders. He faltered, stumbled and fell heavily, Lodovico pinned beneath him.

Yells of protest burst from the mouths of the spectators and many of the men pressed closer to watch the fight. It appeared that Lodovico was in danger, for the Frenchman, in the blind determination of fury, was crawling toward the fire, shoving Lodovico before him as a dog might push an overlarge bone.

Lodovico scrambled under the big Lanzi, trying to gain purchase on the dirt and stop his rush toward the flames. He sank his hands in the Frenchman's hair and brought his head down, using the pressure to lever himself upward at the same time. The Frenchman grunted, then moaned as his forehead scraped the dirt. He pivoted on his knee and tried to wrap his arms around Lodovico's waist in order to drag him back onto the ground.

But as Lodovico regained his feet, he stepped behind the Frenchman, seized one of the burly arms and began to draw it backward and up, forcing the Frenchman to his feet, and then onto his toes.

"My arm . . ." the Frenchman protested in a voice that was little more than an agonized squeak. "My shoulder . . ."

Lodovico tightened his grip and lifted again, ignoring the sound the Frenchman made and the echo of the men around them. "You wished to prove something, Lanzi?" he whispered, holding the bigger man in that wretched position.

"I . . . No . . ." The Frenchman made one frantic swipe with his free arm, then howled as Lodovico raised his captured arm a hand's breadth higher.

"No? Are you satisfied, then? No more challenges?" He kept his grip on the arm, but shifted his weight so that if the Frenchman had any more tricks in his bag, he would be ready for them.

There was no need. The Frenchman nodded many times. "Let me go. I didn't mean anything . . . It was all a lark, is all." His thighs were quivering from standing on his toes so long. "Please, Ariosto, let me down."

"No more gambling, my French friend," Lodovico murmured, though he knew every man around the fire was listening.

"No . . . No more gambling." The words came out in high, hissing bursts. He collapsed in a heap as Lodovico released his arm and stood back, looking at the others as if seeking another challenger.

"Yes. You're wise," Lodovico said, the fierce smile still showing his teeth. He looked around him. "Let this be the last of the dicing. We must fight with the zeal of monks if we are to prevail, being reckless only in valor. Those who have lost their arms tonight—reclaim them." He stilled the moan of protest this announcement produced with a quick gesture. "You may think that your honor is here, in a leather cup with bits of bone, but I tell you, your honor is on the battlefield, against the foe. Lost arms will be returned. Money, well, that is another matter, and whatever has been won will stay with the winner. Money is little when lives are at stake." He looked at the Lanzi one last time. "I scorn the contemptible man who holds dice more precious than courage." With that, he turned on his heel and walked through the Lanzi.

Without a murmur, his men made a path for him and watched him in respectful and shamefaced silence.

Cifraaculeo sat in his tent, his long cape of tooled white deerskin pulled around him. The enclosure was redolent with strange aromatic gums that blacked in a brazier nearby. From time to time the high priest of the Cérocchi rocked, making noises in his throat. His white hair, usually neat, was disheveled and darkened with smuts and his face had the closed look of those close to death.

"How long has he been like this?" Lodovico asked Falcone in a whisper. They stood together near the doorflap, both reluctant to venture farther.

"Since the guards were set last night. He told Lincepino that he wanted to locate the forces of Anatrecacciatore before we penetrate into this forest any more deeply." Falcone was clearly distressed. He regarded Cifraaculeo with uneasy eyes, his fingers moving over the breastplate of hollowed bones strung with golden beads that was the armor of most of the Cérocchi and Pau Attan. It was a soft, clicking noise, not unlike the sound of rosary beads moving through devout hands.

"And he entered this state then?" Lodovico felt a grue of fear slide up his spine.

"Yes. He chanted a few sacred songs, drew his cape around him and sat, even as you see him now. I know that priests have powers and talents that most of us cannot achieve, but this . . ." He let his hands fall to his sides. "I have been watching him since our guards were posted and there has been nothing—nothing. He moves back and forth a little, and once spittle drooled from his mouth, but otherwise . . ."

"What is it you think?" Lodovico asked, not wishing to mention the terror that had touched the Cérocchi's heart.

"I think that he had sent his spirit out to spy on Anatrecacciatore, and that the sorcerer has caught it and holds it prisoner, and will only return it as his creature, and a spy among us." Falcone had whispered this, as if they could be overheard by the high priest. "If Cifraaculeo is enthralled, then no one is safe."

Lodovico nodded slowly, and said quietly, "When I sought to conquer the Great Mandarin, I saw something like this. There were Magi who could send their souls wandering over the whole of the earth. They wore strange hats and their cloaks were dyed with saffron. Everyone was awed by these men, and treated them with utmost respect. Almost always the souls of these Magi would return and then they would preach with great wisdom. But occasionally, some demon would seize the soul while it was on its journey and corrupt it, or subjugate it to its evil purposes, and then the Magus became a ravening beast, more feared than a mad dog. He would frighten the people, attack them, maim and kill them. Sometimes the Magus would become salacious and would assault his people in other ways, abusing their chastity in unspeakable ways." He watched Cifraaculeo as he spoke, looking for any response—a twitch, a change of color, a tremor, that would indicate that his spirit had once again entered the husk that was his body.

"Do you believe it could happen to Cifraaculeo?" Falcone's hushed voice pleaded with Lodovico to deny this danger.

"I pray it will not be," he said evasively. "But I have seen too much to seek a false hope. He must be guarded. He must be watched. If he awakens soon, see that he is fed and made ready to travel with us. If he does not awaken, a litter must be made for him."

"But do you think he might run wild among us?" The breath was almost stopped in his throat.

"I don't know," Lodovico said after a moment. He had already taken one step away from the tent into the chill of the dawn. "But I tell you this, Falcone. If he has been snared by Anatrecacciatore, I pray that he will run wild."

Falcone's expression was shocked and he was about to utter a protest.

Lodovico cut him off. "What better spy to send among us than your own high priest? Mice are all very well, but a man, a man of much power, a man respected, admired and trusted—what better spy than he? Who would be prepared to doubt him? Who would question what he revealed? Who would risk opposing him, with battle so near? Would you be willing to discount what he tells you, Falcone?"

"But I could not . . ." He stopped abruptly. His eyes went from Lodovico to Cifraaculeo and he muttered a sacred name as he stared at the high priest.

"Could not?" Lodovico questioned, his arched brows

raised. "What if you must, my friend?" He could feel the morning damp soak through the toes of his boots, but there was another, more pernicious cold seeping through him, a cold of terror and doubt.

Falcone did not answer at once. His fingers went back to his breastplate and began to turn the hollowed bones. On his face the expression of worry had been wiped away. "I don't know what to do," he said at last.

Lodovico nodded in sympathy. "I understand. Do you want my advice?" He studied the face of his Cérocchi friend, the clean line of his jaw and the prominent facial bones that lent him the look of a young prophet. Surely, he thought, Joshua had such a face when he stood over the ruins of Jericho.

"I would welcome it," Falcone murmured.

"Very well." Lodovico considered his words carefully. "I do not know how much knowledge is shared by your priests and wizards, but if there is some sharing, then I would gather the wizards and priests of the other people fighting with you, and I would request that each with the gift of seeing in water or ink or flames be set to that work, so that by this evening, we will know how great the danger is."

"You would not move?" Falcone was startled.

"What would be the use? If Anatrecacciatore has possessed Cifraaculeo then what is the use of moving on? If he has not, then we lose little by remaining in order to learn what we may from the wizards and priests." He hoped that Falcone would agree with him, for he did not want to dispute with the Cérocchi prince now, when they were in so hazardous a position.

"The Cicora have a wizard, Fumovisione, who is adept at that skill. And there is a priest from Annou-aigho who has similar abilities. They call him Nebbia-mente, for his mind is a mystery to them all, including himself." Now that Falcone had a focus for action, his previous manner deserted him. He was decisive and insistent. He spoke crisply and his back straightened in answer to this challenge.

"Get them," Lodovico said shortly, taking a last look at Cifraaculeo huddled in his cape, his face vacant as a tree in winter.

Falcone nodded and turned away from the tent of the high priest. He strode away, and Lodovico watched him, musing, wishing he could pray.

Nebbiamente came first. He was wire-thin, not particularly tall, a man into his middle years, with a curious expression of care in his deep-set eyes. He listened to what Falcone told him, then went to the tent of Cifraaculeo to see for himself. He returned quickly, his attitude more apprehensive.

"He tells me," Falcone explained to Lodovico when the priest from Annouaigho had spoken, "that he does not know if he can do anything in this instance. He says that Cifraaculeo is stronger than he, and more advanced. Also, he says that his spirit has been gone so long, it would be difficult to follow. He has agreed to do what he can, but doubts that it will accomplish much. He says that so far, there is no way to tell what has happened to Cifraaculeo, and that the prolonged trance may have done no harm."

Lodovico gave a cautious nod. "Is that all he can tell us?"

"At the moment, it is all he knows." Falcone turned away slightly and continued, in something of an undervoice, to speak to Lodovico. "He is very frightened by what he has seen. He has mastered his fright, but he cannot endure more very soon. Believe me, he does not want to pursue the matter at any length. I think that perhaps it would not be safe for him to do so. If there is another way to get the information, I think that is the way we should use. A man driven by fear, as he is, will have his sight clouded. He has admitted that, and I know it is true."

"Yes," Lodovico concurred. "But if this other cannot help us, the Cicora wizard, then we must convince Nebbiamente that he will have to aid us, for then we will have no choice. No matter how terrified he is, no matter how great the risk, he will have to do all that he can, or we will be all of us at the mercy of our enemy."

The priest had been listening attentively, as if concentration alone could give him understanding of the Italian language. Suddenly he interrupted and spoke to Falcone quickly, excitedly.

"What is it? What has he said?" Lodovico asked when Nebbiamente was silent once more.

Falcone had a measuring look in his eye, and he fingered his lower lip thoughtfully. "He says," he explained after a moment, "that while he does not want to pursue Cifraaculeo into the realms of the spirit, and has made it clear why, for he does not want to be caught in the snares of Anatrecacciatore, he *is* willing to send his spirit over the forest to find the surest and most direct route to the Fortezza Serpente. He thinks that if he does that, he can give you directions so that you, on Bellimbusto, may take us directly there and we will not have to wander through these forests until we die from exhaustion and suffer the attacks of wild beasts sent by Anatrecacciatore to prey upon us. He is confident that he can do this much and not expose himself or the rest of us to the worst of Anatrecacciatore's wrath. However, he warns us that the nearer we come to the Fortezza Serpente, the stronger Anatrecacciatore's power will grow, for that is the land of his creatures, and they are all bent to his will. He says that once the Fortezza Serpente is in sight, we must ignore anything he tells us." Falcone said a few words to Nebbiamente in his tongue, expressing genuine thanks that Lodovico needed no words to comprehend, then once again turned to the Italian hero.

"It may be possible," Lodovico allowed. "If the Cicora wizard is no help . . ."

"Fumovisione is known for his great talents," Falcone said quickly. "He is also known for his temperament. There is no way to anticipate what he will do."

Nebbiamente interrupted them with a few words to Falcone, his manner somewhat vague.

"What did he want?" Lodovico inquired impatiently when Falcone had finished talking to the priest.

"He's going to enter the spirit form, as he said he would. He asks that he be left to himself for a few hours. I have told him it will be as he wishes."

"Certainly there is no harm in it," Lodovico allowed. "Anything we learn now will have to help us." He had dressed in a leather guarnacca that was sewn with metal plates, affording some protection against arrows and other weapons. He had developed the design himself when he had found that Bellimbusto could not easily fly with a man in full armor mounted on him. This was the best compromise that Lodovico could devise, and since that terrible battle with birds, he had determined never to take to the air without wearing it. He had been told that in sunlight he glistened, like Bellimbusto's wings.

"Will you be aloft today, then?" Falcone asked.

"Not until I learn more. I don't want to make myself a target a second time. If we can learn from Nebbiamente or this Fumovisione, then it may be a wise course to take. The forest is vast, and it would take little for the warriors of Anatrecacciatore to hit us on the flank or from behind. We cannot allow that to happen." He touched the steel plating of his guarnacca. "You arm yourself with bone, and I with metal, but we fight the same enemy. We must be armed against more than the weapons that will be used against us: we must be vigilant against the wiles and the sorcery of Anatrecacciatore."

Falcone had taken a few steps back toward the tent where Cifraaculeo sat in ghastly, untenanted silence. "This may be the least of it," he remarked without looking at Lodovico.

"I realize that," Lodovico responded at once. He felt his scabbard across his back where Falavedova hung. "Armor is not enough. Watchfulness may not be enough. Never have I known so despicable a foe. He is without honor, and cares only for dominion."

Falcone reached the tent flap and looked in. The fires

in the braziers were dying and the cloying resins were less apparent, though still strong enough to be offensive. He pulled the flap open a little farther and looked at the high priest. "We must keep this a secret for as long as possible. Once the camp knows of this, many of them will lose heart. I do not wish to be disparaging of my own men, but it is true."

"There are those among the Lanzi that would not fight if His Holiness the Pope said that such battle was ungodly. I know your reservation and I respect it." Lodovico stared at Cifraaculeo. How could anyone determine what had become of the high priest of the Cérocchi? That deathly stillness that was not death. Those closed eyes that did not move behind the heavy eyelids. He realized that the high priest had, in some unknown way, exceeded his powers and was now constrained, by a potent, arcane spell, to deal with horrors that Lodovico could not possibly imagine.

"We cannot wake him. It would be disastrous to try. His spirit might never again find his body, and he would be in this state until his flesh began to rot." Falcone closed the tent flap abruptly and looked away toward the camp.

The men were starting to waken. There were the sounds of voices and scuffles growing steadily louder. The night guards came in from their posts along the perimeter of the camp and called to their morning counterparts, a few making coarse jokes, others demanding food before they could seek their mats for an hour of rest.

"You had best tell them that we do not march today, at least not at once. Put them to work on their weapons. It will not be wasted effort. I'll have my Lanzi check all their saddlery and other tack. That is also necessary and will occupy them well." Lodovico was about to start across the camp when Falcone's hand on his arm detained him. "What?"

Falcone nodded toward a strange, portly figure coming through the camp beside Lincepino. He was dressed entirely in clothing made of bark and as he walked, he gestured extravagantly, almost, Lodovico thought to himself with barely concealed amusement, as extravagantly as an Italian.

"Fumovisione," Falcone said quietly, indicating the bizzare little man.

Lincepino, a resigned, respectful expression on his face, led the wizard up to Falcone, and waited for a break in the stout man's stream of words to present him to the Prince. At last Fumovisione's ramblings came to an end and he looked expectantly toward Falcone and Lodovico.

"This," Lincepino sighed, "is the wizard of the Cicora, Fumovisione, and this is Falcone, Prince of the Cérocchi."

At once the voluble man began again, waving his arms, his voice rising and falling as if in endless song. His face was cherubic though his bright eyes were old.

After a bit, Falcone interjected a few terse questions and held the flap of Cifraaculeo's tent open for the wizard to enter.

"Does he always talk?" Falcone asked Lincepino, and was answered with a nod.

The flap rose again and Fumovisione bustled out. He had left his enthusiastic manner in the tent with the silent high priest. Now the childish face was somber and the voice forceful. Even his gestures had changed characteristics and were direct. He began to pace, and now that rotund body was not comical. He spoke at length, answering the occasional questions that Falcone put to him. Lodovico recalled the Mongol general he had fought once, many years ago, and found the similarity between Fumovisione and that general unnerving.

When the talk was finished, Falcone motioned Lodovico to come closer. "He will help us." This terse announcement was unnecessary, but Lodovico made no retort. He glanced toward Fumovisione and gave him a short bow.

"That was well done," Falcone said, then changed

his tone. "Fumovisione has warned us that Cifraaculeo is indeed becoming a pawn of Anatrecacciatore. He told me that it would be useless to kill him because the spirit would not die with the body and might be of greater danger if the man is dead. He has seen ghosts and other phantoms bring madness to an entire city. He has declared that he will not permit that to happen here. He is going to perform a rite that will protect Cifraaculeo. When he awakens, he will have no memory and be like an infant. We will have to give him constant care. But while he is so, he can do little to hurt us or to aid Anatrecacciatore. You must understand that Fumovisione does not wish to do this, and has informed me that he finds the task repugnant, but the alternative is too dangerous to allow it to occur. He has also said that he will make special amulets for all the men on guard to wear that will give them the gift of sight and enable them to know which animals are possessed by the magic of Anatrecacciatore and which are only animals."

Fumovisione was following this, nodding and giving occasional emphatic grunts accompanied by sweeping gestures. There was mud on his squat, muscular legs and his bare arms were beaded with dew, yet he seemed unaware of this, his whole attention on Falcone.

"I would not mind having such an amulet," Lodovico said, half in jest.

Falcone relayed this request and waited while Fumovisione considered the matter and then made a terse statement on the question.

"He thinks it would be unlikely," Falcone interpreted for Lodovico. "Your gods are not our gods, and your vision is not as ours. He said he would not know what to invoke for you."

"Well, it was a thought." Lodovico straightened himself and looked toward the camp again. "I must inform my men that we won't be breaking camp this early, and set them to work on their tack." He nodded toward Falcone and Fumovisione. "Tell me any progress you

make. It is crucial now, I think." He left them before
they could protest and walked quickly to the Lanzi.

It was midafternoon before he saw Falcone again.
The Cérocchi Prince came striding through the clusters
of men, stopping now and again to address a few words
to one of the warriors. He was regal in his Cérocchi
armor and bearskin leggings, and his proud head was
carried erect, confident. It pleased Lodovico to see
Falcone so much the master of this situation.

"How is it?" Lodovico called from the temporary
stables where he had been rubbing Bellimbusto's black-
and-bronze wings. He had taken off his guarnacca and
was wearing only his shirt, hose and calzebrache. Amid
the tight, dark curls on his chest there lay three medals
on a narrow gold chain.

"Good news, I think," Falcone announced loudly
enough for the men nearby to hear.

"Good news is welcome," Lodovico agreed and stood
aside for Falcone to join him. Once in the shadow, he
asked softly, "How bad is it?"

Falcone shook his head. "Bad enough. Cifraaculeo
has not yet . . . returned. Fumovisione has not been
able to find or free his spirit. He has said that it will
take longer. He has indomitable will, that strange little
man. If I were to fall in battle, I could find many worse
leaders for my men."

Lodovico, too, had sensed the power in the Cicora
wizard, and gave him due respect. "A good man in a
fight. Well, if he cannot master this sorcerer, then we
are most vulnerable. What about taking away your
high priest's memory? Is he still going to do that?"

"What choice is there? Otherwise we are certain to
have a spy in our midst, and one with so high a rank.
Fumovisione will begin the rite before sundown."

"That's something. I have been thinking this afternoon, what a wretched state we would be in now if
Cifraaculeo's spirit had returned to his body, the slave
of Anatrecacciatore, with no one aware of it." He had
taken time to say thankful prayers for this deliverance,

but the magnitude of the danger still impressed him. God had been merciful and Lodovico hoped that He would continue to guard him and his men—all of his men.

Falcone shuddered and the breastplate clicked and rattled. "Yes, that occurred to me, too. I felt my heart go numb in my breast with the realization of what might have happened."

The two men stood silently together, each lost in their private reflections. Falcone was the first to break the silence.

"I have one thing that should please you." He held out a roll of white birch bark which he had carried here.

"What is it?" Lodovico took it and pulled it open. There were a number of charcoal lines on it, forming a crude picture.

"Nebbiamente sent it to you. For your flight. This, he tells me," he said, pointing to a number of connected humps, "are the hills where we are now camped. He says that these two hills are at either end of this ridge. These valleys, the long narrow one, and this broader one, are a day's march from here, and the water there is pure and there is game to hunt. Beyond, he says that this is a river, and these, smaller rivers that feed into it. And here is another range of hills." His finger pointed out these features, and slowly the drawing took form for Lodovico.

Falcone indicated a long sinuous shape near the top of the drawing. "And this . . ."

Lodovico's veins filled with pride, with the confidence that had been draining from him for the last two days, since that disastrous battle in the air. He smiled and his chestnut eyes glowed. "I know what that is," he said in resonant tones. "That is the Fortezza Serpente."

La Realtà

Damiano di Piero de' Medici was wearing a giaquetta of red Venetian silk and his leggings were particolored red and black. He stood in the antechamber at his Fiesole villa, tapping his long fingers impatiently on the table where Lodovico had spread out books. He regarded the poet evenly as he came into the room, and said, without preamble, "You are sending your son to Paris?"

"He leaves in two days," Lodovico answered, puzzled by the inquiry, and the manner. He saw that Damiano was noticeably thinner and white shone in his dark hair like a gloss.

"You're probably wise to do that." Il Primàrio looked down at the books. "For Margharita?"

"Yes. She learns quickly. As you see, Marsilio Ficino and Luigi Pulci already." He indicated the *Morgante Maggiore* lying on the table.

"And the *Platonic Essays,* I assume?" Damiano said, picking up the Ficino and opening the volume. "Yes. My grandfather told me that Ficino kept a candle burning before the bust of Plato. Or was it Socrates? He regarded Socrates as a saint, in any case." With a sudden motion, he closed the book and set it aside. "You decided on Paris for Virginio."

"Yes." It took considerable courage for Lodovico to

speak again. "Why do you ask? Is there some reason?"
He wanted to know how much Damiano had learned
of Virginio's difficulties with the Cardinale, but could
not bring himself to frame the question.

"No reason, really. There are times when I see the
sons of my . . . friends doing well. Then I remember my
own sons." The old pain shaped his features. "I have
nephews, of course, but it is hardly the same thing." He
dropped into the chair beside the table, where Lodovico
usually sat to instruct Sir Thomas More's daughter, and
idly picked up a few of the parchment sheets, glancing
through them before looking at Lodovico, one brow
raised in speculation. "Margharita's work?"

"Yes. I have had her writing her own essays. She is
a most intelligent woman, Damiano." He let himself
come across the floor and take the smaller, harder chair.

Damiano stifled a yawn. "You're pleased with her
progress?"

"For the most part." He was quite curious now, and
somewhat disturbed. The visit from Damiano was unexpected, and Lodovico could not think of any reason
il Primàrio would want to see him, and in such grand
clothing. "You are traveling?" he ventured.

Damiano laughed shortly. "No doubt you want to
know what I'm doing here."

Lodovico stiffened. "It is your villa, Primàrio. You
are our host, we are your guests. How could you not
be welcome here?"

"If I interrupted your working, I don't expect you
to be glad to see me." He fingered the edge of his
ornamental sleeve. "Well? Did I interrupt your work?"

With a guilty flush, Lodovico nodded. "A few verses,
nothing to bother about." It was a clumsy lie. His head
was still echoing with the grandeur of his new fantasy.

"May I see it?" Damiano held out his hand for the
parchment sheets half-hidden by Lodovico's arm.

"They're not ready yet, but if you insist . . . You are
my patron." Reluctantly he touched the sheets. "I don't
have the right to question or object, if you want . . ."

"Per gli arcangeli!" he burst out, but did not rise.

"Will you abandon your pride for a moment? I am here seeking respite," he went on with some asperity, "and I refuse to wrangle with you, Lodovico. I have disputes enough awaiting me in Firenze. If you don't want to let me see your work, well and good. I will not argue with you. I don't *want* to argue with you." He picked up the volume of Luigi Pulci's work and thumbed through it, not truly reading.

Lodovico wished he had not offended Damiano. He considered reaching across the table and handing him the incomplete pages as a peace offering, but could not bring himself to do it. Instead he cleared his throat, saying, "I have had a letter from Sir Thomas this week. It was brought by a dyer coming to Firenze. He made good time, I think. Would you like to read it?" The three, closely written and tightly folded sheets were tucked into a slim book of Giovanni Pico della Mirandola's essays. Lodovico opened it and held up the letter.

Damiano's brows rose. "What has he got to say?"

The first part of the letter was filled with traveling details, projected dates of arrival and departure in different cities of Russia.

"Ah, here." Lodovico found the place and began to read. " *'Poland and Austria seem content to follow Italy's lead for as long as the truce with the Turks continues to be honored by both sides. The main concern of the Dukes here is the continuing religious conflicts in the German states. There have been rumors that Savonarola is dead, but his great age makes such gossip inevitable. He preached at Easter and his followers burned a dozen Lutherans immediately afterward. The Elector could do nothing without endangering himself. So far Savonarola has attracted few Poles to his cause, but with German monks traveling here regularly, there is legitimate cause for worry. Though I am a good Catholic and opposed to the enemies of the Church, I could wish that Luther had lived somewhat longer in order to stop the hysteria of these religious wars. If Luther had been willing to be reconciled with the Church before his death, Savonarola's followers might*

not be so determined in their persecution of the Luther-
an converts. As it is, the atrocities here rival those in
Spain. . . .' Then he says that some of the German
leaders would welcome a breakdown in the truce with
the Turks because it would give both the Savonarolans
and Lutherans a common enemy to fight. Then there's
a description of the provisions for the journey. Nothing
you do not know yourself. He asks that his family be
given guards for any journeys they may take beyond
Italia Federata."

"Naturally. That's all arranged."

Lodovico turned the page over. "Here's something.
About your son. Would you like me to read it?"

Damiano's eyes were weary with old pain. "Why
not?"

"Let me find the place," he said, reading quickly to
be certain that there was nothing too unpleasant. "Ah,
here. *'As part of the Austrian contingent, Leone de'*
Medici was one of those in the company that forms our
escort to Minsk. He has a caustic wit and is not well
liked by his comrades . . .' There's some mentioning of
the nature of the escort, and the condition of the
roads . . ." Lodovico said as he read of Leone's gambling excesses. Until Leone had left la Federazione, his
gambling had been the subject of constant quarrels and
embarrassment to Damiano. "There's more here. *'Leone*
de' Medici remarked that he was not anxious to return
to Firenze, but had almost decided to join his brother
Renato for a time. He said that he thought Gianpiero
Frescobaldi might come into France and they would all
stay at Nemours until something more attractive was
offered them.' That is all he has said about Leone."

"France. Nemours," Damiano said slowly. "France."

"Leone is not foolish enough to try to return to Italia
at this time," Lodovico hastened to assure Damiano.

"That wasn't my concern," he responded, shaking off
the melancholy with determination. "What else does Sir
Thomas have to say?"

"There is a comment here that may interest you.
'Word has reached us on the road that Spain is seeking

allies against Italia, but as yet none of the rulers approached are anxious to defy the Pope and stand with Spain. While it is true that the Spanish holdings in the Far East are increasing, and their two colonies in Africa are most prosperous, without colonies in the New World there is little chance that they will have sufficient to offer an ally that would compensate for being under interdict.' He also has reference to the Low Countries. *'It is rumored here that the Dutch might be willing to join with England against France, if proper terms can be agreed upon. I don't give much credence to the rumor because I know Henry Tudor. He is anxious for an alliance with Russia and will not easily settle for less. Mistress Boleyn's child will seal the bargain. As I recall, she should deliver in August or September, so it may be that you will know soon whether a Russian Princess will come to England or an English Princess will go to Russia.'* "

"I haven't had word on that," Damiano said in the silence. "I haven't had word on a great many things. I am," he went on rather distantly, "on the road to meet the court party of the Doge of Genova. Ercole is going to honor me with his presence again. In this weather, too."

"Why did you choose to ride in the heat of the afternoon?" Lodovico could not resist asking.

"I don't know. Penance, perhaps. A need to be alone. There were very few people on the road." He slouched in his chair. "Is there anything else from More that has bearing on the state?"

"Not really. He has found copies of a great many Italian books in Poland. He discovered a number of interesting manuscripts. There is a Swedish scholar in Warsaw who is very promising. A Turkish jewel merchant has opened a business in Minsk. The King of Denmark is said to be buying French cavalry companies. Apparently Denmark and Sweden fear what may happen to them if Russia and England become allies." Lodovico looked over the rest of the letter.

"He has already warned me of that—not but what

it was unexpected. He also tells me that Ippolito Davanzati sends messages to Roma with great regularity. Which of my relatives does he write to, I wonder. If he is intelligent, it will be to Clemente, but I am not convinced that Ippolito has thought so far ahead." He stared at the dusty toes of his boots in silence.

The day was hot and the listless breeze did little more than stir the air enough to spread the heat throughout the valley. There were summer smells, so intense they were almost visible, flooding the afternoon. Here in the antechamber it was cooler, and the shutters were half closed to ensure there would be some refuge from the implacable sun.

"Do you think it wise to continue your journey? You're enervated now, and another hour in the saddle . . ." Lodovico tried to give il Primàrio the firm smile that would indicate he knew best.

"It's tempting, but there are other considerations." He continued to stare at his boots. "Many other considerations."

"They must be important," Lodovico capitulated, feeling inane.

"I certainly hope so," Damiano answered, his voice thickened with a fatigue that went far beyond the tiredness of his body. "I feel I've been in a bath, I'm so wet. My shirt is soaked through and this giaquetta will be equally wet in another hour. But what else can I do? Ercole is an officer of la Federazione, a very high-ranking one in a critical area. I would insult him unbearably if I did not ride out to meet him. I have an escort of Lanzi waiting at San Gregorio already, and a dozen courtiers at the villa of Giovanni Tornabuoni. We'll gather there, feast, and in the morning proceed in state to Firenze." He sighed heavily, as if the prospect of lavish entertainment sickened him.

Lodovico pondered if Damiano wanted him to join the party, and was about to ask when Damiano went on.

"We will banquet late tonight, in the larger courtyard of Palazzo de' Medici. Ercole has got it into his head that he would rather stay there than at Palazzo Pitti, though why, I can't imagine." He pulled his plumed hat from under his arm and propped it on his knee. "Christ alone knows what Barbabianca wants."

"Do you wish me to try to find out?" Lodovico asked in a rush.

Damiano stared at him, then chuckled. "You? Well, he would never suspect you." His chuckle turned to laughter. "Gran' Dio, Lodovico Ariosto a spy!"

"You made one of Sir Thomas," Lodovico snapped, and was shocked to see the quick, sobering change his words brought to Damiano.

"Yes, I made a spy of that good, honest man. If I could have thought of any other way to accomplish the task, I would have done it." He rubbed his jaw, grimacing. "That was a reprehensible act, but it is done and I have convinced myself that it was necessary. But I will not make a spy of you, my friend. I wish to leave this world with at least one man uncorrupted by me." He tapped the plume and set it nodding. "I have spies in my cousin Cosimo's household, and a most attentive nephew at the Papal court, but it does not please me. What would these men be, if I did not have need of them? My daughter Pia, in her nun's habit, is still my spy. Will God forgive me that, do you think?"

This sudden, grim turn of mind alarmed Lodovico, who said lightly, "Who suspects a poet?"

"No one," Damiano sighed, "and I would not want to give them cause. Fiesole is a sanctuary more secure than the Church," he said, looking around the antechamber, at the plain white walls and painted ceiling beams.

"You do not want my help?" Lodovico asked, not quite disguising his hurt. It was galling to think that he would not be permitted to assist il Primàrio, to be trusted by him. What could he do to convince Damiano that he could be useful, when Damino believed that Lodovico was only capable of writing verse and plays, of teaching Italian to Margharita, and not able to make his way in the subtle world of the court? He lifted his chin, showing the worst of his freshly trimmed beard, and ducked his head quickly.

"Want your help?" Damiano echoed. "You do help me. Knowing that you are here, removed from the sewer that is Firenze, that helps me. I think it may be the one thing that keeps me sane. You are my assurance that . . ." He stopped and drew a long breath. "Lodovico, my second cousin covets Firenze. Indeed, he covets Toscana, all of la Federazione. It is not enough for him to have the seven tassels and red hat, he wants more temporal authority."

Lodovico bit back a remark about the other things that Cosimo, Cardinale Medici coveted, fearing Damiano's response.

"I know this. I *know* it. But I can find nothing. I am learning how wars begin. There are moments when it would be so easy to order the Lanzi to seize one of the cities where Cosimo has allies. I would feel then that I had accomplished something. But waiting, searching, knowing and having no proof . . . !" His hands came together and tightened as if around a throat. "Benci has discovered two of the Cardinale's spies in my household and has got rid of them for me, but he admits that he is baffled. He has tried to place men in unsuspect stations in the Cardinale's followers, but has not succeeded." Again he studied the feather in his hat, then tapped it to set it nodding once more. He gazed at it, abstracted, and when he spoke, his voice seemed to come from a long way off. "My wife. My wife is in France. She has said that she is going to Nemours, to my uncle's estate there, as part of a diplomatic mission." He was fascinated by the movements of the plume. "That is a lie. Graziella has left me." Suddenly he looked at Lodovico. "There is a French nobleman, very handsome, very rich, not consumed with statecraft, not wedded to his country, who is besotted with her, as I have been. He is to be her host. That is the name we give it. He has a wife somewhere, making this respectable. His estate is conveniently near Fontainebleau, which will continue the fiction of the diplomatic visit for a little while." He bit the inside of his cheek. "No one knows this, not for certain, though there are the inevitable rumors. No one knows." His face was blank now, and his dark, long-tailed eyes averted. "I sensed this was coming, but I never thought it would actually happen. It seemed impossible. Graziella, leave me? Why? For whom? So far, I have told only you. My confessor does not know. Benci suspects, but I have not confirmed it. I will maintain the pretense as long as I am able to." He cleared his throat. "My wife and my sons . . . And Ercole Barbabianca is waiting for me to greet him and give him lavish entertainment." There were tears on his face, but he did not notice them. "I have told myself that it is wiser she is gone, for if there is treachery—and I fear there will be treachery—she will be safe. I will have spared her that. And once she is a widow, she need only wait a year . . ."

"Damiano!" The shock which had made Lodovico silent lost its grip on him. He took his friend's hand and squeezed it in his own. "You must not wound yourself." How inadequate the words were! He wished he could find a more eloquent expression, some profound comfort that would ease Damiano's lonely suffering.

"Must I not?" Damiano inquired sardonically. "Why?"

"For . . ." He faltered. "If you're willing to lose your wife for Italia Federata, then it is for the sake of the nation that you must not. If you cannot for your own sake." Lodovico had felt his eyes fill as Damiano told him of Graziella's desertion. Now the shared hurt was keen within him, and he saw the anguish of il Primàrio reflected in himself. He forced his voice to be steady. "Stay here for a day. Give yourself a respite from the other. One day will not make a difference."

Damiano pulled his hand away. "You know I can't do that. Ercole would be deeply insulted and rightly so. Since I have chosen Italia Federata, I must accept her terms." Again he wiped his face, but this time he looked

at his wet hands with bemused surprise. He had not
known he wept.

"I will send a messenger and say that you have been
taken ill and must rest here." It was a desperate idea,
and a foolish one. Damiano shook his head. "I will go
myself, and surely I can make them believe me."

"I am more touched than you know, Lodovico. I
doubt if anyone else would offer this to me. But I must
leave." He got to his feet, pulling his hat from his knee
and placing it once more on his head, paying no attention to the angle so that the plume dangled down toward the back of his high, stiff collar. "I stopped here . . .
because I had to have some little time to myself, and
the company of a friend. You have been a better friend
to me than I have ever had, a better one, perhaps, than
I could possibly deserve." He grabbed Lodovico by the
shoulders and embraced him once, harshly, then thrust
him away.

Lodovico stood, astounded, thinking frantically for
ways to keep this grieving man with him a little longer.
"Alessandra will want to see you. She is at the market-
place, but will return shortly. You must let her see you.
She'll be very disappointed . . ."

"I will see her, but not now." Damiano regarded Lodovico with curious compassion. "You really should
go with your son, and if I were less greedy, I would
order you to leave when he does. But my charity has
limits. Against my nobler inclinations, I intend to keep
you here. I pray God I will not regret my decision."

"Damiano?" Lodovico blinked at this condemnation.
"I promise you I will not compromise you. I will keep
your confidences." He said this stiffly, wondering why
Damiano should be so unjust after trusting him. "Nothing you have said, nothing, will be repea—"

But Damiano interrupted him, despair in his face.
"You misunderstand me. It is not you I reproach, but
myself."

For the third time that afternoon Lodovico found
himself without words. He stood in the center of the
antechamber and watched while Damiano hastened to

the door and went out into the stultifying heat of the afternoon.

Virginio tied his cloak to the back of the saddle and checked the buckles that held his wallet to his belt.

"Now you will be certain to choose your inn carefully," Alessandra was saying as he worked. "And stay away from tavern wenches. Too many of them are poxy, and I will not have my son infected with the French disease. Find yourself an honest girl and treat her well." She put her hands on her hips to show how firm her orders were.

"Messer' Ariosto . . ." said the understeward on the horse beside Virginio's.

"He means you, my son," Lodovico said gently when Virginio did not give the man his attention.

"Messer'?" A slight smile curved Virginio's mouth. "Messer' Ariosto. I suppose I am." He turned to his parents and allowed himself to be hugged by each of them, then stepped back.

"Send us word when you have found lodgings," Lodovico reminded him.

"Yes, of course. I'll have Guido"—he nodded toward the understeward—"bring a message."

"There is some money set aside for you at the Paris branch of the Medici bank," Lodovico went on. "You're not to use it frivolously. Il Primàrio has given it to you for your education and for your advancement in the future. He has great expectations for you. Do well, and you will have his patronage and the patronage of his heirs for life."

"I understand," Virginio said patiently. He had been told this several times already.

"You're anxious to be on your way, then." Alessandra gave her son a last hearty kiss. "Be off then. But write to us. Remember, I can read, too. Do not write only to your father."

Virginio swung up into the saddle, grinning with pride. Damiano had sent him a bay gelding from his own stable with a certificate of ownership, so that the

horse was Virginio's, not de' Medici's. The bay was
well trained and answered the rein easily. "I go to
Genova, then along the coast, then to Avignon. From
there to Orleans and then to Paris. I have your letters
of introduction in my saddlebags."

"Very good." Lodovico smiled toward his son and
felt a certain loss. When Virginio rode out of the courtyard, he would no longer be his boy, but Messer' Virginio Ariosto. The boy would be gone forever. He
patted the bay's neck. "Travel safely and well, and
God go with you," he said.

"Thank you, father. God keep you and my mother
safe and well." He turned away and signaled to Guido.
Then, without another word, he set his heels to the
bay's flanks and the horse sprang forward, the hooves
clattering on the courtyard stones. Guido followed behind him.

Lodovico had put his arm around Alessandra's shoulder and they stood together in the courtyard until they
could no longer hear the sound of the horses.

"He's gone," Alessandra murmured when they had
stood in silence.

"Yes." Lodovico nodded. He turned to kiss Alessandra's forehead, took her in his arms a moment, then
let her go. "He'll do well, wife. He's a fine boy."

She said nothing, as if not entirely convinced by her
husband. "I don't know," she said to herself. "He's
been well enough until those weeks in Firenze . . ."

"Don't be worried," Lodovico said heartily, afraid
of precisely the same thing his wife was. True, in
Firenze he had refused the offers and returned to his
father's house, but might not Paris, so far away and so
tempting, give him a different attitude? It was one thing
to ride an hour from the Porta San Gallo, from a city
where Virginio was not a stranger. In Paris, he would
be removed, by distance and his foreignness. In Firenze
Virginio had decided not to trade his body for political
favor. He had seen for himself how those who had
could profit. What would France hold out to him? And
would he make the same choice? It was useless to ask

these questions, he told himself, because Virginio would do as he saw fit, not as his mother or his father or his confessor might wish.

"You're not certain, are you?" Alessandra asked. "But what can we do now? If we bring him back, he will not forgive us. He must learn to make his way in the world . . ." She said this as if by rote, and did not finish the platitudes she was reciting.

"You've been a good mother. I've wanted to be a good father. What more can we do?" He shrugged and stared out at the garden, feeling old.

Margaret Roper was distracted at her next lesson. She answered the questions Lodovico put to her but paid so little attention that it was quite impossible to make any progress. Her vellum copybook had two large smears across the page she had prepared, yet she hardly noticed them. Once she put a hand to her head as if it ached, and another time she sighed for no reason.

"What is it, Margharita?" Lodovico inquired when he had endured more than an hour of this.

"What? . . . Nothing." She bit her thumbnail.

"You, who are so bright a student, work so shoddily and say that there is nothing disturbing you? I can't believe that." He folded his hands and waited, as if prepared to sit thus for the entire day.

"It was not unexpected . . ."

"What was not unexpected?" He watched her as she tugged at a wisp of hair that had escaped from her headdress. "Won't you tell me, so that we may resume our lesson?"

Margaret placed her hands together as if in prayer. "I don't know if it's wise . . ." Her firm mouth trembled. "We had word from England yesterday. King Henry has learned of our arrival here and is not pleased. He informed us—including my father—that we are exiled and may not again set foot in England. He has signed the proclamation. He has declared us traitors." She said the last so softly that Lodovico, sitting near her, could barely hear her.

"But you did not want to go back to England, did you?" He felt a welling of sympathy for this woman. "You came here to be free of your King's wrath, didn't you?"

"Yes, of course," she said as she continued to pull at her hair. "But this is different, don't you see? Before we would not go back because we chose not to, but now we are forbidden to, and the price of returning is execution."

Lodovico listened to her attentively. He was aware of her plight, but until this moment had not realized that there were such dire consequences to their actions. "Your King isn't so much a fool. Sir Thomas is a brilliant man, and no King is stupid enough to place pride before genius."

"You don't know Henry Tudor." Margaret's face hardened. "That whore he married will drive him to it, now that she is near delivery. She wants no stigma attached to her bastard. Henry is hoping that the Grand Duke of Muscovy will accept an alliance with this child. He has both sons and daughters. That way he will both cement his relations with Muscovy and remove Mistress Boleyn's child, whatever it may be, from the succession. Compared to that, what is an honorable Chancellor?"

Lodovico was not shocked, and that alarmed him. A year ago, even in Damiano's court, he might have felt revulsion for the shameful behavior of the King of England. Now he was bitter but he no longer could muster a sense of outrage. He put his hand on Margaret Roper's shoulder. "The Pope will not allow it."

"The Pope has nothing to say about it. Henry has broken all ties with Rome and he will not change his mind. He can be the most *mulish* man." Her blue-gray eyes were brighter than Lodovico had ever seen them and her voice had taken on the sharpness of authority. "He will take any liberty, use any device, perpetrate any evil if he thinks it will serve the Crown. And the Crown, of course, is himself. He was a handsome enough youth, and he is a fine figure of a King, but there is nothing behind that façade but corruption." She had picked up her copybook and now she slammed it down on the table with the full force of her anger.

"Margharita!" Lodovico had half risen from his chair and was staring down at her. "Numi! What passion you hide within yourself." He tried to laugh. "You must not let the King distress you. He is insane, and madmen must not distress you."

"This particular madman is King of England," she said through her teeth, though she lowered her voice.

"But it cannot last. He has the Pope against him, he has argued, even, with the Protestants, they say. His own people must be in turmoil. How long can such a king reign? A year? Two? Five? It cannot be long, not when he has set aside his wife and taken his mistress to his bed as his Queen. Someone will oppose him and it will be over. Then you and your family will go home again to the praise of your people." He was afraid that it might take longer than five years, but he was very certain that if half of what Margaret Roper told him were true, Henry Tudor would be supplanted before the start of the next decade, seven years away.

Margaret gathered her hands into fists. "I hate that man!" she whispered with venomous softness. "I hate him. He has treated us with arrogance and contempt. He has made a mockery of the finest man in his kingdom. There is no one who has cared more for the safety and protection of the Crown than my father, and if King Henry thinks that Richard Rich will serve him as well . . ."

"Richard Rich? Riccardo Ricco?" In either form, he did not know the name. "Who is he?"

"The new Chancellor of England! Oh, yes. Not content with banishing Sir Thomas More, King Henry has appointed Richard Rich his successor. This is the very man who provided Henry with the legal excuses to exile our family. The Chancellorship is his reward. It is Henry's way of telling the world that he will have no one around him with an opinion that does not concur with His Majesty's." Her voice was quite still, a deadly cutting quiet that pierced like fine, honed steel.

"It will not last," Lodovico promised her.

"Not even if Henry forms an alliance with France? It would be possible once arrangements have been made with the Grand Duke of Muscovy. Henry imagines himself an Emperor striding the world around. Russia to the east, and then all the English claims to France reasserted. Before my father left, he warned me that it could happen just that way."

"The King of France is no idiot," Lodovico said, soothing her. "Your Enrico will not be able to convince him that they are united in their goals. France has other problems to contend with—Spain would take it badly if France opened negotiations with England. You saw the letter I had from your father, and I am certain that Damiano would let you see most of the reports he has received."

Margaret pounded the table with her fists once. "I am generally a calm and self-possessed woman," she announced to the room. "Yet when I am here, and I think of what Henry Tudor has done to my father and our family out of pique, all the emotions I have rise in me like bubbles in boiling water."

Lodovico was relieved. The worst of this tempest was behind them. "Poets are said to be made of emotions," he reminded her with his most tolerant smile, and wondered if it were so.

"I also understand," Margaret went on in a more reasonable tone, "that il Primàrio's son was said to be in England. I had that from Cecily Howard, who is a lady-in-waiting to Mistress Boleyn."

"His son? Which one?" Lodovico was suddenly cold. The remote troubles of that distant island had not touched him, but with this revelation, he felt the whole might of Henry Tudor become a threat. If one of Damiano's sons was there, and decided to cause trouble, he could find no more effective way than to keep King Henry apprised of Medici family politics.

"I believe it was Renato." She frowned over the name.

"That's the second one." He remembered the boy he had taught. Renato had a facile wit and a superficial charm that masked his inner rage. "Does Damiano know of this?" It was difficult to speak to il Primàrio about any of his sons, but he hoped that in this case, someone had told him about Renato.

"I showed him the letter. He said nothing. He was displeased." She paused, giving Lodovico a quick, knowing glance. "They're none of them in Italy, are they?"

"Leone—he was named for his uncle the Pope—is, I believe, in Austria or Hungary. Arrigo was reported to be in Spain, but that was a year ago. And now you say Renato is in England." He found himself wishing he could return to his little room, to his desk and his papers for the joy of losing himself in his work, in a world where sons were assets to their fathers. "There has always been difficulty with them. From the beginning. Yet Damiano's daughters are women of learning and sense and integrity."

Margaret took one of the sheets of vellum in her hand. "I wish I could write to my father, but there is no way, I suppose."

"We know where he is going to be, but it is not possible to send messengers after him on the road. If we were to do that, Damiano might as well send a delegation to the Grand Duke of Muscovy himself. We have his letters, and will for a time yet. Be grateful that so much is possible. If we were still at war with the Turks, it would not be safe to make this journey, and impossible to get messages back." He held out a trimmed quill to her. "You may want to write him letters, in any case, and keep them to give to him when he returns. It's not quite the same, but he will be able to read how you learned and what you did as you did them."

"Write him letters and keep them." Margaret gave the matter some thought. "If it were you, Ariosto, would you do that?"

Lodovico could not answer any way but honestly. "Probably not, but I write few letters, only the ones I must. All other writing is saved for my poetry. I don't want to sacrifice one quatrain to a letter." He patted her hand. "Don't let my obsession change your mind. Poets are quite mad, you know."

Margaret smiled at him, but her frown returned quickly. "There was one thing that Sir John Howard said in a letter to my husband, and I don't know whether or not I should bring it to Damiano's attention."

"What is it, Donna Margharita?" He knew from her expression that the matter had given her perplexity.

"Sir John has said that Renato is encouraging King Henry to send expeditions to the New World for the express purpose of destroying the trade that has been established with Italy. Renato knows about the three trading ports, and has said that he could force a surrender with little bloodshed. Sir John doubts that Henry will give Renato the money and ships because he is more interested in Russia and France than the New World." She plucked at an imaginary bit of lint on her dress. "I think if Damian were told, he would be distressed."

"Distressed!" Lodovico wanted to howl with laughter as a dog would at the moon. "Even if such a mad venture came to nothing, Damiano would be incandescently angry." This new treachery, coming so close on the heels of Graziella's departure, would wound Damiano nearly to frenzy. With a great effort he was able to keep his voice level. "He and Renato do not . . . agree. Renato is seeking to . . . ruin his father."

Margaret regarded Lodovico with unconcealed curiosity. "I suppose it would be useless to ask you why this has happened."

Lodovico shook his head. "I am sorry, Donna Margharita. It is not for me to tell you. I will advise you, however, to show the letter to Damiano. No matter how much it distresses him, he should know of it. And I urge you not to ask him too much."

Margaret sighed her acceptance. "Very well." She opened her copybook again. "Please, will you repeat what you told me about the changes in form since the time of Dante Alighieri. I will try to give you my attention."

"Can you simply set your questions aside?" Lodovico marveled.

"Not entirely, no," she said, and there was an unexpected dimple at the corner of her mouth. "But I don't wish to trespass on your good will. It's wiser, I think, if we devote ourselves to Italian."

"As you wish, Donna Margharita." He picked up his well-read copy of *La Divina Commedia* but did not open it. "Donna Margharita, I must ask you—for yourself as well as others—tread carefully. There are traps here that you know nothing of. I'll admit that I don't know the total of them, myself."

"Of course," she said at once. "I have seen life at court before, though the English court is not so . . . complex as the court of la Federazione. Don't be concerned. I have confined myself to discussing important matters with you and Andrew. And Damian, when he initiates such conversation."

"Andrea Benci?" He gestured acceptance. Certainly Andrea Benci in his position as Damiano's secretary knew all that was happening in Firenze and la Federazione. He hitched his shoulder up unhappily. It would be so much easier, he thought, if he could bring himself to like that polished, elegant old man.

"Why? Is something the matter?" Margaret, as always, was quick to read the nuances of Lodovico's expression.

"No, nothing. An irrational dislike." He opened the book and his eye was caught by the sign over the mouth of Hell—*Leave behind every hope, you who enter*.

Nerissa was chopping vegetables fresh from the garden and Alessandra bustled about ladling cubes of chicken cooked with lemons in red wine over saffron rice. Her face was rosy and damp, her hair had corkscrewed up around her face and her limp lace cap was askew on her head, but her smile made up for it all.

"I've so wanted you to stay, Donna Margharita. I wish you had taken time to do this before." She handed a plate to her guest and began to prepare one for her husband. "I hate to interrupt lessons, and usually at the end of them, Lodovico hurries back to his study so that he can put a few more stanzas on paper before he eats. It's delightful to have you here."

"The squashes are ready," Nerissa announced as she wiped her hands on her apron. "Do you need me anymore?"

Alessandra glanced over the kitchen before she answered. "No, I don't think I do, Nerissa. We have everything. You will want to come back in an hour, I would guess. I doubt we'll be through in less time."

"An hour," Nerissa said unhappily. "Very well." She had already untied her apron, and now she hung it on a bent nail before hurrying out into the courtyard.

"Poor Nerissa," Alessandra said as she wiped the sweat from her face with her sleeve. "Those relatives of hers give her no peace. I sometimes wonder if we were right in taking Carlo on in the stables. Well, it's done." She had finished filling her own plate and she nodded toward the plank table with benches near the corner window. "Sit, sit. There's no sense in eating outside tonight. There are far too many insects about. I'm afraid they would have more of a meal than we would."

The table had been scrubbed and it was cooling off. Lodovico took his place at one end of the bench, wiping the board for Margaret Roper. "There, Donna Margharita. It is not perfect, but it won't ruin your gonella now."

Margaret tried to smile but she was was too nervous to carry it off. She stared down at her plate and said, as if reciting a lesson, "It smells delicious."

"Merce di Maria," Alessandra laughed, putting one hand to her bosom, "I hope it is not *that* bad." She settled on the bench opposite her husband. "If it does not please you, you have only to tell me. The vegetables will be served later, but if you would rather have them now, I will prepare the oil and cook them at once."

Shamefaced, Margaret took the spoon offered her and dipped into the plate. "I am sure I will enjoy this," she said with grim determination.

Lodovico looked about. "Wine. Is there a bottle?"

"Did you remember to bring one out?" Alessandra asked, then shook her head indulgently. "Of course you didn't. I reminded you just before you went up to your study. Well, if Donna Margharita will move aside for you, you may get it now. *Not* the new jars. They're very raw still." As Lodovico made his way past Margaret, Alessandra added, "You can also bring out the honey. Doubtless we'll all want to put it on the fruit."

"Do you think that will be necessary?" Margaret asked. "I'm afraid I'm not used to the Italian manner of cooking yet. There is so much more savor to everything that there are times when I think I will never be able to taste anything again." The formality of her manner had lessened, and some of the kindness was in her expression as she looked at Alessandra. "Is it very difficult being a poet's wife?"

Alessandra had a wicked chuckle, not unlike a very loud purr. She chuckled now and her eyes glinted. "Difficult? Well, not as a great many men are difficult. He does not beat me or guard me with terrible jealousy. He does not confine me to the house and treat me as a slave instead of a wife. Lodovico is a brilliant man, and a gentle one. We lived together for almost ten years before we could marry—that was when Damiano became his patron. I know of no man I would rather spend my life with. But, of course, he is infuriating. He would sell his soul for a rhyme. He is forgetful. He lives in the kingdom of his mind more than half his waking hours. He is at once the most and least observant man I know." She lifted her spoon and sampled her own cooking. "I've made better, but this is well enough."

Lodovico stood in the pantry listening to his wife. He was annoyed and touched by her affectionate and unvarnished summing up of him. Was it true that he was forgetful? He had forgotten the wine, but surely that did not mean he was forgetful. He took two of the older jars from the shelves and as an added precaution, read the dates on each. Both were 1523, ten years old. Alessandra called him gentle and brilliant. That was high praise from that intelligent and unassuming woman. But how could he be the most and least observant man she knew? It made no sense. He turned and came out of the pantry.

"Here is the wine. I should have remembered it." He put the jars on the table and looked for a knife with which to pry off the seals.

Alessandra offered him her own knife. "This is sufficient. Use it."

Lodovico took the knife and set to work on the seal. "Is Nerissa eating with Carlo again?"

"Of course," Alessandra said patiently, then explained to Margaret. "Nerissa, our cook, talked us into taking on her cousin Carlo to care for the stables. He was a smith and lost his post when his employer lost his crops. I feel sorry for the man, but I don't know if we should have taken him on. These family matters are always so difficult. He's an acceptable worker, but he isn't willing, if you understand what I mean."

"Yes, I do," Margaret responded. "My father has often said that those are the worst sorts of servants and students—the ones who are capable but who give no heart to it. We had a housekeeper for a time, until my stepmother dismissed her, a woman who knew a great deal about managing a household, and fulfilled her responsibilities, but nothing more. When one of the housemaids broke her leg, the housekeeper would not do anything to help the poor child. I finally had to send for an apothecary for poppy-juice and for the chiurgeon to set the bone. The housekeeper said that she would not be bothered with such things. I've never seen my stepmother in such a rage." She had not been eating, but now she was silent while she took several bites. "This is really very good, I'm growing used to it."

By this time Lodovico had the first of the jars open, and he began to pour the fragrant red Lombardi wine into the earthenware cups set on the table.

"I wonder if this Carlo isn't worse." Alessandra looked quickly over her shoulder, as if expecting to find the stablehand listening. "He's a hard man, and though

Nerissa tells me that he is perfectly reliable, I can't bring myself to believe that."

"How do you mean?" Margaret asked.

"I'm afraid that he bullies Nerissa. She hasn't been herself since Carlo came to work here. She jumps at shadows. I can't help but think that she would be happier if we sent him away, but then he would not have work again, and doubtless he would expect her to care for him . . . This arrangement is probably better, for at least he works for the food and coins he gets. All the same, I wish Nerissa would confide in me. Then I would know what best to do."

"I'll see if Damiano has a place for this Carlo," Lodovico suggested. "That way, if he has other work to do, he will not demand that Nerissa take care of him." He congratulated himself for that solution, and was convinced that there was nothing to say against it.

Alessandra clicked her tongue in exasperation and exchanged a look with Margaret. "And if Nerissa is convinced that we arranged for Carlo to leave, she might wish to leave herself. We must be more subtle than that, my dearest. There is a better way, I think." She gestured toward Margaret. "What do you say, Donna Margharita?"

"It's not for me to . . ." she began, and then she gave the matter her serious consideration. "It might be awkward to have the man offered employment by Damian, though, since this is his villa, it might be reasoned that he is the employer already. Your cook would believe that you had arranged the matter, whether you had or not." She frowned and took some of the wine. "It might be better if some other man offered employment, but it would still be suspicious. Who would have recommended him?"

Lodovico had made his way back to his seat on the bench and was regretting the whole issue. "We can discuss it another time," he said testily.

"Carlo is a strange one," Alessandra said, as much to herself as to her husband and guest. "I wonder, occasionally, why he decided to work here."

"He was hungry," Lodovico said, dismissing the matter.

"But he's a smith. Wouldn't you think he'd look for employment doing smithing?" Alessandra narrowed her eyes as if to see through the questions she had to the truth.

Margaret looked up from her plate. "Well, you say his cousin is here. The work is probably easier, and since this woman is your cook, he is probably living very well." She took another spoonful of rice. "If all the cooking is like this, I do not blame him."

"Thank you, Donna Margharita," Alessandra said merrily. "You've probably found the right of it. It's a shame Nerissa is frightened, she deserves better, but . . ." She gestured to show her sense of futility. "We may not be here much longer. By winter, we'll probably be back in Firenze."

"What makes you say that?" Lodovico demanded.

"A feeling I have. You will finish that new *Fantasia* of yours by the autumn, and by then Damiano will decide that he needs his poet back where he can be seen. And you'll want to read the new work. It's always been like that with you: until you finish it, you hide it, and after it is done, you want everyone to hear it or read it." She glanced at Margaret. "Are all men like this, or only poets?"

Margaret laughed. "I've yet to meet a man who enjoys being wrong. This is probably more of the same." She tried to look chagrined, but the unexpected dimple betrayed her. "I should not speak so about my instructor, of course. It's a lamentable lapse on my part."

Lodovico stared into his wine, wishing that the two women would not giggle, or say such things about him. He did not hate being wrong, he told himself. He simply did not wish to show his work until it was up to his standards. As certain artists kept a canvas covered until the work was completely finished. That was not the same as not wanting to be wrong. He drank deeply of the wine. Was Margaret Roper like this with her father? Would she giggle about Sir Thomas while she had her meal? If this were only the midday comestio, then, at the conclusion of the meal, when the prayers were said, he could include a pointed remark about respect. But there were rarely prayers after the evening meal, and most emphatically not when eaten in the kitchen.

"My husband," Alessandra said, touching his arm, "don't fret. We say the things we do out of affection. If you were disliked or feared, we could not tease you." She nodded toward Margaret. "Ask Donna Margharita if this is not so."

"I believe you," he muttered, but could not disguise a tinge of satisfaction in his voice.

Lodovico awakened far into the night. He turned in his bed, his thoughts in turmoil. A fragment of a dream clouded his mind and it took him a few moments before he realized what had brought him out of his sleep—someone was pounding on the door.

Beside him, Alessandra stirred and opened her eyes. "Santa Maria," she yawned. "Who comes at this hour?"

"I don't know." Belatedly, Lodovico climbed out of bed and searched for a chamber robe to throw over himself.

"Nerissa should have got it," Alessandra murmured, petulance in her voice now. "She or Carlo. Carlo must have heard—whoever that is arrive. One of them will get it. They've wakened by now."

The knocking had not ceased. Lodovico muttered under his breath and fumbled about the dark room searching for his robe. At last his fingers closed on the garment and he pulled it from the peg on the outside of the tall wardrobe against the far wall. Tugging the robe over his arms, and feeling for the belt, he made his way back across the room to the table where he knew a lantern stood. He hit the table with his hip, then patted at its surface until he found the lantern. His fingers closed on the steel, and a moment later he struck a spark on the flint. On the second try, the lantern took the flame and there was light in the dark, shuttered room.

In the hall, Lodovico hesitated and called for Nerissa, but the cook did not answer. He shrugged this off uneasily, reminding himself that there were many men and women who, once asleep, would not waken for anything short of a cannon.

He made his way down the stairs and into the entryway. The blows on the door were less frequent but just as determined. Lodovico set the lantern in the niche beside the door and drew back the heavy wooden bolt.

The night was filled with moonlight, the air the color of sapphires. It was warm still, and the sounds of insects and frogs made an eerie chorus in the distance.

"Messer Ariosto?" the man at the door demanded.

Lodovico, still half asleep, gestured and stood aside for the visitor to enter. "Come in. Forgive me. The hour . . ."

"You must forgive me," was the prompt answer from the tall young man. "If it were not urgent, I would never have wakened you in this way." He spoke Italian with a strong accent and his dress was foreign.

"But who?" Lodovico took the lantern and held it close to the stranger. "I don't know you." He felt a slight apprehension as he said this, and wondered if it had been wise to let this man into his villa.

"I am William Roper, Margaret's husband." He bowed slightly and smiled.

"Ah. A great pleasure, though I am curious about the time you've chosen to come to visit me." He put the lantern down again. Now that his interest was aroused, he began to enjoy the absurdity of the situation. He motioned vaguely toward the antechamber and said, "We might be more comfortable sitting."

"Very much so," William Roper agreed at once, and went swiftly into the room.

Lodovico secured the door bolt again and followed this most unorthodox guest, setting the lantern on the table where he put his books and papers when he was teaching Margaret.

"I realize that this is an odd time to come here. You must believe that my mission is urgent." He had sat on the bench along the wall and was reaching into the long, ornamental sleeve of his giornea. He was dressed for dancing, not riding, in sculptured velvet. "I was asked to come in secret."

"And pounded on my door," Lodovico pointed out.

"I had to rouse you. I was told that no one should know that I have been here." His manner now was apologetic. "Damian asked me to do this for him. After all he has done for us, taking in the family and offering protection . . . I could not refuse."

"Damiano sent you?" Lodovico was suddenly alert. What little of the dreamlike muzziness that had clung to him was gone. "Why?"

"He asked me to bring this to you." He had taken a folded and sealed parchment from his sleeve and he held it out to Lodovico. "He instructed me to be certain that you read it so that I may return your answer."

Lodovico took the parchment in cold fingers and stared down at the impressions on the wax seals. It was the de' Medici arms, without doubt. He had seen that seal many times. He broke the wax with care so that the parchment would not be damaged, then spread out the sheet. Before him was the familiar, sloping hand.

"To my friend, who doubtless deserves better from me:

"I am setting aside my principles and must insist . . ."

A sudden disturbance behind him made Lodovico turn. He put his arm across the letter as he looked up into Nerissa's face.

"Master . . . I didn't realize . . . I heard . . ." Her plain, round face was bunched and lined by her distress. "I thought . . . but Carlo didn't . . ."

Lodovico did not attempt to sort out all the fragments she gave him. He chose the last and most obvious of her statements. "Yes. Where is Carlo?"

"He . . ." Her face went a custardy color. "I don't know. I called him. I went to his quarters. He isn't there. He's gone. A girl, perhaps. I don't know." Each phrase came out in pants and Lodovico had the impression—though why, he did not know—that the woman was lying. "I . . . Don't turn him off. He has to stay here. He has to . . ."

"I'm not going to turn him off for wenching," Lodovico said, to quiet his cook. "Any night but this one it would not matter. It's a small thing." He glanced at his guest. "This gentleman needs some wine after his ride. See if you can find him some."

Nerissa clapped her hands across her ample bosom and dragged her chamber robe more tightly around her, then turned, and with a sound such as an enraged mouse might make, fled down the hall.

William Roper laughed quietly. "A nervous woman."

"Yes," Lodovico said slowly, scowling. "A nervous woman." But Nerissa was not often nervous, and when she was, it inevitably centered on her blacksmith cousin. Where had Carlo been? Where had he gone? Why had Nerissa been so . . . frightened? He stared ahead, pondering these questions until William Roper's tactful cough brought his attention back to the letter hidden under his sleeve.

"I gave my word I would watch you read it," Roper said mildly.

"Of course." Lodovico felt slightly embarrassed. He held the parchment up to the lantern and resumed reading.

"*. . . principles and must insist that you return to Firenze. I will expect you within the week.*

"*Forgive me.*

"*Damiano*"

Lodovico stared at the page. He was being recalled to Firenze. His eyes shone and he wished he could laugh. Damiano had need of him at last!

William Roper looked puzzled. "You're pleased?"

"Pleased? I'm delighted!" Lodovico read the letter again, to be certain he had not misunderstood. No. There it was, in that slanting, angular writing. He was ordered back to Firenze. Within the week.

"And what shall I tell him?" William asked. "He was concerned about your work, and said that if you wanted more time . . ."

Lodovico looked up from the page, grinning. "I can finish my work in Firenze. Tell him yes. Tell him that I am grateful."

A strange expression flickered on William Roper's face, but it was gone before Lodovico could identify it. "That's odd. Damiano said much the same thing. He will be grateful to you if you are willing to return."

"Willing?" Lodovico could hardly contain his satisfaction. "I have been hoping for this."

"Damiano asked that I remind you of his warning," William Roper went on, puzzled. "All this secrecy—sending me off in the middle of the night, instructing me to tell no one where I was going, bringing you back to Firenze in this manner. What is the man playing at?"

"At last," Lodovico murmured, not really hearing what Roper was saying. "At last. Grazie al Iddio." He could imagine Alessandra's pleasure when he told her of this summons. She would giggle with joy, and though Lodovico did not like giggling, in this instance it would be welcome. Then he realized he had not heard all that William Roper had told him. "Your pardon. I wasn't listening."

Roper chuckled. "Damian predicted you might well react this way, with joy. It was . . . disturbing." His expression turned inward and his face was troubled.

"Disturbing? In what way?" Was Damiano playing with him, then, and this was a joke? There was nothing in the message that implied it.

William Roper answered reluctantly, speaking slowly. He could not look at Lodovico. "There were tears in his eyes when he said it."

PART III

La Fantasia

Below him, the landmarks were exactly as Nebbiamente had described them. Lodovico grinned his approval as Bellimbusto flew west-northwest over the amazing verdure of this magnificent land. He had passed over the narrow valley some time before, and had marveled at the tall, lance-straight pines and the river which poured through the valley like liquid diamonds. Now he was over the wider valley, and here there were groves of fruit trees, and deer wandered among the trees nibbling on the bounty that drooped eagerly down for them. He thought that Paradise must look so, for he had never seen such abundance.

Yet he was wary. His experience with the birds had shown him that much of the peace was illusory. He was armed now with more than Falavedova: he carried two javelins and a bow. Arrows lay in a quiver buckled to his saddle and there were two long knives tucked into his high boots.

"Remember," Fumovisione had warned him before he had mounted Bellimbusto, "the nearer you come to the Fortezza Serpente, the more you will be susceptible to his power. You must go cautiously, and be alert for any danger." The wizard had given him a piece of bark with many strange signs drawn on it in a multitude of colors. "This may help, but I cannot promise."

Lodovico had taken the bark gratefully and it now reposed under his shirt where the gold medals on their chain lay. While he doubted the charm would be of much use to him, he had been too far and seen too much to despise any protection offered him. He missed his chittarone, for on such a glorious day it would have been a pleasure to serenade the whole of the sky. Fumovisione had warned him against that as well, saying that it would tell all the forces gathered against him that he was coming toward them. "A wise soldier does not advertise his presence."

"I have learned that the hard way," Lodovico had said with a charming smile. "Never fear, I will remain silent, and only *think* my songs as Bellimbusto soars among the clouds."

"We can pray there will be no clouds," Fumovisione grumbled. "You will not be able to see the landmarks if you are within the clouds. You must see the landmarks. Stay away from the clouds."

Though Lodovico knew the advice was good, he found it hard not to protest. "I'll bear this in mind," he had promised, then gratefully swung into the saddle, and with a high whistle, had given Bellimbusto the office and the fabled mount rose into the air with a great flapping of bronze-and-black wings.

His eyes scanned the range of hills on the far side of the splendid valley, and suddenly he saw something that banished the lightness from his heart.

There, on the ridge of the hills, the trees were sere and withered, the grass alternately white and burned. Coming closer now, Lodovico could discern the damage that had been done. The hillside was blighted, and where plenty had been, there was now destruction that would bring famine.

He nudged Bellimbusto and the horse slid away to the left, giving Lodovico a clearer view of the hills. Now he could see the line of ruin advancing, and at the front of it a column of ash-colored men in frosty armor made their way toward the expanse and luxury of the valley, leaving a growing swath of devastation behind them. Lodovico watched in horror as one squad of warriors, at this distance seeming as small as ants, stopped at a small grove of trees and, not content with chilling the life from them, began a savage extirpation.

Would it be possible? he asked himself. If the troops of Italia and Falcone could be set in motion quickly, there might still be a chance to save some piece of this beautiful place. He did not want to think of what those inhuman warriors would do to the valley. Quickly he murmured a prayer beseeching heaven to aid him, and then he tugged at the reins and brought Bellimbusto around so that he faced toward their own forces. Even as he urged the hippogryph to greater speed, he was thinking of ways the soldiers could travel faster. Once he turned in the saddle and stared back at the idyllic danger-filled place, then resolutely set his face toward the east-southeast.

Nebbiamente sat beside the brazier in the center of the tent, saying he wished to listen to the flames. To one side, on heaps of bearskins, Lodovico addressed Falcone and Fumovisione. Though Nebbiamente said nothing, they were all aware that he heard and understood every word.

"How many would you say there are in the company?" Falcone asked when he had listened to the hideous report.

"Perhaps as many as two hundred. I did not want to come too near them for fear they would try to spear Bellimbusto, or worse, call up the forces of Anatrecacciatore to rouse the birds against me." In the dirt between the piles of bearskins Lodovico had scratched a crude map and now he was indicating the movement he had observed. "If we march tonight and a good portion of tomorrow, we should be able to reach the valley by afternoon. Fighting would be difficult, but it isn't likely that we would be able to commence any real assault until the next morning. Perhaps these warriors of flint and frost will not want to fight in the dark any more than we will."

"That may be an error," Fumovisione cautioned them. "They are not men as we are, but potent beings that are not subject to the same weaknesses and laws that govern us. I fear we must assume that they will fight at any time, in any place, under any conditions, until they are broken and unable to move. We must render them immobile if we wish to vanquish them."

There was silence in the tent for a moment as each man grappled with the implications of Fumovisione's warnings.

"We need catapults," Lodovico said with a gesture of despair.

"You mean those machines that hurl rocks at walls? They are not any more use than cannon would be." Falcone glared down at the lines drawn in the earth.

"Then siege machinery of some sort," Lodovico protested. "There are towers that offer protection and give archers a platform from which to shoot . . ." He stopped. "There is also Bellimbusto. I can take him up, and drop stones on the flint and frost soldiers. I am sorry that there are no petards, for a line of those explosives set up at intervals might be very useful. Most of the time they are used to blow holes in gates and walls, but the principle is the same. We could blast the unnatural things to pieces."

"But, as you say, we have no provisions to make them." Falcone sighed, which was as great a show of emotion as he would permit himself.

"Wait," Fumovisione said just as Lodovico was about to get to his feet. "You are too hasty. Give me a moment . . ." He put his first fingers together under his chin, looking like a particularly sagacious baby. "I may be able . . ."

It was at that moment that Nebbiamente spoke at last. "If there are other traps, as if for game—nets, deadfalls, and the like—then it may be possible to harm them."

"No one is going to stand still while you build a deadfall and then walk into it," Fumovisione said contemptuously.

"No, naturally not," Nebbiamente agreed with a vague wave of his hand. "Still, it might be possible for one group of warriors to engage these enemy troops and then fall back, with guidance, of course, and lead the troops of Anatrecacciatore into the snares we set for them." He leaned his head back and stared up into the gloom. "It's merely a suggestion. I am not a warrior, I am a priest. What can I do?"

Falcone was about to fling an insulting remark at Nebbiamente, then stopped and looked once more at the map Lodovico had made. "Let me see. There is a river, you say?"

"There are two," Lodovico assured him, "and both are fed by a number of springs. One of the rivers is here, near the eastern slope of the valley, and the other is approximately here"—he pointed out an uneven line—"down the center of the valley. The western slope has a number of springs, though I suppose they will be useless and unhealthy now that the soldiers of Anatrecacciatore have crossed them."

"What if we use the rivers for our protection?" Falcone suggested, his brow creased in thought. "How do these soldiers fare in water, do you know?"

"There is no way to know," Fumovisione shook his head. "It may not faze them at all. They would be poor soldiers if they could not get wet."

"I haven't seen them cross water, so I can't tell how much it affects them." Lodovico stared down at the map again. "Arrows fletched with duck feathers may stop them. Or the reanimated skins of fallen warriors. We'll have to gamble on that." Though he was apprehensive, he knew he must not reveal it in his manner. He smiled broadly, jauntily. "Our men are strong, well-armed, and committed to this fight. With the help of God, we will prevail."

Fumovisione looked away, saying remotely, "Anatrecacciatore has his god, too, who will aid him."

"The powers of Satan are not equal to the might of God," Lodovico assured him, and got slowly to his feet. "We must gather our captains together and alert them to our plans. That way, should anything happen to any of us, these good men may carry on the battle."

"Nembosanguinoso is waiting in his tent. Lungobraccio can be sent for. I wish we knew what had become of Coltellomela. His men worry for him, and that does not bode well for them in battle. Fierovento will be with his priests now, but I will ask him to join us when he has completed his rituals." Falcone had also risen and inclined his head toward Fumovisione. "Will you speak to the priests and wizards?"

"Naturally, naturally," was the rather distant reply. The wizard remained seated, gazing at nothing in particular. "I feel that we must soon confront the warriors of Anatrecacciatore, and the valley that the Italian describes is, I believe, an excellent place to begin the war."

Falcone set his jaw. "I wish the Cioctau and Iustaga were with us. If Coltellomelma reached Naniaba, they may yet reach us in time to aid us in this fight. Naniaba is to the north, and, I think, behind us. It will be hard going for those soldiers if they set out from there. The terrain is rough and mountainous. They will not know where to find us." He stopped. "I must not concern myself with that."

Lodovico, seeing the resignation and strength in the face of the Cérocchi Prince, felt admiration and sympathy for this great leader. Falcone was young and this was his first real test in battle. He had taken the responsibility without flinching and was carrying his burden nobly. "My Prince," Lodovico said kindly, remembering the many times he had had to take orders from less valiant men, "let us send messengers to Naniaba and any other city where we may have allies. It is not too late to do so. If we must fall back, then we will fall back to a strong defensive force, which is wise. Naniaba may be distant, but a few good men, on horseback, should make reasonable time if they are sensible."

"Very well," Falcone agreed after a moment's consideration. "I will ask Lungobraccio and Nembosanguinoso to choose the best of their horsemen for the journey." Then he turned to Lodovico, smiling. "You are a marvel, my friend. Where others see only defeat and despair, you see a challenge and hope."

Lodovico dared not confide his fears to Falcone, for the Prince was in need of all the optimism he could find. With a great effort that almost overwhelmed him, Lodovico hooked his thumbs in his belt and forced himself to grin. "There is no reason why we cannot triumph, Falcone. I say this, who have fought Djini in Arabia and chimeras in the lost regions of India. Those who are true of heart go forth with the light of God within them, and nothing of darkness can stand against them." As he said this, he thought of his own unconfessed passion for Aureoraggio and felt a gelid fist close in his chest. How could he expect God to lend him the might of the archangels with this sin upon his soul?

Falcone sensed nothing of this turmoil, and gratefully accepted the confident appearance of Lodovico as wholly genuine. He clapped Lodovico on the shoulder. "You are remarkable, Ariosto. I wish I had your certainty and strength."

"But you do," Lodovico assured him with feeling. "You may have more than I."

"If you believe that, you are more of a dreamer than Nebbiamente, there." This was said with a chuckle and some of the buoyancy of spirit that Lodovico had hoped he might restore in the prince. "Come. The captains are waiting for us, and we must not delay." With that, he strode to the door of the tent, motioning Lodovico to join him.

"I will read the omens," Fumovisione announced with a sigh as Lodovico reached the tent door.

"We will need favorable ones," Lodovico warned him, then followed Falcone out into the dusk.

Lungobraccio lived up to his name—his long arms reached almost to his knees. He was dressed with the same armor as Falcone and he carried a large war axe in his belt. Beside him Nembosanguinoso appeared less impressive, for he was smaller in stature and his countenance was less ruggedly distinctive. His eyes, however, held a lambent fury that was lacking in Lungobraccio. Both men rose as Lodovico and Falcone entered their tent.

"There will be battle soon," Falcone announced without preamble. "Your priests will confirm it, if necessary, but I tell you that it is so. We know the place and Lodovico has seen the enemy. It is for us now to prepare ourselves for the fight."

"It is well." Lungobraccio had a deep voice that echoed in his broad chest so that it sounded as if he were speaking into a hollow place. He dropped once more onto his folded legs and waited impassively for Falcone to continue.

Falcone seated himself and at once began to describe what Lodovico had seen. He had just come to the description of the two rivers when Lodovico interrupted him deferentially.

"If you will agree, my Prince, I would like to get my captain of Lanzi to listen, as well. If we all speak together, then more can be accomplished."

Startled, Falcone looked up. "Yes." His reddish skin did not show color changes easily, yet Lodovico thought that perhaps the Cérocchi blushed. "By all means. I should have thought of that myself. Find your Capitano Fabroni at once."

Lodovico bowed elegantly and went quickly in search of the bivouac of the Lanzi.

It was quite dark now, and the various groups of warriors gathered around their fires for the evening meal. Here there were pikemen from Annouaigho poaching fresh-caught fish in venison broth. There the Onaumanient had set their bows and knives aside and were laughing as a haunch of wild boar sizzled on a slowly turning spit. Beyond them, soldiers from Giagaia had turned their curved daggers to cleaning partridges and geese before stuffing them with nuts and thrusting them into the coals to roast. Cica Omini sat with their Pau Attan cousins around a huge pot that simmered fragrantly. Lodovico knew that he could stop at any of these gatherings and share the succulent repasts, but he resisted the temptation. There would be time for that later, when he had finished his talk with the captains. His body protested, his mouth watered, but he continued resolutely toward the far side of the camp where the Lanzi gathered.

Massamo Fabroni was cutting meat from the flank of a wild oxen calf which had just been pulled out of its ember-lined bed of leaves. The flesh was pale and the smell delicious, and from the smile on the old soldier's face, he had been anticipating this meal for some little time. He grinned happily as he saw Lodovico approaching.

"Ariosto! In time to join us. Here." He turned brusquely to his men. "Make room for the man. He does us great honor to share our table."

Lodovico hated to disappoint the man, but knew that the sooner he explained the situation, the less insulted the Lanzi capitano would be. "I'm afraid that I must not accept, though to tell you the truth, I would much rather dine with you than do what I must."

Massamo had just sunk a fork deep into the steaming meat, and he did not look around at once. "How do you mean? There's plenty."

"I can see that, and for that reason, I hope there will be some left when you and I are finished with the business that calls us both away from this delicious meal." Lodovico made a gesture of apology to the other men and addressed Massamo Fabroni. "There is a meeting of the troop leaders, and I must ask you to come with me. We have much to plan before we are ready to meet the enemy, and that hour will be upon us in very short order."

"Battle?" Fabroni asked, his eyes alight. "About time, I say." He set his rough plate aside, tossed his carving knife to one of his corporales, wiped his greasy hands on his leather leggings and gave Lodovico an eager, voracious grin. "I'm your man for battle, Ariosto."

Lodovico answered Massamo's grin with one of his

own. "Then we will do well together, for it is to battle that we go."

Now it was settled. Falcone studied the faces of his captains and raised his brow toward the wizards and priests. Lodovico gripped Massamo's arm, excitement filling him.

"We depart within the hour," Falcone said, his eyes filled with a stern satisfaction. "We will march through the rest of the night, pause for a meal at dawn and march until sunset, when we will once again make camp. It is likely that by that time we will be on the hills beyond the valley where the warriors of flint and frost are now ravaging the land. We will make a holding camp, and before first light, we will prepare for battle. Is that the nature of your understanding, captains?"

All but Nembosanguinoso muttered their assent, but the Cicora captain hesitated.

"What is the trouble?" Falcone asked, watching the calm, hot-eyed warrior.

"I am troubled in my mind," he said simply. "If these warriors are as mighty as the priests and wizards say they are, what is to prevent them from falling upon us in the night and killing us to a man while we sleep? Then our skins will be gathered up for Anatrecacciatore to breathe into and they will be sent in the guise of friends against our allies . . ." He looked at the others. "We cannot rely on mere guards around the camp, for all that the enemy need do is kill the guard, reanimate the skin and pass on to slaughter those asleep. Should anyone wake, there would be no way to tell what had happened."

Lodovico had listened to this with great attention. He could not help but agree with the Cicora soldier, and said so. "He's right, you know. We're exposing ourselves to more danger than is necessary."

Falcone turned to him in some ire. "What do we do, then? We must go forth to meet these soldiers, and we must rest before we start into battle. What can we do but take the best precautions we may and pray that our gods will give us protection against the evil of Anatrecacciatore?"

"You say that we should take precautions, and I agree most emphatically. But I don't think standing guards are sufficient." He recalled the fight he had waged in the air with the birds. "We will need every man in the field on the day of battle. We can't put all of them on watch and then arm them to fight. That would be utmost folly. We must find reliable guards, guards that may not be killed or suborned by any of the enemy. For that reason, I would set a small foot patrol to catching ducks."

The others stared at him, some aghast, some annoyed, one or two amused.

"When the birds came against me, the ducks did not. It has been suggested by your own wizards and priests that the great power of Anatrecacciatore cannot extend to ducks because those birds are the heart of his power, or perhaps the only opposition he can have because of his name. I have seen much stranger things in my travels. Therefore it is possible that his warriors cannot harm ducks either. I have found that ducks are easily alarmed, and when they are they make a frightful din. No enemy could approach our camp without causing these birds to squawk and quack and therefore give us good warning of danger." As he spoke, he felt his confidence in the plan grow. His chestnut eyes were alight with enthusiasm and his voice became more vibrant. "Consider, good captains, the advantages. We would be protected by the very thing that Anatrecacciatore is unable to influence. Short of the Sword of San Michele, I can think of nothing more effective to guard us."

Lungobraccio scowled. "Ducks may be slain. They are not large beasts. It would be a simple matter for the warriors of flint and frost to set upon them and kill them."

"Not before they had begun making noise," Lodovico asserted. "Think of that. Should they be killed—although I doubt that will happen—they will still make an alarm and we may be awakened to do battle. If every man sleeps with his weapons at his side, there will be no need to take extra time to prepare for the fray." He almost laughed. "Some of your men must have baskets in which they carry their supplies. Surely they will sacrifice them to the ducks in exchange for the protection the birds afford."

Falcone had been listening to this in silence and now he met Lodovico's eyes with increased respect that bordered on awe. "I am beginning to believe the stories I've heard about you. At first, I thought that it was the pride of your countrymen talking, not truth, but I see that all that has been said is true. You are the most clever man I have known. *We* should have thought of this. You are a stranger, new to our land and new to the threat of Anatrecacciatore, yet while we sit here wishing to find ways to thwart him, you go to the heart of the matter and give us the solution that we have been seeking."

A flush of pride stole over Lodovico's handsome face and he shrugged eloquently. "If I have been fortunate in this guess, it is because I have been fortunate on other occasions and have brought all that I have learned—at some cost—to bear on our struggles. I am no wiser than you, no more acute, but I have not had to grapple with this evil for as long as you have. I see it differently, and therefore I have had the opportunity to observe your valiant efforts from another view." He smiled at Falcone and thought, with a pang, that were it not for his unrevealed passion for Aureoraggio, this would be the finest comrade at arms he had ever known. There should be no secrets between comrades, but this secret, he knew, he must keep. It would be the most terrible betrayal he could commit, and with battle so near, he must not burden Falcone with this other conflict.

"It is your modesty speaking," Falcone said, misreading Lodovico's sudden reserve. "But I will not bore you by reminding you of your many victories. I will only tell you that no one of my blood has done so much to aid us, and if there is a victory here, it will be more truly yours than any of ours."

The others agreed, though some were distressed to hear such words come from this superb prince.

Lungobraccio rose first. "I will set my men to trapping ducks. They are positioned on the flanks in any case, and it will be a simple matter for them to hunt the water birds." It was obvious that he was not as enthusiastic about Lodovico's plan as Falcone was.

"Excellent," the Cérocchi prince declared and looked meaningfully at the other captains.

It was Fumovisione who spoke next, though the wizards and priests had not been consulted in the matter. "I believe that Ariosto is on to something. I will go into the marshes myself and bring back as many ducks as I can lay hands on. Which may be quite a few, as I have some tricks in my bag that the rest of you know nothing of." There was a twinkle in his eye as he spoke and as he glanced at Lodovico, he winked.

What little resistance there was crumbled under Fumovisione's comments. The captains rose and gave their unusual salutes before leaving the tent of Falcone.

Massamo Fabroni was among the last to go, pausing to say to Lodovico, "I don't know what good this plan of yours will do. It sounds as if ducks are a lot of nonsense, but if that's what you want . . ." He opened his hands to show his acceptance of Lodovico's orders. "If nothing else, we can make a meal of them when the battle is over."

Lodovico did not have an answer for the rugged Lanzi. He considered his comment carefully, knowing that Massamo had a touchy and highly prized sense of honor. "I am not familiar with the strength and weakness of these people," he said at last, more slowly than he generally spoke. "But I know that we must take advantage of every strength we possess, search out new strength, and, if necessary, invent it. I have no illusions about the power and malice of Anatrecacciatore."

It was not remarkable that Falcone overheard this. He came to Lodovico's side. "You are too severe, Ariosto. And I think that you do not quite believe that, not after the birds attacked you."

Caught between Massamo Fabroni and his utter materialism and Falcone's mystic sense of the forces around him, Lodovico struggled to think of a way to satisfy both of them without causing insult to either. "When I was in the air and there were birds around me in so dense a cloud that I could hardly see the light of the sun, and it was as if night had descended most unnaturally, I knew that Falcone had been right in assessing the danger of Anatrecacciatore's power. But I am also aware that it is the pragmatic soldier who is most likely to survive. Pragmatic does not mean realistic, of course. But what realistic man would battle a foeman of flint and frost? Yet it must be done because the alternative is complete capitulation, and that is loathsome to any man who respects himself and God."

Both Massamo and Falcone were pleased with this answer. Falcone smiled slightly. "I must not forget how astute you are, Ariosto. It is part of your genius." He offered his arm to Massamo Fabroni. "We are allies in this fight, good Italian, and I am grateful for your good sense and your willingness to take up our cause as your own. In battle I will take heart, knowing that you will set an example of courage."

Massamo grasped Falcone's arm and for the first time there was genuine acceptance in his eyes. "I am your man to death, Cérocchi."

A great load was lifted from Lodovico's spirits. "Come," he said to the two men. "First we catch ducks. Then we fight."

La Realtà

Ercole Barbabianca glared across the rose hedge at
Ezio Foscari, oldest son of the Doge of Venezia. "You
are cooperating with the Turks against us!" he insisted,
his cherub's face contorted. "You deny it, of course you
deny it, but I have the word of my commanders in this."

"There was some mistake, then," Ezio Foscari responded as he picked out a rose and held it to his face.
"We don't send our ships against friends."

"The friendship between Genova and Venezia is
recent. The rivalry is ancient. Is there not the slightest
chance that one of your commanders, in a forgetful
moment, thought himself in the past? Barbabianca was
not yelling now, but his expression was no less deadly.

"Is it not also possible that such a lapse affected
your commanders?" Ezio Foscari inquired sweetly. He
was in his early twenties, effete in manner and dress but
hardy as a weed, a rangy, fair-haired man with sharp
Foscari features.

"It is a shame that you cannot follow your father
in office," Ercole Barbabianca sneered.

"There is no assurance that I won't. I may be elected.
You, however, having no sons, must hate the passing
days, knowing that no election in the world can pass
your title on to your children." He was using the rose

to gesture with, and his bantering tone made mockery of Ercole Barbabianca's nastiness.

"Both of you, give it a rest," Damiano put in, stopping the exchange. "When I asked you to walk with me in the garden it was not so that you could duel with words." He turned to the man beside him. "Suggest another topic, Lodovico."

Stunned, Lodovico mentioned the first thing that came into his mind. "Has the ship come back from the land of the Cérocchi? It's been more than a year . . ."

Damiano's face darkened and he looked at his two feuding guests. "It got back across the Atlantic safely enough, but ran afoul of the Spanish. The crew was taken prisoner at Barcelona. It was traveling without escort, unfortunately." It was apparent to all three men that Damiano held both Genova and Venezia accountable for this oversight. "There will be other ships, naturally, and in time we may learn what those despicable Spaniards did to our men. Since they gave a royal edict that there could be no exploration of such heathen lands, they have been at pains to interfere as much as possible with our trade. I would have thought," he added in another voice, "considering it was Genova who established the trade, that Genovese ships would protect the place, but it would seem that this is not the case."

Foscari and Barbabianca exchanged uncomfortable looks, and at last the stout Genovese Doge said, "We have many concerns, as you know, Primàrio. It is unfortunate that our Signoria is not always quick to see the advantage in such outposts as Nuova Genova. When we brought the two Cérocchi guests in fifteen thirteen, I was new to my office and perhaps I did not handle the enterprise as well as I might have. It was your grandfather who made the situation clear to me. I recall that he gave me some excellent advice at the time, as he so often did. You probably don't remember. You were very young at the time."

"I remember very well," Damiano corrected him. "I was fifteen years old by then, and already my grandfather was schooling me. I had paid official visits to Paris and Cologne before then, and a year later, I visited Cyprus with the old Venezian Doge. The Cérocchi made quite an impression on His Holiness." He chuckled. "Uncle Giovanni loved the picturesque and strange, and those Cérocchi were better than anything he had seen except the Russian dwarves. He kept them in Roma for the better part of a year. Finally my grandfather had to go and get them and arrange for them to be taken home. There was an agreement with the King of their people and he was determined to honor it."

Ezio Foscari could afford to laugh, and he did. Ercole Barbabianca cleared his throat. "Yes. Well, you've got to be aware, de' Medici, that it was not always possible to have a fully supplied ship ready to undertake such a hazardous journey at short notice."

"Doubtless that is why the Cérocchi returned in one of our ships." Though Firenze was an inland city, she maintained a small fleet of her own at Pisa. "We must have been strangely fortunate to be able to set out so quickly. Strange. I had assumed that Genova would be more capable than Firenze in such things."

Though the embarrassment had occurred almost twenty years before, it still carried a sting.

"It is sad that you did not think to contact Venezia," Ezio Foscari remarked to the air. "We're usually able to put to sea within two days of an order." He favored Barbabianca with a particularly malicious smile.

"Gran Dio," the Genovese Doge muttered, but refused to be drawn into altercation. "We do well with the Cérocchi and their allies," he said in a determinedly hearty manner. "They provide us with a variety of furs and hides, for the most part, and some lumber. There are also artifacts that a few people enjoy, and we purchase some regularly. I think it has been an advantageous arrangement both ways."

"What about a fuller exploration of the country itself? How is that going?" Damiano seemed genuinely interested, for there was a brightness in his brown eyes and he walked more briskly.

"Well, you know that it is not an easy thing to cross the ocean and then set off exploring. The Cérocchi have taken some of the outpost guards through most of their territories, but they are only one of many nations, and not all of them are at peace. We are attempting to make arrangements, of course, but"—his face turned a plummy shade—"we lack the sort of courageous leader who would be able to head such a prolonged venture. We have searched, and I am fully committed to the task, but it's difficult, Damiano. It's very difficult."

Lodovico wished he could bring himself to speak, to ask for the honor of leading such an expedition. He had been listening avidly, thinking of that time, twenty years before, when as a young man he had heard the Cérocchi talk about their homeland. He had been entranced then, and now, in his writing, all he had been told came back with vivid reality. To have the opportunity of going there . . . He did not continue the thought, for he knew that it would not be possible, not with Alessandra and Virginio. If he were a man without family or obligations, it would be different; he could roam the entire world. He also admitted to himself that Damiano would not be willing to let a man, untried and unknown, take on the responsibilities of the venture. And perhaps, he told himself, salving his pride, his skills would be of more use here than in that strange land where he would be, in all practical senses of the word, mute. A poet feeds on words, he knew. If he could not speak, he would be a poor leader.

"How do you see it, Lodovico?" Damiano asked suddenly and Lodovico realized that he had not been listening.

"About Nuova Genova?" he wondered aloud, not certain if the subject had changed or not.

Damiano came as close to laughing as he ever did these days. "I wish I had your gift, Lodovico. I would spend my days in the clouds. Your mind has wings."

"But are we speaking still of Nuova Genova?" Lodovico persisted, not at all certain that Damiano's remarks were complimentary.

"Yes, and all the Nuovo Mondo. Do you remember the Cérocchi? I think you met them." He had stopped beside a statue of a faun and he rested his hand familiarly on the marble shoulder.

"Of course I remember them," he said shortly. "Two men, in their middle years. One spoke Italian quite well, and the other understood a great deal though he did not speak much." He looked at the three men as if expecting them to contradict him. "We discussed many things," he said after a moment. "It is an exciting place, enormous and rich. When the Spaniards sent their first six ships, they came back with rumors of cities made of precious stones, but the Cérocchi told me it was not true." He sighed, recalling again the enthusiastic words of the Spanish monk who had been on that voyage. Lodovico had met him in Torino at a great celebration.

"Of course they denied it," Ezio Foscari scoffed. "You don't expect them to admit they have such wealth, do you? It would be too much temptation. They give us furs and wood and keep their precious stones for themselves."

For once Ercole Barbabianca was in agreement. "They're clever men. I know what it would be like if we advertised our treasures—we would have half the armies of Europe climbing all over us. The German States would stop their civil wars and Spain would turn all their heretics into soldiers until they controlled the wealth they desire." He had folded his arms on his chest and was watching Damiano with a reserved anger.

"Such discretion," Damiano murmured, addressing the marble faun.

"Well," Barbabianca went on belligerently, "they are not fools, and they know enough to protect themselves—don't tell me otherwise. There may well be cities of diamonds in the forests, but the only way we will find them is to go there. Sadly, the Signoria of Genova does not agree."

Ezio Foscari studied the Doge of Genova. "We have many good men in Venezia who might like that opportunity. They are greedy, but what else can you expect?"

His polite and cynical laughter was interrupted by Lodovico's unexpected outburst: "There is honor!"

Barbabianca regarded him in disbelief, and Foscari absolutely guffawed. Lodovico felt his face darken in unaccountable shame and wished he could flee. What had he said that warranted such derision? He had often heard these men praise honor, declaring that without it all other virtues lost their worth.

Only Damiano did not laugh. He looked evenly at Lodovico, his brown eyes filled with an emotion that was not quite pity. "Yes," he said slowly after a moment. "There is honor."

The amusement filling Barbabianca and Foscari stopped at once, wiped away by the seriousness of Damiano's voice. There was an awkward silence, and Ezio Foscari gazed down a nearby path as if he longed to use it for escape. At last Ercole Barbabianca looked squarely at Lodovico.

"I knew there was a reason that most rulers are suspicious of poets," he said without hostility. "You have reminded us of matters we would prefer to forget."

Was that what he had done? Lodovico was not sure whether he should be amazed or offended. Was the Doge of Genova serious, or was this a subtle insult? He tried to find an appropriate retort. "If rulers forget honor, then they cannot hope a poet will save them." It was too weak, he thought, or too petulant.

"Sadly, you have the right of it," Damiano sighed.

There was a tension in the air now that had not been there before. Barbabianca glared at the pebbled walkway while Foscari flung his rose away with sudden violence.

"Come, gentlemen," Damiano said, spuriously laconic. "It is too hot to stay here. Inside it is much cooler, I promise you." He indicated the pathway back toward the Palazzo Pitti.

"Yes, it is too hot," Ercole Barbabianca muttered. "I suppose your poet is coming with us?"

Lodovico felt this rebuff as a blow. "I did not intend . . ."

Damiano silenced him with a gesture. "He is good for my conscience," he said enigmatically. Then he turned down the hedge-framed walk and without waiting for the others to follow, started toward the garden terrace of the palace. Lodovico had almost to run to keep up with il Primàrio, and as he did, he saw, to his consternation, that Damiano's shoulders drooped, bowed under a heavy, invisible burden.

There was a shiny film of sweat on his upper lip, but other than that, Andrea Benci was cool and elegant. His brocaded giaquetta was in the French fashion, with a beaded and jeweled codpiece and padded shoulders. Slashed sleeves and bodice showed his silken shirt of pleated pale blue silk, and his hose were banded and padded, very short, the height of fashion. His white hair had been trimmed into the current shorter mode and his beard, the color of silver, was perfectly groomed. Lodovico hated the sight of him.

"Cosimo, Cardinale Medici, is waiting to see you," he said to Damiano with a courtly bow.

"Yes, yes." Damiano was reading a message and did not look up at once. There were two deep lines between his brows.

With utmost diplomacy, Benci said, "He has said it is too important for him to be kept waiting."

Damiano set the vellum sheet aside. "It is always too important for him to be kept waiting." He paced down the library. "Very well, very well, bring him in. The sooner he gets it over with, the sooner he'll be gone."

In the last few days Lodovico had noticed this shortness of temper in Damiano that was a new development. He put his book aside and got to his feet. "If you want me to leave . . . ?"

"Christ, no." Damiano answered at once. "I may need a witness, if my cousin is bringing me news from Clemente." He put his hand to his brow and rubbed once, then looked at Andrea Benci. "Show him in, by all means."

Andrea Benci's mouth was slightly pursed, but there was nothing in his expression to reveal his thoughts other than that. He turned away and was out of the library.

"How do you bear his obsequiousness?" Lodovico demanded, knowing full well that his dislike of the man extended to much more than his manner.

"It's useful," Damiano said distantly. "I hate to admit it, but I have no idea what Cosimo wants to discuss with me. There are spies in his household, of course, but they have provided me very little in the way of information of late. He's being very careful. That worries me." He walked down to the largest of the tables, an enormous piece of furniture of carved oak. He took one chair behind it and sat, as if in state. Seeing Lodovico's scandalized expression, he winked. "I need to bolster my position, and since Cosimo is a Prince of the Church, without a crown and scepter, this is the best I can do."

Lodovico was about to protest what he felt was sham when the door opened again and Andrea Benci announced Cosimo, Cardinale Medici.

Cosimo was rigged out in full ecclesiastical splendor, as if he, too, had determined to muster every badge of authority he possessed. He saw Lodovico and his face soured. "Cousin," he called out. "I had hoped we would be private."

"We are," Damiano responded with his most affable smile. "Lodovico is my confidant, and if I cannot trust him, then I cannot trust myself." He indicated a chair for the Cardinale. "Eminenza." He most pointedly did not kiss Cosimo's ring nor request his blessing.

Cosimo was unruffled by this insolence, but there was a shine at the back of his prominent eyes that smoldered. "I was pleased that you were willing to make time for me." He waited for an answer.

Damiano let him wait. "If it was so urgent . . ." he said when the silence had lengthened.

"Yes." He looked down at his satin shoes. "I bring a message from our kinsman, His Holiness Clemente the Seventh."

"And what does my father's bastard first cousin want?" He asked this so flippantly that Cosimo could not respond with anger. It took him a moment to collect himself. "His Holiness has decided to extend an invitation to Lazaro Frescobaldi to return to Italia Federata under his personal protection." He relished saying this, knowing it to be a direct countermanding of Damiano's orders.

"My brother-in-law," Damiano said quietly, "is a danger to Italia Federata. He has been in the pay of both Saxony and Spain. If he returns, he will use it to his advantage and you may be certain that it would not be to ours."

Lodovico had heard that implacable note in Damiano's voice before, and each time he was struck anew by the ruthlessness that lay just below il Primàrio's geniality. He could see now that a greater determination possessed Cosimo, Cardinale Medici. It was a cold fire fueled by ambition and frustration, unhampered by pity or compassion. The second cousins glared into each other's faces.

"It is the hope of His Holiness that through Lazaro, who is now a monk and given to a pious life . . ."

"Pious!" Damiano snorted.

". . . and dedicated to the good of God and the Church, a way may be found whereby Spain will once again resume her place among the well-loved Catholic nations . . ."

"Losing revenue, is he?" Damiano inquired harshly. "Spain won't jump to the lash anymore, cousin. They've had a taste of their own power and they like it. What would it profit them to make peace with Roma? You don't see the German States rushing to do it, do you? It's a monks' battle there, and see what it has gotten them. Two Kings and an Elector assassinated in the last eight years and Wittenburg in ashes. Bavaria burned four thousand heretics last year. Guicciardini warned me that there will be more. Is that what our Papal cousin wants, cousin? Or is he more subtle than that?" There was a flutter at the corner of his eye, but that was all that betrayed his agitation. Damiano had not changed his authoritative posture and his voice had not altered pitch.

"If we're to talk of heresy, Primàrio," Cosimo said smoothly, though his face was the color of sculptor's wax, "you stand in mortal peril yourself. Your remarks here—oh, do not fear I will repeat them, though you may regret allowing Ariosto to stay—would send you to the stake in Madrid."

"We are not in Madrid," Damiano pointed out. "We are in Firenze, in a nation that has been cobbled together out of a dozen warring states. If the Pope turns his back on la Federazione, then we may as well begin the Requiem, for Italia Federata will be in her death throes in less than a year, and those greedy wolves in Austria and France and Spain will be on us to devour us. Is that what Clemente wants? Is it?" He leaned forward and struck the table with the flat of his hand. "Well?"

"Cousin, such choler." His laugh rustled like dry leaves. "His Holiness has the Church and her sanctity at heart . . ."

"That's a change," Damiano put in, and went on without letting Cosimo continue, "Giulio is a clever man—I've never said otherwise. But he's venal. Don't bother to deny it. I grew up watching him. I don't criticize him for it. Considering the political difficulties he is handling, he's much more useful than a saint would be. Spiritual men do more good in hermits' cells than in the Chair of San Piero."

"Then you will cooperate?" Cosimo inquired in his most self-deprecating manner.

"Will I help bring Spain back into the fold? No. Will I welcome Lazaro Frescobaldi? No. Will I participate in the destruction of la Federazione? No." He met Cosimo's eyes frankly. "And you knew when you came

here that I would not. Tell me, cousin, what do you
really want of me?"

Cosimo, Cardinale Medici, paused a moment. "Make
me your heir."

"What?" Damiano demanded. "My heir?"

Before he could say more, Cosimo went on. "Your
sons are lost to you, though they live. You need not
deny it. There are only your grandsons, and they are
very young. How old is Pierfrancesco? Eight? And
Giuliano? Six?"

"I was *my* grandfather's heir," Damiano pointed out
in an elaborate appeal to reason, but Cosimo would not
be stilled.

"That was another time. And, if you will forgive me
for pointing it out, you are not Lorenzo. When he died
he was an old man, and you, coming to power, were
in the first strength of your manhood. Which of your
sons is a candidate for the Papacy? Lorenzo had Giovanni, and it was a formidable alliance. Could either of
your grandsons handle the reins of state? Of course
not. They would be hampered, controlled, set about
with regents and protectors until there would be no
escape for them. You recall what happened in Milano
when Il Moro was regent for his nephew—the nephew
and his family disappeared. It might well go the same
way for your grandsons."

"You're assuming that I will not live to the same
old age that my grandfather did," Damiano said, but
could not bring himself to make light of the warning
implicit in Cosimo's words.

Lodovico felt cold spread through him as he listened.
The library was pleasantly warm and a bowl of roses,
full-blown, stood on the mantel sweetening the air, but
it meant nothing to him. He was certain both men had
forgotten his presence and he wished now that he had
taken the opportunity to leave. His eyes, he thought,
must have frozen in his head and would be like ice or
marbles if he should topple. He feared he would never
see anything but this library and the two men in it,

locked into their mutual hatred with a force that exceeded passion.

"There have been, as you yourself have pointed out, assassinations in the German States. More than one person has plotted against the King of France and it is only a fluke that he is still alive; he has always learned of the danger in time and was able to avert the peril. That is because he has been willing to listen when advice was given him," he added significantly. He permitted himself the tiniest smile as he watched Damiano's apprehension.

"You're telling me that I may be killed." He said it flatly and showed no fear. "That danger has existed most of my life."

"I merely warn you," Cosimo de' Medici said, with a little less confidence. "You're fooling yourself if you think that you are safe."

"I have never thought that." His tone was drier, and his smile was now condescending. "If this is to persuade me to see the advantage of having you my heir, you are not being very wise, cousin."

The Cardinale bristled visibly, which startled both Damiano and Lodovico. It was an indication of the depth of Cosimo's feelings that he would forget himself so much. "I am protection, cousin. I am high in the Church and I have the ear of Clemente. I might be able to convince him that Spain should be left to herself."

"And, knowing Clemente, you might not be able to. A very capricious man, my father's cousin's bastard." He enjoyed Cosimo's discomfort at his reminder of the Pope's illegitimacy.

Cosimo's hands had closed into fists and the knuckles were white. "You are arrogant and prideful, Damiano. I will not forget this. Spurn my request if you dare. Willingly or unwillingly, you will have me after you. I am a staunch ally, and I am a formidable enemy."

"Arrogance and pride run in our family," Damiano said with grim amusement. "Since we are being bald-faced now, I take leave to tell you, my cousin, that I am convinced that you would be more destructive to la

Federazione than plague and war together. If that draws the battleline, so be it. But while we are issuing warnings, let me warn you that any attempt on your part to interfere with the running of the state will be met with the sternest rebuke I am capable of. I will have you detained in Roma as long as is necessary. Do not doubt that His Holiness will aid you. Remember that he was at Giovanni's side when he was Leone the Tenth, and la Federazione is as much his dream as it was Giovanni's and Lorenzo's. Endanger Italia Federata and you will find yourself in a monk's cell. I would not want to do this. There are rifts enough in la Federazione without bringing family politics into it. Yet, should I learn that you are determined on this lunatic course, I will stop you." There was no doubt that he was serious. His voice was even and matter-of-fact. His eyes met his cousin's unflinchingly.

"Very well." Cosimo, Cardinale Medici rose. His face was chalky and about his mouth there appeared to be a white line. He could not entirely keep the tremor of rage from his words. "You execrable cur." He was silent, as if readying himself for a vituperative tirade. His breath came quickly, hissing.

Damiano did not move. One arm rested on the table, the other was extended negligently on the arm of the chair. His face was set into stern but calm authority. Impassively he studied his red-garbed second cousin, giving no response to the bitter obduracy that Cosimo divulged. When he was certain that the Cardinale would not launch another assault, he said, "If there is nothing else you wish to discuss, Eminenza . . ."

Without a word, Cosimo di' Medici turned on his heel and stroke from the room.

As the latch clicked, Damiano sighed, and brought his hands together. He sat looking abstractedly over his interlaced fingers. There was an isolation about him, a remoteness that jangled Lodovico's already overwrought sensibilities.

"Primario . . ." It was difficult now to think of this man as his friend, his patron; he was too separate, made an exile in his own country through the gravity of his office.

"San Egidio, don't you start on me," Damiano said in a voice so exhausted that Lodovico could hardly recognize it.

His aversion, which had been increasing all through the terrible interview he had witnessed, was replaced by a sudden, guilty rush of sympathy. "No. I won't." He should have realized that what Damiano had done was a performance, created especially for an audience of one —his second cousin. His attitudes, his aloof demeanor were assumed with the same skill and purpose an actor might choose to portray a King. Lodovico got out of his chair and went to stand beside the table where Damiano sat. Hesitantly he put a hand on Damiano's shoulder. At that moment il Primàrio reminded Lodovico of Virginio in those days after his retreat from the same august Prince of the Church who had just left the library. The acrimony he had felt for Cosimo grew more intense. The Cardinale had left the effluvium of his malice on two of the men he treasured. That officer of God's Church, he thought with vehemence, is a rapacious, pernicious reprobate. "Sodomite!" Lodovico whispered as his indignation grew.

Damiano brought his head up sharply. "What did you call me?" There was sufficient apprehension in his manner to startle Lodovico.

"Not you," he protested. "The Cardinale." He read nothing in Damiano's enigmatic expression, and decided impulsively to tell il Primàrio of what his kinsman had attempted. "My son . . . while he was here in Firenze not so long ago, attracted the Cardinale's attention . . ."

The telling was long and painful, with many awkward silences and sickening hesitations when Lodovico felt as if he were falling over a cliff or being drowned in a well. His mouth was dry and his tongue moved behind his teeth like a wooden paddle. Halfway through this shameful tale, he wished he could stop. He should have never begun, he told himself. He might well compromise his son, if any word of this conversation should become known. His eyes darted nervously about the room and he set his teeth.

"Go on, Lodovico," Damiano urged kindly. "I am familiar enough with Cosimo's antics that you will not disgust me, I give you my word."

Lodovico very nearly blurted out that he feared not for Damiano but his son's reputation, but for once he contained himself. He resumed the story, recalling the late night arrival of Tancredi Scoglio.

"Scoglio . . ." Damiano repeated. "He's one of Benci's lot, isn't he?" He scowled at the flowers on the mantel. "My secretary should have taught the lad more discretion."

"But it was Benci who brought Virginio to the Cardinale's attention," Lodovico objected, letting his rancor show for once. "Benci does not like me. He wants to embarrass me. He'll use my son if he has to, if he cannot compromise me directly." He was foolish to say this, he knew he was foolish. Inwardly he cursed himself for this petty indulgence of spleen. He would destroy his credibility with Damiano, he was sure of it. At the least he would be returned to the villa at Fiesole, if he was fortunate enough to keep Damiano's patronage at all.

"Yes," Damiano said calmly. "I'm aware of that. It's not as extreme as you imagine, but it would take a man much blinder than I can afford to be to overlook the battle beween you two."

"But, then, why? . . ." Lodovico hoisted himself onto the table and tucked his legs under himself, tailor fashion.

Damiano gave Lodovico a long, faintly sardonic stare. "As comforting as it might be to be counseled only by men who agree with each other and with me, I was taught from childhood on that a leader who insists on such sycophancy breeds his own ruin. It is unfortunate that Benci cannot see your virtues and your worth because he does not understand men who do things for reasons other than political ones. You, to complement him, are not willing to tolerate his political

talents. I am selfish enough to want both of you near
me. Between you, I will keep on the path I must tread.
Neither of you walks it, but without both of you, I fear
I should quickly lose my way."

"But Virginio . . ." Lodovico began, and stopped
as quickly.

"That I was not aware of," Damiano said, his brow
darkening anew. "I should have paid more attention.
But as you have your differences and blindnesses with
Benci, so I have them with Cosimo." He propped his
chin in his hand. "I'll have to watch that more closely,
I fear."

"If it had been a minor matter," Lodovico went on,
chagrined. He thought that perhaps it would have been
better to keep the matter to himself and trust that distance and time would favor Virginio.

"This is not a minor matter. It is true it's a very little
thing, but if Cosimo is so indiscreet and audacious that
he approaches young men who are not . . . available,
then he must be watched."

Lodovico agreed and after a moment told Damiano
the rest of it, not omitting the painful confrontation he
had had with Virginio that brought the sordid matter
to light. "I have faith that the worst that was damaged
was Virginio's vanity."

"You know," Damiano said thoughtfully as he regarded Lodovico, "there are many fathers who would
have told their sons to accept the Cardinale's offer. A
great deal of advantage is to be gained in such arrangements."

For a moment, Lodovico could not move. He was not
sure he could breathe. Then, with a calm that startled
and pleased him, he said, "There are such men, yes. I
have heard you speak of them as despicable. I do not
think I could ask my own child—my only child—to
make himself a whore to his own ambition, or to
mine."

"You struck home on that one," Damiano acknowledged with a gesture. "It is true enough that I find such
men contemptible. Whores are not lovers, certainly.

But perhaps I'm too severe. I can't point to my own sons with pride, so it may be that those fathers who guide their children into venality do well by them." His expression was once again melancholy, introverted.

In a desperate attempt to turn Damiano away from the reflections that were tormenting him, Lodovico said, "Would you prefer to see them parading with the catamites in Piazza delle Belle Donne? Think of Renato with his lips carmined and his hair dyed blond, arranged in curls."

Damiano's painful chuckle stopped him. "You've made your point, Lodovico. Don't belabor it, I beg of you." He got to his feet and thrust his hands through his belt. "I need time. And I haven't got time. I haven't got the information I must have. The wolves are following my scent, I fear. But what wolves?" He stared away, through the windows, beyond the gardens and orchards and fortified walls.

Lodovico got down from the table, noticing that his heel had scarred the fine wood. He buffed at it with his sleeve surreptitiously, but the mark remained, a silent reproach for his clumsiness.

"Do you know Carmelo di Lozza?" Damiano asked suddenly.

"No," Lodovico answered, trying to place the name. "Who is he?"

"He claims to be a prophet," Damiano went on as if he had not heard Lodovico, "which I take leave to doubt. His parents were part of Savonarola's sect before he was sent away. They were very strict, given to fasting and prayers and mystical dancing. That whole group was fanatically austere. No ornaments on the clothes or in the home. No luxury in food. No music that is not religious. No sport. No art. No jewelry. Carmelo falls into trances, they claim. I have heard the gibberish he speaks and it sounds no different to me than the raving of madmen. Yet he has a small and devoted following."

"Why do you ask?" Lodovico was disturbed by the excessively religious. As a boy, reading the lives of the saints, he had been filled with the conviction that it was not zeal but vanity and unsound mind that provoked many of them to the outrageous acts credited to them. He had not been back in Firenze long enough to learn of this man, he decided, admitting also that he would not want to know too much of such a person as this Carmelo di Lozza.

"Benci tells me that it's becoming popular with the younger officials to attend this Carmelo's meetings . . ." Damiano remarked, frowning.

"Tell the Prior that you would rather he not allow . . ." Lodovico began only to be interrupted.

"He's not in any order. He claims to detest the profligacy of monks. Give him a pulpit and he might change his mind." He drew his hands out of his belt and folded his arms. "What concerns me is that this man is full of praise for Cosimo. He has been saying that only a man in the Church is sufficiently wise and farsighted to be capable of leading la Federazione in a godly way. It would seem that he does not know my cousin well. Yet, he is certainly the Cardinale's creature. Observe him for yourself, for after what I have learned today . . ."

"Do you mean that you believe the Cardinale has corrupted this Carmelo di Lozza?" Lodovico was prepared to think ill of Cosimo de' Medici, but was shocked, nonetheless.

"Oh, no, nothing so blatant as that. Men like di Lozza are not corruptible. But they are manipulable. They can be used more successfully than the most contumelious rascal alive because men such as Carmelo di Lozza fancy themselves acolytes, servants of a great truth, and will endure anything for it, anything at all. If they can be convinced that such a man or such a group or such a nation will further their one great truth, they will follow that man or that group or that nation all the way to the gates of hell." He cocked his head to the side as if listening to faint whisperings. "I wonder who convinced di Lozza that Cosimo de' Medici serves the same truth that he does. For whoever that man is, he is a greater danger to me, to this state, than a dozen of Cosimo."

"Has anyone spoken with di Lozza?" He felt something stir in him, not quite worry, not quite anger.

"Whom would he confide in?" Damiano asked wearily, meeting Lodovico's eyes for a moment.

Though Lodovico nodded, he wanted to ask Damiano why it was not possible to find someone who might persuade di Lozza that it was Cosimo, not Damiano, who was the more sinister man. He compromised, suggesting: "Do you think he would listen to me? You are my patron, there is no disguising that, and I am often in your company. But everyone knows I am inept when it comes to politics. Under ordinary circumstances, our close association might turn against you, but if I tell him something of what passed between the Cardinale and my son, then he might not ignore what I say."

Damiano considered this. "I had planned to send Benci, but perhaps you are right." He fiddled with the lacing on his sleeve. "Don't force him to listen to you, Lodovico. Men like di Lozza won't tolerate that. But if it turns out that there is opportunity . . ." He gave Lodovico a speculative scrutiny. "He disapproves of poetry; you know that."

"There are times I think that half the court disapproves of poetry," Lodovico said, trying to make light of this remark.

Unexpectedly, Damiano laughed. He put his hand on Lodovico's shoulder, saying in an undertone, "Very well. See what you can learn from him. But it may be best not to discuss Virginio's encounter with the Cardinale. Di Lozza might take a notion to denounce the boy, and that would be unfortunate." He removed his hand and stepped back.

"If that is what you wish, I will," Lodovico said, and his heart was troubled.

La Fantasia

A stealthy hand parted the reeds; water lapped against the hiding place. There was a sudden lunge, a cry, a squawk, the rustle of feathers and hoarse quacks of consternation, a subdued shout of triumph and an insistent shushing.

"We got two of them," Massamo Fabroni announced in a loud, gravelly whisper that carried across the marshy backwater of the river as effectively as a shout.

"There were more, but they're gone," Lodovico answered sharply, then as quickly relented. "It's good that you caught them. Another five and we should have enough."

Massamo held up a large sack that moved and bulged most strangely, and a new sound arose from it, a distressed cackling. Massamo held up the two ducks that flapped in his hands. "I feel a damned whoreson fool, Ariosto, but if this is necessary . . ."

Taking the sack from the Lanzi captain, Lodovico held the mouth open a moment while Massamo Fabroni thrust the two new ducks into it. The sack writhed and the noises grew louder. "We'll take these back anyway. If the others have fared as well, there should be ample ducks for all of us."

"The only place I would consider ducks ample is in a cookpot," said Massamo as he slung the sack onto his shoulder. "Ducks, of all things. Ducks!" He chortled and began to wade back toward firm ground.

"Per grazie Dei, be careful," Lodovico said sharply. It was dark and the way was hazardous. He had been given stern warnings from the Cérocchi and Pau Attan of the perils of the swamps. There were voracious serpents, deadlier than the asp, that waited in the tangled vegetation of the shore to surprise their victims. It was said that these snakes struck so quickly that there was almost no time for a cry before the venom rendered the unfortunate insensible, and the serpent dragged the body under the water so that it might consume its prey in comfort. Fumovisione had described a gigantic lizard, like the crocodiles of Egypt, that lay still on the water, having the appearance of a log, that could tear a man in two.

"Fables for children," Massamo pronounced as Lodovico reiterated the warnings. "Where are the lizards, tell me that?"

"Far from here, I earnestly hope," he said with a quiet laugh. "Indeed, I hope that all the monsters they have described to me so vividly prefer to stay abed at night and will not trouble us in any way."

"You've the right of it," Massamo exclaimed. "The only monsters I want are the ones you can't see."

"That's another matter entirely," Lodovico corrected him, suddenly serious, his chestnut eyes shining with somber determination. "The monsters you cannot see are immeasurably worse than those you can, for no matter how terrible, the visible ones can be fought. How do you battle an enemy you are unable to see? Where is it? What is it like? Where is it armed? Where are its weapons? How does it move? Whenever you face a man in battle, those are the things that save you, whether you think of them or not. Your mind takes note of such details and you are able to defeat the other soldier or demon or monster. I am often reminded of those brave, blind Kings who still went into battle and somehow found glory and victory. What great souls those valiant Kings possessed! I cannot think of them without humility. Who am I, who are any of us, in the face of such commitment and integrity?"

Away to the left there was the sound of other waders and in a moment it was possible to see a party of Cicora soldiers coming along the edge of the marsh. There were six men, two with sacks giving ample evidence that the men had caught a great many ducks. One of the men lifted a hand in lackadaisical greeting. The others were less cordial.

"We're still foreigners to them," Massamo growled to Lodovico, with no attempt to lower his voice. "I know they're good enough fighters, but what will happen in battle, that's what I want to know. I don't mind taking on these wizards and supernatural warriors so long as I know there are loyal men at my back."

Lodovico watched the Cicora men in the gloom and kept his thoughts to himself. If only he did not share Massamo's fear! It was well enough with most of the Cérocchi, but there were so many others, and Lodovico could not deny the apprehension that very nearly overwhelmed him. He tried to recall the problems he had had with the Turkish fighters he had taken with his expedition against the Great Mandarin, but had to admit that he could not offer these troops the plunder that had so attracted the Turks. He did not want to burden Falcone with the problem, for the Cérocchi Prince had much on his mind, and was still new to battle.

There was a shout from the Cicora band, and a flurry of activity. Then one of the men screamed out for help. Lodovico exchanged a quick look with Massamo, then sprinted out of the water. "You take the ducks back to camp and bring help," he called to the Lanzi captain. "I will do what I can here."

Massamo started to protest, then shrugged massively and began to slog off toward the shore, his high boots making a sound not unlike large frogs.

By the time Massamo had set foot on the bank, Lodovico had reached the Cicora, calling to gain their attention as he approached. "Good fighters," he addressed them as he lessened his pace. "What has happened here?" He was hampered, he knew, by his inexpert command of their language, but he had already decided that it would be better to speak in their tongue than in Cérocchi, in which he had by now become quite fluent.

The nearest of the Cicora turned, distressed. "Our companion," he cried, pointing out a dim figure thrashing in the mud some little distance beyond them, "has been seized by the sucking earth."

The others nodded in agreement and the man in the mud cried out in a doleful wail.

"What is the sucking earth?" Lodovico was not entirely certain that he understood the word correctly. Sucking earth sounded very strange to him, though it did remind him of the dangerous sands in the vast deserts of the Orient where he had wandered not so long ago. There he had seen those stretches of sand, in no visible way different from any other area of sand, where, if man or beast set foot, he would be dragged down to a slow and terrible death of suffocation. He went quickly to the edge of the mud, heedless of the warning of the Cicora. In the desert, he had learned that it was possible to save men from the sands, and so it might be possible to save the man in the mud.

"Do not, Ariosto . . ." the nearest of the men cautioned him.

But already Lodovico was pulling off his scaled guarnacca. It was a cool night and he was half soaked. "Hold my feet," he ordered tersely.

Two of the Cicora glanced at each other as if to disavow any idea this clearly deranged foreigner might profess.

"If that is your wish," the man beside him assented dubiously.

"I'll need one man on each leg," he went on, ignoring the protestations that rose from the warriors. "Hold them firmly, and if I tell you to pull, then pull me as hard as you can away from the mud." He did not wait any longer, but dropped to his knees and began to stretch out in the direction of the man who was by now deeper than his waist in the hideous bog. Carefully Lodovico slithered forward until he could feel the consistency of the mud change to a treacherous, jelly-like, smooth and unstable surface. He stopped at once and lay spread-eagled on the clammy mud.

"Ariosto." The Cicora who had spoken to him before sounded impossibly distant, as if speaking over miles of open water instead of two arm lengths of marsh.

"My feet!" Lodovico shouted, and murmured a brief prayer that the warriors would do as he told them. "Hang on. Now!"

The Cicora obeyed him, reluctantly.

The next maneuver, he knew, was the most difficult and the most essential. If he failed in it, he would not only lose the man flailing at the air not far from him, but he might be trapped the same way himself. He clutched his guarnacca, and, holding the cuff of one sleeve firmly in his hand, he swung the rest of the garment so that it might reach out to the man.

At first the garment fell short, but, undaunted, Lodovico mustered his strength to try again. He felt his skin growing cold from the wet that had soaked through his shirt and hose and calzebrache. He tossed the guarnacca again and almost lost his hold on it. He could hear the men behind him mutter among themselves, and it seemed as if the grip on one of his ankles lessened.

"Hold fast!" he shouted and swung the guarnacca with all his might.

The garment arched through the air, the metallic scales shining in the muted light from the Cicora's lantern. It fell swift and true, the cuff of the sleeve landing within reach of the man caught in the mud.

The Cicora gasped and one of them uttered words that, though Lodovico did not understand them, could only be an oath. "We are holding you," the leader of the group assured Lodovico, and the tightness of the hands on his knees and ankles attested eloquently to this.

"You," Lodovico said to the trapped man, not allowing himself to be distracted from his purpose by the enthusiasm of the men behind him. "You must take the end of the sleeve, just there." He waited, tense, while the man scrabbled for the cuff. His chest was growing icy from the dampness. "Have you got it yet?"

The man nodded frantically, and rasped out a few garbled words. "He has it," the spokesman of the group interpreted.

"Very well," Lodovico said, deciding that it would be best for the man in the mud to hear the instructions plainly and in his own language. "Tell him that I am going to start to pull him toward me. I will pull very slowly at first. Tell him that he must do nothing. All that is necessary is that he maintain his hold on the sleeve. Be certain he understands."

The Cicora relayed this, and there was an anxious burst of words from the trapped man. "He says that he is still sinking."

"I am aware of that," Lodovico responded as calmly as he could. "Tell him that it is not important and that it will not be for long."

The man did as he was told, then said to Lodovico, "What must we do now?"

"Hold me until I tell you otherwise. Do not let me slip." It was perilous now, he realized. The first tugs were the most difficult, and the most essential. If the mud had not gripped him too completely, it would be a routine matter to pull him from it. Lodovico knew that it was senseless to jerk at the guarnacca. It would not help the trapped man and it might tear the sleeves off the garment. He drew the sleeve toward him until he felt the cloth grow taut, then he began slowly increasing the pressure. "Don't let me move!" he ordered the men holding him. He felt the first, slight shift that told him the man was no longer sinking. Lodovico took heart and dragged on the guarnacca with more force than he had dared use at first.

The trapped man shouted something, shook his head wildly and tried to scramble out of the mud.

"No!" Lodovico cried out, and felt himself start to slip toward that ominous stretch of quivering dampness. "Hang on!"

There were frantic hands on him and a hubble of voices.

Lodovico slid a little farther and he felt his elbows start to sink, a gentle, seductive plucking from the ravenous, deadly marsh. Then he very nearly released the cuff he held. He could hear the trapped man shriek terribly, but it was a temptation that came from his fear. To sink down in that! Only the knowledge that he would condemn the man on the other end of the guarnacca to just such a hideous death kept his fingers closed tightly on the fabric. He had stopped moving now, but for the sliding of his elbows. "Do you have me?" he called, glad that he could keep his words steady.

"Yes," came the prompt answer, from a voice that was strained and unnaturally high.

"Good. Now, tell that man that he must not move again. He must lie still. If he moves again, I don't know whether I'll be able to pull him out." He gradually pulled the guarnacca taut again while the Cicora explained to his trapped friend what had been said. "Are you certain that he will not move?" He asked the question in trepidation. He doubted if he could sustain another such disruption.

"He will lie still," the man behind him said with cold authority.

"Excellent." He wrapped the end of the sleeve more tightly around his hands. "We try again." The sweat on his brow was as gelid and slimy as the mud around him, but Lodovico hardly noticed it. All his concentration went into the strength of his arms, of that steady pressure that would mean the difference between life and death to the horrified Cicora warrior in the sucking mud. His breath hissed over his clenched teeth as he strove to keep up the hauling force.

First there was a sound like a kiss, then another,

more like a belch. The jellylike surface of the marsh shuddered, and the trapped man began to reappear. His hands were locked in the sleeve and his face was set in a grimace worse than the rictus of death.

At last the man was out as far as his hips and Lodovico, seeing this, yelled with all the energy left in him: *"Pull!"*

The Cicora who held him obeyed at once. They dragged him back, over the mud and marsh grass, towing him and their comrade away from the mud and well onto the solid ground, coming to rest only when Lodovico's shin bounced against an exposed tree root.

The man who had been trapped lay on the ground, his knees drawn up to his chest. He shook as if gripped by ague and in the feeble light of the lantern, his skin appeared to be the color of slate.

A commotion nearby attracted the attention of the little group before Lodovico could suggest ways in which the rescued man might be revived. There was a clatter of breaking branches and twigs trod underfoot, and then a large company of men burst upon the scene.

First of their number was Massamo Fabroni, his wide face shiny with sweat and worry. Immediately behind him came Falcone, who, judging from his well-soaked leggings, had just returned from catching ducks himself. Lodovico could also make out Nebbiamente's benign features, and Lungobraccio's distinctive armor.

"Ariosto!" Falcone shouted, and hurried forward.

In the next moment, everyone began to speak, and after the cacophony had crescendoed unbearably, Lodovico shouted for quiet. "There is a man hurt here!" He raised his arms as he shouted and now, he saw that his shirt was caked with mud. Looking down, he had to laugh. "Nome del Dio," he said. "I look as if I had just crawled out of the grave."

"That isn't humorous," Falcone snapped.

"Of course it is. It is only when you cannot laugh that the joke is gone." He turned toward the man huddled on the ground. "This man knows that better than any of you, but he came too close to be able to laugh. He's a very brave soldier." Lodovico went down on one knee beside the man. "It is over," he said gently, and tried to pry the straining hands from the sleeve of his guarnacca.

"We foolishly had not brought our nets," the Cicora who had spoken to Lodovico was saying to Falcone. "When we were returning from the hunt, we grew careless and Accettafosco was caught by the death-well."

The rest of the Cicora party, hearing this, added their impressions, and then let the man continue. "We were at a loss, for in the dark we did not know how far it was safe to venture without being similarly trapped."

"Accettafosco," Lodovico said quietly to the fallen man, "you are safe. You are free."

"If it were not for Ariosto, surely our comrade would already be hunting with his ancestors. While we debated among ourselves how best to proceed, this good man had stripped off his garment and was crawling toward Accettafosco." At this confession, he looked abashed.

The men with Massamo and Falcone stared at Lodovico as he rose from the prostrate figure. "I know I am a fright, covered with mud as I am," he said with a hesitant smile, "but I trust you will excuse me." He looked at all the warriors gathered in the narrow clearing. "Accettafosco must be bathed and warmed, and I would like the same for myself. And," he added diffidently, "if one of you would be kind enough—though I would not blame you for refusing—to lend me a cloak. I am soaked through and I'm quite cold."

Falcone signaled imperiously. "Any man here would be honored to have you accept his cloak." He turned to the Cicora warrior. "Nettocchio, I charge you with the task of caring for Accettafosco. See that he is bathed at once. We will march at midnight, so he must be ready by then." As he rapped out these instructions, he drew his own cloak from around his shoulders.

"My Prince," Lodovico said as it was held out for him, "I cannot. It will be ruined."

"Take it, take it," Falcone insisted before turning to those who had accompanied him and Massamo Fabroni. "I have heard mutterings from some of you, whispers that we are not to trust the Italians who fight beside us. There are those of you who think that they would abandon us at the first real danger. Is there any of you who believe that now?" His piercing eyes challenged them all to answer. "Come, I give you the opportunity." He extended his hand as if offering consent to any who came forth. "No one? Not one of you thinks that Ariosto is a fraud and a coward? Yet I have heard those words, I thought. How was it I was so misled?"

Lodovico felt a great humility possess him. He held Falcone's cloak in front of him, staring at the fine doeskin and splendid ornaments on it. He felt that his presence sullied it, and turned to Massamo. "My friend, may I have your cape?"

The Lanzi captain goggled. "A Prince's cape is better than mine," he sputtered.

"But I am a soldier, not a Prince," Lodovico pointed out with a gentle smile. "Your cape is more fitting."

Falcone began an amazed protest, but Lodovico handed back the beautiful cloak. "If, at the end of the battle, you wish me to have it, then give it to me. For the test of valor will be passed and we will be wholly aware of whether such an honor is merited."

Reluctantly, Falcone took his cape. "It will be as you wish. At the end of the battle, if we are both still alive, it will be yours."

Lodovico smiled gratefully at the Cérocchi prince. "I thank you, Falcone." He was already sliding Massamo's cape about his shoulders. "Soldiers' capes endure much abuse, and this will make little difference." Then, quite suddenly, he wiped his hands as clean as he could on the sides of his thighs, then put one hand on Falcone's shoulder, the other on Massamo's. "Look at us," he said, amusement glinting in his fine chestnut eyes. "What foe can overcome men like you?"

"Or like you?" both men responded at once, and, all three caught in the heartening glow of brotherhood, they went together through the crowd out of the clearing by the marsh, accompanied by the cheers of their men and the muffled quacking of ducks.

La Realtà

Amid the gorgeous velvets and brocades, the man was conspicuous for the absolute simplicity of his white woolen lucco. Carmelo di Lozza walked the length of the banquet hall of the Palazzo Pitti, looking straight ahead, apparently unaware of the susurrus of whispered speculation around him. He was not more than twenty-five; his hair was clipped raggedly short to demonstrate his humility and renunciation of worldly vanities. Yet what there was of his hair was flaxen blond and it glistened like a halo. His face was as aloof and as beautiful as a Botticelli saint, and his eyes were deep, serene pools of cerulean blue.

"Why doesn't he complete the allusion and wear a crown of thorns?" a voice in the crowd sniggered loudly.

From his place by the sideboard where he was pouring wine for Margaret Roper, Damiano spoke sharply. "I have given instructions to you all that there will be no disrespect. If you cannot abide by that, you must leave." He let his voice drop back to normal conversational levels, though in the sudden quiet it carried throughout the hall. "There you are, Margharita. Italia Federata has no finer vintage to offer you."

Margaret was already flushed and the rosy hue deepened. "I am sure it is superb."

"God rewards true faith," Damiano responded impishly. "I trust our vintners can do as well." He was resplendent tonight in a long farsetto of sea-green silken damask over narrow, knee-length slashed Venetians. Two years before, the high Spanish ruffs had been all the rage, but since Clemente had put Spain under interdict, the fashion had changed and now Damiano showed himself at its forefront with a wide, ruffled collar of French lace. His silk leggings were held by embroidered garters fastened below the knee, and he was shod in soft, duck-billed slippers. He allowed Carmelo di Lozza to catch his attention at last.

"I was summoned," di Lozza said. He had a beautiful voice, as well, and he was clever enough to use it.

"Yes." Damiano regarded him steadily. "I've heard amazing things about you, di Lozza."

"And I of you," was the answer.

Damiano studied the man more closely. "What am I to infer from that remark?" He indicated the impressive gathering. "I have no secrets from these people—and could not have even if I desired a few—and anything you might say to me in private can as well be said here."

Carmelo di Lozza reluctantly looked around. "I would not change my answer for the convenience of your followers, de' Medici. I am only a tool in the hands of God." He cast his eyes down. "You cannot awe me with your fine company and your riches and your luxurious viands. I have seen the flight of angels, and I know that earth has nothing to compare to it."

"No doubt," Damiano agreed. "We do the best we can, however." He motioned to Lodovico, who stood off to the side. "Come here, my friend. I want you to listen to this saintly man."

Lodovico obeyed unwillingly. When he had been told
the day before of the plan for this evening, he had
found the whole idea distasteful, and now that the confrontation was underway, he recoiled from it. He
could not bring himself to defy Damiano in this place,
with his enemies all around him. "I am here, Primàrio,"
he said as he touched Damiano's shoulder.

"I am glad of it, good poet." He lifted his voice so
that it would carry through the drone of conversation.
"You are a man of genius and wisdom, Lodovico. There
is a special gift of vision that is the blessing and the
curse of poets, and you have it in abundance. And
therefore, you will be more knowledgeable than I, than
most of us here, in this case. Until now you have had
only your Muse to counsel you, but now the choirs of
heaven may add their efforts to your inspiration." He
turned back to di Lozza. "That is one of the many
things I have heard about you, that you speak with the
angels. Do not, I pray you, disappoint us."

Inwardly, Lodovico shrank from the sarcasm Damiano heaped on the man in white. He wanted to tell
il Primàrio that it was a tactical error to alienate this
self-proclaimed visionary, but he had listed all his objections already and knew that it was fruitless to do so
again. He muttered, "I want nothing from this man."

"Lodovico!" Damiano admonished him. "Who else
may we rely on, if not you? My cousin Cosimo is not
here, so we have no officer of the Church who is of
high enough rank to judge the merit of this man. Without the Cardinale, we have to improvise, and you yourself have told me before that poets, saints, and madmen
are all brothers."

Di Lozza was gazing at Lodovico, and for an instant
his candid blue eyes narrowed in scrutiny. "So you are
the idolatrous poet Ariosto."

"I wouldn't describe myself that way," Lodovico answered good-naturedly. He was determined not to be offended by any challenge di Lozza offered him. "I am a
good son of Holy Mother Church, or I try to be."

"That is not good enough. It is easy to say in this

company, in this room." Carmelo di Lozza permitted his gaze to travel through the room, over the guests and the furniture and the paintings and the statues. "Surrounded by luxury, supported in your vices, you confess with pride and then you commit them afresh, supported and encouraged by the man you call il Primàrio."

"Vice? Luxury?" Lodovico demanded, the unnecessary accusations stinging him. "This is the first new giornea I've had in five years. My wife and I live simply, because we must. Yet I know that I am fortunate. My patron is not a whimsical man, and he is generous. I am encouraged to write what I wish to write and not what he would like me to write. There are few poets who can say that. If you rebuke me for what you see as privilege, then remember that without this so-called privilege, I could not realize my art. If I had to break my back digging in the earth, or ruin my eyes weaving cloth, or wear out my learning attempting to teach recalcitrant children, then all I would ever have done is scribble a few lines that would be forgotten. But this man and this court offer me a haven, so that instead of a few sheaves of incomplete verses, I have now a body of works, of epics and plays and romances . . ." He was as astounded as the rest of the gathering at this outburst, and was not certain where it would lead.

Di Lozza cut him short. "These things in which you take pride are ornaments of Satan. You do not dedicate your work to the Glory of God. You say that you are supported. So would you be in a hermit's cell, in a cloister, but no, you must have worldly acclaim for your profane writings."

"That's not so!" Lodovico cried out because he feared that it was.

"Then it would be better for you to leave this place, this city, and live in obscurity rather than spend your time in creating lying tales of heathenish cowards for the delight of these degenerate wastrels." He said this calmly, with that strange composure that was as distinctive as his clothing.

"My tales aren't lying. They're romances, fictions . . ." His ire was rising and he was aware that in some subtle way this imposter in white was baiting him. He tried to recall all his good intentions, all the admonitions he had given Damiano on the benefits of tolerance, but none of them came to mind.

"Are they parables to show the Will of God? They are not." Di Lozza tucked his hands into his ample sleeves and gazed down at the intricate parquetry of the floor. "Why do I subject myself to this, to the shame and the ridicule of you impious villains?" A dreaminess stole over his features and he smiled slightly. "God, my God, You have mandated a task that fills me with trepidation. Guide me."

Lodovico was prepared to dispute further with di Lozza, but he felt Damiano's hand on his arm and heard a soft, restraining word in his ear.

Carmelo di Lozza sank to his knees and the banquet hall grew silent. The man in white was trembling and his head lolled back. His features were contorted now, as if in pain or ecstasy, and his breath was loud in his throat. "O God, O God, O God," he intoned.

One of the courtiers tittered nervously.

"Sin, sin, sin, all around me. Cleanse this place, I beseech You. The stench—ah! The chastening rod and scourge must be felt. There must be good men to lead, men of God, not the world." Suddenly di Lozza began to weep. "I mourn for you, Firenze. Lost, benighted, led into the trackless wastes of degradation." There was spittle on his lips and his beautiful voice was harsh, high and grating. "There must be one to lead them back. Your Princes on earth, my God. Send us Your Prince to be our Prince!" With this last frantic plea, Carmelo di Lozza toppled to his side, shaking, sobbing, his face unrecognizable.

Damiano stared down at him. "Who has told him this? Who has made him believe?" He spoke softly though it was hardly necessary in the eruption of sound that filled the banquet hall. He beckoned to Lodovico. "When he comes to his senses, take him into the withdrawing room upstairs, the one with the two Verocchio bronzes. I'll see that you're not disturbed."

"I don't want to talk to him," Lodovico said, averting his eyes. "I know I wasn't supposed to get angry, but when he said my work is lies, well . . ." He was abashed, realizing how completely he had disappointed Damiano. His intentions had been good, he told himself defensively. But he had been provoked beyond anything acceptable.

"You pleased me very much, Lodovico," Damiano said candidly. "I had not expected that—of either of you." He glanced swiftly around the hall. "I had better have the musicians start playing dance tunes or there will be chaos here." He was about to move away when Lodovico stopped him with a question.

"Primàrio, what if he will not talk to me? After what passed between us . . ." He gave a helpless jerk to his shoulders.

"After what passed between you," Damiano said with mirthless laughter, "he will undoubtedly want the last word." He moved away through the crowd and stopped only to talk with Margaret Roper before motioning to one of the servants.

Lodovico squatted down beside the twitching di Lozza. He noticed that no one in the crowded hall was willing to come near them. With a sigh he watched the distorted, angelic features, waiting for the seizure to pass.

Andrea Benci held the door to the withdrawing room open. "I hope that you will not be long," he said to Lodovico, making a point of ignoring di Lozza.

"We will be as long as is necessary, but no longer," Lodovico assured him, and waited while Carmelo di Lozza went through the door. He could not resist turning to the old courtier and adding, "As il Primàrio's secretary, doubtless you have other duties to attend to."

"Doubtless," Benci snapped. He glanced once at di Lozza and muttered a few words under his breath.

"Have the understeward supply your wants," he added before slamming the door closed.

Di Lozza had gone to the window and stood looking out on the evening. The last of the sunset had faded from the sky and only a blush in the western sky hinted that the day had just ended. He refused to acknowledge Lodovico's presence.

Lodovico selected one of the four chairs and sat in it. There were candles and a lantern to light the room, which pleased him. He would have liked to have something to read, but there was nothing in the chamber but statues and paintings, so he contented himself with staring at a *Flight into Egypt*. In this light and at this distance, the edges were softly blurred and the color stood out boldly.

"Paintings," di Lozza announced, "are idolatrous."

"Perhaps they are, if you are seeking idols." He said it mildly, more to indicate he had heard than to make comment, and so he was surprised when di Lozza rounded on him in fury.

"I tell you that they are damnable! They are tools of the Devil! They are sent to confuse the people into error and sin!" At each of these statements, he struck his fist into the opposite palm.

"But the saints have said that there is much that painting can teach us," Lodovico said, hoping to calm the man.

"They were in error. God despises those excesses. He needs nothing more than the earth and sky to teach us His lessons. The rest is vanity. Worldly men don't understand that. Only men of God know. Men of God see beyond the world." He shook his head. "If a man's servants speak against him, if they give warning in their hearts, it must be God at work. Loyal servants defend their masters, as priests defend God. If there is no reform . . ."

"If there is no reform," Lodovico prompted when it seemed that di Lozza had lost track of what he was saying.

"Savonarola tried it, and he was sent away as punishment. He was a willing, ardent servant of God who cared nothing for the world, who sought to end the corruption around him. A Godless Pope and a reprobate Prince sent him to Saxony. Yet he was not silenced. I will not be silenced. You may send me away, but still the servants will know that the master is degenerate, and they will accomplish . . ." Quite suddenly he stopped. "You don't believe me, do you?"

"No," Lodovico answered gently.

Di Lozza accepted this mutely. He began to walk around the room, pausing at each statue and picture to look at it. His expression was that of a man looking into a charnel house and his nostrils were pinched by the spiritual stench.

As the man in white made his censorious tour of the room's treasures, Lodovico watched him. What was it about di Lozza that disturbed him so much? Was it simply that he had attacked Lodovico's work, which was more painful than if he had attacked with swords and cannons? He had to admit that was probably the case. Yes, Lodovico told himself, when it came to his work he was touchy as a bear in spring. He tried to be philosophical and find amusement in his antics, but he could not. He could laugh at the unkempt state of his beard and the run in his silken leggings, but he was unable to detach himself from the words he scribbled on paper. Words on paper! Ephemeral things, he thought in a stern way, but the rush of his pulse denied it. He stared at di Lozza, forcing himself to concentrate on the man, to put his inner debate aside. There was something he must do. He cleared his throat.

"Tell me—you said that when a man's servants speak against him it bodes ill."

"And so it does," di Lozza affirmed. "It is the part of the servant to be loyal to an honest and Godly master."

"Yet you said that there were servants who spoke against their master. Did you mean il Primàrio when you said the master?" He knew the answer, but he could

think of no other way to get the man to discuss what
he knew.

"I meant all those who are without true faith and
who plunder the Kingdom of God with their blasphe-
my." He had stopped beside a small, gilded Madonna,
a fresh-faced, placid young woman in a garden dan-
dling a sober-miened infant on her knee. The work was
by Fra Filippo Lippi and regarded as a great treasure. Carmelo di Lozza perused it, his lips tightening.
"A disgrace. The man was no more a monk than you
are. He littered all Toscana with his bastards! But he
dared to paint Maria in all her purity."

Lodovico wanted to suggest that it might have been
the only way Lippi could experience purity, in that
serenely stupid and vacant woman. He turned the con-
ceit over in his mind and thought it was worth exploring. Innocence and ignorance were often assumed
to be the same thing, he noted, and yet they could not
be. Then he remembered what he had to do. "Were you
speaking in metaphor about servants, or have actual
servants been talking to you?" he persisted.

"I am no priest. I hear no confession. But there are
those who are troubled in soul, and they come to me
when they can find no succor in this venal city. They
tell me that the churches are stuffed with pomp but the
Majesty of God is missing. I have said that it is because
the state is guided by an ambitious and worldly man.
The churches are tainted with the desecrations of the
civic leaders."

"What servants?" Lodovico asked, determined to
stay on the subject.

"Knowing ones," di Lozza answered smugly. "I am
not so foolish as to listen to every complaint as valid,
or to assume that a dissatisfied scullery maid has legitimate cause for her protests, but highly-placed men, who
are close to . . ." A crafty look came into his eyes and
he looked away from Lodovico. "It does not become
me to speak of it, for though I have no vows to keep,
yet I regard what has been said to me as protected by
the seal of confession."

"Then why tell me at all?" He knew the answer, even if di Lozza did not, and it disappointed him. Up until that moment, di Lozza, in his own way, had been boasting. He did not tell of his great deeds, but he did revel in his influence. So Carmelo di Lozza was a fraud, whether he recognized it himself or not. It was an effort for Lodovico to contain his indignation. Here was a man posing as saintly, but who was as engrossed in manipulations and the wielding of temporal power as any of the greedy courtiers in the banquet hall. He wanted to grab the pleated front of di Lozza's lucco and shake him as he would a disobedient child. What caused Lodovico the greatest distress was the realization that part of him had wanted di Lozza to be genuine, to be nothing but a misguided but well-intentioned man in the throes of a religious passion. Lodovico felt cheated and sullied.

Di Lozza had picked up a small ceramic figure, a study by the great, irascible Buonarroti. He turned it over in his fingers, his face intent. "He is at Roma, is he not? With the Pope?"

"Yes," Lodovico answered. "Clemente has known him since they were boys. Buonarroti is older, of course."

"He has done much for the Church, hasn't he? He's not a priest, either. I have heard the Cardinale say that he would like to see more sacred works in Firenze." He put the figure back on the narrow table.

Lodovico, recalling the terrible interview he had witnessed, had nothing to say. He looked down and discovered that there was a rip in the front of his giornea, very small, but still a rip. How had it happened? he wondered, thinking back over the evening and the one previous occasion he had worn the garment. He could not account for the tear, but there it was, reproaching him. He pressed the rent together with his fingers, as if the cloth could heal itself.

Di Lozza turned away and went back to the window,

refusing to speak again until the understeward knocked on the door, more than an hour later.

Margaret Roper stared at the Papal seals on the letter handed to her. Giulio de' Medici had been taught penmanship by the finest calligaphers in Firenze and a simple request looked like poetry in his elegant hand. She had kissed the wax impressions under his signature when it was given her, but could not bring herself to read the missive.

"My once-removed first cousin wishes you to come to Roma," Damiano explained. "He has sent me his instructions. I gather that your father wrote to His Holiness and told him what he was doing in Russia. Because Henry is not likely to receive Sir Thomas kindly, the Pope is extending his hospitality to your entire family until such time as all of you are properly welcomed in England."

Lodovico, looking up from the papers Margaret had given him, drew in his breath sharply. Henry Tudor had thrown down the glove when he had divorced his wife Katherine and married Mistress Boleyn and now the Pope was taking up the challenge. Open defiance of the Church would not be tolerated. Lodovico glanced at Damiano, but il Primàrio's face was a polite mask and he could read nothing there.

"But why?" Margaret Roper asked finally, the very question that burned in Lodovico.

"He says that he wishes to honor your father and his family for your steadfast faith. You are an example to Catholics everywhere. It's in the letter." Damiano had folded his arms over his chest.

Lodovico's apartments in Palazzo Pitti were on the south side of the north wing, three pleasant, light rooms overlooking the terrace and the enormous gardens. Damiano was adding a third orchard higher up the slope and there were dusty tracks through the flowers to the incomplete plantation. It was a warm day, with early autumn sunlight flooding through Firenze like the gilt rays in Fra Angelico's paintings. Until the messenger had arrived, Lodovico and Margaret had been enjoying what they still called a lesson, but had become an erudite conversation. The arrival of the messenger changed that.

Margaret bent her head over the page and studied it as if she had no knowledge of Latin whatever, and was trying to find one recognizable word. "I don't understand," she said slowly and looked toward Damiano for an explanation.

Damiano refused to meet her eyes. He strolled to the nearest window. "His Holiness doesn't like Henry Tudor usurping his authority. He feels the King of England is overstepping himself." He stared out into the afternoon. "I think that he has every intention of settling the question of Papal supremacy once and for all. Spain has been a necessary evil, and the German States, well, no Pope has known what to do with the German States. But England, that is another matter. If England's rebellion is tolerated, then who might be next? France? He can't allow that."

"But how will this serve him?" Margaret demanded, then flushed. "I am sorry, Primàrio. It may be that we are an embarrassment to you. My father implied as much in one of his letters . . ." In her confusion, her Italian faltered and she spoke in English. "He told me that your situation is awkward with Clement."

"I gather from what Lodovico has told me that Sir Thomas was very much troubled by the differences between my Papal cousin and me." He picked up the letter. "It is not only the King of England he is asserting his power over, but the Primàrio of Italia Federata, as well. Church and state don't run in harness well in Italia." There was a hurt in Damiano's eyes as he looked from Margaret to Lodovico. "Neither is willing to match pace with the other."

"But His Holiness is a Medici, isn't he?" Margaret asked, bewildered.

"Yes, and a member of the senior branch, but a bastard. There is the difficulty. Within the family, he is in a slightly subordinate position because of the illegitimacy, though he is of my father's generation. Yet, because he is of the senior line, he is in a slightly superior position to, say, my cousin Cosimo, and Cosimo is his inferior within the Church as well. No doubt there are times Giulio would be happy to see Cosimo in my place." He waved his hand in dismissal. "Never mind, Margharita. You and your husband may remain here, if that is your desire, but I fear I must comply with the Pope's request and send at least part of your family to Roma."

Margaret smoothed the soft fabric of her dress. She had adopted the Italian fashions entirely now, and her light-brown hair shone under an embroidered cap. "I would not want to be separated from my stepmother and my sisters and brother. I am certain that William would prefer we stay together, as well. Forgive me, Premier. We have had nothing but kindness from you . . ."

"Your father might dispute that," Damiano said quietly.

"He understood," Lodovico put in. "He assured me he did, and saw that it must be for the best."

"Did he, my friend?" Damiano put his hand on Margaret's shoulder. "You're a daughter worthy of your father, Margharita. I can find it in myself to envy him you."

Margaret had been at the Italian court long enough to know how things stood with Damiano and his sons, and so she did not answer at once. "It is my fortune to be very like my father," she said at last, picking her words with care. "I think that another man might have found me to be a hoyden and disobedient. God was kind to us." She folded her hands and assumed the appearance of tranquillity, though her eyes burned.

Whatever Damiano might have said was stopped as Alessandra bustled through the door. She was carrying a small basket of mending, and her hair was escaping from the netting that covered the coiled braids. "Ah!" she cried when she saw Damiano. "Next time you must warn me."

There was an uneasy moment while Lodovico shifted in his chair, and then he shrugged. "I didn't know myself until Damiano walked through the door. It was a usual lesson afternoon . . ."

"Your lessons!" Alessandra beamed at Margaret. "I am so pleased that they have continued. I was afraid that, even back in Firenze, with Virginio off in Paris, I would never see a young face or hear educated conversation. I was afraid that I would have to pass my time among the women who speak of nothing but servants and sewing and trinkets. But having you here." She sighed happily and settled into a high-backed chair near the window. "I'll try not to interrupt. Do go on." She had already opened the basket and was selecting a thread from one of several wound on wooden spools.

"We weren't doing lessons," Lodovico said when Damiano and Margaret had refused to speak. "There has been a message from the Pope."

"Nothing disagreeable, I hope?" Alessandra asked. "His Holiness is a little high-handed at times." She chuckled. "Do you remember the time when he came to a governing convocation with half the Papal court? High Mass every morning in Santa Maria del Fiore, full rituals in all the churches, and all the whores in the city tottering between bed and confessional for most of April."

Both Lodovico and Damiano smiled and nodded, but Margaret Roper was scandalized. "How can you speak of the Pope in this way?" she demanded, starting to rise.

"He's family, Margharita," Damiano explained patiently. "And the Papal court is well enough known in la Federazione to have rid most of us of our illusions about it. In England it may be deemed that these are wise and holy men, wrestling Satan for the benefit of the souls of the devout, but in Italia, we know that power is a more potent intoxicant than wine, and that the Church draws ambitious men as the moon draws the tides."

"But the Pope is the voice of God on earth," Mar-

garet protested. She touched the golden crucifix at her
throat as if to ward off danger.

"He is also Giulio de' Medici in a nest of della
Roveres and Farneses and Colonnas, all of whom have
reason to want the Papacy for themselves, and all of
whom wield enormous temporal power." Damiano
gazed down at her. "The Church, my dear, owns a
great deal. She has land and ships and houses and treasure. She is very rich in a way that no nation can be rich.
A nation must send soldiers to protect her people, must
concern herself with their lives, but the Church need
only promise the hope of Paradise and collect tithes as
tributes."

"That's heresy!" Margaret got to her feet. "I have
read the writings of Clement. He is a good man, worthy
of his elevation and firm in his faith." Her voice had
gone up as her excitement grew.

"How much I wish," Damiano sighed as he took
Margaret's hand, "that I had only to make elegant
speeches on valor and honor to have those virtues appear in the men around me. His Holiness discusses
faith, and his followers kneel in awe and ask nothing
more than the words. He is protected by his pomp as
surely as he would be by stone walls and incantations."

Alessandra shook her finger at il Primàrio. "You're
becoming a cynic, de' Medici." Her hands were full of
white linen and her words were muffled because of the
pins held in her mouth.

"No, Donna Alessandra," he said in a tone so quiet
with pain that the room was still, "I am not cynical—
I'm frightened." He released Margaret's hand. "I will
miss you, Margharita. More than you know, I would
like to take issue with my Papal cousin over you and
your family, but it's not possible. The risks are too
great." He turned away and motioned to Lodovico.
"Spare me a little of your time, good poet. I need to
clear my mind of politics."

"Go on," Alessandra said, motioning her husband toward the door. "Margharita and I don't have much

chance to talk together, and I'm sure you would not want to hear what we say about you."

Passing her chair, Lodovico patted Alessandra's arm fondly. "You're very good to me," he whispered.

"Go on, go on," she ordered him brusquely, smiling with pleasure.

The road along the back of the extensive gardens was little more than a gardener's track; dusty, rutted and maintained only by the passage of gardeners to and from the newly planted orchard. Damiano walked slightly ahead of Lodovico, occasionally holding an untrimmed branch so that it would not snap back at Lodovico. "I hope that we won't be overheard here," Damiano said when they had gone some distance from the Palazzo Pitti.

"Trees and bushes have no ears," Lodovico said, thinking it was silly to put it that way. He watched Damiano, concerned. The line between il Primàrio's brows was cut deeper, more permanently into his forehead and the downward turn of his mouth was becoming habitual. His laughter was shorter, harsher than before and there was a restlessness about him that increased daily. Lodovico had thought at first that he had imagined the furtiveness that had come into the Firenze court, but he realized now that it was more severe than he had known. Here in the warm afternoon sun with the wind full of rosemary and blown roses it was easy to forget the treachery that soiled everything, like a lingering odor of decay.

Damiano stepped to the side of the path, down a little-used and partially-overgrown series of stones that gave access to a little creekbed, dry now, but in winter filled by rain. Balanced on two stones was a weathered plank that served as a bridge when one was needed. Heedless of his pleated linen farsetto cut in the short-waisted Flemish style, with rosettes for buttons, he sank onto the wide, dusty board, his melon hose and canions scraping on the splinters. "Come. Sit beside me. I don't imagine we'll be disturbed here."

Lodovico obeyed, listening to the board groan with some trepidation. "Why must we be so secretive?" he asked. He could feel his new silk leggings snag and run as the plank bent a little under their weight.

"Do I seem unreasonable to you, to sneak away from my own house and cower in the back garden? My house is filled with spies and the friends of my enemies." He kicked at the gravel in the creekbed. "I don't know who among them may be trusted. I thought I did once, but I am no longer certain."

It was foolish to deny this and Lodovico did not make the attempt. He fingered his wilting embroidered collar, searching his thoughts for words of comfort, and found none. "There has been more trouble?"

"Yes." Damiano stared at his rose-colored boots. "I've been trying for weeks to discover which of my staff are in the pay of my cousin, and so far I have found only three. Yet there have to be more. The contents of my letters from Sir Thomas are known to Cosimo and Foscari, and the letter I had from Sforza might as well have been cried through the streets." He rubbed his hands briskly, as if to rid them of dust. "I spoke with Margharita about this, and she has admitted that she has not been as careful with her father's letters as she might be. That is a remarkable woman," he went on in another voice. "I wish there were time to know her better. But my cousin has other plans, and I must accommodate him."

Never before had Lodovico heard such bitterness from Damiano. He shook his head in disbelief. "Can't you object?"

"And play into Cosimo's hands? What I told Margharita was the truth. With Cosimo in my place, Giulio would have control of all la Federazione, and that's a great temptation. Italian armies could then be sent to quell the Spanish, and the French would have to cooperate. All that is needed is that I be gone. I have treaties and agreements with these countries. If I approach France for soldiers, Genova will secede from la Federazione. The Pope can force Genova to tolerate the situation, using the threat of excommunication if necessary. He can order the ships of Venezia and Napoli to sink all English vessels. He can cancel the importing agreements with the German States, all with the might of the Chair of San Piero. I can only appeal to reason and sense." He pushed himself off the board.

"Damiano," Lodovico said after a moment, "are you truly convinced it is hopeless?" He could feel the blood pound in his ears as he asked.

"No." He walked a few steps down the dry creekbed. "If I truly believed that the cause was lost, I would stand aside and let the old rivalries and feuds break out again. Italia at war would put half the Cardinales in Roma at one another's throats. Clemente would have no time for France or Spain or the German States. Italia would be fragmented into principalities and petty states again, and at the mercy of the rest of Europe. Cosimo could have Firenze then. I've lost my sons and my wife to this city, this country. How many friends do I have, aside from you? Benci? Margharita?"

"But you're doing nothing," Lodovico said. "What good is it to indulge in self-pity if it leads you to defeat?" He had not meant to be harsh with Damiano, for he sensed the suffering that festered in the man before him. The sharpness of his voice surprised him, and he was saddened by the coldness Damiano assumed.

"Self-pity? Does it seem that way?" As he turned away, he put his hands to his eyes. "Who is doing this, Lodovico? Who? Benci has his men everywhere. He brings me reports daily, and yet I am no closer to knowing than before. Must I beg you to listen to me? Then I beg you." Now his words were harsh. " I love la Federazione. If I were convinced my death would guarantee her survival, then I would die gratefully. I would," he vowed, dropping his hands to his side and meeting Lodovico's eyes unflinchingly. "But to have lost so much already and to lose la Federazione as well . . . Must it come to that? Dio mio, if I could only walk away from it. If I could watch it all and never know anguish."

Lodovico had not doubted Damiano's dedication or sincerity, but hearing him now, in this desolate place, he was moved by his friend's courage. It was not the valor of battle, but the unending refusal to be defeated that marked Damiano's struggle. For Damiano there was no glory, no trumpets and laurels, only the precarious survival of his beloved Federazione. He stood up and put his hand on Damiano's shoulder. "I'm not much of an ally. My mind is in the clouds more hours of the day than it is on this earth. I do not understand the devious ways of political men. But I will, I promise you with my soul, Damiano, do all that I can to aid you, and will stand by you as long as you will have me there."

Damiano put his hand over Lodovico's. "I could not wish for better beside me," he said, kissing Lodovico's cheeks as he would a belted and titled military commander.

La Fantasia

Pinpoints of light moved through the forest; a whispering, rustling, murmuring sibilation accompanied the light. The army of Nuova Genova, of Cérocchi, Pau Attan, Cicora, Cica Omini, Cesapichi, and Onaumanient with the men of Giagaia and Annouaigho was on its night march .

Falcone was in the van on foot, leading the magnificent sorrel charger he would ride in battle the next day. Beside him Lodovico marched, his hand holding Bellimbusto's reins. The hippogryph was anxious to take wing and occasionally pulled restively at his bridle. On the other side of Falcone, Massamo Fabroni led his destrier and two pack mules. He had donned his breastplate and had his sword buckled into place. Several paces behind them, six Cérocchi soldiers carried a litter in which rode their high priest, Cifraaculeo, silent and remote, lost in those reaches beyond the world and senses.

Lungobraccio was between the litter and Falcone, and he bore, as did many of the warriors, a basket of woven reeds in which a duck rested. So far the walk had been quiet. Messages were passed regularly down the ranks of warriors. These were given in murmured code words at specific intervals in the hope that such precautions would make it more difficult for the forces of Anatrecacciatore to penetrate what few defenses they had.

The ground had been rising gently for some time and the river marsh was left behind. Now the path grew steeper and there were outcroppings of stones that thrust up between the trees, blocking the advancing army. Falcone gestured for a halt and signaled for a hurried consultation with his captains. He stood with Lodovico while the word was passed, and was relieved when, shortly thereafter, the leaders of the fighting companies came silently through the night to hear him.

"We will have to go in single file, I fear," Falcone said. "Ariosto has suggested that we move in five columns. That way, no one man will be exposed to the full might of the enemy if we are discovered. We will also be able to move more swiftly in five columns than in one. We must be careful to see that our swordsmen are ahead of our spearmen, and that they are ahead of the archers. That way, if we must, we can take up our fighting positions without endangering our own men more than they are endangered already." He gave Lodovico a swift look and was pleased with the confirming nod. "Lungobraccio, you will take the southernmost column. Nembosanguinoso will have the next one. I will lead the middle column, Massamo Fabroni will be at the head of his own company of Lanzi, and Ariosto will take the northernmost column. We will have to be certain that there are ducks enough in each column, for it would be an easy thing for Anatrecacciatore to send his spies and reanimated dead among us while we are in columns. The ducks may be able to give us sufficient warning." He had kept his voice low as he gave his orders, and now his words dropped to a whisper. "Also, assign a priest and a wizard to be at the front and the rear of a line. What the ducks cannot perceive, they may be able to."

Lungobraccio turned his head toward the litter that bore Cifraaculeo. "And him? What of him?"

"We will carry him. It is a risk we cannot avoid," Falcone said, the worried expression on his handsome features at odds with the cool authority of his words. "If we leave him behind, he will be in great danger, from wild beasts as well as Anatrecacciatore. You say that he is vulnerable now, and I will not dispute it, but I would prefer to have him where I can see him than to leave him and not know what has become of him. He has power we overlook at our peril." The young Prince was standing very straight, his bone-and-bead breastplate shining faintly in the subdued light from the lanterns. He hooked his thumb around the hilt of the dagger at his waist.

"What if he is being used by Anatrecacciatore at this moment?" Nembosanguinoso growled under his breath.

"It's possible," Lodovico said, speaking up for the first time. "But both Nebbiamente and Lincepino say that such is not the case. Fumovisione has surrounded Cifraaculeo with charms and enchantments to protect him from any more of Anatrecacciatore's malice. If there were not a battle to fight, the wizards and priests would be able to save Cifraaculeo from the grip of the force that binds him now."

"I don't like it," Nembosanguinoso said forthrightly, and a few of the captains agreed with him.

"Neither do I," Falcone cut in. "We haven't the luxury of choice now. I will give orders that Cifraaculeo is to be carried in my column, so that if there is danger, I will bear the brunt of it, and I will have him in the middle of the line. It will be more difficult for changes to occur unnoticed if he is there."

As the lantern lights flickered, the captains looked at each other, and at last accepted the ruling of Falcone. Each voiced his assent, and each turned to pass word to his troops of the change in marching.

One man remained behind. He was the Cicora, Nettocchio, whose companion Accettafosco Lodovico had pulled from the sucking mud. He stood before Lodovico and Falcone, indecision on his face. "Prince, I have to ask this of you."

"What is it?" Falcone inquired, looking impatiently toward the huddled group of Cérocchi warriors waiting for him.

"This man Ariosto saved the life of my friend. Both of us would like to march with him. We know that you have every right to refuse this request, but I implore you to let us to do this. How else can we vindicate our honor, but to fight beside the man who has done so much for us?" He did not expect an answer to his question, for he knew that Falcone could not deny him.

"You have two more men for your column," Falcone told Lodovico after he had translated the request. "Nettocchio and Accettafosco want to fight with you. I advise you to take them. It's a matter of obligation. They wish to pay the debt they owe you."

Lodovico had understood a few words of the Cicora, and he weighed the problem. "There is the question of language," he said cautiously. "In battle I cannot wait for a translator to give them my orders." He stared hard at Nettocchio. "My orders will be in your tongue or in Italian. They . . ."

Nettocchio interrupted. "I know some Cérocchi. So

does Accettafosco. Simple orders are no problem. Put us with a few Cérocchi and we will do well enough."

When this had been explained, Lodovico considered again. "It may be possible."

It was Falcone who hit upon the solution. "I will give you four of my men as your guard. It will be a great tribute to them. We will have Nettocchio and Accettafosco come with them, and everyone will be satisfied. If you are satisfied."

"It is fine with me," Lodovico consented. "Have your men report to me as soon as possible. And, if you are willing, I would like to have Nebbiamente with my column."

"Not Fumovisione?" Falcone asked, surprised. "I thought you'd want . . ."

"Nebbiamente," Lodovico said firmly. "He is a strange one, no doubt, but I think that he see things the rest of us cannot. On the northernmost column, we may have need of his special gifts. And you will have to keep Fumovisione near Cifraaculeo or expose yourself to added hazard. There is no telling what Anatrecacciatore might try to do once he realizes what we're attempting." His smile was more of a courageous show of teeth than an expression of humor. "Let me have Nebbiamente. He will be better with us."

"As you wish," Falcone agreed, and motioned to Nettocchio. "You will have your chance. Come with me." Falcone nodded to Lodovico and turned away toward the waiting soldiers.

Shortly thereafter, Lodovico had moved to the north side of the army and was busy with the job of getting his column in order.

When the army had stopped at midday, it had regrouped while the meal was eaten and the captains conferred. Falcone had worried about the slowness of their progress, but Lodovico took a more heartening view of the matter.

"These are rough hills," he reminded the Cérocchi Prince, "and we have had to move more cautiously in this terrain. When moving in columns, progress is less apparent because the lines are strung out so far, yet, I assure you, we are doing well. One more range of hills and we will be at the valley where the warriors of flint and frost await us. By this time tomorrow we will all have tasted battle." He looked somber. "Do well to think of that, my friend. Battle is the great test, the true test of courage. If you are to lead us, you must be ready for the fight."

"I am," Falcone said without hesitation. "I long for this battle, to face at last this enemy who has been so deadly. It will give me true satisfaction to see his soldiers bleed and die."

"Do these warriors of Anatrecacciatore bleed?" Lodovico asked.

"Or die? I will find out presently." His mouth was set in a firm line, and he began to walk toward the fire where a meal of trout and pork simmered on spits.

Lodovico hung back. "If you do not object, Falcone, I want to take to the air. It would be bad for us to encounter the warriors before we are prepared for battle, and I think it may be possible that we're being observed more closely than we realize."

"Do as you must," Falcone declared, and then softened his brusqueness. "I welcome any intelligence you bring us, for to be truthful, I am apprehensive about our position. An hour ago Cifraaculeo screamed out once and Fumovisione declared that we had crossed a barrier."

"What sort of barrier?" Lodovico wondered, and resolved to speak to Nebbiamente about it before he took Bellimbusto aloft.

"He could not tell me." Falcone's eyes grew hard.

The power of fear, Lodovico thought, and in his heart he prayed that God would lend him courage and fortitude to face whatever lay ahead. He no longer had his guarnacca with the metal scales, for the sucking mud had ruined it, but he had donned a breastplate and hoped fervently that it would be enough. He could not expect Bellimbusto to carry more weight if he were to be able to fly in battle. "Perhaps if you ask him again, or ask the others?"

"Perhaps." Falcone walked away toward the fire.

Nebbiamente stood beside Bellimbusto, his hand caressing the feathered neck. "He is a wonder," he said to Lodovico without turning around.

"That he is," Lodovico concurred. "It is one of the great joys of my life that I have had such a mount."

"Surely there are other joys?" Nebbiamente protested gently, his long, thin arms moving expressively. "One who has seen as much as you have must have learned . . ."

Lodovico's brilliant eyes filled with stern amusement. "You've traveled in realms far stranger than any I have known, and what have you learned: to enjoy the few treasures of life, as I have. You value honor and the love of comrades. Bellimbusto is such a comrade."

"An excellent point," Nebbiamente said rather vaguely. "You will fly today?"

"Yes. We must know how much nearer the warriors of flint and frost have come. Your special sight would be useful now, good man. I need every advantage I can find." He moved around the hippogryph to check the girths and bridle. "Any protection your skill might bestow would be most welcome."

There was an amused turn to Nebbiamente's lips. "I understand that your god is known for his jealousy. Might not my aid work against you in his eyes?"

Lodovico had pulled a portion of dried meat from his ample wallet, and this he offered to Bellimbusto, who took it in one gilded claw and nibbled at it daintily. "There are those who think that, certainly, but I hope that the other opinion is correct. It is also said of God that He is merciful and forgiving. I doubt that He could object to my arming myself with all the protection available."

"In that case . . ." Nebbiamente stood back and made a few, peculiar passes with his hands. A dreamy look had come over his face and he whispered bits of words as he began to circle Bellimbusto and Lodovico. His smile became beatific.

Bellimbusto raised his head from the morsel clasped in his talons and gave Nebbiamente a long, even stare. Then he finished the meat and lowered his head, as if in tribute. His bronze-and-black wings were held bowed out from his body and his large eyes glittered.

"He approves of whatever you're doing," Lodovico observed, and saw that Nebbiamente had not heard him. He shrugged and reached for the reins. Then, with a lithe and graceful movement, he swung up into the high-fronted saddle. From this vantage point he looked down at the sweet-faced priest. "I thank you, Nebbiamente. It may be that I will not return, for our enemies grow stronger. If I do not, will you do what you can to see that the priests of my God know I am lost so that they may offer their prayers on my behalf?"

Some of the somnambulistic vagueness left Nebbiamente's face. "Yes, I will do that, if I am alive." He made another strange gesture, then stood back as Bellimbusto spread his wings.

Bellimbusto flew quickly, sensing his master's urgency, his enormous wings resonant as drums as he clove through the sky. Twice he shied when birds drew near, each time giving a distressed cry that was echoed in Lodovico's heart.

The last ridges were quickly traversed, and then Lodovico could see the wide valley of two rivers where he thought the battleground would be.

But at first he did not recognize it. Gone were the beautiful fruit trees and the gardenlike tranquillity. Now the place was arid, blighted by the awesome, unnatural beings who fought for Anatrecacciatore. The earth beneath him was barren and the few trees still standing were like the flayed victims of the cruel Moors of old, for they had been stripped of fruit, flower, leaf and bark. Lodovico gazed down in horror at the desolation that had so utterly blasted the beauty of that broad valley. His chestnut eyes grew dark with anguish and tears as he saw the inexorable annihilation of the land. Off to the south, a straggling group of the warriors of flint and frost razed the last of the flowering shrubs, and as they passed on, the grasses withered.

Quite suddenly, Lodovico came to himself. It was necessary that he return at once to Falcone. The battle could not be fought here, for the splendid valley was already lost. The only hope now was to occupy the highest ridge and defend it to the last man. He twitched the rein, and Bellimbusto, eager to obey, canted down the sky and soared over the grim line of Anatrecacciatore's hideous army.

As the shadow of the hippogryph touched the soldiers, a number of them looked up. Lodovico could not hear if words were exchanged, but in the next moment, three stone-tipped arrows were soaring aloft.

Bellimbusto shied and evaded the arrows, but he had lost altitude in the maneuver and was well within range of bow shot. The warriors below did not wait, but loosed another volley, and Lodovico heard the cry of Bellimbusto as an arrow grazed his flank. A moment later, his own cheek stung as another arrow shot by. Lodovico put a gloved hand to his face and drew it away. There was a great deal of blood on the embroidered leather. He wiped impatiently at his face and dragged on the rein to bring Bellimbusto around and out of danger.

More arrows raced skyward, but by now, Bellimbusto was in a steep upward climb, hooves, talons and wings all seeming to claw their way higher into the sky.

A last, spent arrow nicked Lodovico's shoulder, and then they were beyond the reach of the bows of the unnatural army. Lodovico eased his pressure and shifted his seat so that Bellimbusto could fly horizontally. He turned in the saddle to watch the warriors of flint and frost as they started to make their way up the first line of hills, and he realized with a sinking heart that they would move quickly, ruining all in their path, leaving nothing but bare earth behind them. Lodovico had to admit the advantage of that, for surely Falcone's army could not advance to fight Anatrecacciatore in his stronghold of the Fortezza Serpente if there was no forest, no cover, no food, no game to support his troops on the march.

The steady beat of Bellimbusto's flying was broken and the hippogryph wavered in his course. One wing was dragging, moving sluggishly, and Bellimbusto was beginning to pant. His movements were labored and he began to make an eerie wail with each breath he drew.

Lodovico tried to calm the great beast with his voice, but Bellimbusto seemed hardly to hear him. At last, as he stared at the wing, he saw that an arrow was lodged in it, and that blood coursed down it, staining the feathers a crimson as intense as the sunset sky before an east wind. Slowly, so as not to give Bellimbusto greater hurt, he signaled him to descend. The hippogryph gratefully slid lower.

How far was it now to Falcone's camp? Lodovico asked himself. In all the evasion of arrows, he knew that Bellimbusto had moved off the line of flight Lodovico had tried to maintain, and now he feared they were much too far to the south. He nudged Bellimbusto and the stalwart mount swung to the north, flying painfully as he strove to carry his master to safety.

La Realtà

There were three heralds in the Camera della Signoria: one was in the full regalia of Milano, the city arms and the Sforza arms sharing the embroidered splendor of his tabard. The second was from Napoli with the rampant blue lion of the king. The third was from Sicilia, but wearing the arms of the Duca of Calabria—a black wing wielding a red sword on a gold field. They stopped before the dais where Damiano sat, and bowed in recognition of his office. They then performed the same courtesy to the men gathered there. To the far left, the Lion of San Marco identified the Venetians, and the ship and keys to the far right marked the Genovese contingent.

"What is it you want?" Damiano asked icily. "You're interrupting a proceeding of la Federazione."

"I apologize for the intrusion," said Muzio Maggio, the herald from Napoli. "I don't know what the task of our Milanese brother is, but I know that my Siciliano counterpart and I come on a similar errand." He had the herald's carrying voice, and in this high-ceilinged room his words were as clear and understandable as if they sat at table. "I come at the behest of my king, who bids me inform you that it is the intention of Napoli to withdraw from la Federazione."

Damiano regarded the herald Muzio Maggio with

amazement and disbelief. "Withdraw from la Federazione? What is this nonsense?"

"No nonsense, de' Medici. It is the intention of my master, the King of Napoli, to join with the King of Sicilia for the purpose of forming a separate state. My master respectfully submits that the needs of Napoli are not the needs of Firenze or Venezia or Milano. Our fighting men are forever at the beck and call of the north, our merchants are always in competition with those of Genova and Roma. It is not to our advantage."

"And Manrico forgets so soon how the Genovese ships protected his trading fleet from pirates?" Damiano asked gently before turning to the assembly. "This unexpected . . . development is not part of our agenda, but if you will all agree, I think it would be best to hear these heralds out."

From his place at the rear of the room, Lodovico could see the hard glitter of Damiano's eyes and his throat grew tight in sympathy. Damiano had been prepared for treachery but not for this. He wished he had seen the heralds before they entered so that he could stop them, so that there might have been time to warn Damiano, so that he might have found a way to change their minds. He reminded himself that was foolish for heralds acted at the behest of their masters, not from their own convictions. It might well be that all three men in their heraldic uniforms felt that their masters were mistaken, but it was not the function of their office to say so. Lodovico sunk his chin on his chest and watched.

There was general assent from the delegation, though Cesare d'Este of Ferrara raised an objection. "If we refuse to hear these men until tomorrow, it could be that our actions will anticipate their grievances and this . . . gambit will not be necessary."

Damiano glanced over the men before him. "D'Este has a point, but I think that it might be well to let them speak now. If the Kings of Napoli and Sicilia have already made up their minds, it would seem any redress we might offer comes after the fact."

Lodovico wanted to object, though he attended only on Damiano's sufferance. He wished to plead with the men in the chamber that it was too cruel to ask a man to preside at his own destruction, for without doubt the loss of the south would disrupt la Federazione completely. Italia Federata was Damiano's faith and sustenance and family. The disgrace of Leone, Arrigo, and Renato was nothing to this.

Muzio Maggio bowed to the chamber. "In the name of my King, I thank you for granting me the opportunity to deliver the message I am mandated to present." He looked toward Damiano.

"Speak, then." He had leaned back in his chair, an abstract frown creasing between his brows.

"After consulting the wisest and most experienced men in his realm, and having given the entire question his whole attention, the King of Napoli has, with the knowledge and consent of his advisers, decided to demand the return of his army from the Venetian borders, and to withdraw his kingdom, militarily, mercantilly, legislatively and scholastically, from Italia Federata and to form with the King of Sicilia a separate and distinct alliance under terms more satisfactory to the King's Majesty." At the conclusion of this speech, Muzio Maggio offered a lavishly sealed scroll to Damiano. "My master commands me to present this document to you, saying that it contains precisely the same message I have just delivered and carries the full weight of his will."

Damiano stared at the scroll as if he had never seen one before and did not know what to do with it. He laid his staff of office beside the sealed document and said distantly, "I will inspect it . . . later. I will have to consult my Console, for unlike your King, I need more than my own will in order to act for la Federazione."

In the Venetian delegation, Ezio Foscari had been listening with increasing agitation. In the silence that greeted Damiano's remark, Ezio got to his feet. "So Napoli wishes to withdraw her troops from what she calls the Venetian borders. Those are *Italia's* borders.

They are perilous. We have Slavs and Turks and Bul-
gars to contend with there. We need an army twice the
size of the one we have now. And I remind all the delegates and the heralds that it is Venetian gold that pays
the soldiers." He looked around him, turning from one
group to another. "Do you remember what it was like
before the truce? We keep that truce with honor but we
protect it with arms." His next appeal was to Ercole
Barbabianca, who was dressed in his robes of state.
"How many skirmishes did you have with France before
la Federazione made it possible for you to defend your
borders? Genova was in danger of being a French
province, a vassal of a foreign King. If any kingdom
principate, duchy, county, republic or municipality is
intact in this country, it is because of la Federata. If you
are all so short-sighted that you cannot see that, then
we are lost." He stared at Damiano as if he might say
more, then sat down and refused to acknowledge the
cheers that greeted his words.

"And you? Is your message the same?" Damiano
asked, his voice slightly thickened, of the Sicilian
herald.

"Essentially it is the same," the herald affirmed.

"Is any detail significantly different that it would require you to recite the contents of that scroll you are
unquestionably going to present to me?" His hand had
tightened on his staff of office and Lodovico wondered
if Damiano might be tempted to use it as a cudgel.

"The documents are very nearly identical, de' Medici.
If you like, I will forgo the recitation if I am assured
that the Console will be formally presented with the
scroll and it will be read before sunset tomorrow." He
offered the scroll to Damiano, who took it as if it were
venomous.

"They are determined to force us to act so quickly?"
He was looking at the Sicilian herald, but as he continued, it was apparent that his words were intended for
all the assembled delegates. "My grandfather was asked
why he refused a title when he had been offered one
a second time, and it was his response that the arro-

gance of nobles is legendary, and when it was wed to power, it was the most potent drug ever developed and was deadly to reason. I had not, until now, realized how accurate he was. Manrico imagines himself the victor in this, but I tell you, and you may tell your master, that he has authorized his own destruction with this folly. The same is true of Rafaele. Tell them to remember this day when Tunisian pirates seize their ships and burn their villages."

The men in the room heard him out in stillness, and for once there was no whispering, no significant, side-long glances.

"You," he went on, addressing the Milanese herald. "If you bring me more of this idiotic irresponsi—"

Orfeo Dardo bowed, and dared to interrupt. "No, Primàrio, I do not. I am sent with a message that was brought to Milano by a Polish emissary. Francesco Sforza, my master, read the message and sent it on to you as quickly as I could ride here. The Polish messenger wished to deliver the scroll, but my master reminded him that he did not have the access to you that I have."

"What is in the scroll, Dardo?" Damiano snapped.

"This is an official document from the English mission to the Grand Duke of Muscovy. It informs the Italian state"—he chose his words discreetly, Lodovico thought—"that Ippolito Davanzati was killed by a sword wound during an evening of . . . debauchery. The man who killed him is being held by the Russian state for execution." He faltered, staring toward the windows.

"Go on," Damiano said, his words devoid of feeling.

"I am most truly sorry to tell you this, Primàrio. Believe me." He held out the scroll, and as Damiano leaned down to take it, he said softly, "Leone de' Medici killed Ippolito Davanzati."

Damiano's hand closed convulsively around the scroll and his face became a mask. "Leone de' Medici killed Ippolito Davanzati," he repeated clearly. "Dardo, tell your master that . . . that I appreciate his haste. There is no way that such an act could be excused or concealed. Assure your master that the proper . . . acknowledgments will be dispatched at once to Poland and Russia." He started to rise, then stopped, remembering where he was. "I . . ."

Andrea Benci, who had been sitting at his writing table to the side of the delegation, got to his feet and came around the end of the table. "Delegates of la Federazione," he said at his most urbane, "considering the grave nature of the documents presented by the heralds, perhaps it would be wise for you to declare a recess, and for the Console to meet in the morning immediately after Mass, to consider the proper response to Napoli and Sicilia."

"Sensible," Ercole Barbabianca agreed, and motioned his delegation to follow him from la Camera della Federazione. The Genovese contingent was the first to depart.

The men were uncharacteristically quiet as they left, most exchanging only a few, whispered words. Cesare d'Este approached Damiano's place on the dais, and he murmured something to il Primàrio that brought a grateful, tortured smile to his lips.

At last the room was empty. Lodovico rose and came across the floor, thinking that his soft-soled shoes made more noise than he would have thought possible. He stopped at the foot of the dais and looked up. "Damiano," he said when he had waited in silence some little time, "come. Let's go home." It was, he thought, like addressing an invalid or a lost child. The unblinking stare Damiano directed at the three scrolls on the table before him was a blind one.

"I will be in the secretarial offices, if il Primàrio should want me," Andrea Benci said to Lodovico without attempting to speak to Damiano.

Lodovico was incensed at this treatment of his friend. "If you wish Damiano to know a thing, tell him yourself." How much of this irate response came from his own dislike of Benci he did not know, and in this instance he was not willing to examine his conscience.

Andrea Benci looked affronted. "I did not wish to trouble him with such a minor matter." He delivered his rebuke with the expression of one who has experienced the ultimate boorishness. "If you are not willing, however . . ."

"Damiano is present and hears you." Lodovico turned away from Benci and refused to look at him again.

"Primàrio," Benci said with a bored sigh, "I will be in my offices if you should need me."

"Thank you," Damiano murmured, and looked up from the scrolls.

Lodovico turned back just in time to see Andrea Benci favor Damiano with a slight, respectful bow. He felt himself fill with rage as if his vitals were swollen with it. What effrontery! What self-serving arrogance! He wished he had the courage to shout at Benci, but he could not—not now, while Damiano had the look of one with a relentless fever devouring him. He contented himself with a short, caustic laugh.

Andrea Benci glared at Lodovico, then trod across the room. At the door he turned, as if the matter had just occurred to him. "My festa this evening. Do you think I should cancel it?"

This question roused Damiano. He glanced once again at the scrolls, then slammed his palm on the table. "Per San Giorgio, no! Those scum in Napoli and Sicilia would boast of it for years. Have the festa, and be sure that all of the Console attends. I will not allow those disloyal knaves to garner any satisfaction from their rashness."

As he bowed his acceptance of this order, Andrea Benci inquired, "And you, yourself? The matter with . . . your son . . . you may prefer not to join us."

Damiano hesitated. "I will tell you later." He was looking now at the third scroll.

"As you wish. I am confident that no one will expect you, and you may be sure that neither Napoli nor Sicilia will take credit for your absence." Again he gave the slight, subservient bow and then withdrew, taking care to secure the great double doors behind him.

"So." Damiano picked up the scroll from Milano. "Leone killed Ippolito Davanzati. Why? Or did he have a reason?" It was apparent that he did not expect an answer. "Why so foolish, my son?" He tapped the scroll on the table but made no attempt to open it. "Lodovico," he said in another voice, "what is the method of execution in Russia, do you know?"

"No, Damiano." It was an effort for him to speak, and meeting the misery in those brown eyes was more than he could bear.

"Well, doubtless someone will." He got to his feet, walking like one who has been long abed.

"The scrolls, Damiano?" Lodovico pointed to the three lying on the table.

"Leave them. No one will touch them. They're mere formalities, in any case." He had come down from the dais. "I need . . ." He did not say what he needed, and Lodovico was too wise to ask.

Margaret Roper heard the news in stunned silence. "Your son . . . *your* son killed one of the Florentine escort?" she demanded when Damiano had told her all of it.

"There seems to be no doubt of it." He walked away from her, toward the nearest pedestal on which stood a Verocchio satyr with his grin, his potency and his pipes. "I have to tell the others, Margharita. They must know. It is perhaps just as well that you are leaving for Roma next week." He was unable to smile, and after the first attempt, abandoned all pretense. "Lodovico, have the others assembled in the courtyard?"

"Yes, Damiano." His eyes felt hot for want of tears, but he had told himself sternly that his grief would have to wait until later, when he and Alessandra were alone and he would not disgrace Damiano. He went to the study door and held it open.

But Damiano was not quite through with Margaret yet. "You will hear many rumors, and a few of them may be true, but I ask you to remember that I have never told you anything but the truth. Perhaps, when he returns, you will tell your father that for me, as well." He had taken her hands in his. "Will you do that, for a friend?"

"You will do that yourself, Damian," she said.

"Perhaps," was his answer as he stepped back, releasing her and starting toward the door where Lodovico waited.

"The trouble with Naples and Sicily won't last," Margaret called after him. "England has been plagued by Scotland and Ireland for centuries, but we have all survived. This is more of the same."

"Do you think so?" Damiano asked without turning, and he was out of the room before she could protest. He put his arm through Lodovico's. "I could wish that just one of the Console were as faithful as that woman," he remarked wistfully as they walked down the corridor. The walls were filled with paintings, and where there were no pictures, the wall itself was decorated with interlacing designs. "I've always liked that da Vinci," he went on inconsequently. "It's a pity he didn't finish it, but then, he finished very little. Still, his starts are more splendid than most of the completed work of others." He stopped a moment and looked back at the study door. "Did you notice? She did not ask me about her father. A fine woman, Margharita Roper."

"The household is waiting," Lodovico reminded him gently. "The longer they wait, the more alarmed they will become."

Damiano nodded. "For a poet, you are an astute man, my friend."

There was no way for Lodovico to answer this. He muttered a few, jumbled syllables and pulled his arm free of Damiano's as they started down the short flight of narrow stairs that led to the expanse between the two wings of Palazzo Pitti.

"I think now that my grandfather was wise to prefer Palazzo Medici," he said before he started out the door. "The old place is more like a fort than this is. We could lock and bar the gates and hold off half the city if we had to." This was mentioned lightly, as if in jest, but

Lodovico knew how little humor there was in Damiano's words, and before he could frame a reply to this, Damiano had stepped out into the sunlight to face his waiting household.

"You will help no one if you do not eat," Alessandra was scolding Lodovico as he sat at his writing table, several sheets of unfinished verse scattered around him. "You have obligations to Damiano. You accepted them, and you must honor them. For one thing, you must do your work. You are his poet, not his conscience. For another, if you are weak and snappish—and you get that way when you skip meals, Lodovico, you know you do—you cannot aid him as he must be aided now. You are indulging in pride and vanity, my husband, and these are sins." She put the tray she was carrying down on an uncluttered corner of the table. "I expect you to eat this. There is pork and vegetables in savor sanguino, and some new bread." For a moment her exasperated manner faltered and revealed the worry it masked.

Lodovico reached over and patted her hand. "You are a good wife to me, Alessandra. You're a good woman. You must forgive me for my . . ." He stopped and searched inwardly for the word, but it eluded him. "I will eat, I promise you."

"See that you do," was her kindly, gruff answer. She watched him until he cleared a place for the tray and moved it. Then she hurried toward the door.

As Lodovico picked at the meal, his thoughts wandered. He could not bring himself to remember the morning, and the terrible messages of the heralds. Instead, he tried to imagine what Virginio was doing, what lodging he had found, what he had seen in Paris, how he liked the Université. He gazed out the window at the hills, touched now with a burnished autumn bronze. The first few leaves were falling, spangling the ground like gold coins idly and munificently flung along the walkways of the garden. All of the roses were gone. In the orchards, Lodovico's near-sighted eyes could

barely make out the men on ladders who brought in
the bounty of the trees. It had been a good year, and
the harvest was abundant, and only those who feared
an early rain predicted anything other than plenty.
Lodovico realized with a start that Sir Thomas More
might well have arrived in Muscovy by now, and thought
that it would be a pleasure to read of that distant and
fabled city.

On his plate the food had grown cold, though he
hardly noticed it. Lodovico began to gather up the
pages on the table into a neat pile. He tried not to
look at what he had written, but now and again, a
phrase or a few lines would catch his eye and he
would stop to read them over, his critical eye searching
for imperfections which he found all too often for his
taste. Perhaps no one but himself would see the awkward phrases and infelicitous images; the work would
need revision, and he thought back to the twelve years
he had spent in revising *Orlando Furioso*. He could not
feel stimulated by the prospect of another such dozen
years, though he knew that once he had. Testily he put
the pages aside, then broke off a bit of bread and put
it to soak in the congealing sauce.

When the door opened he did not look up, thinking
it was Alessandra coming to hector him once more.
Guiltily, he popped the chunk of bread into his mouth
and began to chew vigorously.

"Lodovico," Damiano said as he came into the room.
"I need you to come with me. Wear your best clothes."
He himself was magnificently dressed in a long silken
farsetto in the dark-red of mourning. There was a black
mourning wreath on his brow and white mourning bands
on his elaborately puffed and slashed sleeves. His
Venetians were the same dark red and the slashing
showed linings of white satin. On a gold collar he
wore the badge of la Federazione—a knotted rope
worked in plaits of gold and silver. Lodovico had never
seen him wear the badge at any time other than full
state functions.

"Where are we going?" Lodovico asked as he got to his feet.

"To Andrea Benci's festa, of course." He watched Lodovico closely and saw apprehension, quickly concealed, tighten his face. "Do not be concerned, my friend. I will not behave stupidly. I am on guard against such things now."

"Very well," Lodovico responded cautiously. "Will you tell me why you are going?"

Damiano gave him a swift, acute stare. "Because I don't want to create any more doubts than now exist. If I stay away, it will only add fuel to the fires started by Napoli and Sicilia. I can't let that happen." He folded his hands and studied the elaborate rings that flashed on his fingers. "I have little in reserve now. I had thought that when Sir Thomas returned, there would be time and information enough to shore up the breaches in la Federazione. I hadn't realized how far our enemies had come. Sir Thomas, if he left Muscovy tomorrow, would not be here in time to divert their intentions. So," he said more quietly, "I made an honest man a spy for nothing."

Lodovico recalled the troubled tone of Sir Thomas' letters, and could not find the words to deny this.

"And my son—my damned child—has given the dissident members of la Federazione the lever they need to turn us back to the old ways of petty, belligerent states. When Sir Thomas returns, he may well find Austria and Spain picking our bones." Damiano's voice had grown louder again, and ragged. He breathed deeply. "I am going to the house of Andrea Benci for his festa, where perhaps I may learn something to save us. I must do this." He dropped his hands to his side. "I am depending on you to help me."

Lodovico pushed the tray aside and put a little iron figure of San Giorgio on the stacked pages. "I will need time to change," he said.

As he bowed his two late-arriving guests into his banqueting hall, Andrea Benci said in an undervoice,

"Primàrio, do you think this is wise? With what you have undergone today, might it not be better if you kept . . ."

Damiano stopped him. "I am dressed in mourning. You need not fear that I will forget myself."

"I did not mean to imply that, Primàrio," Benci assured him, and allowed Damiano and Lodovico to precede him through the tall double doors to the two huge rooms where the festa was being kept.

Music and conversation faltered as Damiano strode into the room, and in the middle of the floor a few of the dancers missed the figure of the bel riguardo in the peregrina. Taking advantage of this, Damiano strolled into the banqueting hall and gestured his greeting.

Immediately the activities were resumed, but at a quickened, fervid pace, as if all in attendance had been caught napping and were determined to make amends.

Lodovico reached Damiano's side as a group of young men came hurtling across the room. He recognized Tancredi Scoglio among them, and his lips tightened to a thin line. "Damiano . . ."

The back of Damiano's hand touched his shoulder and Lodovico was silent. "Good evening," he said to the young men.

"Primàrio," one of them blurted out, his words not quite clear. "There is a rumor in the city. They say that Ippolito Davanzati is dead. They say that . . ." He realized then to whom he spoke and the rest was lost in mumbling.

"They say that my son Leone killed him," Damiano finished for him, and only Lodovico sensed the iron control that kept his voice even. "That is what I have been told, and considering the source I have no reason to doubt it. As you see, I mourn my son. The message was three weeks old when it arrived and by now the execution must have been carried out."

"A pity about Ippolito," Tancredi said boldly.

"A great pity," Damiano agreed.

"And good riddance to . . ." Tancredi began, but one of the others hushed him.

"Per la Virgine, Scoglio, remember who it is," one of them hissed, and Tancredi muttered a few words under his breath and crossed his arms in a manner at once defiant and sulky.

Lodovico looked about, seeking a means to extricate Damiano from this company, but everywhere he looked, he saw the same eager voracity, the same destructive hunger that shone in the faces of these young men. He tried to fold his arms but the huge padded sleeves of his giaquetta made this extremely difficult, and he was reduced to planting his hands on his hips, thinking that this bulky silhouette was a great nuisance, and wishing now that he had selected a more restrained fashion for his most formal clothes. He listened to the young men ask questions and waited for Damiano's answers.

"I don't know," Damiano was saying to one of the Strozzi youths. "I was not informed of the nature of burial services given Davanzati. They are of the Orthodox faith, but I hope that God can translate from the Russian as He does from the Latin. Perhaps the Poles had a priest in their train, in which case, a Mass will have been said. I've already dispatched orders to Santa Trinità for Masses for Davanzati, and for prayers for my son."

"I'd think you'd be relieved," another in the group said insolently. "A son like Leone must be an embarrassment."

"You're drunk," Damiano countered mildly, but Lodovico could see the white around his mouth, and heard the tremor in his voice.

"Not so drunk that I don't know a convenient accident when I see one," the voice shot back, becoming more assertive and louder.

"Renaldo Tommassini," Damiano said pleasantly, dangerously, "if you repeat that again tonight, or at any time in the future, you will learn more than you want to know about convenient accidents."

At the mention of Tommassini's name, Lodovico turned quickly, looking into the roistering young men for the speaker. He recognized the man at last, though

Tommassini had frizzed and dyed his hair in the current fashion.

Renaldo Tommassini started to take up the challenge but was quieted by his companions.

"Damiano," Lodovico said softly, "Ercole Barbabianca is in the adjoining room with several of his court. They will be eager to see you."

"Such tact," Damiano said, sotto voce, before bidding the young men a pleasant evening. As they crossed the room, he added, "They were harder to face than I thought they would be. That Tommassini . . ."

"Did you have a falling out with him?" Lodovico asked, puzzled by what had passed between Damiano and Tommassini.

"Falling out? I never had a falling *in* with him. Men of that stamp are not . . . reliable." He paused to nod to an elder Gaetani, saying, "You are a long way from Roma, Signor'."

"True, but here I am more content." He had the grand manner of the old aristocracy, and though his head was bald and more than half his teeth were missing, he conducted himself with a grace that enchanted Lodovico as he watched him.

"You are very kind," Damiano said, touching cheeks with the old man before continuing on with Lodovico.

"But," Lodovico said, resuming his question, "if you do not trust Renaldo Tommassini, why did you use him as a messenger?" He could still remember that highhanded young man demanding Sir Thomas' letters, and he had to fight down the impulse to denounce Tommassini in front of all of Benci's guests.

"What do you mean, use him as a messenger? I've never employed him in any way." Damiano had stopped walking and was looking at Lodovico with sudden intensity.

"But . . ." Lodovico began, and then saw their host coming toward them. "Not now. We need privacy."

Damiano was about to protest, but changed his mind with one crisp nod as he allowed Andrea Benci to catch his attention. "Many of my guests have spoken to me about the signal honor you've done me, Primàrio. I wanted to thank you for this tribute. At such a time, it would be wholly understandable if you were to overlook such courteous gestures."

"It isn't flattery alone that brings me here," Damiano replied with a slight, cynical smile. "There are a few political matters that, like it or not, I must attend to before sunset tomorrow. It will be easier to manage this if I solicit opinions informally rather than wait for the meeting of the Console tomorrow."

"Quite sensible," Andrea concurred, "and yet, I still am honored that you visit me, as you could have easily commanded the presence of the Console at Palazzo Pitti this evening." He gestured to the banquet hall. "I am sorry that I had not the opportunity to remove the garlands and replace them with wreaths, but . . ."

"Under the circumstances, it is not to be expected that you would make such a change." Damiano indicated the French pinks set out on the sideboards. "It would be a pity to waste those blooms when you must have gone to great effort and expense to procure them."

Palazzo Benci was a fairly new structure built south of the Arno near the Porta San Miniato al Monte. It contrived to be both imposing and unassuming, for though the rooms were large, there were few ornamentations on the walls and the furniture was ostentatiously simple. The only displays of extravagance were the flowers. Andrea Benci beamed at the sideboards. "Indeed, Primàrio. They were brought from Genova in special cases so that they would bloom at the right time. I am pleased that you noticed."

"I noticed," Damiano assured him, and Lodovico heard the implacable coldness in his voice.

Apparently Andrea Benci did not, for he went on, "There are not many here who recognize the worth of those flowers, and though it does not become me to say it, I believe that the staggering cost was worth it."

"Staggering cost," Damiano repeated. "You have been more successful than I realized, Benci."

At that, Andrea Benci chuckled, though Lodovico

thought it rang false. "Not successful, merely careful. I do not waste my gold on fripperies," he said, running his hand down the velvet panels of his long giornea. "I allow myself occasional luxuries, such as those flowers, and for the rest, I keep strict household. I've told you my thoughts on the matter before."

"Yes, you have." Damiano moved restlessly, his fingers beating out a tattoo on his leg. "Benci, I wonder if you will be good enough to aid my purposes this evening?"

The smile that Andrea Benci gave in response to this request was genuinely delighted. "Of course, Primàrio. It is my function, is it not, to aid you?"

"It is," Damiano agreed at once. "Then, I would appreciate it if you would assign me a withdrawing room or antechamber where I may speak with the Console members attending your festa. That way, I will not interfere with your pleasures and there will be no awkwardness about my mourning attire." He waited, his face set in mendacious good fellowship, while Andrea Benci considered his request.

"Yes," he said a few moments later, "there is a room which is not in use this evening. You have seen it before, I think. There are two tapestries hung in it. It's on the west side of the building."

"I know it," Damiano said at once. "The room with the tapestries. Excellent. With your permission, I will go there now, and shortly I'll send Lodovico to summon whomever I need to consult. That way, there will be few interruptions."

Benci frowned. "I will gladly put one of my staff at your disposal. There is no need for Ariosto to . . ."

"I would prefer that Lodovico do this for me. He has more address than you or I do." It was blatantly untrue and all three men knew it. Yet there was no way for Benci to deny it without setting himself in opposition to Damiano.

"Of course, Primàrio," he said stiffly, and gave a bow. "I will not detain you." He turned on his heel and strode swiftly away.

Lodovico watched him, feeling a certain reprehensible triumph within him. He could tell by the set of Benci's shoulders that the old courtier was furious and dared not express his wrath. He was gloating a little when he saw Renaldo Tommassini approach Andrea Benci. The distance was too great and the company too boisterous to hear what was said, but even Lodovico's near-sighted eyes could tell that Tommassini was upset. That did not surprise Lodovico, considering what had passed between Damiano and Tommassini such a short time before, but what startled him was the manner in which Andrea Benci responded. It was obvious that Benci did not want to speak with Tommassini, indeed, not want to be seen with him. Il Primàrio's secretary cast one anxious glance around the room, and then hurried away from the rowdy young man.

"Lodovico; quickly," Damiano whispered softly, pulling at Lodovico's voluminous sleeve.

"At once," Lodovico said, blinking to recall himself. He fell into step beside Damiano as they left the banquet room through a side door. "Damiano . . ." Lodovico began, wanting to put his thoughts into words.

"In a moment," Damiano insisted. He looked up and down the hall they had entered. "It's too easy to be overheard. The room with the tapestries. How convenient!"

"Damiano," Lodovico said again, determined to make his friend listen. "I will speak softly. But you must listen. It's important."

"Yes. I am listening," Damiano said. "It's about Andrea Benci, isn't it?" He pounded one fist into the other palm. "Benci. Benci. French pinks."

Lodovico was very nearly distracted by this. What had French pinks to do with anything? But he resisted the urge to ask and said, "That man Renaldo Tommassini, when I was at your villa in the country. He came there once and asked for Sir Thomas' letters. He said that you had . . ." Then he remembered. "No, he said that your secretary had sent him. Damiano . . ."

"I know. I know." They started up a narrow stairwell. "Benci. So he sent Tommassini. Did you give him the letters?"

"No," Lodovico said with a spurt of satisfaction, and though he knew it was not his perspicacity but his offended pride that had stopped him, he permitted himself a moment of self-congratulations. "His manner insulted me, and I said that I would give the letters to you myself." Which, he knew, was more or less the truth.

Damiano clapped one hand on Lodovico's shoulder. "You humble me, my poet-friend. I do not know what inspired such loyalty in you, but I will thank God for it on my knees every day of my life—however long that may be."

This addition stopped any protestation that Lodovico might have made, and he felt the apprehensive cold, which he had kept at bay with assumed confidence, return with bone-numbing keenness.

At the top of the stair, Damiano motioned for silence, and led the way down the hall. He stopped at last before the curtained entrance to a corner chamber. "The room with the tapestries," he said caustically. "But who needs doors in the house of an ally?" He pulled the hangings aside and gestured to Lodovico to enter. "It will take him a few moments to dispatch ears to this room," he went on softly, then flung one of his jeweled rings across the room. *"Political whore!"* He said the words softly but with such vehemence that Lodovico reacted as if Damiano had shouted. "Cozening, recreant traitor!"

"Damiano!" Lodovico stepped back, horrified.

"Benci. Benci. Benci. It was there all the time and I could not see it. My secretary! By all the devils in Hell!" He rounded on Lodovico. "Self-effacing, submissive, willing . . . !" There were three chairs in the room and Damiano sank into one of them and put his clasped hands over his eyes. "Blind, blind! Christ forgive me for my unpardonable stupidity." His voice broke. "Jesu, how could I not have seen it? How?"

Lodovico crossed himself and felt his eyes brim. He tried to find a few words of solace, but his tongue would not obey him and his mind stubbornly refused to provide him with what he wanted. Instead, he could feel a part of himself—and at that moment, he loathed himself for it—step back from this appalling room and watch it, cataloguing the weight and color and sound of despair so that later he could remember it in his writing. He bit the insides of his cheeks deliberately, forcing his attention to immediate action. With unsteady strides he crossed the room to the chair and Damiano. "Oh, my friend," he whispered, and he crouched beside the chair to put his arms around Damiano.

When the worst of his torment had passed, Damiano opened his hands and looked down at Lodovico with reddened eyes as he drew a shuddering breath. He opened his mouth to speak, but said nothing. With his thumb he sketched a blessing on Lodovico's forehead. "You deserve more from me than this, but it is all I have."

"Then I am richly paid," Lodovico said as he stood once more. His knees cracked, and he was able to chuckle at it. "Age," he explained unnecessarily.

Damiano nodded. "Age." He straightened himself in the chair. "Well, let us play this travesty through to the end. Who knows, I may even accomplish something."

Lodovico wanted to tell Damiano that he had already subjected himself to enough, but he knew it was useless. "Whom would you like to speak with first?"

"If Cesare d'Este is here, it may be wise to bring him first. Otherwise I will have to choose between Ercole and Ezio, and no matter which one is selected, the other will feel slighted."

"And Benci?" He hated to ask the question, but could not bring himself to return to the banquet room before he knew what Damiano intended to do.

Il Primàrio's face tightened as he took a deep, hissing breath. "Benci. Yes, Benci. There is nothing I might say that he will not be privy to by morning. He is ior later, my friend. For the moment, I will have all I can handle with Ferrara, Genova, Venezia, and Milano."

La Fantasia

As he neared the edge of the Cérocchi encampment, Bellimbusto suddenly faltered and plunged. Lodovico was thrown from the saddle to fall heavily, stunning himself as he struck the earth. He had a vague impression of men running toward him before he lost consciousness, and when next he opened his eyes, Nebbiamente was holding burning feathers to his nostrils and Falcone had his hand on Bellimbusto's reins.

"What happened?" the Cérocchi Prince demanded of Lodovico without preamble.

Lodovico shook his head as if to clear away the reddened swirls that crowded his mind and sight. He motioned awkwardly for Falcone to draw nearer, and then forced himself to speak. "The warriors . . . the flint and frost warriors . . . they're coming . . . I've seen them. They're closer . . . through the valley already . . . We've got to get to the . . . highest ridge and secure it. Anatrecacciatore's army travels much more rapidly than I thought it could . . . They are on a fast march and I do not think they will rest until after they have fought us. If they rest at all." He attempted to get up, but Nebbiamente restrained him.

"A bit longer, Ariosto," he cautioned. "You're badly bruised by your fall."

"Badly bruised," Lodovico said contemptuously. "If

bruises are the worst I suffer this day, I will count myself the most fortunate of men."

"Then you think it will be today?" Falcone asked, his face quite serious.

"I think it must be today." He hated to lie on the ground when there was so much to do. "I have no time for this!" he declared impatiently, but allowed the priest to smear a vile-smelling grease over his forehead and wrap two lengths of cloth around his brow.

By the time he was on his feet again, he was feeling more himself, and was able to answer Falcone's questions coherently and with greater lucidity than he had been capable of when he had come out of his swoon. Already warriors were hurrying on tasks set them by the Prince, and there was the unique exhilaration that is the prelude to battle. Each man moved with purpose and there was a shine in their eyes that revealed their dedication more eloquently than any words could.

"And the valley is completely desolated?" Falcone was asking.

"Yes, sadly. It was a beautiful place when I first saw it, but now it is as wasted as the desert, sere and barren." He felt anger on behalf of the blasted valley, two days ago a near-Eden, and now devastated.

"The warriors do more than take lives, then." Falcone looked over his shoulder at Bellimbusto who limped after them. "They have hurt your mount, as well."

"They have." A deeper rage ignited within him, for Bellimbusto was his prize, the one token of victory that was dearer to him than any medal, honor, or glory that had been awarded him. He stopped and reached for the bridle.

"What are you doing?" Falcone asked, sincerely concerned.

"I am letting him go," Lodovico said as he began to unbuckle the girths of the saddle. "I can't let him fall into Anatrecacciatore's hands. I will send him off, and when the battle is over, if I am still alive, he will come back to me. He has done it before." He tugged the high-fronted saddle from the hippogryph's back. "As soon as I am finished and he is in the air, I will give you all my attention so that we may prepare for the battle. But I must . . ." He was drawing off the bridle now, and Bellimbusto pressed his gilded beak against Lodovico's shoulder, a distressed sound like a mew accompanying this touching gesture of affection.

"If you do not survive, what will happen to him?" Falcone was clearly more distressed than callous, and the abruptness of his question was prompted by affection.

"There is a legend that says when such a creature gives his fidelity, he will return to his fallen master and carry him to their unknown haven for a hero's burial." Lodovico rubbed the gorgeous feathered neck. "I would like to think that such a destiny awaited me, but I doubt I'm worthy of such tribute, if it does exist."

Falcone put his hand on Lodovico's shoulder. "You underestimate yourself, Ariosto, for if you do not belong in such a place, then there is no one who can aspire to it."

Lodovico smiled sadly as he hung Bellimbusto's bridle over his arm. "Perhaps that is why the place is a legend," he suggested. Then he patted his mount and checked the wound on his wing one last time. "You'll do well enough without me aboard," he told Bellimbusto. "Very well, then, off you go!" He slapped his mount's rump, but Bellimbusto did not rise in the air. He turned his enormous, reproachful eyes on Lodovico and gave a little, scornful snort.

"He has a will of his own," Falcone observed.

"Don't defy me now," Lodovico said to the hippogryph as his eyes stung with unshed tears. "You cannot fight with such a wing, and if you were here, I would worry for you, and not care for my men and the ordering of the battle as I should. You must go, Bellimbusto. When it is over, come back, but for now, get you to safety." He laid his hand on the beak as he would have patted a horse's nose, and then he once again slapped the rump.

Reluctantly Bellimbusto spread his great black-and-bronze wings, and slowly he rose into the air, wheeling once over the camp and then turning eastward.

Though he knew he could not spare the time, Lodovico stood for a little while watching until the hippogryph was nothing but a smudge against the glowing sky.

Cifraaculeo had been muttering unintelligibly for more than an hour by the time the troops of Nuova Genova and Falcone's army had reached the highest ridge of the hills. His bearers had exchanged anxious looks and at the first opportunity, Fumovisione was sent for.

The fantastically dressed wizard bustled up to the litter, making haste with his customary energy. He had been talking to the bearers and as he neared the litter, he spotted Lodovico with Nettocchio and called to him to join the rest. "We're seeing disturbances," he explained with gusto. "We're within the area of force controlled by Anatrecacciatore. Half the ducks we brought with us have died."

"Half?" Lodovico repeated, incredulous. "What killed them?"

"The malice of Anatrecacciatore. It's fairly obvious that he is vulnerable to ducks. He can't manipulate them, so he kills them. I wish I knew what force the ducks control that he is so threatened by them. The secret is in his name, but try as I will, I can't see the nature of it." He sighed his exasperation and motioned to the litter bearers to move away so he could approach the white-haired old man. "Yes, he's saying something, all right. I don't recognize the tongues, but that isn't surprising." He leaned close to the high priest of the Cérocchi and gave the man his full attention.

Cifraaculeo sat with legs tucked under him, his face blank as if in sleep, his eyes open and gazing at infinite distances. His mouth barely moved to emit the quiet gibber that had made his bearers distraught.

"No, I can't assess it," Fumovisione said as he stood back. "Pity. He might have something worth under-

standing. I will say this, though," he added thoughtfully as he regarded his afflicted colleague, "I'd be careful about believing what I saw, if I were you. Spells
like this one can manifest in some alarming ways. Anatrecacciatore has some skill with spectres and phantoms. You'd do well to be wary."

Nettocchio, who had overheard this, put his hands
on his hips. "That is not encouraging with the flint and
frost warriors only two hours away from us."

The priest shrugged. "You may not wish to hear it,
but better to know than to be taken unaware. If your
brother came to you and said that you must lay down
your arms, what would you do? An honorable man
would listen to his brother, and open himself to attack.
Be certain that you carry an arrow fletched with duck
feathers, and if such a form presents itself, offer the
arrow to it. If it will not take the thing, then you know
it is a spectre conjured by our great enemy, and deadly.
The priests and wizards will be ready to deal with such,
but you must be on guard or we will not be able to come
to your assistance."

"The man is wise," Lodovico said, for he saw the
warriors doubting the bark-garbed priest. "In such a
battle as we now face, we must overlook nothing, for
surely we will be in the gravest danger the entire time."

Nettocchio supported this. "Listen to Ariosto. We
should be the ones to tell him, but we are so filled with
terror that we will not defend ourselves properly." He
tugged an arrow out of his jeweled belt. "See. I have
such an arrow already and I would sooner part with
my dagger and battle axe than with this arrow. We do
not yet know if our weapons will harm the soldiers of
Anatrecacciatore, but we have learned that the ducks
have a virtue he cannot easily overcome." He returned
the arrow to his belt and looked at the others challeng-
ingly.

"Listen to the Cicora," Fumovisione advised the men.
"And hasten to get your arrows. The time is short." He
approached Cifraaculeo one more time, and said to

Lodovico in a whispered aside, "This bodes ill, Ariosto. It bodes very ill indeed."

Farther down the slope the branches were snapping and groaning as the flint and frost warriors began their ascent. Lodovico stood beside Falcone behind a hastily assembled fortification of piled rocks. "I have never liked waiting," he remarked in the dread-inspired silence.

"Nor I," Falcone agreed.

Some distance down the hill there was a rending moan and a crack not unlike lightning. All along the front line, the soliders, Cicora, Cérocchi, Onaumanient, Pau Attan, Cesapichi, Cica Omini, Italians, looked uneasily about while the priests began their most sacred incantations. Caged ducks huddled together, feathers ruffled as if against cold, though the afternoon was warm.

"It was a tree," Lodovico said quietly. "They break them and then kill them with frost."

Immediately there came more of the hideous crackings as the warriors of flint and frost encountered the wooded stretch of the hill. The sound of their marching was clear now, the most inexorable sound that Lodovico had ever heard.

One of the scouts who had ventured down the hill to watch the progress of the enemy came streaking back to the makeshift ramparts and vaulted over the piled stones. His face was as pale as any Lodovico had seen in this land. The scout shivered, gave a cry and fell, foam on his lips and his limbs twitching. A Pau Attan wizard hurried forward to deal with the unfortunate scout.

"Do you see any of the others?" Falcone asked.

"No," Lodovico said, and the response was echoed all along the line of defense.

"Ah." Falcone turned away toward the verdant hills behind him, as if to assure himself they were still there. When he once again faced the approaching enemy, he said to Lodovico, "I wish you would take the cape I offered you."

"I will," Lodovico said as he drew Falavedova from its scabbard. "When I have earned it."

There was no time to say more: the warriors of flint and frost broke through the trees below and began to climb toward the crest of the hill where Falcone's army waited.

As his sword struck the first warrior, Lodovico nearly cried out in pain and despair. The metal clanged off the cold, stony creature and nearly flew out of his hand. He grasped the hilt with both hands and swung with the flat of Falavedova, aiming for the head. The impact jarred him, but he had the satisfaction of seeing the head fly off and roll back down the hill.

The body of the warrior remained standing, its enormous, ponderous arms bringing a huge mace up to dash out Lodovico's brains.

Lodovico ducked quickly, his mind in turmoil at what he was witnessing. He could see the other men struggling with the forces of Anatrecacciatore, and many of them were being beaten by opponents who should have fallen still, but who continued to fight while any part of them could move. Eerie wraiths of steam rose from the bodies of the warriors of flint and frost, surrounding each of them with a halo of fog which only made them more horrible.

"Break them apart!" Lodovico shouted, hoping that over the ring of metal on stone, someone would hear him. "You can't kill them, you can only break them!"

Nearby, there was an answering shout from Massamo Fabroni, and his words were yelled again to the Lanzi fighters.

Falcone was beleaguered by two of the monstrous fighters, as Lodovico, in a desperate action, forced the flint and frost giant he was fighting back against the crumbling stone fortifications in a lucky move so that the headless figure overbalanced and toppled down, breaking as he rolled. Lodovico did not pause to enjoy this most ephemeral of victories, but plunged in beside

Falcone to save him from the pressing strength of Anatrecacciatore's army.

"We need hammers, not daggers," Falcone panted, his arm bleeding from where one of his opponents had grazed him with the stone axe he carried. His white deerskin cape was dappled with rusty smears.

Lodovico did not reply to this, but made a daring thrust at the shoulder of the nearest flint and frost warrior. The blow was true and the icy arm flew off, crashing down the hill and raising eruptions of dust, though the din of battle covered any sound the arm made.

The warrior's other arm was already swinging, and Lodovico could not entirely escape its fury. He was struck a glancing blow by an enormous fist, and the cold of it pained him more than the hardness. He staggered, almost blundering into Falcone, then, with a muttered prayer, he lunged again at the warrior, this time aiming for the joint of the knee. His first attempt was unsuccessful and the point of Falavedova clanged harmlessly on the stone. Lodovico recovered himself and let the full weight of the sword fall backhanded against the side of the joint as the warrior took an aggressive step forward. The stones parted and the warrior of flint and frost smashed to the ground, missing Lodovico by less than a hand's breadth.

"The joints!" Lodovico shouted at Falcone, who nodded as he brought his mace into play, slamming it on his adversary's elbow so that the lower arm cracked. Half of the flint still dangled from the body, but it had lost much of its volition and at Falcone's second stroke, the entire limb shattered and the flint and frost warrior paused.

That hesitation was enough. Lodovico levered his sword into the waist of the warrior and leaned on the hilt with all his strength. There was a grinding noise, loud enough to carry over the clangs and shouts and screams around them. The upper torso wobbled, rocked and tumbled, the weight of it upsetting the legs as well.

Another such warrior was in the place of the one that had fallen, and now Falcone and Lodovico mounted a double attack. Lodovico searched for weaknesses, chinks in the imposing figure, and where he found them, he pushed his sword deep and pressed it. Falcone was not far behind him, beating his mace on the frost-rimmed arms and legs. This time the warrior went down quickly.

They were strong, they were deadly, they were heavy and huge, but they were stupid as well, and Lodovico hoped for the first time that there might be a way to prevail against them. He shouted toward the band of priests, and to his surprise, in very little time, Nebbiamente stood beside him, his face wide with a grin. By that time, Lodovico and Falcone were striving to bring down yet another of the foe. Between grunts as he thrust Falavedova deeper into the hip joint, Lodovico shouted instructions to the little priest, who nodded at each specific.

"It's the joints! The joints! Don't try to best them— break them in pieces!" His throat ached with shouting and his hands were red with cold as his sword cooled in the frosty stone.

Nebbiamente hastened off, and somewhat later Nettocchio hurried up. His left arm hung uselessly at his side and the white of bone protruded at his shoulder. "The priests!" he cried out. "The priests are coming!"

Lodovico could take no time to ponder the meaning of it, and decided that it was the senseless maunderings of one dreadfully wounded. He had not looked about to see what had become of the defenders of the ridge, and he forced himself not to do so now. He pressed on the hilt until the sword sang and saw Falcone stumble, upset by a rolling hand of one of the broken warriors. "Don't stand on them!" he cried out, his voice a ragged caw.

Falcone dropped to his knee, and Lodovico could feel the flint and frost warrior turn slowly to deliver the fatal blow. There was nothing he could do to prevent it, he feared, but he realized he had to take action. He had only his sword to fight with, and it was thrust deep into the enemy soldier. With the power that comes only in extremity, he began to twist the hilt of Falavedova, to turn the blade and throw the foeman off balance. The steel thrummed and squealed, and then began to move. Encouraged by this accomplishment, Lodovico summoned all of his inner strength and increased the pressure.

The warrior of flint and frost stopped his attack on Falcone and moved toward Lodovico, mighty arms swinging into a deadly curve.

Falcone tried to move away, but one of the fragments of the fallen flint and frost warriors had pinned him to the ground and the Cérocchi Prince was unable to free himself.

"San Michele, San Giorgio, San Vladimiro, aid me, aid me, aid me," Lodovico prayed as he strained against the hilt of his sword. He watched the massive arms come toward him, he felt the first weight of their impact, and then Falavedova wrenched the last bit and Anatrecacciatore's warrior broke into pieces, shattered from within by the twisted sword.

And a twisted sword Falavedova certainly was. Now the long steel blade bowed and turned. Lodovico lifted it to look more closely and felt all the intensity of the blow he had been given catch up with him. His vision blurred and he thought he could see Accettafosco coming toward him, a maul in his hand. Lodovico had a definite impression that there was more danger, but he could not respond. His mind was filled with dire warnings and every sense told him that his peril was graver than ever. Yet he could not stop himself. The inner clamor went unheeded. His knees buckled and he fell forward.

A hand touched his, gently. He opened his eyes and through the haze that hovered, smokelike, around him, he thought he saw Aureoraggio bend toward him, a smile curving her beautiful mouth, her lovely form lithe as a willow in a spring wind. He could not hear what she said, but he knew she wanted him to rise. For some reason it was more difficult than he thought it would be.

Some force held him down, some weakness he feared
was enchantment made water of his bones. Yet Aureoraggio motioned to him to come, and he felt the sweet
longings of his unspoken and unavowed love well in
him. He reached to take her hand, and though she was
too far for this, he willed himself to overcome the in-
comprehensible lassitude that held him in thrall. She
moved ahead of him, pointing the way to a place where
they would be together.

It was delightful to follow her, to walk beside the
most lovely creature. He was troubled that he could not
see her clearly, but it was all part of his weakness and
would pass. He realized that he should have some re-
morse for this betrayal of Falcone, but he could not find
it within himself, and did not look for it.

How lightly they went! How gracefully she moved!
How full of joy he was! The only blight on his pleasure
was that he could not get close enough to gaze on her
more fully. The glamour was radiant about her, so
splendid that she herself was indistinct . . .

And then he saw the six warriors of flint and frost
coming up the slope toward him, and Cifraaculeo lay
at his feet, Accettafosco's lance transfixing him to the
earth. Duck feathers, secured with twine to the long
shaft, shuddered still from the impact that had felled the
high priest of the Cérocchi.

Lodovico was immobilized, disgrace and disgust en-
gulfing him. He had been unwary, he knew, and the
shame of it overcame him. The very thing he had warned
against had happened to him. He had known the hazard
and had succumbed. The enchantments of Anatrecacciatore had found out his desires and worked upon
him, as all sin must work to the detriment of the soul.
From up the hill, behind the broken fortifications, Lodovico could hear men shouting to him. He could not
respond to them in any way, though he knew the battle
continued by the sounds of wood and steel striking
stone, and the shouts of the wounded. He was the one
who had made these brave men vulnerable. He had led

them and failed them. Bitterness more profound than
chagrin rose like gorge in his throat.

Anatrecacciatore's warriors lumbered nearer, the
leaders of the second rank of fighters who were certain
to prevail if ever they reached the summit of the ridge.

In the depths of his soul, Lodovico knew he had to
expiate his folly, his transgression. Perhaps, if he could
catch the approaching warriors of flint and frost at a
weakened moment, they could be bowled over and
sent plummeting down the hill into their fellows. Lodovico smiled now, satisfied that he could make amends
for his culpability. Taking up his twisted sword, he
looked over his shoulder one final time at those great-
hearted, valiant men of Falcone's army. Massamo
Fabroni had just brought one of the flint and frost warriors to its knees and was smashing the stone head
with repeated poundings with his steel flail. Falcone
himself stood at the top of the rickety battlements, his
bloodstained white cape flung back from his shoulders.
He answered Lodovico's farewell salute with one of
his own.

Then the great Italian captain and poet, Lodovico
Ariosto, with his battle cry *"Omaggio!"* on his lips, a
prayer of gratitude in his soul, with exhaustion, wounds,
dishonor forgotten, rushed down the hill toward his
enemies.

La Realtà

Lodovico overset his brass inkwell as the door to his chamber slammed open, the handle leaving a long impression gouged in the wall. He moved quickly to push his pages aside, then looked about helplessly for a rag.

"I am not going to play into my cousin's hands so easily!" Damiano announced to the air in fury.

In desperation, Lodovico took the pillow from his chair and dropped it onto the pool of ink. "Your cousin . . ." he asked as he righted the inkwell.

Damiano's tightened jaw worked, then he answered, "My cousin. Who else? I sent a message to Graziella in France, to tell her about . . . Leone. She will have heard by now from others, but I couldn't let her have it on rumors . . ." The softening of his expression was gone and he turned on his heel, starting to pace the length of the small chamber. "And now I hear that I have written to ask for asylum in France, that I am going to flee Firenze! Cosimo will have to do better than that."

"You mean that the Cardinale is saying that you will leave?" Lodovico said incredulously. "Impossible. You are part of Firenze."

"I would prefer torture to exile," Damiano said, so quietly and so firmly that there was no doubt that it was the truth. "If they want me out of Firenze, they will have to remove my coffin, for I will go no other way."

341

Lodovico patted the pillow to be certain it soaked up all of the ink, then he picked it up and set it, blackened side up, on the wide windowsill. "Cosimo isn't so foolish, is he?"

"Not foolish—ambitious. *I* was foolish to underestimate his ambition." He paused at the far end of the room and peered into the next chamber. "Alessandra is not here?"

"She's gone to the Mercato Nuovo. She wants to buy a cloak to send to Virginio. She's worried that with winter coming soon, he won't be able to find a woolen cloak in all of Paris." He smiled at this and hoped to see a similar amusement in Damiano's face, but could not find it.

"Mothers believe such things," Damiano remarked, not at all interested in what Lodovico had said. "Did I interrupt you?"

"I was very nearly finished for the day, in any case. If I have time tomorrow, I'll do the rest . . ."

"Tomorrow Cesare d'Este is planning to leave for Roma. There's a ceremony planned for the occasion." He stopped at one of the bookcases and negligently began to read titles. "I will miss him. I don't always agree with d'Este, but I have been grateful for his presence. He's more reasonable than Foscari and less vain than Barbabianca."

"He is also richer and has no foreign border but the sea," Lodovico observed dryly.

"Oh, Gran' Dio, not you too? What is this cynicism?" Damiano asked with more disappointment than disgust. "I had hoped that you would be the one man who would not be tainted by politics."

Lodovico wanted to defend himself, to explain that he was neither cynical nor sophisticated, but he dared not. "I have been listening, and you must remember that my first patron was Duchessa of Ferrara. Lucrezia Borgia never made any secret of the d'Este wealth, and Alfonzo used to drink to his only foreign border. I may not understand the subtleties, but I had eight years there, and even I learn, after a while."

"Don't mock," Damiano said, sounding suddenly very tired. "There's been too much of it. And I've been one of the worst offenders."

In the last few days, Damiano had been subject to these erratic shifts in mood, so Lodovico did not feel the alarm he might have at another time. It was part of the burden of his office. "I wasn't mocking, or perhaps only myself. I am too grateful to the d'Estes to mock them."

Damiano said nothing for a time. His pacing slowed to restlessness and the ire went out of his eyes. "The English party leaves tomorrow for Roma. It's probably for the best, but . . ."

"Speaking of English," Lodovico interrupted, "I had word from a correspondent of mine in Ghent that he has heard that Mistress Boleyn has been delivered of a daughter. The news isn't official, since he is not part of the English church or court, but it is a rumor."

"A daughter." Damiano rubbed his chin. "That will mean he will try to betroth her to the Grand Duke of Muscovy's heir. Poor Henry. He must be infuriated. He's got that half-Spanish daughter, that sickly boy, and now another daughter whose legitimacy is questionable, to say the least. He might be wise to bury her off in Russia where she cannot be an embarrassment to him." There was real interest in him and he came back to Lodovico's writing table. "When did you get this? What else does your correspondent in Ghent have to tell you?"

Lodovico was pleased at Damiano's attentiveness. "Most of it has to do with books, I'm afraid. I've asked him to find me copies of certain volumes, though he has not had a great deal of luck doing so. He was offering me a volume of French letters purported to be by the monk Abelard, though he says he doubts they're genuine."

"Have done with books!" Damiano said impatiently. "What is his news of the world?"

"There is little of it. He told me about the daughter of Mistress Boleyn, and said that there was a group of Savonarola's followers in the Low Countries, but that few were interested in their preaching. The old monk is rumored to be ailing, but you know that. The Low Countries are not sure how long their independence from Spain will last. The Emperor does not like his possessions chopped up into separate jurisdictions, but with Spain under interdict, there is nothing he can do and retain his title."

"If Charles had his way, he would march straight to Roma and cram the interdict down Clemente's throat. I suppose I should be grateful that he and François hate each other. If they could work together, Italia Federata would be in more trouble than it is." The gravity had come back to his face, and his momentary delight faded away. "The heralds left this morning with the full Console petitions to both Kings, offering to redress wrongs and provide for any inequities. I think the gesture is a mistake, but the Console voted for it. I have never before wanted despotic power, but when Ezio Foscari began his lurid tales of what would happen if the border guards were lessened by so much as one man, he could have suggested that each member of the Console crawl to Manrico and Rafaele to kiss their feet, and it would have been approved. You should have heard him. His imagination is vivid, I promise you: cities sacked and burning, ragged families fleeing the vengeful Turks, children spitted on swords, women ravished by hundreds of men in every conceivable way, churches desecrated, goods looted and destroyed—his invention was without bounds. Oh, I know there is genuine danger from the Turks. There has always been danger. But the truce is successful, and if we have a little time, we can reinforce the border patrols without using soldiers from Napoli and Sicilia."

"What soldiers?" Lodovico asked.

"Well, we can get some from your precious Ferrara. There are two excellent companies of fighting men there who are used primarily now as military escorts. There are such companies all through the Papal States. If we use half of those, Napoli and Sicilia can withdraw their men and we will still be completely protected." He stopped to look at a map of the world Lodovico had pinned to the wall. "There are many places where we can get troops, if we must have them."

"Of course," Lodovico concurred, and added helpfully, "If it were important enough, the Lanzi companies could be withdrawn from Nuova Genova."

"Lanzi companies? There are less than fifty Lanzi in the Nuovo Mondo." Damiano gave his harsh laugh. "I know, to hear Ercole speak of it, we've taken half his army there, but truly, there are very few. What do we need them for?"

"Well, Nuova Genova . . ." Lodovico began, trying to put his objection into words. Nuova Genova was large enough, prosperous enough to need protection.

"San Benedetto! Nuova Genova! Six brick houses and a warehouse with a pier on a sandpit at the edge of a swamp!"

Lodovico did not dare to give Damiano back his admonition against mockery, but he could not disguise his expression.

"Have you been listening to Ercole's extravagant fancies?" Damiano asked, more kindly now that he saw Lodovico's shock. He came away from the map.

"I . . . no . . . but I . . ." How could it be that Nuova Genova was as Damiano said? It was part of Damiano's current difficulties, he decided. It might very well be wise to modify his enthusiasm for the city unless it became necessary to recall to the Console's minds that the limits of Italia Federata were far-flung indeed. Nuova Genova had a cathedral and palazzos, piazzas and high walls. He knew it as certainly as if he had seen them with his own eyes. The pages of his new work were stacked on the table and he put a protective hand over them. He wanted to explain to Damiano that he understood when there was a discreet knock at the open door and Andrea Benci, perfectly groomed in burgundy velvet, came into the room.

Damiano tightened his mouth to the approximation of a smile. "Yes? What is it?"

"You must pardon me," he said politely, though Lodovico felt each word was a calculated insult. "There is a messenger from England, and I thought perhaps you would wish to see him at once." Benci had ignored Lodovico, but now he turned to the poet. "Unless this conversation is more important than il Primàrio's obligations to la Federazione."

Damiano intervened before Lodovico could respond. "That will do! Undoubtedly the messenger comes with the tidings of Mistress Boleyn's safe delivery of a daughter. Though what we are to do in answer to this news, I do not know." He nodded at Benci's annoyed surprise. "You see, there are things one can learn from poets." As he reached the door, he called out, "Tomorrow, there is a leave-taking reception for Sir Thomas' family. Quite small. After Mass."

"I'll be there, if you like." Lodovico was still smarting under Damiano's cavalier attitude about Nuova Genova.

"Of course I want you there," Damiano said sharply, then gave his attention to Andrea Benci.

Lodovico sat alone in his chamber, his papers untouched at his elbow. He had told Damiano that it was foolish not to clap his secretary in chains as soon as his treason was discovered, but Damiano had said that would be unwise. There were other men in the conspiracy, men who were linked with Cosimo, Cardinale Medici, and perhaps all the way to Clemente VII. With such men, it was best to be cautious, Damiano explained as he and Lodovico strolled past the vendors in the Mercato Vecchio. That had been several days ago, and at the time, Lodovico was dubious. Now, he was frightened. It was Damiano's intention, he knew, to send a private letter to his uncle the Pope about the matter, and then to act against Andrea Benci. That would mean Andrea Benci would have another six days to work his malicious plans. Lodovico rose suddenly, new determination in him. He would stay near Damiano, as near as he was able. That way, il Primàrio would have some genuine protection. He had suggested that

the Lanzi should be alerted to the coming arrest, but
Damiano had refused. "I might as well post an announcement in every tavern in Firenze as tell the Lanzi
my intentions." Though Lodovico understood this, he
could not remain inactive. True, he was not much of
a fighter, but he was better than no one. He weighted
the papers on his writing table and left his chamber,
trying to recall where he had put the hunting dagger his
father had given him when he was a boy.

There were four carriages drawn up in front of the
Palazzo Pitti. They were large, covered vehicles with
enormous rear wheels and bodies high off the road.
Each was drawn by a team of four horses, from the
Medici stables.

"You're not to worry about changing horses," Damiano was saying to Margaret Roper as the traveling
party emerged from the palazzo. "I have teams all along
the road to Roma. The drivers know where, and they
carry full authorizations. Medici vehicles are familiar
throughout la Federazione. I've also arranged for a
small escort of Lanzi. Our roads are in general quite
safe, but as you're foreigners . . ."

"Of course," Margaret said in her forthright way.
"Foreigners are easy prey, are they not? It is very good
of you, Damian. We did not look for this courtesy."

"Nor did you look to go to Roma," Lodovico said,
a little sadly. "But His Holiness has need of you." It was
a polite lie, and he could tell that Margaret knew it. "Go
safely, my dear. I never thought I would enjoy teaching
a novice the Italian language, but you have shown me
I was wrong." They were nearly the same height and
touched cheeks easily.

"I will always be grateful to you. When you see me
next, you will probably lament how badly I have done
without you." Her tone was light and her words were
brave, but at the back of her eyes there was deepest
sorrow.

"When next we meet." It was more difficult for the

tall Damiano to touch cheeks with Margaret, but he did, his hands at her waist to lift her for this courtesy.

"You have been very good to us, Premier," William Roper said when Margaret had stepped back. "I'm certain Sir Thomas will be pleased when we tell him of all you've done."

"Are you?" Damiano said, this touching of cheeks more perfunctory. "You must ask him, then. Though he may surprise you." The irony was lost on William Roper, who had gone on to Andrea Benci to wish him well. Damiano's secretary accepted the praises lavished on him with self-effacing condescension.

The rest of the family made their thanks, Sir Thomas' wife, Alice, saying that Italy had turned out to be more pleasant than she had heard it was, which was a great compliment for that stern and sensible woman.

Footmen handed the travelers and three servants into the carriages, and Damiano walked to the first one, where Margaret Roper was seated. "I have a Hungarian carriage-maker, Margharita. He comes from Kocs, where the best are made. You will travel quite comfortably, I think."

She stuck her head out the square window. "It is luxury, Damian."

They exchanged smiles, and he said, almost as an afterthought. "You have that note I gave you?"

"I will see that it is delivered. If I can, I will do it myself," she answered promptly. "I wish there were more . . ."

"It is much more than I should ask of you," Damiano said, cutting off her words. "If there were another way, I would use it, but . . . You are kind, Margharita. More than you know." He stepped back from the carriage.

"Damian . . ." she began, but he had already lifted his hand in farewell. She relented. "Damian, Lodovico, thank you. Until we're toge—" The last words were swallowed up by the crunch of the horses' hooves and the rumble of the wheels on the flagging, and the jingle of harness as the carriages got under way.

Damiano stood watching the four splendid vehicles

as they moved south along the Via della Santa Felicità. There were large numbers of people on the street, many wagons and carts, so the carriages went slowly threading their way through the traffic. "The Lanzi will meet them at the Porta Romagna," he said to Lodovico, though he did not look at him.

"It's good of you to give them escort," Lodovico said because he had to say something and could think of no way to express the sudden loss he felt, a loss he sensed was much greater for Damiano de' Medici.

"I hated to send the note with her, but there was no one else." The Kocs carriages were out of sight, hidden by the rise of buildings.

Lodovico looked around guiltily to see if Andrea Benci had overheard, but the secretary was walking into the door of the Palazzo Pitti. "Why take the risk of telling me that," Lodovico admonished Damiano in a lowered voice. "If you had been overheard . . ."

"It doesn't matter," Damiano said with an affectionate chuckle. "I have a lie ready for any question. Andrea Benci accomplished his own business with the second driver, and he would not expect me to transact the delivery of secret papers in front of my home. He thinks he's the only one subtle enough to do that. Also, I made certain he learned that I had a packet given to the Lanzi capitano, and he's convinced that is the important message." He looked at Lodovico and patted his shoulder. "I was born to this game, my friend. I've been blind, but I knew the game was going on. Chide me for my lack of esthetic appreciation, not my clumsiness at politics."

"Would you listen?" Lodovico wondered aloud.

"Most certainly," Damiano answered at once. "I would be happy to hear you out. You don't know how much I miss wrangling about philosophy and art. My grandfather always made time for it, even when the old Repubblica was on the brink of war. I've lost sight of it, which I never meant to do . . ." He started for the door which a footman held open, waiting for il Primàrio to enter.

Lodovico followed him. "Would you like to have such a discussion? Tell me." It was not the time to ask Damiano, he was sure, but there was no time that was right, so he seized the opportunity and salved his conscience with the assurance that if Damiano rejected the idea, it was because it had been put to him at the wrong time. He passed through the door a few steps behind Damiano and almost ran into his friend, who had halted in the vestibule.

"Yes, I think I would like to have such a discussion," he said after a hesitation. "San Jacopo knows that I need a diversion." He glanced speculatively at Lodovico. "All right, we'll do it. Come to my study tomorrow afternoon. I've got to meet with the local Gonfaloniere and some others for comestio, and there is to be a discussion after the meal, but I have time after that. I was going to spend it riding, but this will be better. Come to my study an hour after comestio. If I'm not there at once, wait for me."

"I will," Lodovico promised, satisfied that he could fulfill both his obligation to Damiano—who, after all, was his patron—and his private vow to stay close to his friend.

"An hour after comestio tomorrow," Damiano stated, pointing a finger at Lodovico in punctuation.

"In your study. Yes."

"Good." Without another word, Damiano turned away and went off down the long hall toward the state drawing rooms leaving Lodovico grinning with the first real hope he had known in days.

"You're not working," Alessandra said as she looked up from her sewing.

"I'm thinking." Lodovico had propped his elbows on the table and his quill was bridging his hands as he stared out into the night. There were only two lanterns in the room, one by Alessandra's chair and the other hung over Lodovico's table so that he sat in a soft puddle of light.

"The ink on your quill is caked." It was not an accusation. Alessandra set the shirt she was stitching aside. "You've been lost all evening. Is anything wrong? Are you well?"

"Of course I'm well," Lodovico assured her, answering the easiest of her questions.

"Then what is it?" Her old buff-colored camora was golden in the feeble light, and the harsher signs of age in her face could not be seen. She looked very much the way Lodovico remembered her when they had met at the d'Este court. As he recalled, she had been wearing a damask the color of jonquils that made her light-brown hair seem to be lunar gold. She had read one of his plays, he remembered, and asked him intelligent questions. They had not been allowed to marry, but she had come to live with him before the summer was over.

"I've always liked you in yellow," he said inconsequently. He was pleased that she was intuitive enough not to ask for an explanation.

"It was sad that Donna Margharita had to leave," Alessandra remarked a little later. "I had wonderful talks with her. It's so refreshing to meet a woman who isn't boring. She was interested in more things than children and households and Saints' Days. I hope it's possible for her to return one day."

"I hope so, too," he said, and could not shake off the melancholy suspicion that it would never happen.

"She'll do well in Roma, but it will take her time to learn. Roma is a special place." Alessandra had started to work on her sewing again.

"You've only been there twice," Lodovico reminded her gently.

"It was enough. Margharita Roper will hate it at first, but she may have the talent for . . ." She gestured aimlessly, her needle a shining point of light in her hands.

"Not intrigue?" Lodovico asked, hoping that he had not found the correct word. It was true that Margaret carried a letter for Damiano, but that surely did not mean that she would learn to fawn, flatter, lie, coquette and manipulate with the lamentable gusto of so many Roman women.

"No, not that," Alessandra exclaimed, exasperated. "No, I mean that she might find a place in that other Roma, where learning and antiquity and virtues are treasured. There are a few of the old families who have such a life, and should Donna Margharita be fortunate, she will discover them before the rest of Roma engulfs her."

"She has a strong will. She will not be overcome by it," Lodovico said rather weakly, for he hated the idea of Margaret in that holy, pernicious city.

"She should do better than simply learn to resist!" was Alessandra's answer. Her needle jabbed into the linen and she gave a little yelp, then pulled her hand free and stuck a finger into her mouth.

"Are you hurt?" Lodovico asked.

"Not badly," Alessandra replied indistinctly.

"Is the shirt for Virginio?" he inquired, not caring but eager to show his wife that he was concerned with her.

"Of course." She had peered at her finger, licked it once, then, apparently satisfied that there was no serious damage, she went back to stitching. "I found a fine cloak for him, and I thought I would finish this shirt to send at the same time. Damiano said that he was sending a messenger into France at the end of the month, and he would give authorization for a package to Virginio." Her smile deepened as she went on. "If the report from Padre Gregorio is right, Virginio is doing very well for himself. When he called yesterday, I was so frightened that he would tell us that our son had gone the way of so many others and spent his days in mischief and his nights in debauch. Instead, he brings word that Virginio is acquiring a reputation for scholarship and at the same time is known as a good fellow. What more can I wish for him?"

Lodovico could not admit it to Alessandra, but he had shared her fear, and when the Augustinian priest had come with news, he had fought the urge to send him away. Now, he was glad that he had been willing to listen to the traveling prelate. "It was good of him to stop," Lodovico agreed.

"My husband," Alessandra said with a sigh, "how is it that you can spend hours scribbling about the most fabulous adventures, but when you are discussing your own son, you become nearly mute?" She did not expect an answer and got none.

For a time Lodovico busied himself cleaning and sharpening his quill, though he was not aware of these simple, habitual actions. His mind drifted to the endless snows of the Russias, and to Sir Thomas More in those deadly wastes, still believing that he was obligated to Damiano de' Medici for the safety of his wife and family. Damiano, Lodovico decided, had been right. The confrontation could not wait until the exiled Chancellor of England returned to Firenze with the private gleanings of his travels to report to Damiano. The ink had dried on his pen again as Lodovico gazed out into the night where a ruddy and insubstantial image of himself in the narrow panes of glass seemed to hover in the branches of the distant trees.

Damiano was late, and so Lodovico had passed the time deciphering Leonardo da Vinci's backward hand in one of his notebooks which Damiano had had bound in red leather. Most of the drawings were concerned with a variety of vehicles that Leonardo apparently thought could be made to fly. He was just finishing the description of the function of wings in birds when he looked up, hearing a hasty, unsteady step in the hall. He marked his place with one finger and holding the book closed with the rest of his hand, he half-rose.

The footsteps stumbled, and Lodovico, unreasonably alarmed, put the books aside, and drawing the little dagger he had appropriated that morning from its sheath on his belt, he went toward the door, just as Damiano lurched through it.

Sobbing, his face sallow as old ivory, his left arm held against his side, Damiano was unaware of anyone

else in the study. He fumbled for the latch and nearly
fell as he tried to swing the door closed. "Dio. Dio. Dio.
Only two. Only two," he breathed as he leaned back
against the door as if to hold himself up as much as to
assure himself it was closed. His mouth was an agonized square, his face waxen and smooth.

The shock which had immobilized Lodovico at the
sight of Damiano left him so suddenly that he had to
catch himself on the table to keep from falling. "Damiano . . ."

For the first time, Damiano's vision cleared and he
saw his friend. He groaned at the sight of him. "No.
Oh, no." Then he staggered away from the door, leaving a long, wet, red stain on the green-and-gold paint.

Lodovico saw the blood but could not bring himself
to accept what it meant.

"The table," Damiano panted as he tugged at it
futilely. "The door. Jesu, only two of them. If I'd had a
sword . . ."

"Damiano, what happened?" Lodovico demanded as,
belatedly, he reached out to aid him.

"The door!" Damiano insisted. "As you love Christ,
block it!" He half-fell toward a chair. "They were waiting for me, all of them. Benci, that nephew of his, the
lot of them. The Gonfaloniere, Manrico's bastard, all
of them." He put one hand to his side with the same
wide-palmed touch that an infant might use on an unexplored thing. It came away red and he nodded to himself, leaning back.

As he struggled with the heavy table, pushing at it
without success, his right hand still clutching the little
dagger, Lodovico managed to ask, "What did they do?"
He knew well enough what they did, he told himself
furiously: they had attacked his friend.

"Hurry. Hurry. They'll be here soon." His eyes were
closed now and there was a sheen on his face, like the
blighting touch of frost.

The writing table in Damiano's study was designed to
be moved by two men, and the parquetry floor was uneven. Lodovico was able to push the imposing piece of

furniture a quarter of the way across the room toward the door when he heard running footsteps far down the hall.

"I should have paid that Burgundian to kill him," Damiano said weakly, more to himself than Lodovico. "He would have done it. I should have paid him. A Borgia or a Sforza or a della Rovere would have paid. I thought it was wrong. Despicable. Then this." A spasm shook him. "The door, for God's sake!"

Lodovico looked frantically about and saw at last the candelabrum in the corner. It was taller than a man, of ornate iron. He fairly ran across the room and grabbed the candelabrum, tilted it and began dragging it back across the study. He could feel his arms tremble with the unaccustomed demand of this effort and his unacknowledged fear. The sound of iron against wood was hideous and ordinarily would have put Lodovico's teeth on edge but now he barely noticed it.

"The study!" shouted a voice far down the hall, and the sound of running feet grew louder.

Part of the pedestal of the candelabrum caught against the carved foot of the table and Lodovico tugged and grunted, working it free, refusing to listen for the approach of the men pursuing Damiano.

"Perdonami, perdonami Iddio," Damiano muttered as he tried to sit straight in the chair. He caught sight of Lodovico just as the foot of the candelabrum came free and Lodovico gave an involuntary cry of relief. "And you, my friend. Forgive me. I didn't think that this would . . ."

Lodovico had no time to answer and little inclination to speak. He was too busy with the candelabrum, and was convinced now that if only he could drag it a few more paces, he could block the door with it. The little dagger felt hot in his hand and he had skinned his knuckles on the elaborate iron, but he would not drop the weapon. He steadfastly refused to think of what might happen once the door was blocked and more ambitious, bloody men gathered outside it.

He had almost reached the door when it started to

open. Shouting some unknown word of blessing or curse, Lodovico thrust the candelabrum ahead of him, using it like a multitipped pike. Candles broke, scattering white flakes of wax over the floor, and the iron dug into the painted wood just where it was smeared with blood. Lodovico pressed down on the metal, determined to wedge it tightly against the door.

"The footprints! Look! Blood!" one of the voices announced distinctly, excitedly, as if the speaker were half drunk.

"Lodovico . . ." Damiano was saying with careful, painful effort. "While there's still time. I forgot you'd be here. I didn't intend. I never intended you to have to . . ."

Now there was a pounding on the door, done first with fists and then with sword hilts. Lodovico shot one worried glance at the latch, then looked back at Damiano, who had lifted his sanguined hand listlessly. "The window. You can get out. They don't know . . ."

"It's two storeys to the paved courtyard," Lodovico reminded him unemotionally.

"Climb down. I beg . . ." Damiano whispered.

Lodovico wanted to weep, to shout at the enraged men on the other side of the door to be silent, for they would have their wishes soon enough. He could see death lying over Damiano's face, as if the body had been invaded by a stranger. But he could not say it, not to the men bludgeoning the door, not to Damiano, pale in the high-backed chair. Instead he tried to chuckle. "Climb down? At my age? If we wait, someone will come."

"Someone is here." Damiano coughed once and shook his head. "Cosimo will come. When this is over. Cosimo will come."

There was a scraping and splintering, and fingers pushed eagerly through the first little cracks in the wood, searching for whatever had blocked the way.

"We need more room!" one of the men shouted, and the hacking was renewed by fewer, stronger arms.

Lodovico went to the foot of the candelabrum once

more and pushed against it, not sure that it was enough to stop the men if they actually chopped the door into pieces. He said as he worked, "There are men who will not allow this, Damiano. There are men who will be outraged, all over Europe. They will hasten to you as soon as they learn what is happening here." He could not hear Damiano's answer, if there was one. He put all his strength into blocking the door though his hands were blistering with the effort and the edge of the dagger nicked the fleshy part of his palm.

A section of wood gave way and a padded and slashed silken sleeve of periwinkle blue pushed through the jagged space. There was a short sword in an embroidered glove, and it slashed blindly, wildly about. Lodovico had to resist the urge to grab for the blade, confine it, and slap the hand that held it. He felt himself about to laugh and knew that he must not.

"Only two. Not enough. Tried for Benci. No good; Benci wouldn't have been enough," Damiano remarked casually, dreamily. "I'd have to get my cousin as well. But only *two* . . ." The faint voice choked. "I didn't want to have to do it that way. I wanted to prove . . . to prove . . . ? my grandfather's ideals . . . were right. It should be possible to . . . govern with reason and sense . . . It should . . . It *is* . . . But Benci . . . Why Benci?"

The short sword was withdrawn and the assault on the door continued. Lodovico tightened his hand around the dagger and waited.

"My cousin . . . Benci . . . They could have been killed . . . but . . . if I did that . . . where would it stop? . . . Where? . . . And now this . . ." His voice had faded to a shadow of sound, and Lodovico did not hear more than five words of what Damiano was saying.

The hole in the door was wider and more weapons and arms appeared.

"It could have worked," Damiano said wistfully, though he was unaware that no one could hear him.

Lodovico had wanted to listen, had tried to, but his mind was on the door, at the buckling panels. He could

not think of what he ought to do. How did he, a man
with only one short dagger, defend himself against half
a dozen men with swords? "Damiano!" he called, wishing that il Primàrio would think of something more he
might do, wanting his friend to know that he was standing by him.

With a shriek the door burst its hinges, splintering
around the candelabrum, and three men stumbled into
the room with drawn weapons held at the ready. The
first to turn was thick-bodied and coarsely dressed—
with sudden indignation, Lodovico recognized the smith
Carlo, and just behind him, the elegant figure of Andrea
Benci. The third was a young man not known to Lodovico, a handsome youth dressed in the Roman style.

Lodovico had intended to place himself between
these invaders and his stricken friend, but one swift
glance told him that was useless now: Damiano sat
quietly in the high-backed chair, dark eyes turned toward the window, head to one side. He was very still.

With a sound born of despair and fury, Lodovico
thrust the young man aside and lunged at Andrea
Benci, the dagger in his hand darting forward like a
serpent's tongue. And then a coldness possessed him,
a cold more intense than any Lodovico had ever known.
His side, his back, his jaw ached with it, and he could
not move anymore. Without a murmur he fell forward
across the fallen candelabrum.

Il Trapasso

The battle was not yet over. Lodovico could hear, seemingly at a distance, the advancing steps of men, some moving quickly, others more slowly, accompanied by strange shouts and excited words.

"We've done it!"

Lodovico thought he must have lost his weapon or he would be part of the battle, the celebration. He had given his word to Damiano and he was afraid now that he had not accomplished what he had vowed to do. There was more he must do, things to be finished, but he could not find his weapon.

"Benci?"

"No good. The blade went too deep."

Was that Benci speaking? The voice was not polished. It sounded like one of Massamo's Lanzi.

"Benci was right: the poet was in on it."

Benci, Lodovico thought contemptuously. Benci, Benci. A cowardly old man, a subtle, incorrigible villain. He let others do his fighting and himself fled real danger. He was a treacherous man. Lodovico had never liked him. He was too neat. There was something else, a thing his right hand remembered, but he could not describe, though he took a sullied pride in it.

"Renaldo, stop it. He's dead."

Lodovico wanted to protest, but he had fallen

359

through some accident, in some manner he could not recall, and was now unable to rise. There was too much cold in him to rise. One of the warriors of flint and frost had pinned him to the ground. It would take help for him to get up again. The cold was heavy upon him. But he sensed that the battle was stopping. The clash of metal on metal and stone had almost ceased. He thought he saw boots approaching him.

"Leave him. Just cover him up. With all that blood . . ."

Damiano was hurt. He remembered that now. Damiano had been wounded and Falcone would not bring his army in time because the warriors of flint and frost were holding them at the crest of the hill. Damiano needed a champion. He had tried to do what he could. He had tried to break through for Damiano. He had not completed that, and it rankled.

Something fell across his shoulders, something light. Falcone's cape. They had brought him Falcone's cape. His eyes filled with tears. Falcone's cape. It would take time to free him from the grip of the warrior of flint and frost, though he hoped they would do it quickly, for the cold was growing even more oppressive and the cape was not sufficient to warm him.

"They've got to be moved. We need them out of here."

And quickly, quickly, Lodovico urged silently as his strength ran out of him.

"Thank God we succeeded."

Then the forces of Anatrecacciatore were defeated! His charge must have helped the army. They would have come after him, of course they would have, crying *Omaggio* and striking true to the heart of the evil.

"You should thank the Cardinale."

The Cardinale! What had Damiano's cousin to do with it? How could he have come? He was in Italia Federata. It was not possible.

"Shame about Benci."

"Why? The Cardinale would have got rid of him, anyway. Saves us the trouble."

Cosimo, Cardinale Medici, was a venal, greedy man who was not worthy to fight on behalf of Falcone and Nuova Genova. Just as well to recall him before he did more harm. A man like that would destroy an honorable battle. He wanted to warn the others that they must not rely on the Cardinale, though, or trust him. It would be dangerous to do that.

"And get that thing out of here."

There was a scraping and a shadow fell across him. If only he could rise, could move, if he could help them to lift this immense stone warrior. The shadow was bigger, deeper, darker, and there was a sound in his ears he had never heard before. The cold was worse, much worse.

"Move him, can't you?"

More rustling around him, and the cold. The cold. Something brushed his face and he looked up. Bellimbusto had returned, faithful. The shadow, he thought, had been Bellimbusto. He must have fought honorably, for a hippogryph would never come to a disgraced master. He had expiated his sin, then, surely. Already he felt easier, less oppressed. He knew that he would be rescued now. Bellimbusto would not let him lie in the terrible, terrible cold.

There was one keen instant when the talons reached out for him, to pluck him away, raise him up. One moment only of anguish and loss.

Then they were free again, soaring into the unknown and radiant splendor while around him, above him, within him, the great, thundering wings shone now black, now bronze, now gold, now evanescent light.